Praise for *Disor*

"Funny and insightful, with plenty to say about art, identity, Orientalism, and the politics of academia."　　　　　　　　　　—*The New York Times Book Review*

"The hyperactive satire is so consistently funny it almost makes the reader forget about the serious societal issues that undergird the humor. . . . *Disorientation* does what great comedies and satires are supposed to do: make you laugh while forcing you to ponder the uncomfortable implications of every punchline."
　　　　　　　　　　　　　　　　　　　　　—*The Washington Post*

"[A] literary satire that takes a hilarious and refreshingly honest look at the power dynamics of college campuses . . . This one will have you rolling over with laughter and texting your college group chat."　　　　—NPR, *Books We Love* 2022

"A rollicking, whip-smart ride through the hallowed halls of academia."
　　　　　　　　　　　　　　　　　　　　　　—*Harper's Bazaar*

"The pleasures of Elaine Hsieh Chou's campus satire are in high supply. . . . In the tradition of Donna Tartt's *The Secret History* and Elif Batuman's *The Idiot,* Chou has written a delightful new chapter of dark academia."　　　　—*Vogue*

"As the best comedy does, *Disorientation* manages to highlight uncomfortable truths, capture gray areas and hard lines, and resist sliding into easy binaries of heroes and villains."　—*Vanity Fair* (Books We Couldn't Put Down This Month)

"Hilarious and harrowing . . . Elaine Hsieh Chou's debut novel *Disorientation* is a rollicking satire of graduate-school life, Asian American overachievers, and the peculiar injustices of the university. . . . *Disorientation* is a page-turner studded with razor-sharp one-liners. . . . Its twists and turns propel the plot while skewering topics from anti–affirmative action sentiment among Asian Americans to the jargon-heavy stylings of academic prose to the diabolically chameleonic quality of the American right. Along the way, Ingrid's archival mystery leads her out of her dissertation funk and into a tangle of betrayal and deception that forces her to reevaluate her own self-deceiving beliefs about what it means to be an Asian scholar and an Asian woman in America." — *The New York Review of Books*

"*Disorientation* . . . joins a new wave of campus satires, many of which are written by women, that aren't really satires at all. By exposing their characters' human motives, their frailties and failings, deflated aspirations and unarticulated hopes, they offer something more radical than righteous critique: avenues for empathy and, perhaps, pathways back to community for those who have strayed far away."
—*T Magazine*

"This book has so many stifle-a-strangled-laugh lines you might want to refrain from reading it in a library or a train's quiet car. Chou's novel is a send-up of the polite, cardigan-draped white supremacy of liberal arts colleges. . . . Between hiring a private investigator, staging a break-in, flooding a gender neutral bathroom, and smoking weed with a professor, she uncovers a shocking truth—an act of racism in the academic world that had gone unnoticed for decades. . . . In an entertaining takedown, Chou explores who the university really belongs to."
—*Glamour*

"This funny, fearless debut novel about a student's dissertation on a fictional poet dives into the maelstrom of topical arguments about race and comes up fighting. . . . [*Disorientation*] gets candid about the concept of model minorities, the stickiness of inter-racial dating and the way misogyny violently affects Asian women." —*The Observer* (London)

"[*Disorientation*] is captivating, irresistible, and intensely readable, and what we ultimately come to literature to find. . . . The book expands in scope with each passing page, integrating newer and more experimental forms and swallowing larger subject matter. We begin at the campus novel, at critiques of university hierarchy, and end up considering all of American politics and the evolution of racism, fetishism, and social stratification. . . . What *Disorientation* shows us is that there is power in the page-turner, that literary merit and a unique, propelling story are not mutually exclusive." —*Chicago Review of Books*

"Fans of blistering American satires like Paul Beatty's *The Sellout* and Charles Yu's *Interior Chinatown* won't want to miss Elaine Hsieh Chou's electrifying debut *Disorientation*, which turns the campus novel on its head with its portrait of a Taiwanese American PhD student lost in her own research. Taking on fraught topics like appropriation and the 'model minority' in academia, it goes big in the best way, announcing an exciting new voice."
—*Chicago Review of Books* (12 Must-Read Books of March 2022)

"[A] page-turning, thrilling satire of American academia, tangled in literary mystery . . . Ingrid blossoms in a complex coming-to-consciousness as she discovers racial power dynamics and incommensurable concepts of identity. Chou skewers Sinophobes and Sinophiles alike with wit as sharp as a samurai sword mounted on a white guy's bedroom wall. The writing is almost intolerably funny: intolerable only because the wellspring of *Disorientation*'s satire is our racist reality. As Ocean Vuong writes: 'I know. It's not fair that the word laughter is trapped inside slaughter.' Elaine Hsieh Chou is out for blood." —*The Saturday Paper*

"Both deeply moving and rivetingly funny, *Disorientation* is a master class in satire with surprises around every corner. It is a roaring meditation on the ivory tower and Asian American identity that does not mince words about anyone in its illustrious cast of characters. Chou's first foray into fiction left my mind sharp, my heart full, and my belly weak from laughter." —*Foreign Policy*

"If there is one book you read this year, let it be *Disorientation*. . . . Lucid and hilarious and hopeful and grim; in the same absurd style of Paul Beatty, Elaine Hsieh Chou's intellectually sexy book hits all the hot topic arguments of Asian American discourse and higher education identity politics. She lays out the ideological stakes—the personhood of Asian women as people, not objects—and the threat posed by pervasive and internalized racism." —*The Michigan Daily*

"Addressing weighty issues with humor is quite a difficult task for many writers—but Elaine Hsieh Chou has accomplished that and more in her explosive debut novel. *Disorientation* is hilarious and entertaining, while also examining racism and politics in academia, societal changes, and the importance of telling your own story. It's not every day that we get a laugh-out-loud satire, sharp cultural commentary, literary fiction, mystery, and a relatable heroine in one book."
—Malala's Book Club Literati (April 2022 selection)

"Chou's distinct, self-effacing voice makes for a fun ride into a highly charged realm, with a plot that naturally escalates as she looks into various claims about truth in art, who appropriates whom, the limits of allyship, and how we gaslight ourselves in order to accept everyday racial horrors. Chou reflects a world that's complex and entertaining, one that will leave readers with a renewed perspective." —*Booklist* (starred review)

"Calling [*Disorientation*] merely satire about a racial awakening isn't enough. . . . I was not the same person at the end of reading this book that I was before reading it." —*Book Riot* ("The Best Books of 2022 So Far")

"Chou's debut novel is a provocative, satirical take on academia, full of surprising twists." —*Time* (Best Books of March 2022)

"*Disorientation* takes us on a whirlwind romp that combines academic satire with a whodunnit mystery thriller." —*Electric Literature*

"No one is left spared from critique in Chou's satire, much to the reader's delight. Anyone who has experienced the pretension of academia, thought extensively about racial dating preferences, or reveled in takedowns of white institutions will find much to cackle about while reading these pages. But *Disorientation* shines most in its ability to give Asian American readers an entry point to examine and forgive their own potential hypocrisies." —The Cosmos Book Club

"*Disorientation* is a multivalent pleasure, a deeply original debut novel that reinvents the campus novel satire as an Asian American literary studies whodunnit, in which the murder victim might be your idea of yourself—no matter how you identify. I often held my breath until I laughed and I wouldn't dare compare it or Chou to anyone writing now. Wickedly funny and knowing, Chou's dagger wit is sure-eyed, intent on what feels like a decolonization of her protagonist, if not the reader, that just might set her free."
—Alexander Chee, author of *How to Write an Autobiographical Novel*

"*Disorientation* is an irreverent campus satire that skewers white sclerotic academia, creepy Asian fetishists, and twee boba liberalism, but lastly and most importantly, it's a satire, inspired by recent controversies, about an orientalist tradition and its manifestations today. Helmed by a memorable screwball protagonist, the novel is both a joyous and sharply drawn caper."
—Cathy Park Hong, author of *Minor Feelings*

"Chou's pen is a scalpel. *Disorientation* addresses the private absurdities the soul must endure to get free, from tokenism, the quiet exploitation of well-meaning institutions, and the bondage that is self-imposed. Chou does it with wit and verve, and no one is spared." —Raven Leilani, author of *Luster*

"*Disorientation* is the funniest novel I've read all year. . . . This uproarious tale of a young woman's quest to uncover the truth about the world's most famous Chinese American poet is packed full of sly truths about race, love, and life in general—all of which you're going to miss, because you'll be laughing so hard."
—Aravind Adiga, author of *The White Tiger*

PENGUIN BOOKS

DISORIENTATION

Elaine Hsieh Chou is a Taiwanese American writer from California. Her debut novel, *Disorientation*, was a *New York Times* Editors' Choice Book, a Malala's Book Club Pick, and an Indie Next Pick. A 2017 Rona Jaffe Graduate Fellow at NYU and a 2021 NYFA Fellow, her Pushcart Award–winning short fiction appears in *Guernica, Tin House Online, Ploughshares, LARB Quarterly Review,* and elsewhere. She was a Black Warrior Review Flash Fiction 2020 Contest Winner and an Iowa Review Awards 2020 Finalist. Her short story collection, *Where Are You Really From,* is forthcoming in 2024.

Disorientation

Elaine Hsieh Chou

PENGUIN BOOKS

PENGUIN BOOKS
An imprint of Penguin Random House LLC
penguinrandomhouse.com

First published in the United States of America by Penguin Press,
an imprint of Penguin Random House LLC, 2022
Published in Penguin Books 2023

ISBN 9780593298374 (paperback)

THE LIBRARY OF CONGRESS HAS CATALOGED THE HARDCOVER EDITION AS FOLLOWS:
Names: Chou, Elaine Hsieh, author.
Title: Disorientation / Elaine Hsieh Chou.
Description: New York : Penguin Press, 2022. | Includes bibliographical references.
Identifiers: LCCN 2021011961 (print) | LCCN 2021011962 (ebook) |
ISBN 9780593298350 (hardcover) | ISBN 9780593298367 (ebook) |
ISBN 9780593491775 (international edition)
Subjects: LCSH: Women doctoral students—United States—Fiction. |
Chinese American women—Fiction. | Education, Higher—United States—Fiction. |
Discrimination in higher education—United States—Fiction. | Satire, American.
Classification: LCC PS3603.H686 D57 2022 (print) | LCC PS3603.H686 (ebook) |
DDC 813/.6—dc23/eng/20211015
LC record available at https://lccn.loc.gov/2021011961
LC ebook record available at https://lccn.loc.gov/2021011962

Printed in the United States of America
4th Printing

BOOK DESIGN BY LUCIA BERNARD

To Hsieh Hsiu-Hua, who hid in the mountains,
eating raw cabbage, and survived the bombs

Contents

Part III: Spring Quarter

Part IV: Summer

PART I

Fall Quarter

The Curious Note

On September ninth, Ingrid Yang could be found cramped over a desk, left foot asleep, right hand swollen. She had Xiao-Wen Chou on the mind, so much so, she felt his allusions and alliterations leaking from her every orifice and puddling beneath her. She was sucking on the ends of her hair, then sniffing the damp locks, before picking at the eczema patches on her ankles. Her aching eyes were marbled pink from a sleepless night, punctuated by unnecessary trips to the bathroom. She simply idled on the toilet with her eyes closed, nothing going out of, or into, her body.

Even on the rare occasions sleep visited, Ingrid was plagued by a constant, pinching pain in her stomach. Sometimes she imagined, hopefully, that she was developing ulcers. No one could fault her for failing her dissertation because of stomach ulcers, could they? Pneumonia, then? What about mono? But how to contract these illnesses was another question entirely. The black market was the obvious choice—but then again, so was an undergrad frat party.

Pulling her laptop close, she searched "fastest way to contract mono," followed by "top ten deathly illnesses."

No, Ingrid Yang was not doing well.

She was twenty-nine years old and in mounting debt from her undergraduate degree. Four years ago, she had passed her comprehensive exams and started her dissertation. This year, the eighth and final year of her PhD, her funding would run out—an unhappy situation in any circumstance, but compounded by the expiration of her student loan deferral. Somehow, in spite of all this financial doom and gloom, she had to produce two hundred fifty pages on Xiao-Wen Chou. And not just any two hundred fifty pages—they had to be shockingly original *and* convincing! Enough to pass muster with her exacting advisor and an even more exacting dissertation committee. Enough to secure her the prestigious postdoc fellowship established in Xiao-Wen Chou's name.

But after hundreds of hair-pulling hours spent at the archive, all she had accomplished was fifty pages of scrambled notes on Chou's use of enjambment. Plus an addiction to antacids.

Make no mistake, the problem wasn't for lack of trying. She had come up with ideas of her own! The eternal inner conflict between eastern selflessness and western individuality in Chou's poetry. The immigrant's assimilation into American society as endless negotiation in Chou's poetry. Chou's poetry and the impossibility of cultural translation. Chou's poetry and the longing for irretrievably lost motherland and mother tongue, etc.

The problem was some other scholar had, of course, snatched up the idea first. No other Chinese American poet had been so widely read in America, had been so consistently reprinted year after year. The so-called Chinese Robert Frost was taught to students in high schools and colleges all across the country (and occasionally in gifted middle school classes). In every bookstore and library, a good twelve inches of space was reserved for his prolific work. Even those who wanted nothing to do with literature, who couldn't tell you Chou's name much less how to spell it, had bumped into his poems. In dentist offices, middle-class homes and ethnic restaurants, his quotations adorned boxes of tea, wall decorations and watercolor calendars. Xiao-Wen Chou was beloved—more so after he passed away from pancreatic cancer seven years ago.

What could Ingrid possibly offer on the late canonical poet that no one else had? She had memorized Chou's poems backwards and forwards, riffled through innumerable archive boxes, worn out her copy of his biography, read incomprehensible secondary sources, read them a third time. She had even attended a pricey international conference in New York in the hopes of gently plagiarizing some Argentinian or Swedish scholar's paper. When she was still a TA, she had surreptitiously assigned her undergrads essay prompts that fed directly into her own research. She had let her other interests fall to the wayside, not to mention healthy eating and exercise. She had postponed her wedding for another year. From the moment she woke up to the moment she pretended to sleep, Chouian sonnets, villanelles, odes and elegies consumed her. What more could she do? Hire a ghostwriter?

Alas, Ingrid was approaching the problem as though it held a logical solution, but her dissertation woes were preordained from the start: she had never wanted to research Chou in the first place.

As an undergraduate student at Barnes University, Ingrid had waffled over choosing a major. She plodded along in her general education classes, dozing off in Physics of Music and floundering in Beginning Russian, all while fretting over her aimless, and expensive, academic taste testing. Then, to fulfill a writing requirement, she enrolled in Early 20th-Century Poetry taught by Professor Newman.

Judith Newman didn't walk into a room; the room opened up to accommodate her. She had terrifying pale blue eyes and cropped silver hair and dressed like she was heading to an avant-garde art exhibit in Berlin.

She made the auditorium erect with attention. Even the boys in Ingrid's other classes, who always shoehorned an obscure philosopher into every single discussion in a bid to win their professors' respect, were awed into submission. Judith taught without notes, for one thing, and without the crutch of technology (she pitied her colleagues who relied on Word Art to dazzle and distract). She paced back and forth in front of the blackboard, stopping only to call point-blank on a trembling student. When Judith lectured on modernist poetry, Ingrid was convinced she'd yanked back the curtain of reality. What was once a poem was now an ideological stance on language, war, life, death! She was seduced by the modernist obsession with form over content, the abstract over the concrete (suffice it to say, classes on postcolonial and feminist lit made her feel . . . uncomfortable).

And so Ingrid fell into the arms of her first great love. She spent hours in the library fashioning a poem into something greater than itself. While her roommate performed a halfhearted hand job on a lacrosse player in the top bunk, she hid under her covers with a flashlight in the company of Stein and Mallarmé. Analyzing poetry was *cool*. Did some people *actually* believe a poem about a red wheelbarrow was about a red wheelbarrow when it was *obviously* about existential dread? Like a literary detective, Ingrid derived no greater satisfaction than from spotting what swam beneath the surface of words.

And she was good at it. Her paper "Waste, Différance and the Loss of Center in T. S. Eliot's *The Waste Land*" had nabbed an elusive A from Professor Newman. At the end of the semester, she invited Ingrid along with four other students to dine at her house. And what a house it was! Professor Newman's interior design scheme was in fact modeled after an avant-garde art exhibit in Berlin, unlike Ingrid's parents' house, which was cluttered, tacky and had *zero* stainless steel bidets.

Judith was married to a bearded philosophy professor who possessed dual Italian citizenship and, from what Ingrid could tell, excellent calves. For that evening's dinner, he whipped up homemade clam pasta and a tiramisu that somehow tasted . . . erotic. They were parents to twins who sagely commented on the day's foreign policy scandals, as if they weren't still dependent on training wheels. Gazing at the perfect family before her, woozy with thirty-year-old wine and imported shellfish, Ingrid knew then: she was meant to be a professor of modernist literature. Just like Judith Newman.

Becoming a professor would resolve several of Ingrid's hang-ups, one of which was the intellectual shortage she felt the moment she'd stepped onto campus. While her classmates compared notes about reading Melville and watching Truffaut, she stared down at her lap. Her parents had never bought her such books or rented her such movies. She arrived at college missing half the baggage they'd been prepackaged with.

Then, too, was the latent fear someone like her was not supposed to be good at English. In first grade, she'd been placed in remedial English not because it wasn't her native language, but because she'd been too shy to speak up in class. Then, in sixth grade, her English teacher had accused her of plagiarizing her *Of Mice and Men* book report on the grounds it was "suspiciously articulate."

Added to that, Ingrid was obsessive and neurotic, traits well suited for academia. The real world, or nonacademic world, frightened her with its largeness and unknownness—far better to cozily burrow into old texts, to safely engage with dead authors who couldn't talk back. To live inside the past was to debark from contemporary events and concerns, floating away until she landed on a minuscule, highly specialized planet where only a dozen other beings spoke the same language. Ingrid could conceive of nothing better. She even imagined a new wardrobe to complement her future title as Professor Yang: brooches, practical but devastatingly fashionable eyeglasses, perfume that reminded people of their great-aunt (in a good way).

But when she asked Judith to be her senior thesis advisor, she was met with a cruel shock: Judith was leaving the English department for the Comparative Literature department.

"C-Comp Lit?" she stuttered.

"Don't look so surprised, Ingrid. Modernism and deconstruction and post-structuralism—it's all a dying field," every other word punctuated by a quick half smile. "Now comparative literature, on the other hand. Being able to move between mediums, be it film or graphic novels—that's where the future of academia lies. You have to think past the degree, consider what job opportunities are out there. Academia is a tough game. You'll need a unique . . . angle."

Judith squeezed her hands together, and, Ingrid imagined, her thighs under the desk.

"And your particular background is so *unique*. It doesn't have to be a disadvantage—it can be an *advantage*. Do you understand what I mean?"

Ingrid nodded enthusiastically and jotted down the words "unique" and "advantage" in her notebook.

"Good. I'm glad we're on the same page. In fact, you'd be just right for a new project I'm working on." Judith chewed on the end of her glasses as she studied Ingrid. "Research assistantships are usually reserved for graduate students, but I could make an exception for you."

And so Ingrid, being neither Japanese nor interested in Japan, wrote her thesis on 1920s Japanese silent film. Afterwards, the jump from Comp Lit to East Asian Studies was a relatively short one. When Judith was poached by a more well-endowed university, she left Ingrid with a parting gift: a new academic advisor, Michael Bartholomew, a "dear colleague" of hers.

"I know you're interested in pursuing a PhD," she said. "Talk to Michael. He'll know exactly how to help."

BARNES UNIVERSITY MADE UP the center of Wittlebury, Massachusetts. The private research university was home to roughly one thousand undergraduate students and nearly double the amount of graduate students. Founded in 1889, Barnes was not a top-tier nor a lower-tier university, but a firmly middling institution, propped up by alumni donations, nepotism and one illustrious (former) professor: Xiao-Wen Chou. The campus was attractive, with redbrick buildings scattered between virile green lawns, clusters of neatly groomed trees and a quad designed to discourage protests.

Inside the main library's basement resided the Xiao-Wen Chou archive. Acquired after his death, it housed all the distinguished poet's books, journals, manuscripts, reviews, letters and other miscellany. In addition to the archivist's desk were eight others, each furnished with a globe lamp. The dark mahogany walls were accented with photos of Chou and prints of traditional Chinese paintings, characterized by plum tree blossoms, mountains, cranes and peasants bent over rice paddies. Chou's book covers looked more or less identical, though they also featured flowery fans, silhouettes of dark-haired women and chopsticks resting delicately on porcelain bowls.

Ingrid got up from her desk, left foot still asleep, and hobbled to the archivist's desk. She planned to check out box number fifteen, the same one she'd examined yesterday, and guessed the endeavor would be equally fruitless, but what other choice did she have? She needed to kill time, as if it had a neck she could wrap her hands around until it produced, say, an original and convincing idea.

She stood before the archivist, smiling widely, hoping Margaret Hong would smile back at her. They had never exchanged many words, but Ingrid liked to imagine they shared an unspoken intimacy since she spent significant time studying her instead of the archive materials.

Margaret only ever wore thick brocade embroidered with vulgar-looking peonies, peacocks or pagodas. After stalking her online, Ingrid learned she sewed them herself and sold them for exorbitant prices. In her desk drawer, she kept a packet of salted dried plums she discreetly sucked on and indiscreetly spat out, and yet her ruby-red lipstick never strayed. Ingrid often saw her wriggle her shoes off to stretch her plump toes in their sheer stockings. When she thought no one was looking, she'd reach around to the back of her skirt to unglue her underwear from between her derriere. Word around the archive had it that Margaret was a former martial arts grandmaster but because the rumor reinforced a cliché, no one dared confirm the truth with her.

Most recently, Ingrid liked to picture Margaret and Daryl Abrams-Wu entangled in an illicit affair. Daryl, the lanky archive intern, habitually wore a spiked dog collar, painted his nails black and maintained a long slick of hair strategically placed over one eye.

"I said, did you reserve the box online," Margaret repeated.

The image of her straddling Daryl on the accessible toilet evaporated. "Uh, no. Sorry."

Margaret sighed heavily, as if Ingrid were the most useless archive visitor she'd ever encountered. She walked to the back and returned with a gray box and a pair of white cotton gloves.

"Thanks!" Ingrid said with a forced smile.

Margaret didn't smile back. Perhaps the affair with Daryl had soured.

Ingrid carried box number fifteen to her desk and yawned. For an hour, her gaze alternated between her laptop and legal pad. She wrote one sentence, then crossed it out. Typed another one, then deleted it. Clicked undo, changed a preposition, then deleted it again.

Yes, writing a dissertation was its own level in hell.

She paused her self-flagellation to check her email: yet another message from Michael asking to "discuss the progress of your dissertation." A sharp pang stabbed the lower left corner of her stomach. She junked the email.

After her meetings with Michael, Ingrid always left discombobulated, as though he'd taken her apart and put her back together slightly awry. Their first meeting was indelibly inked into her mind. That spring morning had been muggy, with thin clouds crisscrossing the sky. She was dressed in an ankle-length skirt, an oversized sweater and worn brown oxfords. A tortoiseshell clip at the nape of her neck restrained her tangled and unwashed hair. She was twenty-two years old, nearing the end of her undergraduate degree, and, though exhausted, the prospect of conducting her own research seized her with an excitement second only to the time she'd given herself an orgasm.

She had known Judith would guide her in the right direction. But who was this Michael Bartholomew? She checked her notebook again for directions to his office, located in the East Asian Studies department on the fourth floor of the Humanities Block. She knew little about the department—only that it had come under controversy a few years ago for subsuming the short-lived existence of the Asian American Studies department.

Ingrid pushed open a heavy door and stepped into a dim hallway overseen by twitching fluorescent lights. The walls begged for a fresh coat of paint; the carpet, an aggressive steam clean. She knocked on Michael's door and found him bent over a whistling kettle.

"Gao shan tea?"

A tall, striking man in his sixties, with long gray hair tied in a loose ponytail, he appeared to look down on her even when they were sitting face-to-face.

Ingrid took the red clay cup he offered and blinked. Michael's office wasn't in a state of disrepair; it was bright, open and modern. She was stung by a sudden, intense desire to urinate and searched for the culprit: by the window squatted an artificial bonsai zen garden fountain.

"So, Ingrid, I hear you've decided to torture yourself by doing a PhD?" Michael asked good-humoredly.

Ingrid smiled as though constipated.

"Excellent, excellent," Michael beamed. He leaned back in his silk-upholstered chair. "What do you plan to specialize in?"

"Well, I was thinking modernist poetry. Ezra Pound's translation of Chinese—"

Michael gasped. Ingrid looked around in a panic—had she spilled her tea?

"Oh, Ingrid, Ingrid, Ingrid. I hate to be the one to tell you this, but the English department has claimed Pound. They've made that very clear over the years." When he smiled, his broad teeth loomed over the crags of his face. "I would think twice before writing on one of *their* poets. The English department has proven itself to be, I'll go ahead and say it, a xenophobic department. They're very . . . traditional."

"But my senior thesis, in addition to Japanese silent film, references the overlap with modernist poetic aesthetics—"

"Tsk, tsk, tsk! Why delve into that painful past? If you ask me, the English department behaved shamefully, awarding first place in the Humanities Honors Awards to who was it—oh, yes, Quentin Ferguson—after Judith told me *you* had worked so diligently."

Ingrid glanced at the calendar on his wall: two koi fish intertwined like yin and yang.

"Every department is being defunded. In a few years, I doubt the English department will even exist." Michael chuckled and reached for two silver Baoding balls nestled in an engraved wooden box. "Do you know what department receives *more* funding year after year?"

"Er—STEM?"

"No, Ingrid—*my* department."

"Well, I wouldn't even know what to—"

"Oh, I know what you're thinking: everyone's done everything. Right? Sure, you could write a dissertation about this or that censored Beijing installation artist or the newest documentary filmmaker who went undercover in North Korea. But that won't get you *tenure.* Sure, you could bounce around from adjunct to adjunct position across the country, with no healthcare or benefits." He checked Ingrid's expression before continuing. "A former student of mine once pulled out her own molar."

Ingrid swallowed.

Michael leaned closer. "You know what *does* get you tenure?"

She shook her head solemnly.

"The canon."

"The canon?" Ingrid whispered.

"Xiao-Wen Chou."

"But he's been researched to death!" Without meaning to, she had risen from her chair. She coughed and sank back down.

Though Ingrid didn't particularly like or dislike the father of Chinese American poetry, their first encounter was a supremely uncomfortable memory she'd prefer to forget. In ninth grade, as her teacher lectured on Chou, she repeatedly stopped to ask Ingrid questions like how to pronounce "Xiao-Wen Chou" (er—the way you said it?), where Wuyuan Village was located (somewhere inside China?) and lastly, if she had any firsthand knowledge of "the Chinese American experience" (is this going to be on the test?) while the other students snickered.

"The same could be said for Shakespeare, no? Let me ask you something. What poet is taught to freshmen at this university every year? That Beijing installation artist no one will remember in a few months? Or Xiao-Wen Chou?" Michael let the Baoding balls roll to a standstill and leveled her with his full gaze, partially hidden beneath a low brow.

"I—I just thought I could try something different—"

"Listen, Ingrid, I'm watching out for your best interests. And I'm going to let you in on some confidential information."

She held her breath.

"Professor Zhao is retiring soon. The university's been pressuring her for a while now. They won't fill her position immediately, but they'll be looking for another Chouian scholar in a few years. They'll want someone young and energetic. Someone who's shown her dedication to this department. Do you get my meaning?"

Ingrid nodded rapidly. She understood, as did all her fellow PhD candidates, the endangered species status of a tenure-track position. The very mention of the word "tenure" transformed otherwise respectable students into cannibalistic fiends, ready to slaughter each other over the remaining scraps in academia. And once she obtained tenure, she'd finally be afforded the freedom to study whatever she wanted—

"—and I have no doubt researching Chou will prove fulfilling in more ways than one," Michael was saying. "Many students have told me they feel more . . . connected to their Chinese heritage by delving so deeply into Chou's poetry." He paused. "Wouldn't you like that?"

"I suppose so," Ingrid said, though it came out more a question than a statement.

"I know you have what it takes to turn a fresh lens on an old poet. Judith said you were her brightest student. You have a gift, Ingrid—don't let it go to waste."

"Thank you," she murmured.

"So, what do you say?" Michael poured her another cup of tea.

She drank it in one gulp and smiled weakly.

"Welcome home," Michael grinned.

Was it a coincidence that, a few weeks prior to this conversation, the East Asian Studies department had come under criticism for being "89 percent white, 9 percent Asian and 1 percent other"? Well, it didn't matter. That spring, Ingrid applied to the PhD program and was accepted for the following fall semester, somehow bypassing the usual nine-month application period. For three years, she was inundated with East Asian literature, history and philosophy. When it came time to pass her comprehensive exams, she surprised herself, and her professors, by performing half-decently. She waded into her dissertation first with tempered optimism, and then as the years dragged on, with increasing despair, until her research consisted primarily of scratching and sniffing at herself. By then, seven years after her first meeting with Michael, the tracks leading her from the past to the present had all but been erased. Writing her dissertation on Xiao-Wen Chou was like waking up in a doorless, windowless room without knowing how she'd gotten inside.

TWO HOURS IN the archive passed as though they were two whole days. An obscene noise startled Ingrid; she looked around before realizing it was her stomach. She stood up and walked unsteadily towards the lockers. Tucked inside her backpack was a bottle of extra-strength antacids. Her mouth watered at the memory of their chalky sweetness. For Ingrid, the pastilles incited the same religious ecstasy that others got from snorting real drugs.

The sliding glass doors parted, revealing Vivian Vo. She was dressed in all black, accented with a short asymmetrical haircut and dark lipstick. Though Vivian was only younger by a few years, Ingrid felt doddering and geriatric in comparison, which made her want to trip Vivian whenever they crossed paths. Ingrid readied herself to walk briskly past her, delivering only a detached nod in her direction, when, to her horror, Vivian breezed by her as if she were a potted plant.

Vivian was a fifth-year PhD student and, in that time, had attracted the kind of attention Ingrid had always longed for but had never enjoyed. She had scooped up a coveted fellowship, one Ingrid had unsuccessfully applied for as an incoming student, and had already authored *five* peer-reviewed articles. Ingrid had written only one paper forthcoming from *BUGR*, the *Barnes University Graduate Research Journal*.

The two women were not particularly friendly with one another. To begin with, they hailed from different departments: while Ingrid was in East Asian Studies, Vivian was over in Postcolonial Studies. From what Ingrid had gathered, Vivian's dissertation did not consider Chou's work from a literary perspective, like hers did, but from an "anthropological" one. Ingrid refused to ask her for more details at the smattering of university events they'd attended together; Vivian, too, never solicited details about her research. Perhaps she was simply uninterested, but as for Ingrid, the mere acknowledgment of her only direct competition in the field of Chouian studies at Barnes was enough to suggest Vivian's research was legitimate, which, Ingrid had decided, it wasn't. And yet, she was fixated on proving she was just as intelligent, just as relevant, as "the darling of Postcolonial Studies."

In the drafty hallway, Ingrid rummaged around in her backpack for the bottle of antacids. She chewed three pills and texted her fiancé about his day (hers was going horribly as per usual, she reported). She anxiously stared at her phone until he responded (he was fine, had she remembered to book a doctor's appointment about her stomach pain?), then reluctantly towed herself back inside the archive.

Yet another wasted morning.

She was debating between fried chicken or chili cheese fries for lunch when she finally pulled out the first manila folder and shook out its contents. Eleven pages, instead of ten, spilled onto her desk. Her first reaction was annoyance—lately, she'd noticed archive boxes with misplaced or nonexistent catalogue items. She blamed it on Daryl's inefficiency.

Then, as Ingrid unfolded the yellow piece of paper, she recognized the chaotic handwriting as her own. Her heartbeat rattled. She must have left one of her legal pad notes in there by accident. She glanced around, relieved Margaret hadn't found it; no doubt she would have scolded Ingrid in her maddeningly monotone voice.

On one side was a poem copied out by hand:

"*The Ancestral Hearth*"

The ancestral hearth is lost and so, I only visit
in my dreams.

Here the houses sink into the sloping mountainside,
nestled between rock and tree.

To the north are gentle verdant farms, tea leaves bobbing
in the rain.

To the west, a crane perches on a water-smoothed rock,
watching silvery fish flash by.

To the south, sturdy yak pull carts until dusk,
straining their hooves into the mud.

And there, where pearly stream meets ocher forest,
while the eastern wind whispers for five full moons,
lies the origin of things past.

NOTES

Formally, Chou relies on couplets, one tercet. Free verse. Lots of
enjambment, _again_. What does it mean? Note to self: look up if
enjambment has any similarities with Chinese grammar.

The lost ancestral hearth = Chou is unable to give back his
Americanness

Sloping mountainside = Impending disaster

Tea leaves = ???

Crane fishing = Sustenance and survival . . . The Chinese American
must adapt to his surroundings . . . That's not half bad!

Yak stuck in mud = Life is a boorish, endless struggle

Is the poem about how humans are ripped from the comfort of the
home, thrown into cruel and unpredictable environs, until they die
and are buried into the earth again?

Don't be so juvenile, Ingrid.

Concatenation of protohybridity. Hypertextual palimpsest.
Cultural estrangement, cultural perambulation, cultural
dissemination. Parsing a bricolage of a disintegrated self.

*Liminal translocality. Investing the text with refracted
syncretism. Mapping of interdiscursive historiography.
Transpacific cross-fertilization. A caesura of the self. Imbricated
transitoriness.*

Oh, shut up, Ingrid.

*More literally, where "houses sink into sloping mountainside" must
be Baoshan Stone City.*

The origin of things past = Conception? Maternal figure? Yes!

*A poem about migratory patterns . . . A decomposed compass . . . The
speaker is unmoored . . . He travels across the map of China . . .*

*Stanza three has sixteen syllables. Stanza four, twenty-one. Stanza
five, nineteen.*

*If the speaker moves north sixteen degrees, then west for twenty-one
degrees, then south for nineteen degrees . . . Chou's mother must be
from Shangluoshui!*

The other side of the page was hogged by lopsided circles and slanted
annotations jammed into the margins. Her notes looked like the ram-
blings of a lunatic stalking a victim, which in this case was an innocent
poem. In the middle of the page, a zigzagging line bridged Baoshan Stone
City to Shangluoshui. Chou's poetry contained numerous references to
his paternal family's home in Baoshan Stone City, but only obscure nods to
his maternal "ancestral hearth." Ingrid had felt pleased by this modest
discovery, however hypothetical or useless it was. Trying to siphon meaning from Chou's poems was like pulling teeth. When a red lacquered box
appeared on the page, it was just that: a red lacquered box. No deeper

meaning lurked around the poem's corners for her to expose. Unlike the poets she'd *wanted* to study, with their untethered blank verse that sent words tripping across the page, Chou's poetry had a flat, tidy quality to it. Put plainly, he was boring. This made it all the more difficult to pass off an uninteresting and simple poem as an interesting and complex poem—a sleight of hand that determined the foundation of her academic career.

Truthfully, Ingrid was also beginning to understand Chou had fallen out of fashion. His traditional forms were not daring or experimental. Even his subject matter was quickly gathering dust. The new generation of Asian American poets were writing about the texture of their genitals, gentrification, the gig economy. Chou was, clearly, not the most flashy of subjects.

But here . . . here Ingrid might be onto something. If she couldn't find anything in the metaphorical or theoretical plane to write about, at least she could fall back on an autobiographical approach.

She looked more carefully at the piece of paper. Next to "Shangluo-shui" was a note. Whereas Ingrid's handwriting was in pencil, this was scrawled in bold black ink. Someone had written, "No, stupid. It's Xiaoluo-shui," beside a smiley face.

"No, stupid."

Well! Ingrid blinked several times and peered at the tiny, lopsided face—more like a smirk than a smile. Her cheeks burned. Was it mocking her?

She pulled up a map of China on her laptop, retraced her steps and arrived at the same location she'd originally pinpointed: Shangluoshui. Curiously, Xiaoluoshui was only five degrees to the east. Why would she be off by so little? Whoever had left the note was probably playing a harmless joke on her. She picked up her pencil to cross it out. Then she put it back down—it wouldn't hurt to double-check.

She read the poem again, counting syllables, and paused at line twelve: "The eastern wind whispers for five full moons." The east. Five moons.

The clues had been evident all along: Xiaoluoshui was nestled between a "pearly stream" and an "ocher forest." So it *was* Xiaoluoshui!

Her heartbeat sputtered.

Who had written this? Ingrid looked across the room at Vivian, her head bobbing between a pair of enormous headphones. No other PhD student at Barnes was writing a dissertation on Chou. But why would Vivian of all people help her, albeit by calling her stupid?

Ingrid furtively slipped the yellow piece of paper into her bag and snuck a peek at Margaret. She took exactly two breaks: during lunch at 12:00 p.m., when Daryl replaced her for forty-five minutes, and briefly at 3:00 p.m., when she relieved herself. For the next hour, Ingrid pretended to type notes on her laptop, all the while surreptitiously observing Margaret out of the corner of her eye. At 2:58 p.m., the formidable archivist rose from her chair. Whatever Margaret's quirks, Ingrid had to commend her on the regularity of her bowel movements.

She waited until the heavy door to the bathroom swung shut before creeping towards Margaret's desk, enclosed in a smaller room containing all the archive boxes. She verified Daryl was sufficiently distracted, then flipped around the logbook and turned to September eighth.

Wenli Zhao—a professor in E. A. Studies.

Vivian Vo—that was to be expected.

Noah Steiner—yet another E. A. Studies professor.

Retlaw Ekul Nosbig.

Ingrid frowned. What sort of name was that? She frantically copied the assortment of letters onto an index card and swung the logbook back to its original position just as Margaret emerged from the bathroom, striding her wide swinging steps.

"May I help you," Margaret asked flatly.

"I—I was just returning this." Ingrid pushed box number fifteen towards her. "I love the brocade today, by the way! It's so—so—Chinese?"

The archivist's expression remained unchanged. At that moment, Daryl trundled by with a trolley of books. Margaret smiled so widely at him, Ingrid caught a front row view of her cavity fillings.

When she turned back to Ingrid, she withdrew her smile. "Anything else I can help you with."

"I was wondering if you've had any interesting visitors lately." Ingrid paused. "Any . . . foreigners?"

"What do you mean by 'foreigners.'"

"Visitors from, oh, I don't know"—she looked searchingly at her—"Scandinavia?"

Margaret pulled box number fifteen to her chest and narrowed her eyes. "No."

Ingrid laughed a strange, high-pitched laugh and swatted at the air, where Margaret's arm would have been if she wasn't three feet away.

"Oh, Margaret, you're too much!"

They stared at each other for several moments.

"Well," Ingrid said, too loudly for the silent archive, "you have a nice day now, you hear!" She waved by bunching her fingers downwards and sashayed towards the exit.

The moment Ingrid was out of view, Margaret shook her head and muttered under her breath, "Bitch thinks she's white."

INGRID MARCHED TO the parking lot with unusual resolution in her steps. The outline of a plan had already hatched in her mind: she would follow this bread crumb trail to its tasty conclusion. She would surpass self-satisfied little Vivian Vo. She would hunt down Retlaw Ekul Nosbig. She had convinced herself the person behind the name was her hot ticket out of academic purgatory, her long-awaited savior come to free her from reading about filial piety and bound feet ever again. For beneath her veneer of apologetic passivity, Ingrid Yang possessed a frightening determination to put her Xiao-Wen Chou days behind her. She wanted justice—poetic justice, one might say—from the universe, payback for years of wheeling and dealing in Chinese-y shit. Perhaps then and only then, she could find her way back to who she was before Xiao-Wen Chou had hit her over the head like a porcelain vase.

2

A Benign Coincidence

I ngrid and her fiancé lived in a two-bedroom apartment in Barnes's graduate housing to the south of campus. The living room carpet bore a suspicious pink stain, the radiators clanked and the walls were unseasonably thin, but it was subsidized and in walking distance to the university. Parked beneath the apartment was a rusted chocolate-colored Oldsmobile that Stephen had received on his eighteenth birthday, which they took turns sharing.

By all accounts, Stephen Greene was plain. He had a plain, thin face and plain brown hair. He wore plain glasses and preferred plain clothes paired with plain, unpatterned socks. He had the face of an unremarkable passerby or, when he stood in shadowy lighting, of someone on the sex offender registry.

But to Ingrid, he was perfect.

She loved Stephen's generic features and droning public radio voice.

The way he only ate sugar-free cereal and color-coordinated his pencil drawer. She was uncertain about many things in life, but she knew with utmost certainty that she and Stephen—they were meant to be. This belief had scientific backing: after inputting their preferences for age, race, location, education and interests, an online algorithm had matched them together with a 98 percent success rate.

Prior to Stephen, Ingrid had experienced such bad luck with men, she felt fated to be alone for the rest of her life. Although the idea of being her own significant other enjoyed a certain appeal (take *that* patriarchy!)— here, too, she had imagined a new wardrobe of shawls, autumn tones and tinkling jewelry—Ingrid harbored an innate need to attach herself to someone like a pathogen to a host.

Perhaps therein lay the problem. Her ex-boyfriends had called her hurtful names like "clingy" and "codependent." Her first boyfriend, the Film Studies Major, used to disappear on her for weeks at a time with nary a text message. She had to resort to temporarily changing her major in order to take the same classes as him. When she confronted him in Advanced Film Theory 101, he went into a rage, calling her "hysterical" and threatening to file a restraining order against her. But then he showed up outside her dorm room at four in the morning to say if she didn't take him back, he would start using again (prescription Adderall) and would she forgive him?

She forgave him.

Afterwards came the Engineering Grad Student who had also been her TA for a general education requirement. On their first date, while she mopped up the semen on her stomach, he cried and confessed he'd never gotten over his first love (Ingrid was touched by his sensitivity). The Engineering Grad Student had an impressive sex drive—every single time he saw her, he wanted to have sex. His favored position was gripping her around the throat while her limbs flailed in every direction. She once made the mistake of telling him she wasn't in the mood for sex, and she was afraid it would hurt, and he sobbed for an hour straight, rocking back and forth on the bed, whimpering that her rejection of his advances made him feel unlovable, which brought back all his abandonment issues stemming from his stepmom leaving his dad when he was sixteen. She never made the mistake of saying no to him again.

Next was the Investment Banker, who she'd met through a blind date forced upon her by an acquaintance. He had a kink for watching porn together before they had sex, while they had sex and sometimes after they had sex. Ingrid always had trouble getting lost in the commotion onscreen (she was distracted by the soundtrack and set design choices, which she blamed on her introductory dip into Film Studies), but she said nothing—she'd never shame him for having a kink; she wasn't a *Republican*! The relationship ended briefly when she walked in on him during a blindfolded orgy, but the Investment Banker disclosed that his commitment issues originated from his stepmom leaving his dad when he was sixteen so he couldn't be held responsible for his behavior. The relationship ended permanently when he broke up with Ingrid, citing that he just didn't feel the way he used to about her, but could she return the three-hundred-dollar blender he had bought her because, well, it wasn't really fair for her to keep it now that the relationship was over, was it?, and they were still good friends, weren't they?

She gave it back (and emailed him the warranty).

The finale to her season of dating was the Medical Resident. He and Ingrid met by chance just like in the movies: she turning around and splattering her coffee across his pale green scrubs; he waving it off and asking her to dinner that night. They fell into each other like two bodies of water after a dam is lifted. He was the first boyfriend who pronounced "I love you" while neither drunk nor drugged nor in the midst of ejaculation. Ingrid, too, loved him—intensely and obsessively. The Medical Resident explained love was the reason why Ingrid forced him to act the way he did. He made this known by having her list why she loved him, how she had failed to show it and how she would prove it, mostly while on her hands and knees, though sometimes he allowed her to remain standing against the wall. He occasionally locked Ingrid inside his bathroom (having reversed the lock system) when she had done something unacceptable like failing to inform him of her whereabouts after nightfall. He was also fond of projectile-throwing objects and screaming into her face, spraying spittle across her cheeks, which he somehow managed to do only when his neighbors were out. Then one night, when he smacked her so hard she hit the edge of the entertainment console and passed out, she could finally give a name to what he was doing to her, and left.

After that, Ingrid did not date anyone for a year and a half. She began to actively cultivate her spinster wardrobe and visit animal shelters, calculating that if she adopted a cat every seven years, she'd accumulate a respectable number before menopause.

When she registered on the dating website, she acted half out of curiosity and half out of cynicism. She expected to smugly scroll through desperate profile after desperate profile, feeling reaffirmed spinsterhood was the correct and sensible path forward. But then she was matched with Stephen Greene.

Stephen: who believed in "vanquishing toxic masculinity," who did not initiate conversation by demanding "shaved or natural," who instead politely inquired after her dissertation topic, who traded literary quips with her for a full month before she got impatient and asked him out. Stephen: whose idea of a first date wasn't going back to his apartment to "check out his DVD collection," which somehow always turned into a forty-five-minute blow job, but attending a lecture on the short-eared gray owl native to Massachusetts.

During that first date, they traced their similarities like a connect-the-dots picture. Stephen had grown up in a colorless New England town and was an only child; likewise for Ingrid. His parents were both orthodontists; hers were both government bureaucratic workers. Both faithfully recycled. Both dreamt of one day sponsoring a malnourished child in an impoverished, war-torn country (the more impoverished and war-torn, the better). Their interests—intellectual, cultural, political—aligned in comforting symmetry. Make no mistake, Stephen was not exceptional save for the fact that he was exceptionally unexceptional. But Ingrid had tried men who worshipped their own testosterone, men who had personalities and egos the size of small countries, and look how that had gone.

What she wanted now was someone safe and dependable, someone downright predictable. And who could be more predictable than Stephen Greene? The man had used the same brand of hand lotion for over *eleven* years; surely that sort of brand loyalty transferred over to more personal forms of loyalty. As they grew to know each other (Stephen always stressing he would follow Ingrid's pace when it came to physical intimacy; he had been a self-proclaimed feminist since seventh grade), what Ingrid appreciated most about him was his constant and unfailing benevolence. When frowning, Stephen looked thoughtfully concerned. When upset, like he had ingested one too many dairy products (he was lactose intolerant). He was incapable of raising his voice or slamming the door (it triggered his tinnitus). One got the feeling if he were caught in a fire, he would remain calmly smiling even as the flames consumed his flesh. When a fire *did* break out in Stephen's building and when he in fact calmly smiled as the flames melted a decade of work on his hard drive, that was when Ingrid knew for certain: she could trust this man. Her heart, once thought permanently shuttered, reopened for business and let Stephen take up occupancy.

Soon after, all her old behaviors came flooding back—her need to know what he was thinking all the time, to be constantly reassured that no, he was not going to abruptly leave her in the middle of the night with all her cash and her checkbook like a certain Investment Banker, and no, he was not purposefully ignoring her texts, he had just been alphabetizing the pantry, and yes, he really loved her—and not once did Stephen flee. What other men had found intolerable, he found endearing. He delighted in fussing over Ingrid's every need. When she sneezed, he was there a moment later, a tissue balanced tenderly on his palm. When she woke, it was to breakfast laid out on the table, cooled to a perfect seventy-eight degrees. When they had sex, he performed foreplay exactly as she instructed, gently massaging her entire body from her pinky toes to her earlobes with an index finger. Ingrid, too, was eager to demonstrate her devotion: ordering him vitamins in bulk, showing up at his place unannounced to bleach his whites, cooking him fiber-rich stew for each day of the week.

Stephen and Ingrid clicked into each other's lives like two sturdy plastic furniture parts from IKEA fastening together. You couldn't wrench them apart without breaking something.

THE MORNING AFTER the appearance of the smirking smiley face, Ingrid woke up in an empty bed. She found Stephen pacing the office in yesterday's clothes, his hair leaning vertically like porcupine quills.

"Did you sleep?" she asked.

Stephen shook his head.

"You have to take care of yourself," Ingrid chided lightly. She opened the window to let in fresh air, then gathered the empty coffee cups on his desk. "When do you think you'll finish the first draft?"

Stephen was a professional Japanese-to-English translator, all the more impressive because he could not speak Japanese. Entirely self-taught, he didn't study the language until after college. But despite his insecurities over never having visited Japan and knowing only how to convincingly say "sugoi!" his vocabulary was impressively extensive. She didn't know anyone who worked as hard as he did, perusing the dictionary for pleasure, analyzing Japanese TV shows while taking meticulous notes, compiling his own thesaurus. His diligence was admirable, and it had finally paid off. After submitting a sample translation of three chapters, he'd been awarded the first major contract of his career—Azumi Kasuya's autofiction novel *Pink Salon*.

"Tonight, if possible."

"Tonight?" Ingrid balked. "But tonight's the launch of—"

Stephen chuckled and enveloped her in a hug.

"I know. You didn't think I forgot, did you?"

He motioned at the door. Hanging against it were outfits he had selected for the evening: charcoal-gray slacks and a button-up for him, a soft gray wool skirt and cardigan for her.

Ingrid let out a happy cry. She believed matching outfits for couples were the height of romance.

"I wouldn't miss celebrating you being a published *auteur*," he smiled.

She waved him away and tried not to look too pleased. "Well, I should get some work done, too." As she closed the door, Stephen called, "Don't forget your orthopedic writing cushion!"

With the cushion in hand, Ingrid positioned herself on the living room sofa and opened up her laptop. Thus far, "Retlaw Ekul Nosbig" had led her nowhere in her online scavenging.

When she searched all the words together, she landed on pages of indecipherable coding: "nosbiG paDdig yfiddig . . . etiruajul ekuL sseneku . . . treboR retlAw ailagiboR." When she looked up "Retlaw," she found a British confectionary company and a fourteenth-century composer. "Ekul" brought up an electronic musician and various avatar usernames while "Nosbig" led to misleading results on rhinoplasty. In the muddled haze that accompanies descending into the Internet's depths, Ingrid analyzed Before and After videos for three hours before she grew conscious of her sidetracked spiraling. Retlaw Ekul Nosbig had evaded her again.

The very sound of those six syllables irritated her. Coupled with the insulting note and smirking smiley face, she understood whoever had signed under the phony name in the logbook was playing a joke on her.

"Having a laugh at my expense," Ingrid muttered.

Instead of focusing on her dissertation, she had wasted hours of precious research time on nonsense. What had she been thinking?

THE LAUNCH OF *BUGR*'s fall issue took place in the dean's conference room. The tablecloths, platters of hors d'oeuvres and bottles of screw-top wine did little to disguise the fact that it was a conference room: relentlessly depressing no matter how dressed up.

Still, Ingrid's heart fluttered when she held the journal in her hands and saw her name in print for the first time: "Traces of Bilingualism in Xiao-Wen Chou's Poetry" by Ingrid Yang. She should send a copy to her parents. When her dissertation came crumbling apart and her funding was revoked, at least they'd have that.

She was thumbing through the watery smooth pages when her eyes fell on a familiar name: "Yellowdrama! Or Banal Orientalism and the Enduring Popularity of Miss Saigon" by Vivian Vo. Her ears inflamed. Yet another article? How could any human be so productive? Did Vivian Vo even have time to take a shit?

A low, seductive laugh interrupted her internal fuming. There she was: draped in a black dress that hit her ankles, clunky combat boots, dark lipstick. Surrounded by a circle of worshippers staring at her with spellbound attention. Ingrid instantly regretted her choice of gray cardigan and wool skirt—she and her fiancé had unintentionally matched the conference room.

Stephen wandered back with a plate of mini quiches. "Everything okay, dear? You look upset."

"I'm fine," she said through clenched teeth.

Stephen chuckled. "I can tell you're not fine. What's going on?" When she crossed her arms for a response, he rubbed her shoulders and said, "All right, let's talk about it when we get home. How does that sound? Here, eat one of these."

Ingrid wasn't hungry, but swallowed the mini quiche Stephen held before her mouth. She felt a little better—maybe she *was* hungry and just hadn't realized it.

"Thanks." She smiled gratefully up at him.

"Hi, Ingrid! Hi, Stephen!"

They turned around to see Eunice Kim, grafted into a tight, low-cut dress paired with stiletto heels. Four foot eleven with double D breasts and impeccable false eyelashes, no one ever guessed Eunice was a sixth-year PhD candidate with a prestigious fellowship. Her dissertation concerned Hegelian ethics in K-dramas. Eunice was as carefree as Ingrid was anxious. She was also Ingrid's closest and unlikeliest friend. They'd met after they were instructed to share an office, which permanently stank of wet socks, but their friendship was solidified once they discovered their mutual hatred of Vivian Vo.

"Oh, this is my date, Thad," Eunice announced.

The tall and unsmiling blond man beside her shook hands with Ingrid and Stephen, somehow managing to say hello without meeting their eyes or moving his neck. He wore a polo shirt, khaki shorts and a cordless headset plugged into his right ear.

"Are you also in academia?" Stephen asked brightly.

Thad stretched his arms behind his head and rocked back on his heels. "Nope, I'm in tech."

"Thad is creating a start-up," Eunice cooed while slipping her arm around his waist. The effect of seeing them squished together was unsettling. Their disparity in height created the illusion that Eunice was growing out of his leg.

"What's your start-up?" Stephen politely asked.

While Thad launched into a monologue, Ingrid scanned the room. She caught a glimpse of Michael and quickly lowered her gaze to the floor. Her stomach felt like a nail was being hammered through its pyloric antrum. Every encounter with Michael ended with him asking after her dissertation and Ingrid lying through her teeth. She'd never intended to walk down the dark path of lies and over-the-counter drugs. Yet here she was.

"The published scholar!" Michael boomed across the room. He had seen her. He strode over with his wife, Cixi, in tow. After shaking hands with everyone, Michael clapped Ingrid on the back. The mini quiche she'd consumed levitated an inch.

"Stomach flu doing better?" Michael inquired.

"Oh, yes, thank you," Ingrid murmured. She saw Stephen frown, his lips beginning to part, and elbowed him in the side.

"Have you tried the hors d'oeuvres?" Michael waved over a server. "What do we have here?"

"Seared tuna roll," the server replied. Everyone took one and bit in.

"Ah, I'm getting a hint of wasabi. Anyone else?" Michael asked.

"I taste it, too," Stephen nodded. "Although, I doubt it's *real* wasabi."

"What do you mean?" Thad squinted at him.

"Well, commercial wasabi is horseradish that's simply been dyed green."

"The last time I was in Japan, I visited a wasabi farm in Nagano Prefecture," Michael said. "Absolutely life-changing. The farmer and I—"

"I don't think so," Thad interrupted. "False advertising is illegal." He glanced over at Eunice for approval. She continued scrolling through her phone.

"I can assure you it's true," Stephen persisted. "Real wasabi is very labor intensive to produce. You see, it's made from the plant *Wasabia japonica*—"

"Never heard of it before."

"Surely, Thad, you don't believe if you've never heard of something, it doesn't exist—"

"I'll believe whatever I want," Thad huffed, squaring back his shoulders. "This is a free country, isn't it?"

"Now, now, boys, I tasted real wasabi in Nagano Prefecture. I can be the judge of this." Michael snatched another tuna roll from a passing tray and ate it ceremoniously. He closed his eyes and announced his verdict: "Horseradish."

Stephen smiled pleasantly. Thad crossed his arms.

"Okay, all I'm saying is I've eaten a lot of sushi," Thad backtracked. "Minimum twice a week. My go-to spot is right under my condo. On Thursdays, there's an all-you-can-eat buffet."

"Have you ever been to Yamamoto's?" Stephen countered. "It's our favorite sushi bar in the area."

Thad raised his eyebrows at Ingrid. "Really?"

"Yes, she thinks it's the most authentic in Wittlebury," Stephen answered for her.

When it came to topics concerning Asia, Ingrid always let him take the lead and was thankful he didn't mind. Despite what her dissertation topic suggested, she didn't enjoy discussing sushi or the origin of the fortune cookie or the proper way to feng shui a bathroom or how to say "My name is Geoff" in Mandarin or what her thoughts were regarding the Rape of Nanking.

She concentrated on nibbling whatever was on her plate. What time was it? She searched for a clock in the conference room and realized Michael, Stephen and Thad had crowded together by the refreshments table. She, Eunice and Cixi were left stranded in the middle of the room.

"Cixi, how are you?" Ingrid asked in an effort to be sociable.

"Good," she replied without elaborating.

"I love your . . . jacket," Eunice tried.

"Good."

Ingrid and Eunice exchanged glances. Cixi was often in attendance at Michael's university engagements, though the two rarely spoke to one another. The husband and wife were startlingly different, in both appearance and disposition. Around campus, Michael was considered handsome—at least to those with a yen for shaggy, salt-and-pepper types. He was extroverted and charismatic, commanding and assertive (though he was a bit of an attention whore—when Michael was in the room, you knew it). He never forgot a name or a face, could remember whatever detail you dropped in your last conversation to make it seem like you, just you, were special to him. Unsurprising, then, that he was everyone's favorite professor: the one who yanked a few administrative strings to upgrade your C to a Pass, who turned a blind eye when you showed up to class dead hungover; who let you borrow his faculty parking pass. During Ingrid's first year in the PhD, when she'd failed to win the graduate housing lottery, it was Michael who wangled an apartment for her in the end.

By contrast, Cixi preferred to blend into the decor. A few times, Ingrid had walked past without seeing her, so that when she made a sudden movement, she startled Ingrid. Unlike Michael's public-facing personality, Cixi's was intentionally kept under lock and key for only those she deemed worthy of it. She never smiled and disliked shaking people's hands. Even on semiformal occasions like tonight's, she refused to take off her quilted cotton-padded jacket that had survived the Cultural Revolution. She eschewed makeup, subdued her hair into a tight bun and though she now lived in America, she still looked starved. Cixi wasn't . . . *un*attractive, but she was no beauty, either, her features bare and stern, a large mole pulsing in the upper corner of her hairline. Ingrid and Eunice liked to speculate on how the two had met, what Cixi had been like in her youth (she was fifteen years his junior) when Michael had first laid eyes on her in China. After all, something must have attracted him to her.

"What's new with you, Ingrid?" Eunice asked.

"I've been meaning to tell you—I think I finally found something useful at the archive."

"Oh, I always knew it had to happen one day or another!" Eunice wrapped her arms around Ingrid's waist and squeezed. "I don't know anyone who's worked as hard as you and after all the time you've spent there, you really deserve it—"

"Hello," a voice purred. Vivian had appeared behind Eunice, holding a can of locally brewed beer. Of course; beer wasn't even available at the refreshments table.

"Hello, Vivian. Congratulations on your article."

"Likewise. I'm so looking forward to reading it."

They smiled very hard at one another.

"I see you sent away your white men," Vivian laughed. "They can get a little exhausting, can't they?"

"Wh-what?" Ingrid choked.

Vivian gestured towards Michael, Thad and Stephen. They were still huddled together, deep in conversation over black belts.

"Let me guess," Vivian said dryly, "you got tired of them teaching you about your culture?"

Eunice rolled her eyes and muttered something unintelligible under her breath. Vivian looked her up and down with such a scathing glance, her clothes seemed to disappear. Eunice self-consciously crossed her arms over her chest.

"Oh, no, that's not—" Ingrid stammered. "We're not—they aren't—" She didn't know what to say.

Ingrid hadn't noticed all three men happened to be Caucasian and all three women happened to be Asian, but now that Vivian had said something, she couldn't unnotice it. She looked around the room and counted more couples composed of the same demographic. One by the door. Another next to the journal display. One more sitting down. Well—the pattern was merely a coincidence.

Vivian coughed. "Anyway, I just wanted to say hello. Take care." She wiggled her fingers and floated away.

"Ugh, she's horrible!" Eunice cried the second Vivian was out of earshot.

Ingrid still couldn't speak.

"Let's just forget about it," Eunice said, patting her arm.

She ignored her. "That was weird, wasn't it? I would even go so far as to say openly hostile." To her, calling someone "white" was an act of aggression.

"She's probably just jealous of you."

"Jealous of what?"

Eunice shrugged and slurped the rest of her wine through a straw.

"I can't believe she said—it's so ridiculous—the assumption—" She was furious at Vivian for pointing out something benign that didn't need pointing out, but that now, having been pointed out, had become malignant.

Cixi belched, causing Ingrid and Eunice to jump. They had forgotten her presence.

"What do you think?" Eunice asked.

As though she hadn't heard, Cixi abruptly left them to beeline towards her husband. The moment she stationed herself behind him, Michael sensed her presence without her having to speak.

"Ah, the missus is tired. You know how it is," he laughed. "Enjoy the rest of your night, boys. We'll talk more about aikido next time!"

The mismatched couple walked to the doors, Cixi leading the way, when Michael switched tracks and headed straight towards Ingrid.

"I've been meaning to have a word with you all night!"

Eunice took this as her cue to leave, flashing Ingrid an apologetic smile.

"You have?"

"You didn't respond to my last email."

"I didn't?"

"You know, Ingrid, I do need to see some pages eventually. Can you send something over by next week—"

"Do you know who Retlaw Ekul Nosbig is?" she interrupted.

Michael thoughtfully pursed his lips, looked skywards and slowly shook his head. "No, can't say I do. Why do you ask?"

"I found that name in the archive. I don't know who he, or she, is but I think I'm onto something. I just have a . . . feeling about it!"

"I see." Michael stared at his advisee as if he were a doctor and she were his unruly patient who had gone off her medication. "Ingrid, I'd suggest you stay focused. I know it's tempting to go on a wild goose chase. Writing a dissertation is difficult, you don't have to tell me that—I've written two!" he chuckled. "Wanting to distract yourself is completely natural. But I think you're losing sight of the end goal. That would be very unwise at this stage. Do you understand?"

"Oh. I guess so."

"Now will you forget about this 'name' and focus on your research? I know you're a serious scholar, Ingrid."

"Yes, Michael."

He beamed and clapped her on the shoulder. She unintentionally winced.

"Send me those pages!" he called as he strode away.

Ingrid watched Michael until he exited the room, trying to stay upright as her stomach buckled in pain. She reached into her purse for not one but three antacids, threw back the rest of her red wine, then ambushed the refreshments table to pour herself another glass. She drank it in two large gulps as wine dribbled from the corners of her mouth, then wiped the stains away with the back of her hand. For the rest of the night, her dissertation would be banished to the furthest corner of her mind. She was getting blackout drunk.

INGRID WOKE WITH a throbbing headache. Her mouth was parched and everything, down to her fingernails, ached. When she opened her eyes, she realized she'd passed out on the couch. Stephen had thoughtfully undressed her, buttoned her into her pajamas and tucked her into her hypoallergenic, down-free comforter. With deliberate slowness, she struggled to the bathroom, vomited, then chugged a glass of tap water.

Ingrid slumped back onto the sofa and reached inside her purse for a metal pillbox with painkiller medication. She groaned miserably— overnight, the contraption had expanded into interminable depths. After what felt like hours, her fingers finally alighted on the pillbox. When she pulled it out, however, she was holding a business card.

A memory wobbled on the surface of her brain. Thad had given everyone at the launch party his start-up card, a metal engraved waste of money (and a perfect distillment of his personality) that advertised only his and his company's name: REVER. She was about to flick the card to the floor, when she paused. REVER spelled backwards was REVER. A palindrome.

She sat up and rubbed her eyes, then rooted around in her purse again for the index card and a pen.

Beneath "Retlaw Ekul Nosbig," she flipped the letters around, her penmanship shaky and uneven. Retlaw became Walter, Ekul became Luke, Nosbig became Gibson. Her breath caught in her throat.

Walter Luke Gibson.

A name. A real name!

Ingrid scurried to the office so quickly, she stubbed her toe against Stephen's enormous Japanese-English dictionary. She clutched the edge of her desk and squeezed her eyes shut. Running had unwisely sent all the blood rushing to her head—though on the bright side, she now felt fully awake.

She waited impatiently for her laptop to start. Various applications were still loading when she searched online for "Walter Luke Gibson." The first result was a retired Navy SEAL; he seemed an unlikely Chouian scholar. The second result led to a newspaper column of interviews with authors. The third, a review of a recently published poetry collection.

As Ingrid scrolled down, it dawned on her she'd found who she was looking for: *Walter Luke Gibson is an editor and critic. He lives in San Francisco with his partner and children. Contact him here.*

3

The Most Common Name in the English-Speaking World

Salutations Walter Luke Gibson,

I am a PhD candidate at Barnes University. The other day, I came across your name at the Xiao–Wen Chou archive. I think I found a note belonging to you? Did you visit the archive on September 8? Sorry if that sounds weird. I promise I can explain more over the phone or a video call! Hope to hear from you soon!

XOXO,
Ingrid Yang

INGRID REREAD HER email and cringed. In her excitement, she had sent Walter Luke Gibson a shockingly unprofessional email. A week had passed and he had yet to reply. Well, she could hardly blame him.

She glanced at Stephen, sitting hunched over his desk cluttered with *Pink Salon*, his Japanese-English dictionary, notebooks and pens.

He'd been so immersed in revising his translation, she still hadn't found time to tell him about the rude note, the smiley face, the backwards name. And if she did, suppose he looked at her the way Michael had. Like she was, as the saying went, missing a few screws.

"Do you want to go on a walk?" she asked.

He remained silent.

"Stephen?" she laid her hand on his back.

He severed his attention from *Pink Salon*.

"Sorry, dear. Is everything all right?"

His eyes were bloodshot with fatigue. Ingrid wondered if he had remembered to shower the previous day. Better to tell him when she had something to tell, she decided. Stephen had other things to worry about.

"Yes. I'm just going for a walk."

He nodded, reminded her to dress appropriately for the weather, then turned back to his translation.

When she stepped outside, a chilly wind stung her cheeks and snuck into her jacket. Ingrid hadn't checked the forecast; she wished now she'd listened to Stephen and worn the thermodynamic scarf he'd gifted her last year. She bundled her hands into her pockets and realized she was walking in the direction of Barnes as though on autopilot. She turned down Ainslie Street towards her favorite café, the Old Midwife, named such because it had formerly belonged to an old midwife. Though it was a little shabby and could do with more frequent dusting, students flocked to the café for the worn-in armchairs and couches, free wi-fi and cheap coffee. Ingrid particularly liked the topsy-turvy lamps, the bookshelves open for browsing and the live-in cat, Agatha. She was a temperamental, sticky-furred tuxedo who had once single-handedly thwarted an armed robbery.

Ingrid ordered a hot chocolate with whipped cream and selected a barstool in a corner by the window. Agatha was curled up in the chair beside her. Spending time outside the university felt indulgent, even naughty, but the archive was closed on Sundays.

For the past week, Ingrid had reverted to her old habits. She spent nearly all her time dozing with her eyes open, scratching at her eczema scars and sneaking off to the lockers to throw back a few antacids. Her imagining of Margaret and Daryl's tryst had expanded into a full-fledged saga. They couldn't be together not only because of the age difference (Daryl was twenty-one and Margaret was somewhere between thirty and fifty, impossible to tell) but because Daryl's childhood sweetheart, Grace, had improbably awakened from a coma and wanted to marry him post-haste. Daryl was torn between the two women in his life. The sex with Margaret was filthier and therefore better, but he shared a stronger emotional connection with Grace. She was ignorant of his and Margaret's romping in the archive's accessible bathroom. Daryl had been lying to Grace, pretending Margaret was cruelly making him work overtime even though he was a mere intern. Without realizing it, Ingrid had composed volumes of bad fan fiction without having penned a word. If only she could devote the same enthusiasm to her dissertation.

She took out a notebook, wrote "OTHER CAREER OPTIONS" on a new page and underlined it twice. Triannual K–12 fire drills had instilled in her the instinct to prepare for the worst lest it happen to her unannounced.

She nibbled on the end of a pen and thought.

1. Librarian

She liked books. Though she'd have to go back to school for a different degree.

2. Teacher

Also would require a different degree. Also, she disliked children. They made her nervous and self-conscious, more than she already was around adults. And as a TA, she had started to suspect she lacked the natural authority to teach. Why else would only *her* students, never her fellow colleagues' students, submit their late assignments in the middle of the night without so much as a made-up explanation, address their emails to her with "Hi" and text each other nude pics in class? They didn't even bother hiding their phones beneath their desks like normal, respectfully misbehaving students.

3. Accountant

She wasn't exactly sure what an accountant did, or how to become one, but it sounded like a responsible career. She added an asterisk to it.

4. Housewife

She stared at the word, then laughed a little too aggressively. Agatha meowed, chiding her for the disturbance.

Ingrid had always found it strange that, after marriage, she would be bequeathed this new name: wife. She couldn't identify with the sound the letters produced: "wahyf." The word elicited the same disorienting effect as someone calling her by a different name, like the time the barista at the Old Midwife had scribbled "Yingyi" on her coffee cup (to this day, she still called out "Yingyi!"; Ingrid hadn't dared correct her).

And yet she wanted, fervently, to become Stephen's wife. Much like tenure, marriage would offer her a deliciously concrete sense of security. Even if he entertained ideas about blindfolded orgies somewhere down the line, well, she'd have a legal document issued by the state of Massachusetts proving he was *not* allowed to indulge in such wishful thinking. After the proposal, she had every intention of devoting herself to wedding planning, but of course, the dissertation had different plans.

They had been dating for a year when Stephen asked her to move in together. He prefaced this by stating he supported a modern woman's need for autonomy. Not only had he read *and* bookmarked articles like "Why More Couples Choose to Live Apart," he was the proud owner of a canvas *A Room of One's Own* tote bag. But, he amended, in addition to saving on rent, consolidating their utility bills and therefore helping to reduce their carbon footprint, he hated to be away from her.

Ingrid was won over by this, though she needed no convincing in the first place. Far from being a buzzkill, she found domesticity and all its ordinary routines unbearably sexy. Something about opening a drawer to be greeted by Stephen's 100 percent ethically harvested cotton underwear was . . . *thrilling.* When she caught sight of his designated gargling cup on the bathroom sink, she had to keep from swooning. Surely this was proof Stephen had no immediate plans to leave her.

Given her dating history, Ingrid fell in love with a minuscule disclaimer attached—with abandonment, yes, but knowing in the very back of her mind this kind and sensitive man could be wrested away from her at any minute.

So, two years into their relationship, when Stephen made reservations at the Imperial Seafood Garden a half hour out of town, and told Ingrid to dress semiformal, she came mentally prepared. All throughout the appetizers of braised sea cucumbers and pickled geoduck (Stephen had insisted on ordering for them), Ingrid willed herself to keep from crying. The few times her eyes inadvertently watered, drawing concern, she blamed it on the chili oil. This was her last evening with Stephen—she could sense it. The minute the bowls of sweet red bean soup arrived, he would tell her it was over. He would do it nicely, of course, and like a true gentleman he would offer to drive her back to their apartment even though they were broken up, but he would do it nonetheless.

When the main courses of snow crab and garlic lobster were served, Stephen cleared his throat.

"Dear, I want to talk to you about something."

Here it is, Ingrid thought. She bit her trembling lip.

"I want to begin by saying I understand the institution of marriage was created to control the bodies and property of women. As I'm sure you already know, women were de facto dowries passed from one man to the next. Well, land-owning gentry, anyway—historians say the agrarian classes treated marriage differently—oh, but here I am getting away from myself! What I mean to say is that, even though marriage legally subsumes a woman's name, assets and personhood into her husband's"—here he awkwardly untangled himself from his chair and sagged to one knee—"will you marry me, Ingrid Yang?"

She stared at him in a daze, waiting for his words to reshape themselves into: "It's not you, it's me, let's still be friends, can I have my blender back?" When they did not, she blubbered, "You—you—what?"

Stephen chuckled. "Dear, I'm asking if you will marry me."

Ingrid made approximations of the word "yes" and melted into sobs. She flung herself onto him, forgetting the ring in his hand, and soaked the front of his pale blue shirt. "Thank you," she whispered.

At that moment, she was startled again when her and Stephen's parents barreled into the room, brandishing video recording equipment to document their children's intimate moment. The two families proceeded to eat together. More steaming platters were brought forth, more delicacies sampled. Ingrid was so ecstatic, everything she put in her mouth hit like heroin (she imagined, anyway, never having attempted anything harder than NyQuil).

"You two are so *brave*," Stephen's mother breathed during dessert. "I know interracial couples aren't accepted everywhere in this country—" She blinked rapidly to ward off any unscripted emotions, clasped Ingrid's hand, then after a minute, went on, "But your *love* is stronger than *hate*."

Stephen's father rubbed his wife's back and repeated, "So incredibly brave."

Ingrid's mother and father raised their eyebrows at each other, leaving an awkward silence at the table, which Ingrid's mother duly filled by declaring, "Well, you will have very attractive children!" This set off a casual conversation about dominant versus recessive genes everyone could at last unanimously agree upon.

After the engagement, their relationship transitioned into a higher, more evolved state of being. Ingrid took to letting her upper lip hairs grow to abandon before plucking them. Stephen gave up camouflaging his nose hair trimmer as a high-tech Japanese thermometer. And they fell into oh-so-delightful routine: grocery shopping on Fridays, recycling on Mondays, shower sex every first Wednesday of the month. Ingrid did all the cooking while Stephen did all the cleaning. She refilled the humidifier while he booked their flu shot appointments. After a while, Ingrid could no longer recall her own social security number, designating Stephen as the caretaker of her important records—it was all she had ever wanted.

As Ingrid pictured him hunched over his desk, straining his poor eyes, her heart shivered. She'd go home straightaway and fix him a nutritionally balanced yet flavorful meal!

She tossed back the rest of her hot chocolate and prepared to get up when the café door tinkled. She glimpsed a tall figure with a long gray ponytail and creased her body farther into the corner, then pulled up the hood on her coat.

Michael's voice expanded into the café. "An Americano, black, and whatever this little lady's having."

"A matcha latte," said a quiet voice.

Michael sometimes held office hours at the café; he had done so with Ingrid several times. Her hot chocolate churned in her stomach. She crooked her arm so her right hand rested against her cheek, concealing half her face, and stole a glance at who accompanied him. The student in question had undergrad written all over her, trademarked by an aura of freshness and distracted vacancy. She had short choppy black hair and a backpack laden with stuffed animal key chains.

Ingrid realized they were coming in her direction. She held her breath when Michael's hand reached out to clumsily pet Agatha, who greeted him with a hiss. "Feisty thing!" he laughed. They settled into the two armchairs behind her.

Slowly, Ingrid gathered her belongings. She needed to slip away before Michael spied her. He had sent her another email asking after "those pages you promised me," and she had pretended to have a particularly nasty flu. So that he'd have no doubts about this, she'd described all her symptoms down to the color and consistency of her imaginary mucus.

She was about to uncrease herself when Michael asked the girl, "So, have you thought about your paper topic?" and stayed seated—perhaps she could pilfer an idea or two for her dissertation.

"Um, not really."

"What did you like from the syllabus?"

"I don't know . . . Can we write about a different book? That we didn't read in class?" the girl asked in a hopeful voice.

"I'm afraid not."

"Oh."

"What about Xiao-Wen Chou? What did you think of his poetry?"

The girl shrugged. "It's okay."

"Just 'okay'? Try to be specific, Helen."

"I don't know, it's sort of like . . . stereotypical?"

"I see. Did you read the poems I assigned last week?"

"Yeah."

"What about 'Playground Porridge'? Very moving, wouldn't you say?"

"Oh. Yeah, I guess so."

"What stood out to you about it?"

"I guess the part . . . about being at school."

"Go on."

"About the shame he feels . . . at lunchtime?"

Though most of Chou's poetry veered away from the sentimental, "Playground Porridge" candidly recounted the mix of shame and nostalgia he felt when other children mocked his thousand-year-egg porridge.

"Excellent, excellent. Helen, may I ask what your ethnicity is?"

". . . Chinese . . ."

Michael nodded pensively at this.

"Have you, too, experienced an identity crisis related to being Chinese American, or as Chou said, 'forever caught betwixt east and west'?"

"Uh, not really—"

Michael interrupted, "You know, many students have told me reading Chou, and writing about Chou, helps them connect to their culture as Chinese Americans. And I must say, Helen, you've always been one of my brightest students—"

Michael's voice stretched into a faint echo. Ingrid didn't feel well. She slid abruptly off her barstool, causing Agatha to leap onto the countertop, and rushed from the café. Outside, the streetlamps had been lit. The air was nippier now, too, though she could hardly tell the difference. A heavy cloak of déjà vu hung over her.

At one point, she'd been too terrified to turn around, not because Michael might see her, but in case the person sitting across from him was not a girl named Helen, but Ingrid herself. He had said those words to her, or a variation on them, years ago. Hearing them played back made their once innocuous conversation sound exacting, almost sinister.

Ingrid veered down a side street, not wanting to head home yet. She crossed the road just as the light changed; a driver honked at her.

How had Michael forced Chou into her life? How had she let him? Why *was* she researching a dead Asian man? If Chou were still alive, would he care he was the source of her anxiety and insomnia, her stomach pain and newly acquired wrinkles? She had dedicated years of her life to obsessing over someone who hadn't even known she existed. The truth of the matter came as a sudden slap: her dissertation was nothing more than a one-sided relationship. A pathetic one-sided relationship.

She had interpreted the smiley face note and the reversed name as signs she was on the right path—but maybe they were warning her: quit while you're ahead.

When she arrived home, her fingers and ears were numbed stiff from the cold. She threw open the door to the office, where Stephen was still inclined over his desk, and declared, "I'm going to become an accountant!"

He blinked at her. "What?"

"An accountant," she repeated. Then after a moment, "What do accountants do?"

"Are you feeling all right, dear?" Stephen asked before his eyes widened in alarm. "Ingrid, your nose is all red! I'll prepare the electric blanket and warm you up a cup of miso soup—"

She had already switched on her laptop to look up "how to become an accountant" on the Internet. She would learn to fall in love with numbers; numbers would be her new raison d'être. Numbers—fixed and reliable— would not lead her astray!

A notification popped up in the left corner of her screen.

NEW EMAIL FROM: *wlgibson@gmail.com*

Dear Ingrid Yang,

I apologize for the delay in responding to you. The answer is no, I was not at the Xiao-Wen Chou archive on September 8. I live in San Francisco. The last time I was in Wittlebury was many years ago.

Why do you ask? I admit I'm curious about this note you say belongs to me. If you'd still like to speak, my number is 628-555-8970.

Yours,
W. L. Gibson

INGRID WAITED IN anticipation as the call rang, a cheerful warbling tune that stopped mid-ring as a notification announced, CALL CONNECTING. A man in his sixties wearing a knitted sweater appeared on her screen. As the pixels settled into shape, she realized he was East Asian.

"Hello?" she asked.

"Hi, Ingrid. Can you hear me all right?"

"Yes. Hi. I'm supposed to speak with Walter Luke Gibson," she said dumbly.

The man laughed. "That's me."

A wave of embarrassment washed over her. Of course—he was adopted. "I'm so sorry, I shouldn't have—"

"Walter Luke Gibson is my pen name."

"Oh." Ingrid paused to take this in. "Why a pen name?"

"Well, when I first started out, people didn't want to publish book reviews written by someone with my surname. Now when people meet me, they just assume I'm adopted."

Ingrid nervously echoed his laugh. "So, what should I call you?"

"Luke. Luke is fine."

"Well, Luke, thank you for talking to me. I know this must seem strange."

"No, no, I'm all ears." She walked him through the appearance of the insulting note, the smirking face, his mangled name in the logbook. As she spoke, his smile dissipated. "This sort of thing has happened to me before, if you can believe it."

"Really?"

"Over the years, I've gotten calls from all sorts of places . . . Let me think . . . I once had someone call to say I had returned the wrong microwave. Lots of calls from insurance companies. When it first started, I figured my phone number had gotten into one of those junk mailing lists. But even after I changed my number, it kept happening."

Ingrid rapidly took down notes. "Do you think it's identity theft?"

"That's the thing—no one's ever stolen my credit card."

"Oh . . ." she trailed off. "So, who do you think wrote your name backwards?"

"I don't know. I don't know who's been subscribing me to email chains, either," Luke chuckled. "But I'm curious—you said this note was about a poem?"

"Right. A Xiao-Wen Chou poem. Are you familiar with his work?"

"Oh, sure."

"Have you ever reviewed one of his books?"

"I haven't . . . Surprising, I know. Which poem is it?"

"I have it here." Ingrid read "The Ancestral Hearth" aloud. When she finished, she explained her initial miscalculation. "So you see, I got the coordinates wrong. Whoever left the note wanted me to know the real answer: Xiaoluoshui."

"Could you say that place again?"

"Xiaoluoshui."

Luke reclined in his chair, nodding thoughtfully. "Now that sounds familiar."

Ingrid perked up. "It does?"

"I think I've heard it before in a poem. I used to be the editor of a literary journal. A brief but very . . . insightful experience. I learned a lot about writers and their, let's say, insecurities."

"Insecurities?"

"They sent me some emotional letters. Well, mostly angry, now that I think about it. You know, when a poem had been rejected." Luke paused. "Right, and that name . . . Xiaoluoshui, it rings a bell. Well, I kept a folder of the 'greatest hits.' Fun to read aloud whenever I'm having a bad day. I still do it, though it's all digital now. If you wait here, I'll try to dig it up."

"Take as long as you need." Ingrid crossed her fingers as Luke disappeared from the screen. In his place were floor-to-ceiling bookshelves. Off-screen, a dog barked. After several minutes, Luke reappeared, waving a manila folder. "Found it. I was only the editor for a year, as I said, so there's not too many of them."

Ingrid made to clap her hands, then resisted; she had to act professional. She waited patiently as Luke skimmed through the pages. Occasionally he smiled or shook his head. Halfway through, he sat up straight. "Here it is. 'Dear Mr. Gibson, I received your rejection of "On the Banks of the Xiaoluoshui River," but you did not provide a reason why. As I would like to improve the poem in the future, any feedback is much appreciated.'"

Ingrid gasped at the mention of Xiaoluoshui.

"I kept my response. 'Dear Mr. Smith, unfortunately at this time, we cannot offer personalized feedback. Thank you for submitting to *The Westerly Review*.'" Luke flipped to a new page. "He wrote back: 'Mr. Gibson, as this has been a meticulously edited poem—and I have received comments attesting to its strength—please explain why the poem was rejected on the basis of its aesthetic qualities.'"

"He's starting to sound passive-aggressive," Ingrid remarked.

"Oh, it gets better. I replied, 'Mr. Smith, since you insisted, the fragmented form was arbitrarily chosen, the rhyme scheme overdone, and lastly, the setting of Xiaoluoshui irrelevant to the speaker's intent.'"

"Well said," Ingrid cackled. She assumed no further letters were exchanged, but Luke continued.

"'Mr. Gibson, I don't know why I bothered asking for your feedback when, ever since you became the editor of *The Westerly Review*, its quality has plummeted. Please accept my well-meaning wishes to suck my cock.'"

Ingrid melted into uncontrollable laughter; she had a prepubescent relationship to words referencing genitalia. When she regained her composure, she asked in as dignified a voice as possible, "Do you have more information about his poem?"

"Oh, I have it here. I guess I kept it to remember how bad it was. I'll scan it and send it over."

"That would be wonderful. And this person—do you know anything more about him?"

"No, he never submitted to the journal again. Unless, of course, he used a pen name."

"Did he include his full name?"

Luke flipped through the pages again. "In his initial submission, he signed it, 'John Smith.'"

"That has to be a pen name," Ingrid balked.

"Oh, you'd be surprised. I've met John Smiths in my life. I think there's even an annual conference for them."

"I see." The airy lightness in her chest withered.

"Well, I hope this has been helpful."

She snapped back to attention. "It has. Immensely. I can't thank you enough."

"Will you keep me updated on what you find out? I'd like to know if someone is going around using my pen name."

"Of course. I'll do just that."

AFTER THE CALL disconnected, Ingrid wrote "JOHN SMITH" in her notebook in large capital letters.

Her first instinct was to look the name up on the Internet, but it was immediately squashed by the knowledge that the results would register in the millions. Out of masochistic curiosity, she checked anyway: 1,500,000,000. She didn't know whether to laugh or cry. A strangled noise, some hybrid of the two, slipped from her throat.

She would have to be mad to parse through the John Smiths of the world. Even "John Smith" plus "Xiao-Wen Chou" left her with results in the hundreds of thousands. Next, Ingrid tried "John Smith" plus "Wittlebury." This still led to 100,000 results. She halfheartedly scrolled through obituary notices, white pages, social media profiles and high school football announcements, her heart sinking further and further. Had whoever left the note planned to lead her to this moment of exasperation? To sabotage her time when she could have been conducting *real* research? Anger flared through her chest. Maybe that awful Vivian Vo was the note-leaving bandit, after all.

She made to close her laptop when a pop-up appeared.

The page was electric blue with sunny yellow text. *Looking for someone?* glowed at the top. The middle of the page featured a stock photograph of a magnifying glass poised over a question mark. *Our certified private investigators have tracked down countless missing people.* "Platinum Investigative Associates found my good-for-nothing, child-support-dodging ex-husband. 10 out of 10. Highly recommend!"—Gail from Arkansas. *Call 1-800-FIND-NOW today! Standard phone rates apply.*

Ingrid floated her mouse above the exit button. She was a PhD candidate at a nationally recognized university; she had standards to uphold as a serious and upright scholar. To think someone like her could fall for such an obvious scam!

Satisfaction guaranteed or your money back! sailed across the screen in a blinking banner.

On second thought, it couldn't hurt to try.

4

Yellow Peril 2.0

zumi Kasuya's *Pink Salon* was a work of autofiction, detailing her experience at age eighteen when she worked at a Tokyo pink salon and was abducted by a client for seven days.

The novel had seized Japan's attention, not only for the contents inside the book but the circumstances outside it. *Pink Salon* had spurned the protective screen of traditional fiction: the names of people and places had been left unchanged, including the salaryman who had kidnapped her. The Japanese public was also captivated by Azumi—lithe and beautiful with a round, clear face and mournful eyes. Her employment at a pink salon, notorious for recruiting supposedly unattractive and older sex workers, was astonishing. Out of all Japan's illicit establishments, oral sex brothels ranked at the bottom. Also remarkable about Azumi were her humble origins: born in a rural village in Okinawa, the orphaned daughter of purple sweet potato farmers, she ran away from a group home to Tokyo at sixteen.

"Ingrid, this novel is like nothing else I've read," Stephen said. "It's going to change the landscape of Japanese literature in translation, I know it."

This was what he—what they—had been waiting for: Stephen's chance to break out of obscurity, to earn recognition for his hard work at long last.

"Thanks to *you*," she added.

Stephen grinned toothily, displaying the crooked incisor she loved but that he always tried to conceal. Then Ingrid registered the deepening circles beneath his eyes. She had been waiting and waiting for the right moment to tell him about Walter Luke Gibson and John Smith, but she knew he had more important things on his mind. If he so much as suspected she was experiencing an ounce of distress, he would drop everything to help her. And she refused to do that to him, not now.

"Are you sure you're not overworking yourself? You need to rest." The irony of her words was not lost on Ingrid. She could never abide this kind of advice herself. Perhaps that was why she and Stephen were so well matched; they were similar to the point of being the same person.

"I'll try," he deflected, though she knew the moment she left, he would continue working.

"Can I see?" she asked. She stood behind Stephen, leaned her head against his and leafed through the creamy pages. She had always found Japanese characters more attractive than Chinese characters; likewise, she had always preferred the sounds of Japanese to those of Mandarin. She flipped to the back: half the cover was devoted to Azumi's face, gazing demurely into the far-off distance. Her skin was pale with two spots of peach blush just beneath her eyes.

"She looks so young," Ingrid remarked.

"Only twenty-two years old, if you can believe it."

And pretty, she almost added, but instead closed the book. "Will you meet her? To discuss the translation?"

"I'm not sure yet. She's based in Tokyo, so it seems unlikely."

Ingrid kissed Stephen's cheek as her phone buzzed.

"Who is it?" he asked.

She registered the toll-free 800 number. "No one."

He made a playful grab at the device, but she slipped through his grasp and out the door.

PLATINUM INVESTIGATIVE ASSOCIATES was located in a maze of office buildings: chiropractors, shipping agencies, homeowner associations. Ingrid cut several loops and dead ends around the complex before she found office 201C, an office so ordinary, she'd passed it twice. A receptionist filed her nails behind a counter decorated with a jar of jelly beans and a Garfield calendar. Instrumental music played blandly from a ceiling speaker. Ingrid felt a little disappointed. She had prepared for a scene from the movies, starring men in trench coats and important-looking hats, cigars drooping from the sides of their mouths.

"Do you have an appointment?" the receptionist asked.

"Oh, yes. With"—she glanced at her hand—"a D. Woods."

"Sign in here. Feel free to take a seat."

Sitting next to an artificial palm tree, Ingrid was beginning to wonder if she had taken things too far. What exactly was she hoping for by tracking down this man? She acknowledged on the one hand, it might be nothing more than a distraction—anything to avoid the nonexistent dissertation and Michael's increasingly concerned emails.

And yet, intimate knowledge of Chou's alleged maternal cradle was knowledge privy only to his close associates. Alongside the blatant attempt to hide the identity of the note's author—it was all too purposeful to be random. What had been the motivation? On top of that, Luke had scanned and emailed her John Smith's poem. Although his writing style differed wildly from Chou's, both poems referenced the little-known village of Xiaoluoshui. What if, she mused, Chou and Smith had traveled there—together? She shook her head; she was getting ahead of herself.

Ingrid opened her bag to take out a notebook and pen, coming across her jumbo-sized bottle of antacids, and froze. She had failed to notice her persistent stomach pain hadn't resurfaced in days. For the first time, whenever she thought of her dissertation, she felt . . . hopeful.

"Ingrid Yang?"

D. Woods turned out to be a middle-aged woman with stiff blond hair and dark roots. Her beakish nose complemented her mauve suit-skirt combo, boxy with shoulder pads. She ushered Ingrid into her office and shut the door. Inside, the air smacked of patchouli.

"So lovely to meet you in person."

"Likewise, Ms. Woods." Ingrid struggled to make eye contact with her before realizing she had a lazy eye, then anxiously deliberated over locking onto one eye (but which?) or darting her gaze back and forth between both. She opted for the latter.

"Please, call me Darlene," she smiled. "So, I understand you're in a bit of a pickle."

"I am," Ingrid nodded solemnly.

"Besides the name John Smith, what other information can you give me?"

"The only two things I know, or that I think I know, are"—Ingrid waited for Darlene to record this information; she did not—"first, that he lives in Wittlebury, or has recently visited, and second, that he has a connection to the poet Xiao-Wen Chou."

Darlene pursed her lips. "Could you spell that for me?"

Ingrid wrote down the name.

"Nothing else?" she asked, glancing at her watch.

"Oh, he writes poetry. Or at least used to."

Darlene furrowed her brows together. "And may I ask about the nature of the inquiry? Personal? Professional?"

"Professional."

"I see."

"I'm sorry I don't know more—"

"Never apologize, Ingrid. Especially not when it concerns a man."

Darlene stood. Ingrid looked up at her, unaware the meeting had concluded, before getting up unevenly and knocking over a framed picture on Darlene's desk: a cross-stitched kitten in a basket with "Purroud Feminist" embroidered below.

"I'll be in touch in a week with a list of individuals. We can narrow it down from there." Darlene opened the door and winked. "Yolanda will take care of you."

As Yolanda snapped her gum, Ingrid wrote out a check for three hundred dollars and wondered if this was what people called a mid-life crisis.

FOR THE NEXT WEEK, as Ingrid waited for Darlene's call, she dutifully slogged to the archive. Each day, she checked out a box for the sake of appearances, but returned it untouched. She knew nothing in that stuffy mausoleum could save her from her dissertation woes. She was onto something greater than Chou's use of enjambment now.

But because she could not ogle the ceiling all day, she focused her energies elsewhere, in a more . . . creative fashion. By Friday, she had written eight thousand words in a document entitled "Taxes" discreetly enclosed in a folder entitled Taxes.

> The garden was dark at midnight. Dante pinned Marguerita against the castle's walls and inhaled her fragrant womanly scent.
>
> "Not here!" Marguerita cried.
>
> "We are alone now," Dante breathed. He planted kisses down Marguerita's quivering collarbone.
>
> "What if someone sees us!" she cried again, smothering his head inside her bosom.
>
> Marguerita's Mound of Venus throbbed with ~~moist~~ anticipation as Dante's ~~manhood~~ member pulsated hotly against her thighs.

"Take me, Dante," Marguerita moaned. She did not care if Graciela discovered them—she would not stop. She *could* not stop. "Now, Dante, now!"

He hoisted her onto a low stone wall and pulled her brocade dress to her waist, revealing delicate lace panties. She unlaced his leather britches and reached for his

"Aren't you the busy writer?"

Ingrid quickly snapped her laptop shut and turned around to see Vivian.

"I can hear you typing all the way from across the room."

"Sorry, I'll try to be more quiet," she mumbled.

"I take it your dissertation is going well?"

"It is," she replied, lifting her chin slightly. If by dissertation, Vivian meant soft-core archive erotica. "And yours?"

"Very well."

"Shhh!" Margaret was standing up at her desk, her index finger pressed furiously to her pursed lips.

"Well, I'm going outside for a smoke," Vivian shrugged.

"Er—me, too," Ingrid whispered, though she abhorred cigarettes. The thought of closing the unspoken but hostile distance between them was repugnant, but she was beginning to understand avoiding Vivian was counterintuitive—she might have useful information on Chou. Maybe even John Smith.

Outside on the library steps, Vivian passed her a cigarette from her pack. Ingrid inhaled feebly, coughing and flapping the smoke from her face.

"You okay?" Vivian asked. She looked at Ingrid like she was an automated toy that runs around in mindless circles at the mall.

"I'm fine," she wheezed. "It's just that I usually smoke . . . menthols."

Vivian raised an eyebrow.

When Ingrid had finished pounding her chest, she asked hoarsely, "So, you're also researching Chou?"

"Yeah."

"What's your dissertation called?"

"Pleasing the White Master: Traditional Asian American Literature and the Good Little Immigrant Myth."

Like all her titles, it seemed unnecessarily combative. Ingrid deliberated over asking her to elaborate, when Vivian asked, "And yours?"

"Oh. I don't really have a title yet. Still figuring things out."

Vivian exhaled smoke and nodded.

"But I think I found something strange—in the archive," she heard herself saying. She hadn't meant to broach the topic so suddenly, but something about Vivian annoyingly made her want to . . . impress her.

As Vivian turned to look at her more attentively, she suppressed a smile; for once, she knew more than her. The feeling was so toothsome, she tried to draw it out. "Haven't you ever noticed missing documents? Or how the catalogue doesn't always match up with the contents of a box?"

Vivian shrugged. "Oh, that? It's just Daryl. He's not the most organized intern." She took out her phone as if to signal she'd completely lost what little interest she had in Ingrid a minute ago.

"Right." Her cheeks burned. How had Vivian demoted her modest victory into something so mundane? She inhaled again, managing not to cough uncontrollably, and said in as nonchalant a voice as she could muster, "You've been researching Chou for a couple years now, right? Have you ever heard of someone named John—"

A ringtone interrupted Ingrid as Vivian held her phone to her ear. "Hey, babe. You're here?" She scanned the opposite street. A figure rested against a motorcycle, head encased in a black helmet. Vivian waved and crushed her cigarette beneath her heel.

"Is that your boyfriend?" Ingrid asked in a faux conspiring voice. She was dying to know what kind of man could put up with her.

Vivian regarded her with that same wearily bemused smile.

"No, girlfriend."

She frowned. But Vivian had said "babe," though she supposed women called each other all sorts of pet names, nowadays—

Vivian registered her confusion. "I'm gay."

Ingrid blushed. "Oh, right. Of course." She hesitated, unsure if straight people saying the word "gay" was offensive. "I don't mean 'of course you're gay,' of course, I only meant—"

"I have to go," Vivian said, her voice as sharp-edged as her liquid eyeliner. "See you around."

She walked down the steps, kissed her girlfriend, then swung onto the back of the motorcycle, looking like she was in a commercial for an expensive brand of European espresso. The motorcycle thundered down the quiet street, attracting stares from other students. Ingrid reflexively reached up to pat her hair, wondering how many days ago she'd washed it, then looked down to see her socks didn't match. Impressive how, without saying a single word, Vivian Vo could make her feel so small.

AN HOUR LATER, Ingrid had kicked off her shoes, unbuttoned her pants and flopped onto Eunice's couch drinking boba, an activity they treated as a sacred ritual: Earl Grey milk tea with pearls, 70 percent sweetness, no ice, for Ingrid; and lychee rose green tea with aloe vera, 50 percent sweetness, half ice, for Eunice. In the background, a flat-screen TV played their favorite reality show *A New You*, where contestants rejected after first dates were given makeovers and a second chance.

"Vivian's a lesbian," Ingrid said in a rush, the moment a commercial came on. She muted the TV but kept watching, entranced by the happy-go-lucky actors who claimed their lives had been changed by a new allergy pill: *"Lucidax: Clear Up Your Reality!"*

Eunice didn't seem surprised, instead groaned, "That explains why she's so cool."

She was loath to admit this indisputable fact.

"Well, it's going to be a lot harder to hate her now. It would be, like, homophobic," Eunice added.

She deflated miserably into the couch cushions. "I know. And this weird thing happened when we were talking. I had this urge to . . . impress her."

Eunice gasped. "I've had that feeling, too!"

"It's like she makes me feel stupid, and then I really want to prove to her I'm not."

"I know!"

They laughed and fell into an abrupt silence.

"Anyway," Ingrid said after a moment, "we don't like her."

"No, we don't," Eunice said firmly.

Though neither of them said it aloud, they both understood there were two varieties of Asians: Asians like Vivian and Asians like themselves. And that the two varieties eyed each other warily: the former with pity and the latter with resentment for being pitied. For instance, whenever Ingrid saw Asians from the Postcolonial Studies department flocked together on campus, with their loud pins, posters and chants, she made a point to stare very hard at the ground, as if it were the most interesting thing in the world.

She wasn't sure if Eunice reacted the same. Ingrid regarded her like a rare, undiscovered species: the most popular people in her high school spoke their respective diasporic mother tongues with flawless fluency; Eunice, for instance, was perfectly bilingual in Korean and English. She grew up in a suburb of southern California, attended schools that were 90 percent Asian, never wanted for freshly rolled gimbap or all-you-can-eat Sichuan hot pot. Ingrid had discovered boba and shrimp chips through Eunice, her first real Asian friend. Once she got over the foreboding feeling that consuming Asian snacks with another Asian person ran the risk of making you too Asian, Ingrid succumbed to the delights of her culture's delicacies.

Still, she remained in awe of Eunice's . . . comfort with her Koreanness.

Her own high school experience was all too similar to that of American teen movies: the most her character could hope for was the role of a sidekick in someone else's story.

But despite the stark differences in their upbringings, and their sense of fashion, they shared a near identical acceptance of the state of the world and their positions within it.

"Eunice?"

"Uh-huh?" Her eyes were glued to the TV. Today she wore hazel contact lenses.

"Do you think what I'm doing is crazy? I mean, with hiring the PI?" Last week, Ingrid had come clean to Eunice about the string of strange clues. Unbottling everything had felt good, not least because it anchored the note and the backwards name in reality rather than inside her head.

"No, honey, you're not crazy," she said, still absorbed by the TV.

"If I needed your help, would you help me?"

Now Eunice's eyes locked onto hers. "Of course, *anything*." An ex-member of the Korean Christian community, Eunice harbored a streak of devoutness she now applied to secular areas of her life.

Her words only marginally lightened Ingrid's despair. She slumped back into the couch cushions and closed her eyes.

"Hey, I know what will cheer you up," Eunice exclaimed.

A weak "what?" rose from the cushions.

"A makeover!" Eunice pointed at the TV with her foot.

"I don't know . . . I should probably go soon."

"But it's not even dark yet—what would you do at home, anyway?"

Ingrid pictured the silent apartment, where Stephen was fully immersed in his translation.

"Oh, all right."

AN HOUR LATER, Ingrid scrutinized a stranger in the mirror. Bronzer and highlighter had been applied to the hollows and angles of her face. She had industrial-strength false eyelashes. Volumized hair that could get up and walk away, lead a fulfilling life all its own. Lips plumped up and slathered in a shade of matte lipstick called Ex-Wife. Her eye makeup, "a sexy smoky eye," Eunice had promised, was composed of gradient black patches stamped under her newly intimidating "catch me outside" eyebrows. The dark eyeshadow helped conceal the twin strips of eyelid tape pasted over her eyelids. Ingrid had not known about this unique invention until Eunice excavated it from her makeup kit. Her monolid eyes were transformed, slightly sunk into their sockets, making them appear larger and rounder. Eunice confided in Ingrid that she'd worn the tape all throughout high school before her parents agreed to let her undergo double eyelid surgery in South Korea.

To complete her makeover, Ingrid wore gray-violet circle contact lenses Eunice had received as a free sample. Taken all together, she looked like she frequented nightclubs with long VIP lines and men who altered their Subarus. She looked like her name was Michelle or even, in a certain light, Tiffany. Most certainly not an Ingrid.

"So, what do you think?" Eunice asked, barely controlling her excitement.

Ingrid opened her mouth, but no words escaped.

"Well, *I* think you look amazing! I can give you some of my extra makeup and show you how to do it yourself, it only takes me like an hour each morning—"

Eunice's voice receded into the background as the mirror beckoned Ingrid closer. Most of the makeup was too excessive for her taste, yet, she had to admit, something about her eyes was mesmerizing . . . They were the eyes of a stranger implanted into her face, like a too-real mask. Uncanny. Unsettling. She . . . liked them. But more than the eyes themselves, she liked the idea of becoming someone else. A new and improved Ingrid.

Eunice was about to document her transformation with her camera when they heard a sharp rap on the door.

"Yo, Yoon, where'd you put my car keys?"

Eunice's younger brother leaned against the door frame. Ingrid knew only two things about Alex: he was studying for his JD at Barnes and he was always listening to Yung Chigga (a Chinese American rapper with bleached dreadlocks) with the volume cranked all the way up.

Eunice tossed him the keys.

"Hi, Alex," Ingrid said. He was dressed as he always was: sweatpants, sweatshirt, backwards baseball cap. A diamond stud blinked in his left ear.

Alex stared blankly at her. "Have we met?"

Eunice burst into laughter. "It's *Ingrid*!"

Alex's mouth hung open. "Whoa."

He wandered into Eunice's room and picked at the objects littering her vanity table. He held up the roll of eyelid tape like it was a dirty tissue and shivered. "I thought you threw this shit away."

Eunice snatched it from him. "Why do you care?"

"Why do you wanna look like white people?" he retorted. Alex shook his head as he slouched towards the door. Just before closing it, he bowed and barked, "Take honor in your culture!" as if he were a character in Disney's 1998 *Mulan*.

Ingrid automatically laughed, then abruptly stopped, confused. Eunice threw the door open, yelled, "That is *not* what we are doing!" and slammed it again.

"Sure, okay," Alex yelled back.

Eunice turned to Ingrid. "Ignore him."

But she was already peeling off the eyelashes, the tape. The thrill of beholding her new eyes now tarnished by shame.

DARLENE PRESENTED INGRID with two John Smiths: the first was a man who'd won a spicy noodle–eating challenge at Mr. Foo's Chinese Fast Food and the second was a grassroots community organizer. He was also the author of a monthly online newsletter with ties to China. They both agreed she should seek out the second John Smith, the likeliest candidate. Ingrid had hoped for a phone number or an email, but Darlene provided her with only an address. "He's off the grid," she shrugged, passing her a piece of torn-off receipt paper.

The following day, Ingrid drove to an unfamiliar area so far on the edge of town as to be considered an unofficial backyard shared between Wittlebury and its neighbor, Fallowtown. After passing a car impound, a go-kart racing track and a flea market, she pulled up to a flat expanse of trailer parks. Had Darlene given her the right address? She checked the piece of paper again and saw at the bottom: "trailer 16." So she had.

The trailers were all charmingly decorated in specific themes. One was a year-round ode to Groundhog Day; another was draped in hanging plants; another was painted the sherbet hues of a sunrise. Strewn throughout the park were ingenious sculptures and flowerpots constructed from scrap metal, car parts and other recycled items. After wandering around for several minutes, Ingrid arrived at trailer 16, which also advertised a theme: America.

The entire trailer was festooned in American flags. A giant flag billowed from a pole, miniature flags stood at attention around the perimeter and flag curtains obscured the windows. The trailer was quiet, no sound of chatter or a TV or a radio. On the door hung a clipboard with a pen dangling from a frayed piece of yarn. Ingrid inspected it more closely before recognizing it as a petition:

WARNING: YELLOW PERIL 2.0!

The Chinese are taking away jobs from decent hardworking Americans. Soon there will be ZERO factory jobs in the U. S. of A. Why are there no American cell phones? That is because the Chinese took them. Why does everything say it was Made in China? Because the Chinese want WORLD DOMINATION. They will not stop until they

get it. If they own the world economy, they own us.
When the Chinese take over, COMMUNISM will take over.
Say goodbye to FREEDOM and DEMOCRACY. The only way to
stop the ASIAN INVASION is to destroy China NOW. You
think you can reason with them? The Chinese are SHEEP,
ROBOTS and SPIES. They do not know how to think for
themselves. When China gives the signal, 1.39 billion
Chinese will execute a plan of total and complete
world domination. Sign now if you want to STOP CHINA
and SAVE AMERICA!!!

*Add your email to receive my monthly newsletter

Only four names had been collected: "Bob and Mary," "John Smith" and in the same handwriting, "Joseph McCarthy (deceased)." She stepped away from the clipboard as if it were radioactive. Was this some kind of joke? She took out the piece of paper from her pocket and double-checked the address: no mistake there. And clearly the man's name was John Smith. But he couldn't be the likeliest candidate; it must be the man who'd won a noodle-eating competition. If *this* John Smith knew the Xiao-Wen Chou archive existed, he would have set it on fire by now. Or at least called in the National Guard to detain it for treason.

She pulled out her cell phone to call Darlene, but didn't get past "May I speak to—," when a man yelled from inside the trailer, "Who's there?"

Ingrid startled and hung up; from the quiet, she had assumed no one was home.

"I said, who's there?" the man repeated.

She froze—should she engage with this clearly unhinged individual or make a run for it? But then she turned over the piece of paper in her hand, calling to mind the latest amount she'd forked over to Darlene's coffers. If she was going to pay such a steep price for her expertise, she might as well make use of it.

Ingrid cleared her throat. "I'm looking for a John Smith."

A long silence followed before he spoke again. "How did you get this address?"

"Sir, could I please speak to you? It will only take five minutes," she said through the door.

"No solicitors. Can't you read English?"

Ingrid lowered her gaze: a bright red NO SOLICITORS placard was tacked to the bottom of the trailer door. "I'm not a solicitor. I just want to ask you some questions about Xiao-Wen Chou."

"Who?"

"XIAO-WEN CHOU," she enunciated slowly and loudly.

"What did you say?" he bellowed. "Are you coming over to my house to speak the enemy's words to me?"

"I'm sorry, I, uh, think there's been a mistake—"

The door smacked open, releasing the stench of wet dog fur. The man was shirtless and potbellied. His hair invoked a friar's: bald in the center and ringed with woolly tufts. In his hand was an oversized wooden mallet—had he been tenderizing meat just before this or was he repurposing it as a makeshift weapon?

His eyes widened when he saw her. "Chinese commie! Chinese commie!" he hollered, not so much at Ingrid but into the trailer park at large, as if to alert the other residents.

"I'm not Chinese," she shouted back, "I'm Taiwanese!"

"What, now?"

"I said, I'm Taiwanese," she repeated. She was simply stating a fact—it just so happened during this particular moment in time, standing unarmed in front of this anti-Chinese madman, being Taiwanese was a fortunate coincidence. *But* . . . if Ingrid were being entirely honest with herself, she *liked* correcting people who assumed she was Chinese in any circumstance; they were mistaken, she was *Taiwanese*—as if that introduced an enormous gulf between anything negative associated with China and herself.

The look on John's face was proof this declaration had not made the slightest difference. Perhaps he thought she was pro-KMT? In that case, explaining she wasn't on the side of "the enemy" should do the trick. With her eye on the meat mallet, she said in a casual, friendly tone, "Oh, don't worry—I'm pro-independence. Totally against the One China policy. My parents say the CCP is like 'a bully that throws tantrums,'" she chuckled. "And don't even get me *started* on their human rights violations—"

He narrowed his eyes at her. "You can't fool me. You don't look Aboriginal. You're an ethnic Han Chinese!" Ingrid raised her eyebrows, impressed. Most people didn't know anything about Taiwan, let alone its sticky history. Still, she wondered if she should engage with John on this point of contention, recite a recent article her father had emailed her framing Taiwan as a political collective, but he was back to shouting: "And I don't care what you say you are, I know you're a commie! I heard you speaking your Chinese code. Who sent you?" He peered past Ingrid, then twisted his head around to squint at the sky. "How many others did you bring?"

"Sir—I'm American, I'm not—wait, you really think I'm a *foreign spy*?" The outlandish nature of John's statements had thus far held anger at bay, but now Ingrid felt a hot lash of it. She had never taken a DNA test but she probably was "an ethnic Han Chinese." After all, two of her grandparents and two of her great-grandparents had been born in China before moving to Taiwan. Regardless of her feelings about the CCP, didn't she have an obligation to stand up for her ethnic group? Or was excessive ethnic pride frowned upon these days? She hardly had time to process her thoughts when it became clear she had said the one thing she should not have.

John's eyes bulged beyond what she thought humanly possible. "I knew it. I knew you were a spy!" He spanked the air with his mallet like it had done something naughty. "Now get off my goddamn property! Trespasser. TRESPASSER!" He directed his screams at the other residents again.

Ingrid swiveled her head around, seeing people start to step out of

5

The Versatility of Tampons

Ingrid had always depended on women like Darlene Woods. They were teachers, doctors, friends' mothers, school counselors, supervisors: women who knew how to pat her hand with the perfect amount of pressure as a testament to their bottomless sympathy. Her whole life, they had looked out for Ingrid in a symbiotic relationship of nurturer to nurtured, guider to guided.

"He was really aggressive," Ingrid said, forgetting to suppress the tremor in her voice. She was so distraught, she no longer registered the waves of patchouli rolling across Darlene's desk. "I felt . . . threatened."

"Men," Darlene sighed deeply. "If I could do without them, sweetie, trust me, I would. I can't tell you how many times I've had to stand my ground, Ingrid. The male ego is very fragile. So that's what you'll have to do when you see him again: stand your ground."

"When I see him again?" Ingrid frowned.

"Well, yes."

"But he's not the person I'm looking for, I'm sure of it!" she said, all too ready to repaint yesterday's fiasco.

"Ingrid," Darlene said very slowly, "it's him." Her skirt-suit combo of the day was aquamarine, paired with a bulky gold necklace of seashells.

"But I really don't think—"

"I verified the other John Smith's alibi for September eighth: he was in Tallahassee at an oyster-eating contest. The John Smith you met was in Wittlebury on September eighth. There's no other explanation. I've found our man." She flicked her wrist to check the time.

"Please, Darlene," Ingrid implored. "You have to believe me"—she glanced at the kitten cross-stitch—"woman to woman. This John Smith has absolutely no knowledge of Xiao-Wen Chou. He's certainly not a poet. And he's," her voice wilted to a barely audible mumble, "anti-Chinese."

"He's what?"

"Anti-Chinese?"

She waited for Darlene's expression to react, but it remained serenely blank. "It's a free country, sweetie," she said lightly.

A crack formed in Ingrid's carefully controlled exterior. "But he said all Chinese people are robots and sheep! And—and *spies!*"

Darlene's eyebrows jerked slightly, as if they weren't opposed to the idea.

"He wielded a kitchen appliance at me! He even called me—" She bit her lip; she couldn't bring herself to repeat what he'd shouted after her. "It was offensive . . . it was even . . . maybe . . ."

Now Darlene's eyebrows said, "Oh, let's not bring in the R word."

"It was offensive," Ingrid repeated.

Darlene said in a honeyed voice, like that of a kindergarten teacher, "Ingrid. I know this isn't what you want to hear. But sometimes the person we're looking for doesn't turn out to be the *kind* of person we hoped they'd be. That doesn't mean it's not them. All right? The last thing you want is to let yourself get distracted by your emotions. It's a man's world out there—you have to toughen up."

Ingrid tried to formulate a counterargument but could not summon the energy. Her confrontation with John had left her feeling flattened by a steamroller. Now Darlene, with her mountainous shoulder pads and fuchsia lipstick, was suctioning up all the oxygen in the room.

She gave it one last attempt. "So there's really no one else?"

Darlene perked up. "Well, if you want to expand your search outside of Wittlebury, we could certainly do that. You'll just have to talk to Yolanda about extending your contract." She smiled provocatively and fingered the seashell necklace around her throat. Ingrid felt her checkbook cowering in her purse. That morning, she'd received the first of what would no doubt be several threatening letters from the federal government about paying back her student loans.

The last thing she wanted to do was thank this woman, but she said, "Thank you," before slumping towards her car. What an utter fool she had been. She had withdrawn money from her savings account to be harassed by a conspiracy theorist and cheated by a woman stranded in 1985. And she had no one to blame but herself.

THE NEXT DAY, Ingrid skipped going to the archive and fused herself to the sofa, watching reruns of *A New You*. When Stephen asked what was wrong, she fumbled over how to tell him the truth. Instead, she said her period had started (true) and described her cramps as a construction site erected in the left wall of her uterus (also true).

"What can I do to help?" Stephen asked eagerly.

He proceeded to attend to her every need, adjusting the thermometer just so multiple times within the hour, preparing a hot-water bottle, ferrying over endless cups of herbal tea, buying a new loaf of bread when she complained her toast tasted "unhappy."

But Saturday was the start of the two-day-long Japan Expo in NYC, which Stephen religiously attended each year. Ingrid had accompanied him once and never returned, the frenetic noise, blinding lights and cosplay crowds too apocalyptic for her taste. Stephen insisted he'd gladly sell his ticket and stay with Ingrid this weekend, but she forbade him—he had wasted enough time fussing over her instead of his translation.

"Just go," she whined. "I'll call Eunice to come over for . . . girl time."

Stephen, respectfully mystified by the enigmatic rituals between women, was won over by this. He restocked the refrigerator, washed the dishes and did a load of laundry before he left. Like a concerned parent, he reassured her he'd check in every few hours.

But the moment he shut the apartment door, Ingrid couldn't help but feel a drop of relief. Although self-pity could be magnified when others corroborated it, in truth it was best enjoyed alone. Now she could sink into her lowness, really swim around and bathe in it. She also had no intention of calling anyone.

So she was surprised when, minutes later, Eunice appeared on her doorstep partially hidden behind an overnight bag as large as herself. "I'm here for girl time!" she squealed, already dressed in pajamas with her hair corkscrewed into pink rollers.

"Oh. Hey." Ingrid let herself be hugged. Eunice's Energizer Bunny energy was annoyingly infectious.

"So, what do you want to do?" she plopped onto the sofa. "I brought margarita mix. Oh, and weed brownies Alex made. I've also got"—she dug around in her bag—"illegally downloaded K-dramas."

NINE HOURS LATER, Ingrid and Eunice were tapering off their high and lying supine on the living room rug. *My Once and Forever Springtime Love* played on the TV.

"So now I've wasted all this time," Ingrid moaned.

"Don't say that."

"It's true. I should've been working on my dissertation. Michael will kill me now."

"We'll kill him first!" Eunice said brightly.

"I just really thought I was onto something . . . Didn't it seem like it was, I don't know, more than a coincidence?"

"It was," Eunice shouted, "it was!"

Ingrid sighed. "Oh, well."

They lay in silence, Eunice peering worriedly at her friend, when she suddenly shot up. "Wait—just because Darlene couldn't find the real John Smith doesn't mean he's not out there."

"But I don't have any more money to keep paying her."

"I know." Eunice paused dramatically. "We have to find him ourselves."

"What are you talking about?"

Eunice waved her small hand at this. "Let me think." She scrunched up her face in concentration. "Let's say the person who left the smiley face was John Smith. Right?"

"Right."

"So Smith must have come to the archive before."

"I guess so."

"And he must know a lot about Chou."

Either she was still high or Eunice was repeating facts in a circle. "Okay . . ."

"So," Eunice said, leaping up and trampling on a pizza box, "so Smith must be . . . invested in Chou somehow, right?"

"Yes . . ."

"Wait, I lost it."

Ingrid hauled herself up from the floor to sit cross-legged. "It's all right, Yoon. Thanks for trying to help me. Hey, are you going to finish that slice?" She started reaching for it when Eunice swatted her hand away. "The archive is really fancy, isn't it? Like an art gallery or something."

"That's true."

"So, who's paying for the upkeep?"

"I don't know . . . I never checked."

"Well, can people make donations?"

"I think so."

Grabbing her laptop from the coffee table, Eunice looked up the archive's website. On the upper right corner was a tab labeled *Support Us.* "See! They do take donations."

"I don't know what you're getting at . . ." Ingrid kneaded a patch of eczema on her ankle.

"We have to find out who's donating to the archive. They must keep a list of that sort of thing. And if we see the name John Smith . . . then we'll know he really *did* come to the archive!"

"Then what?"

"Then we'll take it from there."

Ingrid had no rebuttal to this. "Okay," she said, relenting, "but how do we find the list? Ask Margaret for it? She's still mad at me for getting the hiccups last week."

Eunice sighed. "Ingrid, honey, haven't you ever seen a heist movie? We have to *steal* it!"

Ingrid's spell of hopelessness slowly dissipated, replaced by her rabid hunger to excise Chou from her life once and for all. "How do we do that?" she asked, though she already knew the answer.

"We break in, of course."

AS FAR AS Stephen knew, the effects of "girl time" were exceptionally potent. He woke to Ingrid sitting at the kitchen table, breakfast already made, her head bent over a colorful mess of papers, humming.

"What are you doing?" he asked.

"I've had a breakthrough."

"For the dissertation?"

"For the dissertation," she smiled handsomely.

Stephen appeared relieved at this, then kissed her and left to work on his translation. He hadn't noticed the papers were rough sketches of the library's layout. Ingrid was proud of herself for having fabricated this thoughtful white lie; she hadn't made Stephen worry for nothing.

The following night, Ingrid and Eunice began staking out the archive. They recorded when Margaret arrived and when she left: always at the exact same time. Daryl, too, kept regular hours. They understood this regularity was key to successfully breaking in. The only hitch was the archive went into total lockdown at night. Two security guards patrolled both exits of the library and the archive was protected by an alarm system.

After their stakeout sessions, they convened at Eunice's apartment to hammer out their plans. Alex was always hanging around giving unsolicited advice, but they couldn't meet at Ingrid's place for fear of Stephen overhearing them.

"The solution is easy," Eunice said. "One of us has to be locked *inside* the archive before it closes. Like that book . . . where the two kids stay in the museum overnight."

"And one of them has a violin case?"

"And they eat macaroni and cheese casserole?"

"That's the one!"

"Oh, yeah, I really liked that book."

They smiled, suspended in nostalgia.

"But they were kids," Ingrid said, snapping back to reality. "Hiding in small places was easy for them. Where could we hide?"

"Well, definitely not under the visitor desks . . . Maybe under Margaret's desk?"

"Without her seeing us? I mean, we have to hide *before* she leaves the archive, right?"

"Okay, what about in the bathrooms?"

"The stalls are enormous—you can see everything just by looking at the floor."

"We could . . . remove one of the ceiling sections and crawl into the ventilation space!"

"Eunice . . ."

"Yes, Ingrid?"

"We're not in a children's book."

"And?"

"And we absolutely cannot remove one of the ceiling sections and crawl into the ventilation space."

Eunice sighed and reprimanded Ingrid's lack of childlike imagination, but eventually agreed. After running through various scenarios— including drugging and knocking out the security guards and donning their clothes or constructing an extra-large archive box with a fake bottom à la Trojan horse—they both concluded the easiest way to abduct the donor files was in broad daylight, when the archive was open.

The night before Operation John Smith, Ingrid looked over her heist equipment—a piece of paper and a box of extra-jumbo tampons—and batted away any worries she was "thinking like an amateur," as Alex had unhelpfully suggested the other night.

The simple fact was that, faced with despair versus hope, Ingrid had chosen the latter.

ON THE DAY of Operation John Smith, rain pounded against Ingrid's windshield as she cursed the weather's inconsiderate timing. She met Eunice outside the library at 11:30 a.m., both of them armed with umbrellas and wearing rain boots.

"Why are you dressed like that?" Ingrid asked.

"What?" Eunice pouted. "It's part of my undercover look." She was bedecked in black: black miniskirt, black turtleneck, black beret, black sunglasses. "Plus, black is a slimming color."

"You're not supposed to *look* like you're undercover when you're undercover," Ingrid moaned. She wrung her hands together, difficult when the left one was gripping an umbrella. "Just . . . take off the sunglasses, will you? It's October." Eunice grudgingly tucked them into her bag.

They took the elevator down to the basement and peeked through the archive's glass doors. They would execute the operation if one visitor or less was present; any more and they'd have to reschedule. Eunice was to stand guard outside the doors to prevent anyone else from entering.

"Well, this is it," Ingrid said.

For a response, Eunice winked coyly as if she were in a 1960s British spy flick.

What had Ingrid gotten herself into?

She strode into the archive, trying to walk normally, though this simple action now felt wholly unnatural. There was Margaret presiding over her desk. There was Daryl pushing a trolley full of books. And no one else. She let out a sigh. So far, so good. She stowed her belongings in the locker and texted Eunice to tape the TEMPORARILY CLOSED sign on the archive doors. A moment later, she sent back a thumbs-up.

Ingrid approached Margaret, swathed in a new peacock brocade.

"Hello, Margaret," she said pleasantly.

"Hello. We haven't seen you in some time," the archivist said without any hint of emotion in her voice. Ingrid wasn't sure what her remark was meant to imply. She was a complex creature, Margaret Hong.

Ingrid decided to err on the side of optimism. "Well, it's nice to see you again."

"Can I help you."

"Box number thirty-three, please."

Margaret grunted in the direction of the logbook.

With the box in hand, Ingrid chose a desk by the exit, plucked a random book off the nearest shelf and pretended to read it, not realizing the book was in Braille. The time was 11:46 a.m. Just about a quarter of an hour before Margaret's lunch break. Fourteen minutes passed in painfully slow increments before the clock ticked to 12:00 p.m. Ingrid held her breath—Margaret would leave for lunch now and Daryl would replace her. Any minute now. 12:01 p.m. Surely it wouldn't be much longer. 12:02 p.m. Why wasn't Margaret moving? Ingrid glanced up at Daryl, who stifled a yawn as he shelved books. Panic crept its way into her. Margaret always ate lunch at 12:00 p.m. sharp. What was going on?

Then, at 12:03 p.m., Margaret pulled out a beige shake in a plastic thermos from beneath her desk.

What was this madness? Was she on a liquid diet? But Margaret was beautiful the way she was.

Focus, Ingrid, she commanded herself.

She had snuck in her cell phone, which she slipped from her pocket and wedged between her thighs. She hunched over and saw Eunice had texted her.

Eunice: What's taking so long?

Ingrid: M hasn't left. She's drinking a shake at her desk.

Eunice: Fuck, what do we do now?

Ingrid: We have to wait for her to go to the bathroom.

Eunice: Are you serious? How long does she take in there?

Ingrid: About ten minutes. Wait for my signal.

Ingrid resumed restless book riffling, sweating so much a trickle slid down her neck and into her collar. If she called off the operation, nothing guaranteed Margaret would eat a nonliquid meal tomorrow or the day after. The dearth of visitors was rare, too—who knew when they'd have this chance again. She'd have to rely on the regularity of Margaret's bowel movements more than ever before.

At 12:37 p.m., the archivist rose from her chair and issued a grating "hmm-hmm" noise from her throat. Daryl promptly stopped shelving and took her seat. Ingrid watched Margaret disappear towards the women's bathroom. This was her chance.

Ingrid: She's going into the bathroom. Follow her.

Eunice: What?

Ingrid: Make sure she doesn't leave!

She sprang up from her chair and followed closely behind Margaret. The original target was the women's bathroom, but now Ingrid ducked into the gender-neutral accessible bathroom. She removed the jumbo tampons, already unwrapped and removed from their applicators, that she'd stashed in her roomy sweater. She jammed handfuls of them up the toilet drain, which ached for a good scrubbing and dousing of bleach. She held her breath, but the caustic smell of ammonia still assaulted her nostrils. When the tampons were tightly packed inside, she got up and flushed. Water rose to the brim of the toilet. She flushed a second time. Water spilled over. A few more flushes and the entire bathroom floor had started to flood.

Ingrid sprinted out, wicking water from her hands, and passed Eunice standing stock-still outside the women's bathroom.

"What do I do if she's finished and you're not done?" she whispered.

"Improvise!"

Eunice went in, looking pale and stricken. Ingrid estimated they had five minutes left.

"Daryl," she cried when she saw him at Margaret's desk, "there's been an accident in the gender-neutral bathroom!"

He looked up from his phone with his usual bored-miserable expression. "And?"

"The toilet's overflowing!"

He languidly reached for the landline telephone. "I'll call maintenance."

"You can't!" Ingrid shrieked.

"Huh?"

"I—I already called them and they're on their way!"

"Okay, so—"

"There's water everywhere! It's already leaking onto the carpet. The archive papers could get damaged"—Ingrid's mind raced—"from the humidity! If Margaret knew you jeopardized Xiao-Wen—"

Jumping up from his chair, Daryl practically skipped to the supply closet. Ingrid had never seen him display such dedication during the entirety of his internship.

She glanced at the clock—four minutes left at the most. She yanked open drawers in Margaret's desk. The top drawer on the left: office supplies. The one beneath: files listing the contents of each archive box. The top drawer on the right held packets of dried plums and boxes of floss. The one below was crammed tight with various manila folders: Tax Returns, Visitor Information and, there, at the back, Donor Receipts. Ingrid flipped through the pages while peeking at the amounts at the top: fifty dollars, twenty-five dollars, two hundred dollars, seventy dollars. Ten thousand dollars. She heard a distant flush from the bathroom and a loud "Fuck!" from Daryl as she checked the name of the donor: John Smith.

"Fuck," she echoed back.

She made to stuff the receipt into her pocket, then snapped a picture on her phone instead. She jammed the manila folder back into place. Voices were approaching. Her heart was thumping so loudly, she was convinced it would belly-flop out her chest. No time to walk around the hinged counter that functioned as a barrier to the storage room. She crawled out from under the desk on her hands and knees, reaching her own desk just as Margaret strode back in, Eunice trailing nervously behind her.

Margaret froze when she saw Ingrid. "What are you doing on the floor."

"Huh? Oh, I lost my pen."

"Pens are not allowed inside the archive," Margaret boomed.

Ingrid swore flames flared in her eyes. "Pencil! I meant pencil," she laughed as she awkwardly lifted herself into a chair.

Margaret turned back to Eunice. "As I was saying, I've never taken commissions for the brocade, but I'll have to see what I can—" She stopped in midsentence when she noticed Daryl was missing. "Where's Daryl," she asked his empty seat.

At that moment, he reemerged—platform creepers, fishnet socks and ripped-safety-pinned pants soaked through.

"What on earth is going on."

"The bathroom flooded," Ingrid and Daryl said in unison.

Margaret narrowed her eyes at them. The ticking of the archive clock amplified in Ingrid's ears until she felt certain it was coming from inside her.

"Do you take cash?" Eunice said, rupturing the silence. "I really want to buy the—the one you're wearing!"

Margaret turned to her with interest. "Cash? Well, I suppose I could make an exception just this once."

She walked primly over to her desk, sat down and removed her brocade. Incredibly, she appeared to be wearing a second one underneath. She held out her hand. "That will be ninety-five dollars."

Eunice glared sideways at Ingrid as she opened her wallet.

"Regretfully, I don't have change," Margaret said without the least bit of regret.

The moment Eunice left, peacock brocade in hand, Ingrid returned box number thirty-three.

"Leaving already," Margaret asked.

"I have a medical emergency," Ingrid lied.

An annoyed and damp Daryl appeared beside her. "Didn't you say maintenance was coming?"

"Maybe they forgot—I would call them again. You can never be too sure now, can you, ha ha. Well, I must be off now. Toodle-oo!" Ingrid said, impressed by how natural she sounded.

She rushed towards her locker, grabbed her backpack and ran to the library entrance, where Eunice was leaning coolly against a pillar. She had put her sunglasses back on.

"You owe me a hundred bucks," she sulked.

Sharing one umbrella, they scurried towards the parking lot and waited until they were safely locked inside Eunice's car before looking at Ingrid's phone.

"I've never been so nervous in my entire life. I probably lost two pounds from anxiety," Eunice said hopefully.

Ingrid pulled the photo up.

"John Smith!" Eunice gasped.

She zoomed in. At the bottom of the receipt was a scanned image of a check. She closed her eyes and thought, if there is any good in this world, please let there be his contact information. She opened her eyes. Underneath John Smith's name was an address: 2763 Larkspur Drive, Wittlebury, MA.

"Oh. Too bad there's not an email or phone number," Eunice sighed. "At least we tried."

"What do you mean? Now we can go straight to the source."

"You mean, just show up on his doorstep?" she said slowly. "Remember how that went last time?"

"But that was the *wrong* John Smith."

"Well, what would we even say to him?"

Ingrid paused. When she didn't respond, Eunice continued, "Hi, I think you left a note in this archive. Tell me who you are."

"Well, when you put it like that—" she folded her arms.

Eunice reached over to pat her shoulder. "Don't worry. We'll figure something out later. You should go home and shower now."

"Why?"

She cautiously sniffed her. "You smell like a public park bathroom."

6

"Kumquats on an Autumn Day"

The schoolgirl dress is navy blue and white with a square lapel and a red bow. The child-sized top restricts my full breasts, pushing them painfully upwards. My nipples strain against the thin fabric and my knees ache against the cold linoleum. The skirt does little to hide my bottom. I am not wearing underwear.

Mr. Sasaki likes it when I wear this dress so I always wear it for him. Today he smells like lemons. When I ask him why, he pushes my head down. He does not like it when I talk too much.

I take him in my mouth and think of my childhood home. A yuzu tree grew in the yard between our house and our neighbor's. My mother used to cook the fruit into a sweet jam. In the mornings, she stirred it into hot water with a spoonful of honey. When I think of my mother, I cannot see her face. Only parts of her: a graceful arm, slim ankles, a laughing mouth.

When Mr. Sasaki cums against my throat, I can taste my mother's yuzu jam. I want to laugh, but instead I just think of the act of laughing. My mouth opening and sound tumbling out.

"Do you prefer 'my nipples strain against the thin fabric' or 'the thin fabric imprisons my nipples'?" Stephen looked anxiously up at Ingrid, a pencil caught between his teeth.

"I like the first one more," she said, handing back the manuscript.

He nodded thoughtfully and scribbled a note in the margin.

"It's beautiful, Stephen. I mean, I know I can't read the original but I really feel you've captured Azumi's voice."

He shooed the compliment away, but she could tell how pleased he was.

"It's incredible how the act of translation is the truest act of empathy." Stephen paused. "Oh, I should write that down. Could be useful in interviews." He reached for his notebook.

Stephen had completed his translation of *Pink Salon* and was waiting for proofs from the publisher. Ingrid was happy for him, terribly happy, but he now possessed copious free time—time he looked forward to spending with his fiancée. After carefully considering a number of convincing fictitious scenarios, Ingrid landed on an interdepartmental group project. If she told Stephen everything now, he'd be hurt she'd lied by omission. But if she waited until she got to the bottom of things, if she announced she'd finally unlocked the key to her interminable dissertation, he'd be surprised *and* impressed.

"Really? I thought only undergrads did group projects."

"I know," Ingrid laughed uncomfortably. "That's what I said to Michael—'I thought only undergrads did group projects.'"

"Well, what kind is it?"

She hadn't prepared this much in advance. "What kind is it?" she stalled. "It's a, uh, diorama . . . about . . . autobiography in poetry."

"That sounds fascinating, dear."

She could have ended the conversation there, but found herself embellishing the lie. "Oh, yes. I'm very excited. Our topic is How to Know a Poet Through His Poetry."

INGRID AND EUNICE compiled a list of facts about John Smith: 1. He had intimate knowledge about Xiao-Wen Chou's poetry and, potentially, his family history. 2. He sometimes signed himself into places under false names. 3. He was writing poetry almost forty years ago. 4. He was extremely wealthy.

But they still couldn't figure out: what was his connection to Chou?

In the passenger seat, Eunice set her phone on the dashboard, displayed to Chou's memorial video uploaded onto the archive's website. Ingrid had seen it once, years ago.

"Why are we watching—" she tried to ask, but Eunice shushed her and pressed play.

A delicate swell of a string orchestra ushered in Chou as he emerged from around a corner. Dressed in a brown cotton changshan, he strolled along a path in a Japanese garden, hands clasped behind his back.

"Xiao-Wen Chou: The Person Behind the Poet" unfurled across the screen in cursive.

The voice-over narration began: "Xiao-Wen Chou was an accomplished poet, a beloved professor and a valued colleague. Those gathered here today are already aware of his many accomplishments, titles and publications. Today, we want to honor Xiao-Wen Chou, the person."

As Chou gazed at a koi fish pond, the question "What was he like?" scrolled past the screen.

Michael Bartholomew [Professor and Chair of the East Asian Studies department]: "He was incredibly kind. If you needed anything—help researching your book, moving furniture or just someone to talk to—he was there. He never asked for anything in return, either." (Blinking back tears.) "An incredibly selfless man."

Patricia Lombardi [Professor in East Asian Studies]: (Nodding reflectively.) "Private. Reserved. Quiet. But—unusually sharp. He could read something and, no matter how complicated it was, understand it in one sitting. He had that same skill with people—he was able to see through them. To be honest, it was a little daunting at times." (Laughs.) "But that was what made him special."

Thanavat Thongkor [Former Student and Poet]: "I was, um, sort of terrified of him. I never got up the courage to speak in class. But I started going to his office hours and I don't know what I'd been afraid of. He didn't talk down to me because I was just a student, you know? He spoke to me like an equal. I showed him my poetry—I know now it wasn't very good." (Laughs.) "But he encouraged me. He told me to keep writing no matter what. I, um, I never would have gotten to where I am without him."

The string orchestra recommenced, followed by a series of photographs: Chou receiving his honorary diploma from Barnes, sitting at a banquet surrounded by friends, lecturing in front of a blackboard, bending over an open book, standing at a podium above an audience of hundreds.

The video returned to Chou in the Japanese garden, this time walking along a footbridge and accompanied by the question "What is your favorite memory of him?"

Patricia Lombardi: (Smiling.) "Our first departmental meeting together. I was new and, quite honestly, I was completely overwhelmed. I suggested something ridiculous—I can't remember what—and everyone stared at me. I could've died on the spot. But then Xiao-Wen started asking me questions. At first I thought, oh God, he's trying to make me look even worse. But then I realized his questions were nudging my answers towards a better version of what I'd said. And then I realized he was helping me. No—*saving* me. Afterwards, I thanked him and he said, 'What for?'"

Thanavat Thongkor: "My whole family came to my dissertation defense. Even my grandma, who hates leaving the house. The reception afterwards had a bunch of fancy food but, um, my grandma, she didn't want to eat any of it. So I had been standing there trying to make her eat something, anything, for probably half an hour when Professor Chou appeared out of nowhere. He must have overheard my grandma because he was holding a cup of tea in one hand and a plate of fried dumplings in the other. I have no idea how he got them. Maybe he had a secret supply in his office." (Laughs.) "My grandma never forgot him."

Michael Bartholomew: (Staring up at the ceiling, chuckling.) "I can't choose one memory so I'll say . . . every afternoon we spent together playing Go. He was a master of the game—he could have competed on an international level, if he wanted. I understood this after playing just two, three games with him. But every single time we played, he let me win. Or, he'd let me think he was going to win, but right at the end, he'd leave me with a little exit he'd constructed. Those games were all in good fun, of course—just a pretext to spend time together—but it's another example of his generosity. And that was the thing—no matter how successful he became, he remained the same humble Xiao-Wen."

The video cut to a grainy clip taken from one of Chou's rare interviews. He was in his late thirties, handsome and neatly groomed, in square black glasses, a white shirt and a houndstooth tie. His way of speaking was charmingly stilted.

"What do you believe is the purpose of poetry?" the interviewer asked.

Chou reflected for a moment, then said, "In many ways, poetry serves no purpose. It cannot cure sickness, it cannot end wars, it cannot feed the hungry. And yet, a society without poetry is not a society at all. We need poetry to make sense of ourselves and the world around us. We need poetry to examine, on a microscopic level, beauty and pain and everything in between. We need poetry as much as we need our own humanity."

The video's last shot captured Chou, back in the Japanese garden, sitting pensively on a rock while looking out across a lake. "Although Xiao-Wen Chou leaves behind no spouse or children, he was beloved by all who knew him," the narrator concluded, followed by the text, "Rest in Peace, Xiao-Wen Chou: 1949 to 2009." The screen faded to black.

"Well?" Eunice urged.

Ingrid tilted her head. "Maybe Smith was Chou's rival."

Eunice frowned. Clearly this wasn't the answer she'd expected.

"They were writing poetry around the same time," she went on. "And they both wrote about China."

Eunice dipped her chin as if to say, "Really?"

"And now—and now he wants revenge?"

"By helping people better understand Chou's poetry? That doesn't make sense." Eunice rewound the video by a few seconds and hit play again. "Xiao-Wen Chou leaves behind no spouse or children," she repeated after the narrator. She fixed Ingrid with the deranged look of a mad scientist on the verge of a breakthrough.

"So?"

"So he never got married or had kids."

"I agree it's really sad he died all alone, but there's nothing we can do about that now."

"No, don't you see? He didn't get married because he didn't *want* to— he *couldn't*."

"Huh?"

"Ingrid—he must have been secretly gay!"

"Gay?" Ingrid whispered. She still had trouble saying the word aloud. "Don't be ridiculous," she huffed. She had read Chou's biography, *Xiao-Wen Chou: A Noble Life* by Clark Thompson, four times, front to back, during her four years of hopeless research. Nothing in the pages insinuated he was . . . gay. She opened her mouth to say just that, then closed it. She'd assumed Vivian was straight and she'd been wrong . . . Was it possible Chou had been closeted his whole life?

Eunice dramatically flung an arm across her forehead. "To think Chou and Smith never got to proclaim their love while Chou was still alive! His parents were probably strict conservative Chinese parents—they must have tried to pressure him into marrying a nice Chinese girl—but his love for Smith was everlasting—"

Ingrid knit her eyebrows together as sympathy for the late poet flooded through her. Poor Chou! He had suffered in silence for so long . . . How dreadfully unfair he couldn't be himself during his lifetime . . .

And then, just as quickly, warm self-congratulatory sympathy morphed into low thrumming excitement: Wasn't reframing a canonical poet within the margins very à la mode in academia? A dissertation on homoeroticism in Chou's poetry . . . Why, yes . . . That could work . . . *This* was her hot ticket out of academic purgatory!

"You know, now that you mention it"—Ingrid cleared her throat—"a few of his poems are coming to mind. In 'The Cherry Blossom's Song,' Chou writes about an unrequited love."

Eunice gasped.

"And in 'Kumquats on an Autumn Day,' if I'm remembering correctly, there's a line about wanting to taste forbidden fruit."

"No," Eunice intoned. *"Stop."*

"It's true! I'll pull up the poems right now." She took out her phone. "Oh, I just got a notification: the Old Midwife is having a two-for-one pie sale today."

"Ingrid, how can you think about food right now? Don't you see, we've stumbled onto a major secret! This explains why Smith is so rich. When Chou died, he must have left everything to him in his will. Oh, it's so romantic! Since he couldn't come out, he had a 'best friend' he lived with, except they were more than friends. Like . . . Gertrude Stein and . . . what's her name . . . Alice B. Toklas!"

Ingrid eyed Eunice incredulously. "How do you know about them?"

"I took a seminar on modernist poetry once."

"You did?"

Eunice shrugged. "The professor was hot."

"Wait, why would Chou's secret lover leave a note in the archive?"

"Because it's in his interest for people to, you know, keep studying and writing about Chou. I mean, how else will he get royalties?"

"Oh. Good point."

Eunice beamed and picked up the pair of binoculars on the dashboard.

Wittlebury's most affluent area was home to Larkspur Drive. Besides the plush lawns and ample driveways, the neighborhood eluded any underlying aesthetic. Spanish villas mingled with German gingerbread-like houses, English stone cottages with American Victorian manors. Number 2763 was built in this last style, with a porch, a breakfast nook and a round stained-glass window in the gabled attic.

"Do we have any more snacks?"

Ingrid handed Eunice the bag of cheese puffs.

"Stalking is really bad for my diet," she said cheerfully.

They had discovered it simply involved staying immobile for extended chunks of time. Today was their second attempt staking out Smith's house. They had not seen anyone come or go.

Stalking was also surprisingly easy. In a sleepy town like Wittlebury, the streets were thought safe and harmless. That the stalkers in question were two small East Asian women also didn't hurt. No one saw them as threatening. Ingrid felt, not without some resentment, that even the first graders they'd seen peddling fundraiser candy were perceived as more threatening than them. Anyone who looked at her would have never guessed her trunk stowed a coil of rope, a ski mask and a lockpick set. She glanced uneasily at Eunice. She had only told her about the binoculars.

"The garage door is opening," Eunice yelped.

"Get down!"

They slid low into their seats.

"What if he sees us like this? Isn't that more suspicious?" she whispered.

"We can't show our faces."

"I knew I should have worn my beret and sunglasses," she pouted.

They heard Smith reversing out of the driveway, a pause, then a car whizzing past them.

Ingrid started up the Oldsmobile.

"What are you doing? You didn't say anything about a high-speed car chase!" Eunice scolded, though her voice betrayed her excitement.

Ingrid kept her eyes trained on the slate blue minivan moving at approximately twenty-five miles per hour down Larkspur Drive. All she could see of John Smith was the back of his head, obscured by a white baseball cap. He was proving maddeningly easy to tail. Eunice yawned after several minutes had passed of his overly cautious driving. He fully braked at stop signs, which made Ingrid worry she was shadowing him too zealously. She tried to recall from action movies if she was supposed to let another car act as a safety cushion between them, but on this dull Wednesday afternoon, traffic was light.

"So what are we going to do when he stops?" Eunice asked.

"I guess . . . we'll follow him."

"And talk to him?" She immediately pulled down the sunshield to check her makeup.

"I don't know. Let's play it by ear."

"We should give each other code names!"

For a second, Ingrid thought Smith was heading for the university, her heart rate spiking, when he hung a left instead.

"Okay, what's mine?"

Eunice tapped her chin with a manicured nail. "I think code names have to be something you can shout without anyone noticing."

"Like what?"

"Um . . . 'What time is it?' "

"But how do I know if you actually want to know what time it is? And isn't that a little long to say?"

"Okay, what about 'Hello'?"

"But then people will think you're saying hello to them."

"Oh, all right, *you* try coming up with an idea."

"We could make noises."

"Noises."

"Like, 'hoot hoot.' "

Eunice stared at Ingrid. "Like an owl."

"Well, there are owls in Wittlebury," she said, her tone a touch defensive. "The gray short-eared owl is native to Massa—"

"Look, he's turning in there!"

Cheese puffs tumbled across their laps as Ingrid veered sharply into a shopping center. Newly constructed, the center hugged the freeway's length and boasted a sushi bar, a cell phone store, a Thai restaurant, a boba shop, a Korean fried chicken karaoke lounge and a pan-Asian supermarket—the only place in town that sold Asian products.

"Well, well, well," Eunice said. "Isn't this an interesting development. Seeing as Chou is *Asian*." She tented her fingers together one by one like a fictional villain.

"Is it?" Ingrid asked, parking a few spots away from Smith. "Lots of people like Asian food." The sushi bar, Yamamoto's, was Stephen's favorite.

Smith's white baseball cap bobbed through the ocean of the parking lot towards the supermarket. They followed him into the cool air-conditioned store. Inside, it smelled yeasty and sweet like freshly baked buns.

Eunice grabbed a shopping cart. "This is really convenient, actually, because I ran out of gochujang."

Ingrid opened her mouth to argue, then relented. "Well, I guess we'll seem more natural if we do some shopping."

Before they parted ways, Eunice huddled in close to whisper, "Look for a wedding ring."

While she busied herself gathering groceries, Ingrid kept a tight visual leash on Smith. With only his back as a reference, she sketched a rough profile of him: five foot nine or ten, nondescript blue jeans, running sneakers, faded sweatshirt. He shopped quickly and efficiently, grabbing items off the shelf without having to deliberate. He (and Ingrid behind him) was moving faster than Eunice could keep up with; she surmised her multi-tasking friend was somewhere in the produce section.

The only moment Smith paused was in the kitchenware area. Now is your moment, Ingrid thought to herself, go over there and talk to him. She inched her cart forward. She had to say something that would initiate a real conversation with him. Something unexpected.

"Hello," she said, her voice pitched too loud.

Smith unpeeled his attention from the chopsticks display. He looked to be in his midsixties. He had bloated and sun-spotted skin, hooded eyelids, thin and patchy lips and piercing—for they stabbed some tender part of Ingrid—brown eyes.

"Yes? Can I help you?" he asked impatiently.

"Oh, um, what time is it?" she heard herself saying.

Smith held out his watch. Ingrid snuck a look at his left hand, noting a ring, but couldn't verify which finger it encircled because Eunice had materialized at the end of the aisle, frantically waving a daikon radish so large as to be lewd. Ingrid subtly shook her head at her, which only stoked Eunice's confusion.

"Hoot, hoot," Eunice called loudly, her hands cupped around her mouth. "Hoot, hoot."

Ingrid's eyes bulged. Smith started to rotate his head in the vicinity of the presumed owl.

"Um, well, thank you very much," Ingrid said in a rush. She flew down the aisle, one wheel of the shopping cart squeaking obnoxiously, moving so fast Eunice had to jump out of the way.

"Hey, watch it!"

"We have to leave."

"Did I do a good job hooting?"

"Yes, you were very convincing, Eunice." She looked behind her; Smith was gone. "We should really go now."

"Okay—wait, I forgot the gochujang."

"Are you serious—" Ingrid said, unable to suppress her exasperation. "Oh, just meet me at the checkout line."

She steered the cart towards the shortest line when she saw Smith handing an all-black metal credit card to the cashier. No wonder he could afford a ten-thousand-dollar donation to the archive. As he exited the automated doors, sunlight haloing around his figure, Ingrid smiled to herself: to think she was looking at Xiao-Wen Chou's secret lover in the flesh.

While Eunice loaded her groceries into the trunk, Ingrid composed an email to the head of the Gender and Queer Studies department: "Is it ethical to out someone without their consent because, most unfortunately, this person is now deceased?"

INGRID CAME HOME to a man with a long ponytail sitting at her kitchen table. He wore a white frog-button shirt and black Tai Chi slip-on shoes. She rubbed her eyes. No, she wasn't dreaming: her dissertation advisor was drinking tea with her fiancé.

"Ingrid!" Michael grinned.

Stephen smiled sweetly at her. "Would you like some tea, dear?"

Her eyes darted between the two men as panic roared between her eardrums. Was Michael here to saddle her with more work? Although the E. A. department had over thirty graduate students, she somehow consistently found herself on the receiving end of Michael's last-minute requests to compile a report for him or help him grade undergrad papers or host a diversity panel even though she had never attended, much less hosted, a diversity panel.

Or, Ingrid thought, her pulse quickening, was this an intervention? Like in *A New You*, when a contestant refused to quit her ugly old ways? Had Michael and Stephen uncovered her sleuthing gear? Her recent online order wasn't illegal, was it? She had only purchased the lockpick set because she needed to spend over fifty dollars on the website to receive free express shipping and, well, sometimes she misplaced her keys and calling the locksmith was a hassle and she was quite certain no law prohibited private citizens from owning—

"Ingrid? You don't look well," Stephen said. "You've gone all white."

Even Michael, who by now would typically be reciting an ancient Chinese aphorism, appeared worried.

"Here, sit down." Stephen got up and guided her to a chair. "I'll get you some water."

"What are you doing here, Michael?" she finally squeezed out.

"Oh, I was just in the neighborhood. I thought I'd drop by," he smiled warmly.

Ingrid didn't believe him for a second. She smiled back even more warmly.

Stephen returned with the glass of water. "Excuse me," he said to Michael, "I've got a conference call starting in five minutes." He turned to Ingrid and added, "Azumi wants to discuss the latest draft."

"That's great!" she said, hoping beneath the cheerful chirp of her words, Stephen would hear her plea not to be left alone with this man.

He disappeared into the office and shut the door. Evidently he had not heard it.

"You *are* looking pale, Ingrid," Michael said, sounding unusually concerned. "The stomach flu. Then the flu. Then, what was it, measles?"

"I was never vaccinated as a child," she lied.

Michael bent down to retrieve a paper package by his feet and presented it to her. "Your immune system is very frail—it's undoubtedly linked to having a weak chi. But I hope this helps—consider it a 'get well soon' gift."

Ingrid hesitantly untied the package. Inside were Chinese medicinal herbs and, to her shock, a lavish jar of Korean red ginseng. "Oh—my— thank you," she murmured. The gift was (annoyingly) thoughtful. She felt an unexpected pang of tenderness for her advisor.

He patted her hand. "Anything for my prize PhD student. Now tell me—what's going on, Ingrid? You can confide in me. I'm your advisor— I'm here to advise you." He smiled, exposing his yellowing horselike teeth, and leaned back in his chair. She half expected him to whip out his Baoding balls; she wouldn't be surprised if he owned a traveling set. But Michael simply sipped his tea and fixed her with the same concerned look.

"It's the dissertation," she finally admitted.

"Yes?"

"I've been . . . struggling."

"I've known that for some time."

"You have?"

"I haven't seen a single page of it. That usually means one thing."

"Oh." She tugged at a loose thread on her shirtsleeve.

"But that's why I'm here. Two minds are better than one, no? You just have to let me help you, Ingrid. Here's a thought: we'll start having weekly meetings. Each one will center on a certain aspect, an 'angle,' if you will, of Chou's poetry. Together we'll arrive at a top-shelf idea. I'll make sure Margaret supplies you with the corresponding materials in the archive. And I know, I know—you're worried about the defense in June. Right? But don't forget, I'm the chair of the department, Ingrid, I have control over these things—"

Michael's words faded into an indistinct fog. The thought of sitting in his office week after week, listening to the babble of his zen fountain, making prolonged eye contact with his koi fish calendar, paging through more of Chou's poetry, his unending secondary sources, returning to the dark mahogany interior of the archive, like an expensive coffin, withered something inside Ingrid. She felt, with rare certainty, that she would rather die.

"—which I happen to know is not a topic many people have—"

"No," she whispered.

"Come again?"

"No, Michael, I can't."

He frowned. "Ingrid, my prize student. My foremost Chouian scholar in the making. What is it? Are you having trouble with Stephen? No? Is it something . . . up here, then?" He tapped his skull and dropped his voice an octave. "I can get you an appointment with the best psychiatrist at the student health center. A little Prozac could help in the coming gloomy months. There's no shame in it—one in three doctoral students is on anti-depressants."

Her mind throbbed for how to buy herself time while she figured out who on earth John Smith was. "Michael, I don't know how to say this, so I'm just going to say it." She reached for Stephen's abandoned cup of tea and knocked it back in a single gulp. "I don't know why I'm researching what I'm researching. I don't even remember wanting to study Chou in the first place. The idea was—yours."

She waited for Michael to scold her for attempting to distort the past and shift blame to him for her failures. He might even raise his voice at her. She shut her eyes in preparation, but all she heard was silence.

When she opened them, Michael looked . . . pleading.

"Ingrid, what are you suggesting?" he chuckled nervously. "You're not thinking of leaving the department, are you? Listen, one of my advisees wrote a multidisciplinary dissertation on Chou's verse and *Kung Fu Hustle*. We could certainly follow in a similar vein. Are you interested in comic books? Video games? Virtual reality?" he asked hopefully.

"I don't know."

Michael's expression swerved towards desperation. He raked a hand through his ponytail, pulling up loose strands of gray hair. "What is it you need? More funding? I can try to get you more funding. No, I'll make sure of it. Just say the word, Ingrid."

She waved her hand. "It isn't that."

"Let's not make any hasty decisions," he said. "You've been under a lot of stress. An eighth year of a PhD is a notoriously difficult one. Just give it to the end of the semester, all right? And if you still want to"—he inhaled deeply—"transition out of the department, we'll discuss your options."

Because she wanted Michael to leave her apartment, she agreed. At the door, he held out his arms. She stared at him in confusion (was this a Tai Chi move?) before she remembered what the gesture precipitated. She awkwardly stepped into Michael's arms, whereupon he carefully hugged her while avoiding any body-to-body contact.

"If you need anything, you know where to find me," he winked before driving off in his Ford, the only American-made product he owned.

DINNER WAS CHINESE takeout. As Ingrid picked at her mapo doufu, she made an effort to concentrate on Stephen's updates—his latest draft had been met with resounding approval, the galleys would be ready soon, Azumi was thrilled by his efficiency and speed—but she was mired in her own thoughts.

She pushed aside her plate and cracked open her fortune cookie. The white slip of paper predicted, "Your future is bright." She laughed joylessly.

"What does it say?" Stephen asked. He was still working on a bowl of zhajiangmian.

She showed him the fortune.

"Well, it's true," he said and kissed her on the forehead. She wiped away the residue of black bean sauce with the back of her hand.

"I'm glad one of us thinks that."

Stephen set down his chopsticks. "I'm sorry, dear—here I am blabbering away about the translation. I haven't even asked how your meeting went with Michael. I admit I was surprised when he showed up unannounced, but we ended up having a *delightful* conversation about the Opium Wars." He chuckled. "So, is everything all right?"

Ingrid opened her mouth—the events of the past couple months were tamped down inside her, lodged somewhere between her intestines and her throat—then closed it. "Yes, everything is fine." She made herself smile reassuringly.

Satisfied, he tucked back into his noodles.

"Stephen," she said after a moment, "how did you know you wanted to be a Japanese translator?"

"I've always been interested in the exchange of culture through language." His answer sounded rehearsed.

"Yes, of course. I mean—how do you know *why* you like the things you like?"

"Hm?"

"How do you know it's really your choice to like something and not, I don't know, someone telling you to like it?"

He frowned. "I've always been drawn to Japanese culture."

"Do you know why?"

"'Why'?" He set down his chopsticks again and crossed his arms. "Is it a crime to like Japanese culture?"

"What?" Ingrid sat up straighter and rubbed her temples. She felt the warning signs of a tension headache.

"I don't think I need to justify myself. Japan is an inherently interesting country."

"I didn't mean—"

"Mankind is not meant to be stationary. We are nomads by nature. We have always been drawn to cultures different from our own. And it's ridiculous to argue against the perfectly natural human instinct of curiosity. To suggest we should only concern ourselves with our native—" Although Stephen's tone and volume hadn't fluctuated, he spoke in his version of an angry voice—painstakingly enunciated sentences delivered with a pedantic lilt.

"—which simply breeds solipsism—"

"Stephen," she interrupted loudly, "what are you talking about?"

"I'm answering your question."

"No, you're not. You're talking about mankind and—and nomads. I just wanted to talk about, I don't know, career choices."

"Oh." Behind his wire-framed glasses, he blinked rapidly.

"I'm confused about the dissertation. No, that's not it. I'm confused about the whole PhD."

"Ingrid—I had no idea." He brushed her hair from her face. "I'm sorry. I don't know why I reacted that way—I must be overworked." He paused. "But that's not an excuse."

She contemplated the living room rug. "I know you've been really busy. That's why I didn't want to worry you."

"Do you want to talk about it?"

"Maybe later."

"Would you like a Thai massage instead? You seem very stressed, dear." He reached for her hand.

"It's okay. I'm just tired," she replied honestly. She retracted her hand.

Stephen disapproved of this ambiguous response. "I don't think you should hold it against me that I didn't know what you were talking about, since you failed to communicate what you were talking about."

"I'm not holding it against you. Really, I'm fine."

"Well, your body language suggests otherwise."

Fear nipped at Ingrid. In spite of her faith in Stephen, in spite of how he had unerringly proven his commitment to her throughout the years, she hated to upset him. A part of her, stashed in a murky, hard-to-reach place, worried if she upset him one too many times, he'd leave.

"I'm sorry," she said earnestly. "You're right, I *am* stressed. I would love a massage."

Stephen tucked his chin in and widened his eyes, pouting. "I only suggested it because I'm worried about your cortisol levels. My hands are actually really sore from typing so much lately. I took an online quiz that said I'm a perfect candidate for early-onset carpal tunnel."

"Oh—well, don't worry about it, then."

He sighed. "You know, Ingrid, you don't have to reject generosity when it's offered to you. You *deserve* generosity."

"You're right," she smiled weakly.

He rewarded her admission with another kiss on the forehead. Relief replaced panic. She had been forgiven.

As he pummeled her shoulders and back, she closed her eyes and tried to relax. Ingrid didn't particularly like Thai massages (they felt like her bones were being refitted), but she was careful to make appreciative sounds. After all, Stephen knew what was best for her. Lying beneath his carpal tunnel–prone hands, she felt extraordinarily lucky to have a partner who waived his own needs for hers.

"Sorry, honey, I can't make it today."

Ingrid read Eunice's text message a second time. After an uneventful stakeout, when all they had accomplished was cleaning off an entire box of Choco Pies, Eunice had stopping coming along.

"Oh, okay," Ingrid replied. She debated adding a sad face, then thought better of it. No use in making her feel guilty. Eunice had her own dissertation to focus on; she was set to defend three months after Ingrid. Just because she was potentially giving up everything she had ever worked for by chasing a potentially imaginary goose didn't mean Eunice should, too.

Ingrid started to put her phone away, when it chimed again.

"It was fun while it lasted!"

The very words made all her internal organs sink to the car floor. Their scheming and plotting was more than just "fun." She thought Eunice understood this. Still, she couldn't rightfully be upset—Eunice had donated hours of her time to her shenanigans. And had she asked about Eunice's research? If Eunice needed help? No, she had been selfishly embroiled in her own troubles.

Ingrid looked through the binoculars—still nothing—then tossed them onto the passenger seat. She had been surveilling Smith's house unendingly for two hours, had already listened to half of *So You're Thinking of Quitting Your PhD* on audiobook. She decided to rest her eyes for a little while, parked under this shady tree, with frail autumn light filtering through the leaves.

SHE WOKE UP several hours later. The neighborhood was quiet and dark; every porch light had been extinguished. She kneaded her eyes, yawned and stretched. Both her legs had fallen asleep and her lower spine had an aggravating crick. She checked her phone: seventeen missed calls and three text messages from Stephen: "Where are you?" "Please answer." "Should I call 911?"

Guilt gnawed at her; she had made Stephen sick with worry. She typed back: "Sorry, fell asleep at the library. Heading home now."

After the pins and needles in her legs thawed out, she fastened her seat belt and turned on the engine. Another uneventful stakeout. Maybe Eunice was right—it was fun while it lasted.

She put the car into drive and saw something flicker inside Smith's house. A light. Someone had turned on a light. She cut the engine and sank low, scrambling for the binoculars. She held them up to her eyes, adjusted the blurry vision and saw him.

No—impossible.

"Oh my God," Ingrid gasped. She pushed the binoculars so far into her head, they hurt.

She had seen Xiao-Wen Chou.

"But he's supposed to be dead," she cried out softly as he reached up to close the blinds.

She lunged for her phone, her fingers slipping all over the screen for Eunice's number.

"Ingrid, it's one in the morning—"

"I saw him, Yoon, I saw him." Her hands were shaking and she had to steady them against the steering wheel.

"Smith?"

"I saw"—she could hardly believe the words exiting her lips—"Xiao-Wen Chou."

Eunice was silent.

She barreled on, "I noticed a light, so I looked through the binoculars and saw him in one of the upstairs rooms."

"Ingrid, are you sure? You weren't dreaming? Or seeing things?"

"I'm sure. You have to believe me!"

"But he's dead."

"I know!"

"There was an obituary."

"I know!"

"And a memorial at school."

"I know what Chou looks like and it was him!"

After a pause, Eunice said, "Come over," in an uncharacteristically severe voice and hung up.

Ingrid studied the house again. The room was still lit, but all the blinds had been drawn now. She rolled down the car windows to let in the frigid night air, slapped her face a couple times and drove to Eunice's apartment, somehow managing to avoid killing any rodents in her frazzled state.

Xiao-Wen Chou had a long face, a thin nose and melancholy eyes behind thick glasses. From his youth to his later years, he kept a neat mustache and styled his hair combed to one side. Ingrid had seen him speak once, at a commencement speech during her first year in the E. A. department. But even without having seen him, she knew his face, would know it anywhere. The archive was littered with photos of him. Michael's office boasted an opulent framed photo of the two men grinning side by side. His stately black-and-white profile graced the back of all his book covers. Ingrid knew it was Chou. She would swear her life on it.

A few minutes later, she repeated the words aloud: "I would swear my life on it."

Eunice listened to her describe what she'd seen, more slowly and in more detail, before disappearing down the hallway without a word. Wonderful, I've scared her off, Ingrid thought. Then she heard a loud bang followed by a bout of cursing in Korean. She turned around to see Eunice wheeling a six-by-three-foot whiteboard into the living room and nearly cried from joy. Of course she believed her.

Alex emerged from his room, rubbing his head and squinting against the bright light. "What are you guys doing?" he yawned.

"None of your business," his sister snapped.

He shrugged and opened the fridge.

For the next half hour, Ingrid watched Eunice fill the whiteboard with her round, precise handwriting.

The facts so far were: Xiao-Wen Chou was alive. The unknown questions remained: 1. Is Chou living with Smith or visiting him? 2. Did Chou fake his own death or did Smith fake it for him? 3. Did Chou want to "die" or did Smith pressure him to?

Hypothetical possibilities: 1. Smith and Chou are lovers. Chou faked his own death so they could openly live as a couple without "tarnishing" his legacy. 2. Smith and Chou are lovers. Angry Chou wouldn't publicly come out with their relationship, Smith gave him an ultimatum: fake his own death or lose the love of his life. 3. Chou has an identical twin but they were separated at birth; he is now living with his brother's ex-lover.

Eunice's K-drama expertise was proving exceptionally useful. She stepped back from the whiteboard to examine it. "First, we have to determine whether or not Chou is hiding in that house of his own volition."

"Right," Ingrid nodded. "Er—how do we do that?"

Eunice considered. "If we confront Smith, he might lie. And if we confront Chou, he might lie, too. Stockholm syndrome, you know?"

"Should we tell someone? That Chou is still alive?"

"No, let's not involve anyone else yet," she said sagely. "It might be harder to find out the truth once that happens. There'll be like, police cars and reporters everywhere."

Ingrid jiggled her foot. "So, what should we do?"

She hoped Eunice would say what she was thinking.

"We need more, what's the word, reconnaissance."

Her shoulders sagged. "I guess I could call that PI again," she said with as much zeal as getting a colonoscopy.

"No, honey. We need to wait until Smith leaves, then suss out Chou's living situation."

"So we're breaking in."

Eunice laid the backs of her hands against her cheeks, as if to confirm her body hadn't floated away.

"I can't believe I'm saying this, but, yes. Do you think I'm crazy?"

"No," she smiled, thinking of the gloves, rope, ski mask and lockpick waiting in the trunk of her car.

"You got to be fucking kidding me."

Ingrid and Eunice jumped. Alex had appeared behind them, holding a sports drink and a sandwich. He was doubled over laughing.

Eunice whirled around in her chair. "Stop eavesdropping on us!"

"Do you know how stupid you two sound?" he choked out.

"No one asked for your opinion," she shot back.

Alex paused by the kitchen table, scanning their notes and maps. He stood so close to Ingrid, she could trace the prominent veins on his tattooed forearm.

"What's up with all these Post-Its and binders? You guys are treating this like a cute arts and crafts project."

They shot each other embarrassed glances—neither of them could resist the siren call of stationery.

"You think Scarface had shit like," Alex picked up a pack of scented pastel markers, "*this?* No. You guys gotta start thinking like criminals if you're gonna do criminal shit." He glanced at Ingrid, then back at the table. "By the way, you look better without all that junk on your face."

"Go *away!*" Eunice cried. Alex shrugged and headed to his room. A moment later, she said briskly to Ingrid, "What are you smiling for? Come on, we have a lot to do."

7

Hollywood

The night before Operation John Smith, Part II, Ingrid drove to her parents' house in search of her lucky rabbit's foot. They lived an hour away in the claustrophobic suburb of Putterville, in the same house where Ingrid had suffered through puberty: a periwinkle one-story with two bedrooms and a eucalyptus tree crowning the front yard.

During their first year in Massachusetts, her parents had stayed with one of her mother's cousins. But after Ingrid was born, the one-bedroom apartment shrank exponentially and, because the cousin was expecting a baby of her own, would only continue to shrink. So her father returned to Taipei to continue working and sending them money while Ingrid's mother worked part-time and studied for her associate's degree at a community college.

Ingrid was ten when Bowen—"Bo"—moved permanently back to the US. By that time, she had grown accustomed to her fatherless state. Instead of eliciting excitement, his visits puzzled her, as she never understood why he reappeared and disappeared like a vacuum salesman while her friends' fathers stayed put year-round. Bo was not a loquacious man, which exacerbated the intrinsically awkward nature of the visits—him nodding and smiling at Ingrid as she fidgeted on the sofa, unsure of where to look. Though he was determined to make up for lost time, Bo found talking to his preteen daughter more strenuous than learning a new language in a new country. Instead, he defaulted to communicating with her via articles (usually about space, dinosaurs or old presidents), highlighting interesting passages in hopes of discussing them. The tradition continued to this day, by email, though the articles focused on adult matters now, like "Five Foods Beneficial to Anti-Inflammation" and "Neat Tricks on How to Save Money on Your Next Gas Bill."

Ingrid's mother, Jing—"Jean"—was a quick-witted, brisk woman. Unable to sit still for long, she was always finding excuses to fix things that weren't broken, to dust when nothing needed dusting, to cook when no one was hungry. As a mother, she was indulgent (she never cared if Ingrid watched "unsuitable" TV shows or if she stayed up late reading or if she earned less than stellar grades), but raising her alone, Jean was always preoccupied with her own studies and then with working overtime. Ingrid was babysat by the mothers of children in her same grade until Jean discovered public school daycare. Then, when she entered middle school, Jean determined she was old enough to walk home by herself. On the rare occasions they spent one-on-one time together, Ingrid was so worried she wouldn't be entertaining enough for her restless mother, she became paralyzed and couldn't say much. To relatives who commented on her unsociable behavior, her mother explained she was just shy (but she wasn't shy, Ingrid wanted to protest).

By the time she entered high school, she was fully immersed in all its petty dramas and daily betrayals—scenes that composed her "real life." Her "home life" was the backstage area where she ate, showered and slept; her parents, extras who occasionally wandered through a scene.

And so, at age twenty-nine, Ingrid did not know her parents very well.

She parked beside the eucalyptus tree, fished in her bag for her house key and found her parents in the living room, their faces basking in the ultramarine light of a *Jeopardy!* episode. Jean and Bo were now retired and passed the time watching game shows, jogging and temporarily acquiring new hobbies, everything from basket weaving to cultivating yogurt. But their greatest, most singular hobby, Ingrid knew, was hoarding—an immigrant's tic. Although her thesis was in want of evidence, she hypothesized relocating to a new country was predicated on never letting go of anything from the old one or, for that matter, anything in the new one. She therefore concluded hoarding was a stubborn resistance to assimilation. After all, growing up, her friends' houses were immaculately tidy, with matching soaps and toilet seat covers. Even their clutter, if it existed, was banished into neat, labeled bins. That was the ideal suburban American house: harmoniously sterile. By contrast, her parents' decorating scheme could only be characterized as clashing. Lots of clashing.

"Hi, Mom, hi, Dad."

"Ingrid?" her dad asked. "Is everything okay?"

"Did you eat already?" her mom joined in. "Are you hungry?"

"Yes, everything's fine. Yes, I already ate. No, I'm not really hungry."

Jean looked disappointed.

A minute later, Ingrid held a plate stacked with fruit—crispy Asian pears, sliced oranges, kyoho grapes.

"I just came over to pick something up," she said, discreetly setting down the plate and heading to her old bedroom. Her parents nodded, distracted by the return of their show from commercial break. In the hallway, she squeezed past piles of Taiwanese newspapers dating as far back as her birth, a row of coat stands, a precarious stack of Frisbees, CDs wedged into a shoe shelf.

Ingrid had never bothered to redecorate her room after she moved out for college. The actors and bands she'd once idolized towered down from the walls, their hairstyles and clothes embarrassingly outdated but now, extraordinarily, back in fashion. The shelves displayed certificates, plastic gold trophies and blue ribbons, the kind passed out to everyone just for participating. Her old quilted bedspread was camouflaged with storage bins, while cardboard boxes took up the little real estate available on the floor. Ingrid flipped open a box: expired coupons and appliance manuals. Another: dried-up pens and Lego pieces. She opened the closet in dismay to find more unfamiliar cardboard boxes. She heaved them out one by one, hunting for a shoebox plastered in rhinestones and stickers, and eventually found it hidden behind a shopping bag stuffed with Lunar New Year decorations.

She shunted aside a storage bin and sat cross-legged on her bed with the shoebox in her lap. Most of her K–12 life could be found inside. She had safeguarded all sorts of trinkets whose importance escaped her now: intricately folded notes, raffle tickets, thread bracelets, a mood ring, a cherry-scented marker, a miniature sand art bottle.

Childhood. Ingrid didn't care to remember it. And what was there to say that hadn't been said before? She had grown up in a white neighborhood. She had not had any Asian friends, despite her father's platonic matchmaking attempts with the straight-A daughter of his coworker. At school, she ignored the few other Asian students in her grade as though they were invisible. She pined after the boys all the girls in her grade pined after—sandy haired and hazel eyed, careless and cruel. Her best friends were named Britney, Amber and Megan. They were best friends with their mothers, who allowed temporary tattoos and midriff-baring tops. She worshipped these girls, and so it follows did their bidding, performed for them when they asked, remembered what they laughed the hardest at (an invented character named Ying Ying who worked at a nail salon), learned to make quips before anyone else could make them, because then it wasn't mean, not if she said it first, not if she laughed the hardest out of everyone.

In those years, what Ingrid wanted most was to pass. She swore she would die if forced to wear the hand-me-downs from her cousins in

Taiwan, printed with cutesy cartoon animals and ungrammatical English. After her vision worsened in sixth grade, she threw a tantrum in the doctor's waiting room to forgo eyeglasses for contacts. Above all, she would not look like what people expected her to look like.

She styled her hair the same way, in little twists held back with butterfly clips, wore the same lip gloss discreetly slipped into her pocket at a drugstore, rubbed her skin with the same cucumber-melon-scented lotion and really, in certain moments, she felt just like them, she *was* just like them, how she walked and talked was just like how they walked and talked, who could tell them apart, especially when they interlinked their arms, traded friendship necklaces, spit on their hands and pinky swore to be best friends forever and ever?

But inevitably, people could and did tell them apart. Often it was a joke, or an aside, or a teacher's comment, or a TV segment, or something commanded during a game ("you have to be the Yellow Ranger" when her heart had been set on the Pink Ranger), and the facade's shiny shell would splinter. Sometimes it was as simple as getting ready in a friend's bathroom, their eyes locking in the mirror for a split second, the visual such a resounding indictment of difference, she had to look away for fear of crying. Sometimes it was unsticking the label from a new pencil box, slapping the MADE IN TAIWAN oval on Ingrid's arm and howling.

And then there was the time in fourth grade when Austin Krantz filched a piece of floss from the trash and held it up to Ingrid's eyes, declaring, "Now you're blind," and all her friends acted like it was the funniest joke they'd ever heard. Or the time they displayed various objects in her peripheral vision, astonished each time she correctly identified an object given "how flat" her face was. Or that other time in P.E. when the boys made "kung fu" noises at the precise moment she hit the ball and they joined in and so what could she do but join in, too?

When her friends asked her to "do Ying Ying" afterwards, she somehow found it less funny—though she still made sure to laugh the hardest out of everyone.

But they were also writing her notes signed with a million Xs and Os, calling her on the phone to talk nonstop for six hours, telling her secrets they swore they had never told anyone, brushing and braiding her hair, their fingers gentle and careful, buying her the exact pair of earrings she had wanted from the mall for her birthday, saying "love you" so easily and naturally like they meant it, and maybe they did, and maybe that's what made it harder to unknot their cruelty from their kindness, especially when the two were so lovingly laced together. And she loved these girls back, these strawberry and dirty blond girls with hair on their arms that shone golden in the sun, freckles on their noses, eyes that held a dozen different shades of blue and green in a single iris. She thought they were perfect, and for someone like them to love her, even half the time, had to mean something about the kind of person she was.

What had been her childhood, really, other than a 24/7 performance? She was always looking at herself outside of herself, measuring the pitch of her voice, the loudness of her laugh, the sway in her walk, how she chewed her gum, what to do with her gangly arms, careful, careful on the pronunciation of her *l*'s and *r*'s—she would never stumble over these letters like Jacky Ma, who was mercilessly teased by everyone.

Her existence had been a constant containment of any unchecked or residual chinkiness—this inescapable disease that leaked from her body, face, skin.

None of this is new; most of it is predictable; is it still interesting? When something true is repeated too often, its truth is diluted.

Childhood: tolerated alone, her parents wholly unaware of the microscopic nicks and scrapes she sustained each day.

She fitted the lid back on the shoebox, relieved to lock the past into its rightful place. Unlike her colleagues who delighted in sharing old photos online, Ingrid had zero desire to dredge up her former selves. And what would be the point? Whatever issues she had all those years ago had certainly and unmistakably resolved themselves now, at age twenty-nine.

Ingrid cupped the lucky rabbit's foot in her palm, which, like her, had aged: a little more shriveled and gruesome, a little less vibrantly blue. She ran her thumb over its once soft, now stiff fur.

INGRID'S AND EUNICE'S breaths left frosty trails in the air. A few houses on Smith's street were already strung up with Christmas lights, bright multicolored winks in the night sky.

The reconnaissance phase of their mission had lasted two weeks. Eunice took it upon herself to contact Clark Thompson, author of *Xiao-Wen Chou: A Noble Life*, to ask if he'd ever come across a man named John Smith, but his number in the phone book had been disconnected and his publisher never returned her emails. Meanwhile, Ingrid met with the head of the Gender and Queer Studies department, attended an LGBTQ+ Allies meeting and read the article "The Violence of Outing Someone Without Their Consent." Everyone maintained there was no way to "tell" if someone was gay, and that this notion in itself was harmful, and Ingrid trusted them, *of course* she did, but what else could "love / forsaken and forbidden / evades me / once more / yet still / I yearn" possibly mean?

Reconnaissance was followed by another week of intensive planning and staking out. Neither of them had seen Chou again. As for Smith, he left the house sparingly. From what they gathered, his usual haunts were limited to the supermarket, the gym, the library and occasionally a nearby coffee shop. The night they saw him leave in his minivan, outfitted in running shoes and a baseball cap, a gym bag slung over his shoulder, they knew they had at least an hour.

In the backseat, Ingrid and Eunice wriggled into their all-black clothing. They accessorized their outfits with black ski masks, since Alex had advised them that one, an expensive house in an expensive neighborhood would likely have security cameras and two, they couldn't shed any DNA-heavy hairs. Ingrid's other accessory was a headlamp, although the only available one at the store was for children: bright purple with glow-in-the-dark hippos, which killed the sleek Catwoman look Eunice had planned.

After much debate, including a dramatic interlude of Ingrid begging "please, please, *please* don't make me go in there alone," Eunice insisted on waiting in the driver's seat, should Smith come back earlier than expected.

They sat quietly for a moment, each ticking off a mental checklist.

"Are you ready?" Eunice asked.

Ingrid did not feel ready. Every bone in her body was humming at high frequency. She nodded yes in case speaking resulted in projectile vomiting onto the dashboard.

Eunice squeezed her arm. "You got this."

Ingrid opened the car door, darted towards the side gate, then lifted up the hinge as she'd seen Smith do. The backyard looked unused: a brand-new BBQ set, a patio table and chairs, their striped cushions stacked under a plastic sheet.

She tried the back door: locked as expected. Having picked Eunice's front door at least thirty times now, she made quick work of it, her motions fluid and reflexive. The process was more difficult at night, the icy cold chilling her gloved fingers, but when the last pin fell into place, she turned the doorknob and smiled—she was in.

She willed her eyes to adjust to the blue-tinged darkness, hoping to avoid use of the headlamp unless absolutely necessary. She looked around: she had landed in a kitchen, silent except for the purr of the refrigerator and the clank of the ice machine. She considered checking all the cabinetry for Chou, but surely that would be going overboard. Should she call out his name? No, she didn't want to frighten him off. What was that lemony smell? She inhaled sharply: Pine-Sol.

Enough dawdling, Ingrid scolded herself. She slipped on surgical cotton shoe covers, then examined the lower floor first. In addition to the kitchen was an office with a computer desk and chair, plus a living room, dining room, half bathroom and laundry room. She poked her head in the garage, just to be sure. No trace of Chou. The house was clean, too clean, as though whoever lived there had only recently moved in. Even the

furniture—generic, mismatched—gave off an air of temporary conve-
nience.

She headed upstairs. The house felt gloomier up here, the blinds
drawn, the air recycled and stale. She felt for the lucky rabbit's foot in her
pocket as she toured the four bedrooms, two of them completely empty,
the third stocked with unopened cardboard boxes. "That's odd," she murmured. She went into an eerily bare bathroom, went back out. She had
seen Chou in one of the front bedrooms. The only one she hadn't yet inspected: two French doors leading presumably to the master bedroom.

An enormous bed monopolized the middle of the floor. On the right
nightstand were a box of tissues, some pill bottles, a watch and a framed
photograph: a family portrait featuring two parents and a child. The boy
boasted buckteeth; the parents, feathered hair. Smith's family, she guessed.
Curiously, the left nightstand was bare.

Past the bed was a walk-in closet and, beyond it, an expansive bathroom. Ingrid switched on her headlamp and examined the closet first:
pressed shirts, ties, belts, sweaters. The shaft of light swept across something shiny. She edged closer. In the back, behind a wool coat, hung a
changshan woven from black silk with gold and royal blue detailing. She
fingered the slippery fabric, her heartbeat drumming madly. *Chou lives in
this house.*

She wandered, trancelike, to the bathroom. A Jacuzzi bathtub and a
double-headed shower, two toilets, two sinks and a long vanity table with
a Hollywood-style lightbulb mirror.

Ingrid went towards the latter, intrigued by its cluttered surface. As her
headlamp illuminated the objects, confusion spread through her. Various
wigs nested on foam head stands: one short black one, a longer black one,
a gray-black one, followed by a pure gray one. Strange, she thought. She
bent over the table. Liquid black eyeliner pens. An assortment of brushes.
Bottles of foundation. Concealer pots. Cakes of powder foundation and
setting powder. Was Smith also keeping a woman hostage? But where?
Her eyes traveled slowly up to the attic before she clamped them shut—oh,
why had Eunice made her come alone?

When she opened her eyes, she instantly forgot about the attic, all her fear focused on a box teeming with insects. She recoiled, preparing to kill or be killed, before realizing it was chock-full of stick-on mustaches. She laughed a little. *You're psyching yourself out—calm down.* She took a few deep breaths, then returned to examining the vanity table. Beside the box was a pair of small metal scissors and a roll of clear tape, but fabricated from an elastic material—where had she seen it before?

She noticed, then, three black-and-white photos tucked into the side of the mirror. Ingrid scanned the captions beneath.

"Charlie Chan."

"Mr. Yunioshi."

"Fu Manchu."

She slumped down on the vanity stool in a growing pool of confusion, only to be startled by a loud buzzing. She brought her phone slowly to her ear as though she were under water. Eunice must have been shouting, but her voice was distant: "He's coming back, Ingrid. You have to get out now." Other distant sounds: the gravelly crunch of a car pulling up the driveway. The leaden slam of a door.

Move, she commanded herself, move. But how could she take the stairs without being detected? She heard more steps, a dull creak, a door handle's twist. And something else—music? She scrambled on her hands and knees into the walk-in closet, remembering to switch off her headlight just in time.

Smith strolled into the bathroom, whistling a cheerful tune. From the open sliver of the closet, she glimpsed his legs, the brim of his baseball cap.

Wait—it wasn't Smith. It was Chou.

She accidentally bit down on her tongue, her eyes welling up from the pain.

She watched Chou—he was alive, alive!—sit down at the vanity table as her thoughts spun. Why had he faked his own death? Where was Smith? Did they enter the house at different times so no one would infer they were a couple? And where did the woman in the attic figure into all this? She stared at him intently, blinking away tears, feeling like a perverted voyeur.

If he started to disrobe, naturally she'd look away, she didn't want to see—wait. What was Chou doing?

Still whistling, he reached his fingers under his hairline, pulled back and lifted off a long white wig, then a mesh wig cap. Beneath was a sparse crop of white hair. He must be self-conscious about balding, she reasoned. She lowered her gaze when, in one smooth movement, Chou stripped off his mustache. What was he doing now?

She inched closer to the closet entrance as Chou fussed with his eyes. Was he—peeling something from them? He held down the corner of his left eyelid and tugged at the edge. A strip of tape balanced on his fingertip before he flicked it into the trash can, then repeated the same motion to his right eyelid. His eyes transformed into those of a different man: hooded, piercing brown eyes.

Ingrid covered her mouth to keep from gasping aloud.

As though in a dream, she watched him shake a bottle of liquid onto a cotton round, then wipe it across his face. Without the touch of melanin, his skin had become pale and sun-spotted; his cheeks and nose, patchy and red. The dark, elongated corners of his eyes had vanished. Chou rubbed his face and examined himself in the mirror: looking back was the face of John Smith.

Ingrid's mouth felt horribly dry. She was dizzy with nausea, hardly able to see straight. The whistle's refrain looped over itself, louder and louder, until it grew deafening, until the random assortment of objects on the vanity table clicked into place: Chou was not dead. He never existed.

INGRID WAITED UNTIL Smith had stepped into the shower before crawling from the closet, tiptoeing down the stairs and vomiting into a bush in the backyard. She staggered into the quiet street, thrown by its identical appearance from an hour ago. After what she'd witnessed, how could the world dare to look the same?

"Are you okay? Did he see you? What happened?" Eunice asked in a rush. She steered them quickly away from Larkspur Drive.

Ingrid swigged water from a bottle. "Um—I—I'm fine." She death-gripped her seat belt to stop her voice from shaking. "No, he didn't see me."

"Oh, thank God." Eunice frowned. "What was Smith doing when he came back? You were in there for a while."

"What? Oh, he just, um, brushed his teeth. And showered."

"Did you find Chou?"

"No."

"Oh." Eunice was unsatisfied. "Did you look everywhere?"

"Yes," Ingrid said, hoping she'd quit asking questions already. "I guess—I guess I was wrong," she forced out.

Eunice opened her mouth as though to lecture her, then glanced over at her and asked in a softer voice, "Are you really okay?"

She made herself smile. "Uh-huh."

Ingrid could not bring herself to tell Eunice what she'd seen. Her thoughts whipped back to the vanity table, the photos in the mirror, the sickening image of Smith stripping tape from his eyes. No—impossible. She must have imagined it.

The moment Eunice dropped her off, she walked dazedly into the office and removed a heavy volume from the bookshelf. She flipped to the first page.

XIAO-WEN CHOU'S
COMPLETE COLLECTED POETRY
FIRST EDITION

Introduction by Hayward Bloom

Born in 1949 to Lingyu Gao and Shaoqi Chou, Xiao-Wen Chou emigrated from Yunnan to San Francisco in 1957. His parents opened a Chinese restaurant on Grant Avenue and Clay Street where he helped out after school. What makes Chou's early success even more remarkable is his late start learning English and his lack of a formal college education. After graduating from high school, he worked full-time at his parents' restaurant and wrote poetry in his spare time.

Thanks to Clark Thompson, a retired English professor and frequent patron of the restaurant, Chou's talent for poetry was discovered. Thompson saw him scribbling on a scrap of receipt paper one afternoon and asked what he was writing. Stunned by what he saw, he took it upon himself to ensure the poem was published.

Shortly after the release of his first book of poetry, Chou was invited to be a professor in the newly formed East Asian Studies department at Barnes University. He was a National Endowment for the Arts Fellow, founded the annual Chinese American Poetry Conference and served on numerous literary and educational boards. He published eleven books of poetry, the first at age twenty-five.

Chou's trademark clear and unfussy language situates him within New American Romanticism. Unlike many of his contemporary peers, Chou eschewed formal experimentation, preferring instead what he called "accessing the integrity of an image, memory or experience." And indeed, his poetry is remembered for its unequaled ability to condense complex, profound subjects into simplistic, true forms.

But we are most indebted to Chou for his role in demystifying China and articulating the Chinese American immigrant experience. No other poet so eloquently probed the particular east-meets-west mentality of the "Chinaman-cum-American." Epic poems such as "The Mountains of Wutai" set ancient Chinese mythology against a rapidly modernizing, postrevolution country, while more intimate blank verse poems such as "My Grandmother's Hands" recall Chou's experiences growing up in San Francisco's Chinatown and assimilating into American culture.

Chou's legacy in the hallowed halls of Asian American poetry is indelible. As new Asian American poets leave their mark on today's literary scene, their lineage inevitably traces back to Chou, who took the first bold steps into unexplored terrain, and for which he is rightly remembered as the father of Chinese American poetry.

Ingrid slammed the book shut and laughed. Yes—she must be imagining things.

PART II

Winter Quarter

8

Chinatown Blues

"*Pink Salon* establishes Azumi Kasuya as the most daring young writer in Japan, and Stephen Greene as a translator on the rise— challenging the gatekeepers of Japanese literature with his inventive and unorthodox interpretations."

"*Pink Salon* will do for Japan what Anaïs Nin did for America."

"Brutally explicit and gorgeously written, Azumi Kasuya's work of autofiction does not shy away from the darker facets of Japanese culture."

"Stephen Greene's translation takes liberties with the original text, yet captures the raw poeticism of Azumi Kasuya's voice."

"Kasuya's most impressive feat, and in tandem, Greene's, is transporting the reader into the life of an eighteen-year-old Japanese girl, broadening our insight into this foreign, at times impenetrable, culture. Greene's translation belies a profound understanding of modern-day Japan."

"Astonishing, stomach-churning, unforgettable."

"Ten Must-Read Novels This Spring . . ."

"A *New York Times* Best Seller . . ."

INGRID SQUINTED AT her fiancé. Had he grown several inches? Stephen looked taller onstage, accepting yet another award for *Pink Salon*. He wore a blue plaid suit and pink tie, paired with brown leather shoes he'd spent an hour deliberating over. Had he also—she squinted harder—blow-dried his hair?

Stephen launched into a speech about cross-cultural exchange, knowing the other through language, translation as empathy, etc., while Ingrid noisily slurped the rest of her wine. She stifled a yawn. She'd heard it all before—not only at the apartment, but at all the readings, literary conferences and cocktail parties cluttering her formerly empty social calendar.

"You were wonderful," she said the moment he sat down. They hadn't spoken all evening, having arrived separately at separate times.

"Was I?" Stephen's eyes were agitated. He loosened his tie and drank rapidly from a glass of water. At these events, he was always distracted, half listening to her while his eyes scanned (she felt resentfully) for famous writers in the crowd. But they weren't actually famous—they were only famous in a literary context, which meant 99 percent of the general population had no idea who they were.

"Yes," Ingrid assured him, more brusquely than she'd intended. She checked her watch: just another half hour before the event ended.

"Would you like something from the bar, dear?"

She nodded, pleased Stephen was paying attention to her again. Then, on second thought, she followed after him to avoid the peculiar punishment of small talk with people she wasn't interested in and who weren't interested in her. When she wasn't ignored, she was antagonized with questions about what she did for a living, and then inevitably, what she researched.

"Do you think it went well tonight?" Stephen asked as they fell in line.

"I do, really."

"I wasn't too academic-sounding?"

"No, I don't think so."

"What did you think about the part when I said—"

"Oh, hello. Yes, white for me."

"Me, too. Thanks."

They accepted their glasses of wine, stuffed a few dollar bills into the tip jar and turned around, finding themselves immediately cornered into a conversation. Leaving these events took forty-five minutes or so—as you edged your way to the door, an unspoken law required you to chat with everyone along the way. Whatever happened to writers being unsociable, introverted shut-ins? Ingrid thought grimly.

A redheaded woman was congratulating Stephen. She was another translator, of Bengali literature, who'd been recognized tonight. Her companion, a ruddy-cheeked man in tweed, turned to Ingrid.

"Are you a writer, too?" he asked congenially.

Her shoulders tensed. This question, again. "Not really—sort of."

"Ah," he winked, "a muse, then."

Before she could ask for clarification, he faced Stephen and announced, "At last we meet the Japanese author!"

Both Stephen and the redheaded woman fumbled to correct him as Ingrid said coldly, "I'm not Japanese."

"Ingrid is my fiancée," Stephen hastily explained. "She's Chinese."

A twinge of annoyance bit her. She glanced at the unrecognizable person beside her, smiling a pleasant smile. Of course—Stephen had probably said "Chinese" instead of "Taiwanese" to save her from the hassle of fielding responses like, "Aren't they the same thing?" or "I *love* pad thai."

Genuine confusion contorted the man's brow. "But isn't the book—what's it called, *Pink* something, set in Japan?"

"Well, yes. I don't really understand the question." Stephen crossed his arms, looking openly annoyed.

An uneasy silence weighed in the air.

"Dad, let's get you home," the woman said. She turned to Ingrid and Stephen and whispered, "He's not used to this sort of thing," before whisking her father away.

"That was odd, wasn't it?" Stephen shrugged. "Oh, look, they're serving dessert now. Should we go back to our table?"

"You know, I am sort of curious," Ingrid said, as though she hadn't heard him. "Why Japanese?"

"What?"

"I guess I've always wondered why you chose to study Japanese. And not, I don't know, Chinese."

When he didn't answer, she plucked his untouched glass of wine from his fingers and sucked it down.

"What kind of question is that?" he finally said.

"I'm just saying—if Japanese was your first choice, am I your second choice?" She laughed raucously. During dinner, her salmon had sat largely untouched, leaving a clear path for the wine in her stomach to travel to her head.

"Ingrid," Stephen said calmly, "what has gotten into you?" He looked around to verify no one had overheard them. "I'm going to call you a car."

Good, she thought, I want to go home. She didn't like who Stephen was at these events—or rather, she didn't like how much he enjoyed these events. He was still soft-spoken, good-natured, polite. But suddenly he wasn't inquiring after her general state of being every five minutes. And all these other people were inquiring after him. She didn't like, she realized, how easily he accommodated fame. While Stephen was pushed into the spotlight, Ingrid was receding into the background.

WHAT HAD GOTTEN into her, indeed?

Ingrid knew the answer: she'd discovered the most famous Chinese American poet in the country was a white man masquerading in yellowface. And she was the only person who knew it.

But the right occasion to tell Stephen never arose. To begin with, she had never called anyone, much less him, "white." If forced to describe someone white, she defaulted to "Caucasian" or her preferred term "Anglo-Saxon European."

To tell Stephen the truth suggested she had decided to reveal John Smith's identity. And she hadn't made the slightest decision on the matter—she remained suspended in a morally ambiguous limbo, a tightrope walker teetering on the middle of a fraying rope. Because she knew if she said something, people would get hurt. And if she didn't—well, maybe no one would.

Once the holidays began, she and Eunice had paused their sleuthing. *Pink Salon*'s release was a convenient excuse as to why Ingrid was too busy to dive back into stalking, breaking and entering or other unlawful activities. She had to play the role of supportive fiancée to Stephen's budding literary career. Eunice expressed disappointment, but Ingrid detected a whiff of relief. How could she blame her? For months, Eunice had put everything in her life on hold, including her own dissertation, which—the idea was unfathomable—she *liked* working on.

In the meantime, Ingrid pressed ahead with her normal routine—sending the fifty pages on enjambment in Chou's poetry to ward Michael off, passively absorbing reality TV on Eunice's couch, sullenly returning to the archive under Margaret's watchful eye. But inside she was cracking apart. Her antacid addiction had morphed into an allergy medicine dependence, the newly released pale blue Lucidax pills. The antacids did nothing for her anymore; the "high" they'd induced was no doubt owed to the placebo effect. Lucidax, on the other hand, was a real drug with real side effects ranging from infertility to depression to paranoia. She took the pills to access sleep or, more and more often, a nice, drowsy state of existence where everything felt slightly curtained off. Reality was more bearable in those moments, as though she were watching things happen to her as they happened.

Whenever memories of that winter night muscled their way to the surface, she alternated between denial, disbelief and pity. At times she entertained the notion that the makeup, the wigs, the eyelid tape—none of it meant what she'd thought. Perhaps John Smith only role-played as a Chinese man within the confines of the bedroom. Or perhaps he performed in drag on the weekends as an exhilarating form of self-expression.

Other times, she felt a swell of pity for Smith. He must suffer from a serious condition, she had unironically considered, like dissociative identity disorder. What else could compel a man to become someone he's not? To wear another's skin? His delusion was so delusional, he must have acted without any bad intentions. Surely he never meant to *hurt* anybody, she reasoned, impressed by her incredible sensitivity to mental illness.

And yet . . . slivers of disgust had wormed their way into her subconscious in the form of recurring nightmares. She was always an undergrad student in these dreams. She'd go up to Xiao-Wen Chou at a reading with a book of his poetry cradled in her hands, waiting to be signed by him. He'd smile at her and ask for her name, to which she'd bashfully reply, "Ingrid Yang. I've always admired your work." When he handed the book back to her, his arm would fall off along with it. Then the rest of him would begin disintegrating. His hair would slide off his scalp. His eyes, nose and mouth would topple to the floor. Beneath wasn't a bloody mass or a creaky skeleton—instead a smooth, featureless white surface—somehow far more terrifying.

Swung between these extremes, Ingrid chose to do nothing. She was a coward, she knew, covering her ears to pretend she couldn't hear someone's screams.

But even if she wanted to out Smith, how could she? She'd been too startled by his appearance to snap a photo of the vanity table or to film him removing his . . . makeup. If she wanted evidence, she'd have to break in again. What if Smith had noticed his bushes were drenched in vomit? What if he suspected someone had burglarized his home? What if he had tightened his security measures?

No, she reasoned, covering her ears as the screams rose to an unbearable pitch was far easier. She could convince herself she'd been imagining things; she could forget what she'd seen. The prospect of losing her mind was, contrary to popular belief, as soothing as a lullaby. Her life could continue on its merry little way.

Nothing needed to change.

BARNES UNIVERSITY WAS snow covered in February. The tops of bushes and tree boughs looked neatly frosted. The lampposts burned more brightly against the pure white and the brick buildings deepened to a darker shade of red, lending the campus a gothic touch. Save for the frozen chunks of piss on Frat Row, and the occasional pledge running past stark naked while yodeling the Greek alphabet, the grounds looked like an illustration from a children's picture book.

Ingrid trudged to campus on a Monday morning sausaged into her winter jacket, lined boots, mittens and wool hat, already thinking of the lunch she'd packed herself—a whole-wheat egg salad sandwich instead of leftover cheese pizza, and a granola bar instead of a chocolate Ding Dong. So she was capable of change after all.

Inside the archive, the air smelled humid but not unpleasant, the caramelized, woody scent of old books still the dominant note. She arranged her belongings in a locker, greeted Margaret and Daryl, then settled into her usual desk.

Researching a nonexistent poet was gloriously freeing, Ingrid had found. What did it matter if she was right about Chou's use of enjambment? That was precisely it—it didn't! She could invent all sorts of nonsense and it wouldn't matter. She was no longer plagued by the ivory-tower pressure to produce something original and convincing, much less peer review ready. Would her dissertation contribute to the greater culture? Would it forever alter the course of East Asian Studies scholarship? No! And she didn't care.

Three hours were happily passed in this manner. The once stoppered words flowed liberally in the first draft of her dissertation. Her fifty pages of scrambled notes had grown to one hundred twenty-five of mostly comprehensible text. The working title was "Calligraphic Gestures: The Influence of Chinese Grammar on Xiao-Wen Chou's Use of Enjambment." The page count was fluffed out by gratuitous block quotations, historical pictures, graphs, tables, charts and Venn diagrams. The font was also size thirteen and the margins were 1.5 inches, but that was purely for the benefit of people who couldn't read small print.

Who said the position of a professor was unattainable? She could finish the dissertation, revise it into a book and climb the ladder to associate professor in just a few short years—say, ten or twenty. Tenure, retirement and healthcare—oh, dental, too!—all of it would be at her fingertips.

She cupped her chin in her hands and gazed at Chou's massive portrait hanging on the opposite wall. She just had to make sure no one else found out Xiao-Wen Chou was neither dead nor Chinese. That didn't seem too difficult. Then she peered closer—within the oil painting's gold frame, Chou's hair slid off his scalp, followed by his eyes, nose and mouth. The grotesquely blank face looking back at her caused Ingrid's breakfast to lurch skyward. She dry heaved over her desk.

Margaret lanced her with a glare.

She was fine. Perfectly fine. "I'm perfectly fine," she said aloud.

At this, Margaret looked worried—the first time Ingrid had seen the expression mar her face.

When the clock ticked twelve thirty, she retrieved her lunch bag and headed towards the E. A. Studies lounge, where she could brew herself a hot cup of tea and squirrel away some complimentary egg tarts. An admittedly unnecessary expense, the egg tarts were Michael's initiative. Once a week, he hosted an East Asian literary salon where undergrads crowded around him on the floor, listening to him expound on some tasty morsel of ancient Chinese letters. But, judging from their overstuffed cheeks and the ferocious elbowing happening beneath Michael's line of vision, she suspected they were motivated by free food.

After steeping her tea, Ingrid discreetly bundled three egg tarts into a paper towel, hoping her fellow PhD candidates in the lounge wouldn't notice her. They were almost all men, glasses clad and averse to sports and sunshine, with girlfriends and fiancées living in East Asia. The few times they'd coerced her into squeaking out a word or two in Mandarin, they immediately corrected her pronunciation, only stopping after she profusely thanked them. Whenever they inquired after her research, they looked at her with faux sympathy filming their eyes and patted her on the shoulder. "Aw, good for you," the gesture said, "studying your own culture," as they received five-figure grants to research Chinese thinkers so obscure they had never been translated into English. Naturally, since Ingrid couldn't read or write Chinese, these writers were off-limits to her. In the eyes of her colleagues, a dissertation on Xiao-Wen Chou was child's play.

And yet, at times they turned curiously competitive around her—for instance, if Ingrid happened to mention how her grandmother had survived the Japanese bombs by eating raw cabbage in the mountains, they'd talk very loudly over her about a paper they'd written on that exact topic.

As for the few former PhD students in Asian American Studies, Ingrid never had the opportunity to make their acquaintance. They had all, slowly but surely, transferred to Comp Lit, English or Postcolonial Studies rather than stay tethered to the department that subsumed them.

She made it out of the room unobserved and turned down the hallway. Ingrid knew Michael taught on Monday afternoons, so she was surprised to find him in his office. She was surprised, too, that she paused by his open door to say hello. Perhaps Michael ingratiating himself with her for once (how desperate he'd been at her apartment!) had warmed her to him.

"Hello, Michael."

"Cixi?" His head snapped up. "Oh. It's you."

Had Michael retired his trademark boisterous greetings? She couldn't recall the last time he'd recited Laozi at her. On the contrary, his comments regarding Chou's use of enjambment were nothing but complimentary. But he knew it was complete and utter bullshit, didn't he?

Curiosity got the better of her and she found herself sitting down across from him. Up close, Michael's eyes were swollen. His hair was stringier than usual and a sour, feral smell hung over him.

"Are you all right?" she asked.

He stared at her for several moments. Ingrid looked away, preferring to meet the eyes of his koi fish calendar. Maybe he had only pretended her manuscript was on the right track. Humoring her all the better to humiliate her. Now he would lay it all out, his total disappointment.

"I'm sorry—"

"Cixi left me," Michael said at the same time.

Ingrid blinked. "What?"

"She wants a divorce."

She swallowed her relief. "Michael, I'm—I'm so sorry to hear that."

He drank heavily from his minuscule teacup. The sickly sweet smell of plum wine wafted towards her. Three bottles rested by his feet: two empty, one half-full.

"Do you want to talk about it?" she asked cautiously. She hoped he'd pass on the insincere offer—she had no desire to meddle in Michael's marital affairs. He'll surely demur, she thought, to keep the professional boundaries between us securely in place.

"She met someone else," he groaned, pitching back in his chair and throwing his slippered feet onto his desk.

Ingrid raised her eyebrows. Cixi's cotton-padded jackets came to mind, her painful-looking bun, her distaste for smiling. "Cixi" and "passionate affair" seemed unlikely bedfellows.

"He's a Chinese man. Can you believe it?" he scoffed.

Ingrid's face froze; what was she supposed to say to that? Better to ask questions. "Did they meet in China?"

"No, they met here!" Michael roared. He reached for his Baoding balls and launched them into his trash can one by one like a basketball drill. "He was my former student!"

"Wow—that's—it seems out of character for Cixi?"

"In the end, Ingrid, she was loyal to her kind," Michael said cryptically. "I've been thinking a lot about this. Maybe, at the end of the day, we are always loyal to our own kind."

"Huh?" she glanced at the half-full bottle of plum wine. He hadn't offered her any.

"She wasn't like this when we met, you know." By his melodramatic drawl, Ingrid could tell this presaged a long story. She considered improvising an excuse to leave but then realized: this was her chance to come into some very private, very coveted information she and Eunice had speculated about for years—the origin of Michael and Cixi's love story. Plus, she deserved a break after the gains she'd made that morning vis-à-vis her latest dissertation chapter. She poured herself a generous cup of plum wine.

Michael pulled a plaintive face and closed his eyes. "I was a lonely twenty-seven-year-old looking for love when I landed in Shanghai—"

An hour later, having recounted his "many cultural, intellectual and spiritual contributions to the village of Yuanjia'ao," he finally caught up to the day he met Cixi, four years after his arrival. He was slumped over his desk, the only sign he was alive the occasional rise of his back when he burped.

"You should have seen her then," he moaned. "The absolute picture of femininity. Grace, beauty, virtue. The way she held her chopsticks! The way she walked, her little feet floating above the floor. She was too modest to even look me in the eyes." His dreamy expression clouded over. "But what was the point in marrying a Chinese peasant if she was going to get all these ideas in her head? 'Equality.' 'Respect.' 'Independence.' It's outrageous."

Ingrid, now drunk herself, felt her ears prick. What was Michael blabbering on about? She watched him swing violently around in his chair to face the window, his self-addressed monologue in full effect. "When I brought her here, she was the perfect housewife. Totally ignorant of 'women's rights.' She never talked back or questioned my decisions. She wanted nothing more than to fulfill her cherished husband's every need. For Christ's sake, she undressed me and folded my clothes before we made love!—"

Ingrid felt instantly more sober than she did a minute ago.

"But over thirty years in this country—completely let herself go—only wears floral muumuus—ugly plastic slippers—such thick toenails—clips them on the kitchen table—smells like Mentholatum everywhere—"

"I don't think this is appropriate—"

"—threatens me with the bamboo back scratcher every time I try to touch her—"

"—to talk about with me," she slurred.

"—I was tricked—hoodwinked in my own home—"

"I'm"—she hiccupped—"leaving now."

"—after I gave her everything she wanted—one day off a week—her own monthly allowance—and still she wanted more—"

Ingrid stumbled out of his office. As she shut the door, he continued to address the window. Her entire body felt as warm and clammy as an uncle's handshake. She dipped into the bathroom to splash some cold water on her face. What had gotten into Michael? She understood infidelity and divorce would make anyone act erratically. But even while sopping drunk, he'd been callously succinct in his dissection of Cixi. The way he'd described her when she was a young woman—had he always harbored these sorts of thoughts? And did all men who journeyed to China looking for a wife share similar thoughts? No . . . Surely not! Surely Michael was an outlier. Still, Ingrid wondered how much of his true self he'd withheld from her, despite all these years he'd been her advisor. She turned off the faucet and patted her face dry.

As she left the bathroom, a bright, colorful poster caught her eye: "Xiao-Wen Chou's *Chinatown Blues: A Play*. Open forum discussion. Tuesday, 7:00 p.m. in Auditorium B. Hosted by the POC Caucus of the Postcolonial Studies graduate department. Free and open to the public." Ingrid understood only half the words, which waltzed across the poster. She snapped a picture on her phone.

CHINATOWN BLUES WAS not published or performed during Chou's lifetime. Discovered only after his archives were made public, the play belonged to his collection of late juvenilia. In his thirties, Chou had taken a vacation from poetry to pen a smattering of short stories, essays, plays and a single half-finished novella before remembering poetry was where his talent lay. Ingrid had read these writings years ago, mainly out of desperation, and didn't revisit them after they proved useless. She couldn't recollect her thoughts on *Chinatown Blues*. Forgettable, apparently.

On Tuesday evening, she approached Auditorium B with hesitant, defiant steps. Inexplicably, she also moved with a sideways gait, her back kept perpendicular to the wall like a crab scuttling across an ocean floor. An enemy ocean floor.

The environment felt hostile the moment she entered it. The music—someone rapping about the liberation of her clitoris—was hardly appropriate for a public forum at a university. The signs on display were rudimentary and inflammatory—"oppression" this, "justice" that—attention seeking, that was all. Then there was the entire body of the POC Caucus. Their hair, clothes, piercings, tattoos, pins, ironed-on patches, even their shoes—all of it sneered at Ingrid. She kept her head held high as she walked past them in her sensible brown clogs.

The auditorium was packed. She found a seat towards the center back and took stock of the audience: mostly undergrads, some older students, a few professors—Michael, fortunately, exempt from their ranks. She twisted around and did a double take: hoodie, backwards baseball cap, diamond stud. Alex? He caught her looking at him and lifted up his chin in greeting. She waved back.

A minute later, Vivian Vo strode onstage. Of course *she* was leading the forum.

"All right, let's start," she said, exuding both boredom and beauty. Her offhand confidence was infuriating. Also enviable. "Did everyone read the community rules? We'll go over them again to make this space as safe as possible."

Ingrid pursed her lips. What community rules? Then, as Vivian prattled on, her pinched expression morphed into a full-on pout, her bottom lip engulfing the entirety of her upper lip. She felt thrust into an immersive foreign language program; she couldn't understand a thing. All these acronyms she'd never heard before. Terminology that was, like everything Vivian did, combative. The phrase "white supremacy" was thrown around multiple times with alarming insouciance. And why was Vivian honoring the Wampanoag tribe who had first lived on the land Wittlebury occupied? What did that have to do with anything? Wasn't this forum about Xiao-Wen Chou?

As her unthinkably long list came to a close, Ingrid was slapped by disbelief when Vivian announced, "White people can ask questions but cannot make statements." They could not speak "unless they raised their hands and were called on." Her mouth fell open when Vivian finished by asking the "white people at the front" to give up their seats for the mysteriously long acronyms she'd referenced earlier.

Surely this is discriminatory, Ingrid fumed as her thoughts flew to Stephen. If he were here, would he be subjected to this draconian—this *dictatorial*—behavior? Even with his years of specializing in a foreign culture? His *love* for it? She looked around to see if other people were incensed, but the white—that is, the Caucasian—people in the audience were unfazed. Those in the first three rows quietly exited their seats.

"Tonight's open forum will focus on two main points," Vivian said once everyone was settled. "First on the agenda is the casting of Mimi's character in *Chinatown Blues*." Ingrid frowned. This whole hoo-ha was over a *casting* choice? These people were thirsting after a reason to be offended. "Second on the agenda is whether this play should be performed at all. Zoe and I will moderate as needed." Vivian gestured towards an African American woman with a shaved head and a leather jacket. She looked vaguely familiar.

When a woman in the front row stood up, a microphone was passed to her. "I don't know what there is to discuss. A white woman should not be cast to play a Chinese American character. Period." She sat back down.

Soon another person had the microphone. "To play devil's advocate"— groans rippled through the auditorium—"if Santa Claus can be any race nowadays, why can't people play any role they want?"

More groans.

"I just think this sort of language is divisive," he went on in a cheery voice befitting a cereal ad. "If we're so obsessed with calling each other black and white, how are we going to stop discrimination based on being black and white?"

Vivian spoke into her microphone. "Let's stay on topic: the casting of Samantha Prochazka as Mimi Lee."

Ingrid reached into her purse for a Lucidax pill and dry-swallowed it. A second one. A third, just in case.

"This is about scarcity of representation," someone with a pixie haircut piped up. "I'm an actor. There are barely any roles written for someone like me. So when those roles appear, they shouldn't be wasted."

"But what exactly does representation mean—do you mean this actress has to be Chinese American? Or can she be Cambodian American? Or Pakistani? What about Kazakh?"

"East Asian representation is overshadowing other Asian—"

"Samantha Prochazka's boyfriend is Filipino—"

"Her parents emigrated from Czechoslovakia—"

"—understands Mimi's situation—"

"If it's done respectfully and tastefully—"

"Are you telling me they couldn't find a single Asian American actress to play this part?"

"Samantha was trained at the Massachusetts Theater Academy—"

"—performance as Desdemona in *Othello* was simply breathtaking—"

"—just a school play, not fucking Broadway—"

"Shouldn't the role go to whoever gave the best audition?"

"—director is a Chinese woman who approved the casting—"

"She's from China. There's a difference—"

"—saying she's racist against her own people? How does that make sense?"

"Chinese nationals don't have the same concerns as Chinese Americans—"

"—never had to worry about feeling represented onscreen—"

"It sounds like you're calling her a FOB."

"Do not use that language here—"

"Since when is some white girl flapping around onstage in a qipao and chopsticks in her hair 'acting'?"

"An actor's job is to embody someone else's life, not their own—"

"It's an act of modern yellowface, plain and simple. In my paper entitled—"

"Are they going to make her eyes slanty—"

"—'slanty' is a derogatory term—"

"—literally a shape, so does that mean I'm not allowed to say 'square' or 'circular' either—"

"—can't believe we're still discussing if this is okay—"

"—not the 1950s anymore—"

"—you know what else was popular in the 1950s? Book burnings—"

"Well, speaking as a Chinese American man—"

"Well, speaking as a Chinese American *woman*—"

"Well, speaking as a queer disabled Chinese first-generation child of immigrants—"

"Devil's advocate again here! Are you saying if you're a straight, white, brunette woman who's twenty-one years old, you can only play a straight, white, brunette woman who's twenty-one years old?"

"Linda Hunt in *The Year of Living Dangerously*—"

"—phenomenal performance—"

"—Oscar-winning—"

"Couldn't they rewrite Mimi's character as a white woman married to a Chinese man?"

"Are you fucking kidding me—"

"I think we should boycott—"

"—support—"

"—protest—"

"—should celebrate Asian American art when so few of us—"

"Xiao-Wen Chou is—"

"Fuck Xiao-Wen Chou—"

"—doesn't represent me—"

"Well, he can't represent us all—"

"Who has actually read the play?"

"—so problematic—"

"Orientalist trash—"

"—states that the actors have to speak with a Chinese accent—"

"Oh, fuck that—"

"Hey, my parents have accents—"

"—often used to dehumanize and other—"

"Is having an accent a crime? Are we not supposed to exist?"

"Xiao-Wen Chou is Chinese American, so—"

"—does not grant him immunity—"

"—can't be racist if you're—"

"—just saying we shouldn't fight each other when—"

"Not all skinfolk are kinfolk!"

"I mean, no one would accept white actors performing in *Porgy and Bess*—"

"Yeah, why is racism against Asians acceptable when racism against black people—"

"—a double standard—"

"—not fair—"

"Wait a second, how did we get dragged into this?"

"Don't try to compare our struggles! This isn't a competition—"

"You *always* do this—"

"I don't remember you giving a fuck when our community was hurting—"

"Where were you when that goofy motherfucker had a petition to end affirmative action at Barnes—"

"Who?"

"The Asian dude in the bow tie—"

"Yeah!"

"Where were you when the BSU protested the Pimps & Hos party thrown by the Chinese Association?"

"What are you talking about—"

"Don't deny it, we saw the videos—"

"—Afro wigs and gold teeth—"

"—blaccents and AAVE—"

"How come there wasn't an open forum then—"

"Why should we stand up for you when you never stand up for us—"

"—fought for rights you benefit from without so much as a 'thank you' and now—"

"So you want to help white people in their mission to oppress us—"

"And who says *you're* not oppressing *us*?"

"—too busy colonizing Africa—"

"We must confront anti-Blackness in our communities—"

"But I grew up listening to rap!"

"Oh, please—"

"I feel attacked right now—"

"We're stronger when we're together—"

"None of us are free until we're all free!"

"Don't recite some kumbaya shit at—"

"Martin Luther King Jr. said—"

"Oh, shut the fuck—"

"I don't understand what's happening—"

"Fuck this, I'm leaving—"

"Can I just say, I don't see race—"

"Some of my best friends are—"

"Questions only—"

"Hello? Can anyone hear me?"

"I did not call on you—"

"Sit down—"

"Mom? Can you pick me up?"

Ingrid glimpsed an indistinct figure on the far right of the stage. A man wearing heavy makeup, in a silk changshan and a black wig with a queue. "Xiao-Wen Chou?" she whispered.

Then, darkness.

"INGRID? WAKE UP. Hey. Can you hear me?"

She rubbed her eyes. Drool, tight and flaky, had crusted on the side of her mouth. Alex was gripping her shoulders and staring intently at her.

She sat up. "Where is he?"

"Who?"

"Xiao—"

The auditorium was empty. Had she hallucinated him?

"Are you okay?"

"I—I took these allergy pills. I didn't realize they were so strong."

"How many fingers am I holding up?"

"Um—five and a half?"

He sighed. "I'll drive you home."

When Alex opened the auditorium door, the onslaught of cold was so intense her eyes watered like automatic sprinklers. But she was glad for the night air's stinging bite—she needed to undull her senses. What had happened to her in there? The image of Xiao-Wen Chou had looked so . . . real. Don't think about it, she commanded herself, it was only a nightmare.

"Where do you live?" Alex asked as they crossed the parking lot. "Grad housing?"

She nodded.

Alex pressed his car key, unlocking an ordinary sedan. Given his musical tastes, she had expected nothing less than a *Fast and Furious*–approved vehicle: sleek and sophisticated, with advanced modifications. Instead, a stuffed cat key chain and a wooden cross swung from the rearview mirror. Although his sister had left her faith, he seemed to have kept his. What else had she wrongly assumed about Alex?

"So, what did you think of the forum?" she asked.

"I have thoughts," was all he said. His recalcitrance wasn't unwelcome. She had so many arguments, counterarguments and counter-counterarguments swirling in her head, she couldn't bear to hear any more.

Ingrid realized she had never been alone with Alex. She leaned back into her seat as he reached over her lap to pop open the glove compartment. He took out a tin of mints and chewed one before offering her the same. She absentmindedly pocketed the entire tin, distracted by his cologne: it smelled like the ocean if the ocean were also sexy and aloof.

They drove in silence for a while, Ingrid thinking Alex had no interest in talking to her, when he asked if she liked Mexican food.

"Mexican food," she repeated slowly.

"What, you've never had it before?"

"I have! I love—chi-chimichangas," she stammered.

"Cool. There's this new restaurant that just opened up. El Trasero del Burro—you heard of it?"

"Um—"

"We should go sometime. You free Saturday night?"

"Oh . . . yeah, I think so. Eunice has a mani-pedi appointment, though."

"Who said anything about her coming?" Alex laughed. "You're not making this easy, Ingrid. I'm asking you out. On a date."

All the blood in her face coursed to her cheeks. "Oh—I—you mean, Eunice never told you—" Was it her or was it unusually toasty inside the car?

"Told me what?"

"—haven't had time to plan—"

"Plan what?"

"—impending nuptials—"

"Nup-what?"

"Alex, I'm engaged."

Ingrid examined her left hand: bare. Come to think of it—where had she placed her engagement ring?

"No, she never told me. We don't really talk about this stuff. I just fig-ured you were single. Since you're always at our place eating junk food."

Ingrid laughed weakly as Alex turned on the stereo: a soulful ballad in Korean. He was continuing to surprise her.

After another minute, he spoke again. "So, what's his name?"

"His name?" she squeaked. Alex's expression was illegible to her. Amused? Wary? Or both?

"Yeah." They had pulled up to her apartment complex.

"Stephen."

"Stephen," he repeated. "Stephen what?"

Ingrid coughed. "Stephen Greene."

She fiddled with her seat belt, wondering why Alex hadn't said any-thing, when he suddenly laughed, one sharp bark of a laugh, his head thrown back against the headrest.

She crossed her arms. "What's so funny?"

"I should have guessed."

"What?" Impatience snapped at her.

"That you were one of *those* Asian girls. A white boy chaser, huh?"

The blood rushed back to her cheeks—this time the sensation wasn't pleasant.

"Excuse me?"

"Let me guess—you've never dated an Asian guy." Ingrid remained silent. "Tell me I'm wrong."

She climbed out of the car. "I—I do not have to answer that," she finally said. "Good night, Alex."

He shook his head ever so slightly. "Night, Ingrid."

9

Special Occasion Role-Play

Title: Inhabiting the Other: Yellowface as Corporeal Colonization

Author: Vo, Vivian

Journal: North American Postcolonial Studies Journal (Volume 12, No. 3), pp. 125–49

Abstract: This paper examines the American tradition of yellowface as an inherently political and violent act wherein the Asian body becomes the site of colonial occupation. I posit that yellowface is an imperative arm of the larger white supremacist project: cultural production as national discourse. The colonization of the body, like that of Indigenous land and resources, reduces the Asian body to the status of the perpetually foreign, silenced and powerless Other, or the subaltern, while ensuring the oppressor's definition of the Other is the dominant discourse, and therefore, the only public discourse. All manifestations of "Asianness," including those enacted by Asian Americans, lack true autonomy; rather, such manifestations are limited to regurgitations of colonial fictions: their imagined images, sounds and gestures.

What a snide, holier-than-thou tone, Ingrid thought with unrestrained glee. The journal's decision to publish such poppycock was inconceivable—academia's standards were plummeting, to be sure. What ever happened to intellectual rigor? Was this a supermarket-aisle tabloid or a peer-reviewed article? The point wasn't to titillate but to educate, even if it meant boring the reader to an early death! The new loosey-goosey state of academic publication was, she felt with no sense of hyperbole, sinful.

Though she was alone in her apartment, she looked around before surreptitiously clicking on the download button as if she were downloading porn. Then she settled back in her chair to enjoy a hearty portion of schadenfreude. She would scoff, cackle and sputter. She would highlight particularly outlandish quotations to show Eunice. Together, they would laugh at Vivian's faulty reasoning couched in misleading jargon.

But a curious thing happened as Ingrid read. Her scoffs became fewer and far between. Her cackles more like whimpers. Her sputtering not out of condescension but bewilderment. By the end of the article, a seed of doubt had been planted in her.

Could it be yellowface wasn't an act of dress-up, of playing make-believe, albeit in very poor taste? Was it really, as Vivian posited, "an act of violence against the plundered and erased Asian body"? But that sounded absurd. After all, this was *America*, not some developing third world country where citizens were denied basic civil rights!

Still—still, Ingrid was curious about Vivian's thoughts concerning not a symbolic plundering and erasure of the Asian body, but a real one. Say, committed by a man named John Smith. And what was one morally obligated to do should one, say, happen upon this information?

Ingrid was at a loss for who else to ask about yellowface. Of all the people she knew, only Vivian was (irritatingly) well-versed in the subject. Not that Ingrid could ever tell her the truth about Chou—she'd have to introduce the topic as a purely theoretical conundrum.

She sprang up from her chair and paced the room, muttering under her breath. A couple times, she sat down to tinker with the beginnings of an email, before abandoning it and springing back up again. She moseyed to the kitchen to refill her coffee, forgot why she'd gone to the kitchen, then reattempted the email.

"Dear Vivian."

"Hi, girlfriend!"

"Greetings, comrade."

No, no, no, it all sounded wrong. She needed to talk to Vivian—she shuddered—in person.

"FANCY SEEING YOU here," Ingrid announced. She cursed herself; that hadn't been her planned greeting. On the walk over, she had decided on a cool and classic "Hey."

Vivian was by her locker, removing her backpack and coat. She arched an eyebrow. "We see each other here almost every day."

"Oh. Right. Well—I'm glad to see you."

"You are?" She didn't mask her surprise.

"I wanted to tell you I read your article."

"Which one?"

Ingrid quelled the jab of annoyance in her chest—Vivian Vo and her many award-winning publications. But if she wanted Vivian to lay down her (figurative) arms, she had to act the part of ally rather than foe. "The one on"—she pried the word from her mouth—"yellowface."

"I thought you weren't interested in that sort of thing," Vivian said flatly.

"Oh, I'm *very* interested. I was at the forum on Tuesday. You were"— Ingrid gulped and smiled forcefully—"incredible."

"Really."

"Yes! Very—outspoken."

"Thanks?"

"It was—wow—what do I even say—I mean—those *white* people—am I right?" There—she had said it. The W word. Vivian would have to trust her now.

She studied Ingrid carefully, as though checking for signs she hadn't been replaced by a clone. "I had to take a mental health day after that," she said in a cautious voice. "The environment was really triggering."

"Oh my God, *totally*," she agreed. "So . . . triggering." What an odd sensation, trying out an expression without knowing what it meant. She made a mental note to look it up later.

Vivian abruptly shut her locker. "Was there something you needed?"

"I, um, I wanted to ask your opinion about something."

She glanced at her watch. "Well, I'm meeting Zoe at the Old Midwife in an hour—"

"Perfect!" Ingrid said, a tad too excitedly. She had breached the enemy's walls. "I'll buy you a coffee. Or tea. Or juice—whatever beverage you prefer."

The two women sat opposite each other in threadbare armchairs: Moroccan mint tea for Vivian and hot chocolate with extra whipped cream for Ingrid. Agatha slept on a nearby ottoman, her socked white paws twitching in a dream.

"So what exactly did you want to talk about?" Vivian asked. She sat with her arms and legs crossed, angled slightly away from her. She had also glanced at her watch again even though they'd just sat down. No, Vivian Vo did not trust her. Think, Ingrid, think. She pretended to stretch her arms as she furtively scanned the text on Vivian's enamel pin: WHAT WHITE NONSENSE IS THIS?

"I wanted to talk about the—er, play."

"*Chinatown Blues?*"

"Yes."

"Is this for your dissertation?" Vivian asked wryly.

"Oh, no. *No.* I think the play is so"—she recalled some of the language from the open forum—"*problematic.*"

She checked her expression—unimpressed. "I mean, the thing about the accents!"

Vivian nodded. "It's not just that. The line notes make it clear Chou didn't want the actors to pronounce their *l*'s and *r*'s. The actual dialogue is grotesque."

"Grotesque!" she echoed enthusiastically.

"What did you think of the ending?"

"Ending?" Ingrid asked, unaware her voice had pitched skywards.

"Yeah."

"I have—no words—just speechless, really." *Oh, please don't let her catch me, not when I'm so close.*

Vivian sighed. "Same."

As she launched into an impassioned rant about *Chinatown Blues*, Ingrid slipped into the role of attentive listener. The only responsibilities involved nodding or shaking her head from time to time and parroting back selected excerpts. She prepared to silently mock her in a self-narrated director's commentary, but as Vivian spoke, she was taken aback by the genuine emotion lining her voice. Had *she* ever cared that much about anything?

She was also perplexed Vivian had yet to notice the dearth of original opinions coming from her direction. She likes listening to herself talk, Ingrid realized. She could probably go on for hours—and might have if her phone hadn't chimed.

"It's six already?" Vivian said. She looked, for the first time in all the time Ingrid had known her, flustered. "Zoe's here."

Outside the café, a woman waited next to a motorcycle. The same African American woman who'd stood onstage with Vivian. Now Ingrid remembered where she'd seen her.

"Your girlfriend, right?" she said eagerly. "I've been meaning to tell you I'm really sorry about that day. I shouldn't have assumed—"

"It's all right," Vivian shrugged. She smiled at Zoe and mouthed something to her through the window. "Well, see you around."

Ingrid sensed this rare hour they'd shared together already fading from Vivian's memory. Of course she didn't think of her when they were apart the way Ingrid thought of her with abnormal frequency. Why would she?

"Oh, Vivian? I almost forgot," she said hastily. "I want to help out. With the boycott of the play. I'm all for . . . sticking it to the white nonsense!" She prayed she'd seamlessly integrated the term.

For a moment, Vivian stared at her like she still wasn't sure if she'd been cloned. Then she doggedly closed her eyes, as if repeating a prayer to herself about helping the less fortunate. "Well, we can always use more people." She walked to the door, turning around at the threshold to add, "I'll email you about it."

Ingrid beamed. She couldn't tell if the sweetness of the hot chocolate or Vivian's smile was to blame, but for a moment, she forgot Vivian Vo was her sworn nemesis.

AFTER MONTHS OF hoping Stephen would stop pestering her to spend time together, Ingrid now pestered *him* for never making time for *her*. He hadn't dropped by campus to bring her homemade onigiri for weeks. At the apartment, the situation wasn't much better—Ingrid spent most nights with only the TV for company. Already, Stephen had taken a few weekend trips to neighboring towns and now there was talk of a national book tour depending on *Pink Salon*'s sales figures.

Tonight, though, was Ingrid's thirtieth birthday and Stephen had no choice but to spend it with her. Earlier in the evening they'd dined out at their favorite restaurant—she ordered the tamago and eel combo, he the fatty tuna and vegetable tempura—and now they were at her parents' house for cake. Ingrid preferred keeping her birthday celebrations simple. When too many people paid attention to her at the same time, she felt she had to perform a jig to keep them entertained.

By the front door, Stephen whispered politely, "I can't wait to go home after this." In terms of verbal foreplay, this was as explicit as he got.

Ingrid blushed. "Not *here*."

She didn't visit her parents often, only on birthdays and the holidays (rotated every other year with Stephen's parents). He, on the other hand, loved visiting Jean and Bo, frequently dropping hints he missed her mother's three-cup chicken and her father's almond jelly. She didn't think her parents would mind seeing more of Stephen; at least, not her mother. She had an inkling her father wasn't particularly fond of him, though he'd never outright admit it—the distance between her and her parents stopped them short of commenting on her personal life—and Bo had always been courteous to Stephen, but the nagging feeling resurfaced every time the two men were in the same room.

The front door swung open.

"Mama, Baba, ni hao! Nimen hao ma?" Stephen said, showcasing the extent of his Mandarin.

Years ago, Ingrid had taught him these two phrases, had been touched by his effort to "connect to her culture," as he'd put it. But now a sharp, thorny sensation flared up in her chest. Perhaps she really was developing seasonal allergies.

As her mother and father clasped Stephen by the shoulders while praising how well he looked (had he gained a few pounds? good—he was too skinny!), he responded with an almost imperceptible bow. Had he always done that? Ingrid peered at him strangely out of the corner of her eye. Where had he learned it? She never bowed when greeting her parents.

Everyone maneuvered past boxes of knickknacks, jars of dried snow fungus and stacks of old greeting cards to cluster around the coffee table, their knees and elbows kept close to their bodies for lack of space.

Bo passed around glasses of Martinelli's sparkling apple juice.

"Xie xie," Stephen beamed.

Ingrid cleared her throat. She assumed he'd finished with his display of Mandarin when he continued, "Dajia dou hao ma?"

Now her mouth drooped open.

He caught her expression and whispered in her ear, proudly, "I didn't forget what you said the other night, at the award ceremony." When she remained silent he added, "I downloaded an app to learn Chinese."

Her mother clapped her hands, utterly beside herself. "Ni zai nali xue zhongwen?"

"Zenme shuo . . . 'app.'"

Ingrid's mouth still lolled open, dumbfounded. He could already understand full-blown sentences? His supernaturally fast progression was a teacher's slap on the wrist. If he continued at this rate, he'd understand more than her within a fortnight.

"Wah, ni zhen congming!" Jean complimented him.

"Congming?"

"Smart!"

Stephen pretended to wave her off, then counted to ten, his eyes looking up hopefully at Jean and Bo. Her mother erupted into clapping again. Her father drank more sparkling apple juice. Ingrid crossed her arms, petulant—today was her birthday yet she found herself in a CSL lesson. Was she supposed to sit here all night humoring Stephen's (poor) pronunciation? She suspected her parents couldn't actually understand a thing he said. His tones were all over the place.

"I'm hungry," she announced, hoping to break up their little spectacle.

Jean went to the kitchen, followed by Stephen.

"Wo bangmang ni," he said (poorly).

She shot up in disbelief to follow them into the cramped space.

Stephen had whisked Jean's flowered apron from the stove and knotted it around his waist. He shooed away her protests as he coaxed the cake from its pink box, Jean swatting playfully at his arm, insisting he let her do it, simpering like she was a young girl again.

"No, no, I'm happy to help. You should relax, Mama," he said, switching back to English. "Have you been taking vitamin D? I'll mail you and Bo a few bottles."

What was this madness? Ingrid watched as Stephen poured her mother a cup of steaming hot water, added a delicate squeeze of lemon, then set about carefully dividing the cake into even portions as he urged her to sit down and rest her feet.

"Ni zhen guai!" Jean flattered him.

"No, no, I'm not," he said humbly, as per custom.

Why was Stephen trying to upstage her? Ingrid seethed. Why was he, she wondered, almost in awe . . . acting the part of the perfect filial son?

She, the only person present who was raised by her parents, did not even act half of what was required to be a perfect filial daughter. When she was thirteen, her grandparents on her mother's side had flown in from Taiwan for a monthlong visit, and her parents had all but abandoned hope for her. On the first night, Ingrid, instead of greeting her grandparents first, letting them take the first bite during dinner, asking after their health and prosperity first, had done everything wrong and in the wrong order. While her grandpa recounted a riveting story about narrowly escaping the Communists, she had kept her headphones on the whole time, plugged into her portable CD player. When reprimanded, she had rolled her eyes and moaned, "Ugh, why did you have me in America if you didn't want me to act American?" before fleeing to her room like the preteens she'd seen on Nickelodeon.

Now she watched in disbelief as Stephen enthusiastically unclogged the kitchen sink, encouraging Jean to call him if she ever needed an extra hand around the house. She marched back into the living room and plopped down on the sofa.

"So Stephen is learning Mandarin?" Bo asked meaningfully.

She reached in her bag for her Lucidax pills. Two this time.

"What's wrong?"

"I have a headache," she replied curtly.

Then everyone was singing "Happy Birthday" as lit candles blurred her vision. Ingrid blew them out and, crushing her fists together so tightly her knuckles bleached, made a wish: *I want everything to go back to normal.*

When the cake was served, she ate the first bite like it was a punishment. Her parents had bought it from the bakery inside the pan-Asian supermarket. The mousse (dairy free) was mildly sweetened and the cake (coffee flavored) was airily spongy, topped with a mound of glazed fruit. Consuming sugar had the effect of a tranquilizer dart on Ingrid—she felt instantly calmer. Just relax, she scolded herself. Enjoy your birthday cake.

"—flavors of Asian desserts are far more subtle and refined than their western counterparts—" Stephen said as her parents nodded attentively.

Her fork clattered to the coffee table. He had spoiled something she thought unspoilable.

"Have you ever tried wagashi? No? Ah, that's a shame. Well, it's a Japanese dessert traditionally made in—"

She wanted a cake fattened with processed sugar and butter—no, lard. Something you couldn't eat prettily. Something you had to confront with your bare hands. She wanted a cake so extravagant it would make her nose bleed.

"Ingrid, dear, is everything all right?" Stephen worried. "You've been quiet all afternoon."

"I. Have. A. Head. Ache. Like. I. Said. Before."

He and her mother swiftly began to discuss her iron levels and whether or not she should try acupuncture like she wasn't even in the room. Her father busied himself with packing up leftovers while stealing concerned looks at her, which only further inflamed Ingrid.

She considered making a scene. Throwing an age-inappropriate tantrum. She could smash her glass of sparkling apple juice on the floor (no doubt Stephen would gallop on over with a mop, apron in place). She could walk with very loud, exaggerated steps into her old bedroom and, if she wrangled aside a dozen cardboard boxes, slam the door with dramatic flair. Or she could just start crying into her subtly flavored birthday cake.

Instead, she swallowed a third Lucidax pill.

WHEN THEY ARRIVED HOME, Ingrid stumbled into the bathroom, brushed her teeth with sloppy precision, then ran a bath.

Thirty years old today. How surreal that the Ingrid of last year was unrecognizable to her now. She had been working on her dissertation earnestly rather than flippantly. She had had faith in Michael, and, of course, Xiao-Wen Chou. She and Vivian had never spoken—the idea of them getting coffee together was, truly, unimaginable. And everything with Stephen had been wonderful. But it still was, wasn't it? He had just gotten on her nerves a little today, that was all. No doubt he was acting differently because of spotlight-induced stress. She had watched documentaries on the toxic nature of fame, on how so many promising child stars' careers were ruined by it. She couldn't blame him for something out of his control.

She loved Stephen and he loved her—no need to overthink things.

Ingrid toweled off and entered the bedroom, expecting to hear Stephen's asthmatic snore. He showered in the mornings, a habit she could never get over, so he wasn't waiting to use the bathroom after her. Plus, he had knocked back three cups of baijiu with her parents (it was she who had driven them home).

But Stephen was very much awake. He was splayed sideways on the bed, one leg invitingly crooked open, one arm cradling his head.

"Hello, there," he cooed. He was naked save for the black tie looped around his neck and the wooden ruler standing upright in his free hand. His penis drooped down towards the bedsheets.

"What are you doing," she said quietly.

"You didn't forget, did you? Our little tradition," he winked.

She sank down on the other side of the bed.

Stephen broke his carefully arranged pose to face her. "Ingrid?"

She was staring at the outfit he'd laid out for her: short pleated skirt, midriff-baring top with a sailor collar and a floppy bow, black thigh-high stockings. The outfit was reserved for role-play sex, which they reserved for special occasions like birthdays and bank holidays.

"Are you all right, dear?"

Ingrid had worn the schoolgirl outfit several times before, had enjoyed wearing it, had always looked forward to the next time she could wear it. So why did the thought of putting it on inspire dizziness? Her head felt water-logged. Her vision waxed and waned in quick succession like a kaleido-scope. She swung around in confusion, staggering away from him. Why did Stephen's hair look several shades darker? Was it black now? Did the school-teacher outfit include a wig? And why had his eyes changed? As though the corners were hitched up. His skin, too, had taken on a . . . jaundiced hue.

It was him.

"Xiao-Wen Chou," she whispered. "How did you find me?"

Stephen crawled to the other side of the bed and tried to corral her hands. "What's wrong, dear? What's happening to you?"

"Get away from me!" she screamed. "Stop following me around!"

"It's me, Stephen. Ingrid, please."

"Don't touch me!"

What was he doing here? What did he want from her? Was he stalking her because she knew his secret?

"In unknowing the truth, we unknow ourselves," Chou said wistfully, quoting from one of his poems.

Was that a threat?

Ingrid leapt onto the bed and scanned the room for a heavy object; she had to protect herself. She grabbed her nightstand lamp by the throat, pulling it hard enough that the plug disengaged from the wall. She whipped around to face Xiao-Wen Chou, her arm raised, but was met in-stead with a brutally cold shock. Water dripped down her face and hair. Ice cubes bobbed on the bed's surface. She dropped the lamp with a thud and rubbed her eyes.

Stephen stood before her holding an empty cup, looking frightened. "What was that about?"

She tried to summon the right words, but she was very, very tired. Sleep was enveloping her; she wouldn't fight it. She collapsed on the bed, then grabbed a pillow and muffled it over her head, taking no notice of the water soaking into the comforter.

The last thing she remembered hearing was, "Ingrid, have you been hiding something from me?"

THE PROTESTS AGAINST *Chinatown Blues* coincided with the play's rehearsals, every Tuesday and Thursday night at the Bancroft Theater, located across from the library. Wenli Zhao, the director of the play, had declined to comment on the protests. When rehearsals started, Samantha Prochazka had held on to the part of Mimi Lee. Evidently the open forum had not influenced Wenli's casting choice.

On the night of the first rehearsal, Samantha strode into the theater, eyes downcast, shoulders hunched. Secretly, Ingrid felt bad for her. When she first auditioned for the play, how could she have known it would entail spectators casually launching epithets at her? But, Ingrid reminded herself, while in the company of Vivian Vo and the POC Caucus, she hated Samantha Prochazka. She was undercover, a double agent deep in enemy territory. Her mission: gain Vivian's trust, then broach the subject of (hypothetical) yellowface.

"Pass me that brush," Vivian said.

Ingrid handed it over.

They were painting signs inside the graduate lounge of the Postcolonial Studies department. The interior was . . . different from the East Asian Studies lounge, that was certain. The female and male symbols on the bathroom doors had been crossed out. On the table were pamphlets, stickers and buttons touching on a variety of topics—everything from ancestral farming techniques to astrological signs to why monogamy is a colonial construct. During her brief foray into the world of the POC Caucus, Ingrid had learned the colonizers were not only very busy, they had an impressively wide range of interests. She avoided eye contact with the posters papering the walls, mostly African American women and men, often with raised fists in the air. They made her very nervous.

To better blend into her new surroundings, Ingrid also flaunted newly purchased accessories: shoulder-grazing hoop earrings and a beanie that commanded STAY WOKE.

"Is there something you want to write?" Zoe asked.

Thus far, Ingrid had painted the slogans assigned to her with rote efficiency, her mind glazing over the block letters without ascribing any meaning to them. Zoe smiled encouragingly at her as the other students looked on.

Blood rushed to her cheeks. "Me?"

"Yeah."

"Maybe"—she froze, the cogs in her head working overtime to put herself in their shoes—"'I hate white people'?"

No one spoke.

After a moment, Zoe said in a quiet voice, "My dad is white."

Ingrid balked. "I'm so sorry—please forgive me—I didn't know—"

"I'm just kidding," Zoe winked.

Her relief was immense.

"I mean, my dad *is* white," Zoe said, handing her a blank poster. "Do what you got to do. Speak your truth."

Ingrid was flummoxed. To say "I hate white people" when her fiancé, future family-in-law, friends, mentors and intellectual guides had all been white was bad enough. But her own father? She wouldn't dare.

She looked curiously at Zoe, at the other POC Caucus members. Even though they were always blabbing on and on about miserable and depressing topics like "mass incarceration" and "state-sponsored genocide," they didn't seem miserable and depressed themselves. In fact, compared to the E. A. Studies lounge, theirs was downright lively. They were frequently laughing, singing along with the music, swapping inside jokes (inside jokes she desperately wished she understood—purely for espionage purposes, of course).

She eyed the vegan muffins on the table. Maybe it had something to do with their diet.

Once the signs had dried with the help of electric fans, everyone trooped over to the theater. Though the packed snow had begun to thaw, the air was still glacial. Ingrid hoped they wouldn't stay outdoors for long. Surely in extreme weather conditions, protests were moved indoors for the comfort of the protestors.

She was wrong.

Listening to passersby hollering "go back to where you came from"? Being ogled by campus police from across the sidewalk, suggestively fondling their batons? Having to keep rhythm while shouting sixteen-syllable slogans with flawless enunciation? On top of that, activism was physically exhausting. Standing on one's feet for up to *an hour*? What would she do if she needed the bathroom or a light snack? Holding up signs made her arms ache and chanting made her throat hoarse. She hoped she wouldn't catch a cold. On the other hand, she'd have an excuse to skip Thursday night's—

"Doing okay?" Zoe asked.

Ingrid was disarmed by Vivian's girlfriend, with her generous smile and her openness towards herself, who, unbeknownst to Zoe, didn't subscribe to any of the nonsense she was shouting or waving in the air. But truthfully, the other reason Zoe disarmed her was due to her inexperience hanging out with African American people—or, as everyone in the POC Caucus said so freely, Black people with a capital B. She'd had acquaintances, of course, friends of friends, one colleague . . . But she had never been close with an African American—that is, Black—person. In short, Ingrid didn't know how to act around them.

"Yo, what is *up*, home girl!" she answered.

Zoe laughed. "Man, I hate when white people start talking funny the second they see a Black person."

"Me, too!" she guffawed to cover her confusion.

"Do you come to a lot of protests? I haven't seen you around before."

"Me? Oh, you know, I usually go to, um, indie protests."

"Indie protests?"

"Yeah, not a lot of people know about them."

"Really."

"I went to one for the rights of the, what was it—endangered short-eared gray owl native to Massachusetts."

"Hey, that's cool. If we don't stand up for them, who will?"

"Exactly. Wow, you really get me!" Ingrid contemplated how to initiate fist-bumping Zoe in a display of solidarity. Was the fist traditionally facing down or up? Well, she was wearing mittens so the point was probably moot—

"Ingrid!"

She jerked her head up to see a fur-encased figure: Eunice. Even in the arctic weather, she looked impeccable, ready to guest star in a music video. Her faux fur coat was pure white with an enormous hood. Her four-inch stiletto boots nearly brought her to Ingrid's height and her pink lip gloss was, as always, freshly applied. She pushed her hood back, revealing her honey-colored hair and (today) azure blue contact lenses.

"I haven't seen you in ages!" Eunice cried.

Ingrid registered she wasn't alone. A blond man stood beside her in a polo shirt, windbreaker and khaki shorts. One of her boy toys: Brad—no, Thad, that was his name.

"Hey, *bro*," a protestor called. "How's your app going?"

App? Earlier in the Postcolonial Studies lounge, the hot topic of the day had revolved around some scandal at a new tech company. Ingrid's memory, burdened with new lingo, strained to recall the specifics.

Thad grinned. "It's going great, bro, thanks." His smile stiffened when he realized the crowd was laughing at, not with, him.

"Hey, quick question about your app, *bro*," Zoe said. "If I use the 'Jamaican Me Crazy' filter, does it also make my skin black? Or does it just give me locs, a gold tooth and a Rasta beanie?" Someone low-fived Zoe. "I'm just asking 'cause, you know, I'm already Black."

Ingrid's memory jump-started. The hubbub had been over a cosmetic app by REVER called Your Face But Better, which claimed to enhance your facial features with the same precision as top-grade plastic surgery. The app also offered a selection of "Out of This World!" filters that transformed you into a leprechaun or a cheeseburger or a giraffe. And "Around the World!" filters that transformed you into other . . . ethnicities.

Thad rolled his eyes and said to Eunice, "I'll meet you in the car."

An unexpected gust of shame hit Ingrid. But why? Eunice was her friend, not *these* people. And yet . . . why was "Eunice + Thad" so icky? Come to think of it, why *was* someone as extraordinary as Eunice dating someone as mediocre as *Thad*, who insisted on wearing sandals with socks in thirty-degree weather? What did she see in him?

"Is this what you've been up to?" Eunice asked brightly. Her eyes drank in Ingrid's three-by-three I HATE WHITE PEOPLE sign. "Oh—that's . . . interesting."

Ingrid coughed. Vivian was carefully watching her.

"So, see you next Friday? Boba and *A New You*, right?"

Ingrid stared down at her feet. "I'm busy."

"Okay . . . What about the Friday after that?"

"Um . . . I'll have to check my schedule."

Eunice's eyes darted from the crowd to Ingrid. Her bruised expression was unbearable. Ingrid couldn't bring herself to look at her; she studied the ground again.

After a moment, Eunice said, "I see. Have fun with your new friends," in a quiet voice. Her stiletto boots clip-clopped sadly away.

"That app is legit a crime against humanity," someone said from behind Ingrid.

"These tech bros are fucking scary."

"They don't even know how to be subtle with their racism."

"I swear, next thing you know, they'll be wearing armbands and carrying torches."

Just throw down the sign and go to Eunice, Ingrid ordered herself.

And yet, the way this person in a COLUMBUS WAS A MASS MURDERER sweatshirt was looking at her . . . Like she was in on the joke . . . Like she had been invited at long last to consort with the cool kids in the high school cafeteria . . . It was intoxicating.

Ingrid tentatively laughed along with everyone else. She caught sight of Eunice as she disappeared out the university gates. She could call her later that night, explain how she'd been playing a part she didn't even want to play. But the feeling that Eunice had somehow disappointed her lingered.

What was happening? She set down her sign and tried to discreetly blot the tears from her eyes.

"Hey, you okay?" Zoe asked.

"Yes," Ingrid said quickly. "I'm fine. The cold is just making my eyes dry."

She picked back up her sign, which felt strangely lighter than before.

10

Traitor!

Azumi Kasuya was beautiful. In person, she was a facsimile of her author photo: clear skin, rosy cheeks, perfect posture—it was outrageous. Ingrid had been certain the photo was severely doctored; surely, no one's skin looked that flawless without the aid of technology. Evidently Azumi's did. Even more infuriating, from where she stood, the twenty-two-year-old was hardly wearing any makeup.

Ingrid realized she was gawking and looked away. In front of her and Stephen, separated by towering stacks of *Pink Salon*, stood Azumi and her interpreter, Leila Nassar (fluent in four languages). They were at an event hosted by Barnes University's bookstore. Azumi had come to the US for a three-month-long tour of readings, book signings and conferences and Stephen was to accompany her.

He was in a good mood: *Pink Salon* hadn't budged from the *New York Times* Best Seller list for three weeks. His normally constricted method of smiling, a habit cultivated to conceal his crooked tooth, had grown generous and loose. Even more shocking, twice today, she had heard him laugh out loud—she suddenly couldn't remember if he had ever laughed out loud before.

"After the book signing, Azumi says she'd like to visit Wittlebury," Leila translated.

As Stephen enthusiastically reeled off a list of local attractions, Ingrid scrutinized Azumi's wardrobe: a high-collared dress with a hoop skirt and a bow cinched at the throat. She looked like an eighteenth-century milk-maid. Well, whatever could be said for her skincare routine, she clearly did not know how to dress herself. Was this an attempt to appear child-like? Doll-like?—

"Ingrid?"

"What?" she yelped, panicked she'd been thinking aloud.

"Do you want to come with us to the Wittlebury Museum?" Stephen asked.

The minuscule building adjacent to the town hall, preserving musty old knickknacks no one cared about? No, thank you. She had to preserve her energy in the name of social justice for tonight's protest. She was about to say just that when an image of Stephen and Azumi inside the dim, sen-sually lit museum passed through her mind: he bending over a glass case to patiently explain some knickknack's history as she inclined her head towards his, wide-eyed and enthralled.

"I would *love* to come," Ingrid said through a smile that read like a grimace.

THE MUSEUM'S MAIN COLLECTION was displayed in a single square room. Azumi had requested a guided tour, led by a suspiciously jolly government official. The tour wasn't a bad idea, Ingrid conceded, since Stephen wouldn't have to playact as Azumi's private history tutor anymore. Not that Ingrid cared if he did. She wasn't threatened by a walking petticoat in lace stockings and Mary Janes.

Ingrid conspicuously adjusted her engagement ring to catch the light (she'd found it inside a jar of Nutella), then stood close to her fiancé.

"Ingrid, you keep stepping on my feet," Stephen complained.

"Oh. Sorry."

The guide was droning on about something "—ten thousand slaughtered and the rest relocated, on foot, to a reservation in Oklahoma—"

Azumi had the most annoying habit of holding her hand up to her mouth whenever she giggled. Ingrid fell behind her, glaring at the back of her perfectly coiffed head. The guide's strident voice, the fluorescent lights and the distinct smell of mothballs rid the museum of any intimacy. She wished she'd gone home and taken a nap instead.

"—unusually, Wittlebury was the only Northern town to resist abolition. The mayor was a fervent supporter of chattel slavery. A truly tragic, though undeniably fascinating, part of our local history—"

Ingrid glanced distractedly at a faded photo of five bare-chested men standing on an auction block and wondered if Azumi had eyelash extensions. If so, she had an obligation to announce it. Strutting around like she was born with such lengthy lashes was morally irresponsible.

"—after the Chinese Exclusion Act was passed on May 6, 1882. If you look closely, you'll see six Chinamen being thrown overboard on the SS *Liberty*. Remarkably, none of them could swim—"

Stifling a yawn, she stole a glance at Azumi's slender legs. What kind of diet was she on? She'd go home and research what Japanese women ate in her age range. Naturally, she wasn't about to *ask* her.

"—pictured here are the original founding fathers of Barnes University—"

Azumi chirped something in Japanese and both Stephen and Leila laughed. Ingrid rolled her eyes.

"—only segregated university in all of Massachusetts—"

Why was Stephen pretending he could understand Japanese all of a sudden? What could Azumi possibly be saying that was so amusing? Ingrid stabbed her nails into her palms. I can be funny, too, she muttered to herself, especially if given the opportunity to run through punch lines a dozen or so times.

"—and moving on to more contemporary history, this is the famous Waffle-Dog Factory, established after the former sanitarium burned down along with all two hundred residents. I highly recommend taking a tour. Free samples are included," the guide winked.

At the mention of waffle-dogs, Ingrid's mouth watered with Pavlovian instinct. Before the POC Caucus meeting, she'd stop by the factory and ask for extra butter and extra syrup—after today's ordeal, she'd earned it.

When the tour concluded, Ingrid took careful note as Stephen said his goodbyes to Azumi. There it was again—that imperceptible little bow of his. Wait—it was no longer imperceptible, it was mutating into a full-on bow. He bent over so low, his hair nearly mopped the floor and he tucked in his arms so stiffly, they looked besieged by rigor mortis. What had Azumi done to the poor man?

She bowed back, but hers was a pert nod. Leila placed her hand over her heart. Ingrid smiled coldly and wiggled her fingers in the air.

As she and Stephen headed to their car, she commented lightly, "Azumi must be so busy these days. I suppose she won't have time to see us again, will she? What a shame. I thought she was *so* nice."

Stephen laughed. She stared at him—was that the third time he'd laughed aloud in a single day?

"Azumi said her schedule is wide-open. She wants to visit more Wittlebury sites. I hope you can tag along."

"Well, I suppose I'll have to," she replied tartly.

Stephen leaned down to kiss her on the mouth, but Ingrid angled her head so his lips met the skin between her ear and cheek. Since the night of her birthday, she had not been particularly keen on physical affection.

AT THE FINAL rehearsal of *Chinatown Blues*, the protestors chanted more lustily, flapped their signs more vigorously, eyeballed the actors more mur-

derously. Guarding the periphery were a brigade of non–POC Caucus vol-
unteers acting as a first line of defense between the protestors and any
would-be-violent passersby or campus police. When Ingrid voiced her
confusion about their presence ("Aren't they the enemy?"), Vivian had
matter-of-factly explained that white people willing to risk death was the
only acceptable situation in which they could collaborate.

"Whoa . . . *cool*," Ingrid had nodded. And she'd thought lectures on
modernist literature had high stakes!

Against her will, she, too, felt seduced by the heightened atmosphere:
the razor-thin air vibrated with unseen electricity, the mass of protestors
thronged in organized chaos, eyes dilated, heart rates elevated. Also hanging in the air was the implicit understanding that deep within their basest
selves, they wouldn't hesitate to kick a fellow man in the shins, and if it
came to it, oh, kick they would.

The potential for fisticuffs was abetted by the weather: yesterday's rain
shower left little snow on the ground. Ingrid was trussed in three layers
instead of five, which significantly freed up her vocal cords and range of
motion.

"This stops today!" she shouted, surprising herself.

The other protestors repeated after her in a unified, booming chorus.
She shouted a second time; again they obeyed her call. A third time. The
effect was rather thrilling. Powerful. Addictive. Was this why dictators
hated to be toppled?

Maybe protesting wasn't a "whiny cry for attention" as she'd always
thought.

The more Ingrid hung out with the POC Caucus, the more they rattled
her. She was used to Barnes students wielding ironic repartee and witty
sarcasm as emotional armor; naturally, no one *said* what they meant. But
the POC Caucus members were so . . . earnest. When they discussed im-
plementing a triquarterly reparations plan for black students, they weren't
trying to sound unserious by seriously discussing it—they were serious. A
few times, she found herself forgetting she was a spy in enemy territory,

found herself cracking up at their jokes, found herself asking questions with unaffected curiosity. She didn't know how to mentally categorize such moments. Wouldn't anything less than pure and total hatred of the POC Caucus signal a betrayal to Stephen, to Eunice?

Someone in a white fur coat bobbed through the crowd. Ingrid started, thinking it was Eunice, before the person turned her head. Her heart deflated. They hadn't spoken in over a week now.

Don't think about it, Ingrid.

She looked around—the crowd had doubled in size. More passing students stopped by to see what was going on. Ingrid's protesting duties included handing them flyers and encouraging them to join the cause. One student, a gangly East Asian man, took an entire stack and asked Vivian for the megaphone.

She eyed him. "Identify yourself."

"Timothy Liu: sophomore, econ major."

She crossed her arms. "Why haven't I seen you before? We've been protesting the play for over a week."

"I was in Taiwan, visiting my grandparents."

"Oh, I'm Taiwanese, too!" Ingrid interrupted, always happy to meet a fellow countryman. Vivian shot her a now-is-not-the-time look, then turned back to him. "So, what do you want to say?"

"Just how outraged I'm feeling," he said somberly.

"Well, make sure to vocalize. And keep it short." Vivian reluctantly parted with her megaphone.

But the moment she did, Timothy sprinted up the theater's steps and hollered, "Censorship! Censorship!" at the top of his lungs. "Vivian Vo wants to censor art!"

For a moment, no one moved. Even the shivering trees seemed afraid to shiver.

"How dare he!" Vivian cried and lunged up the stairs, capsizing a few people in her wake. Unfortunately, Timothy was quite tall. He taunted her with the megaphone, keeping it just out of reach as her hand pawed the empty air. Several people had taken out their phones to film the kerfuffle. Timothy was clearly enjoying the spectacle, pumping his arms and shimmying his hips. Then he made the mistake of showing off his dance abilities, dropping low to the ground and popping his knees apart.

Vivian yanked his wrist to her lips and shouted into the megaphone, "For your information, censorship only exists from the top down. The *powerless* cannot *censor* anything. This"—she flung her arm towards the theater—"is called *speaking truth to power.*"

Timothy snorted. "Whatever, libtard."

Her eyes looked ready to slingshot from their sockets.

"What? I thought you believed in free speech," he goaded her. "So you can dish it but you can't take it, is that right? Hypocrite."

Vivian clenched her fists together. "Fucking traitor," she hissed and bit him on the thigh. Timothy screamed and flung the megaphone to the ground, emitting an excruciating squeal. He leaned down to examine his leg; his cotton pants had been ripped through. "You psycho bitch," he panted.

She didn't blink at the insult. "Says the Asian man endorsing Orientalist trash."

"I'm supporting Chinese American *art* written by a Chinese American man and directed by a Chinese woman."

Vivian laughed, stopped abruptly, then laughed again. She wrested herself free from the protestors restraining her by the arms and marched up to Timothy. He flinched as she stuck her face in his.

"If you honestly think this play was written by an Asian man," she said, her voice low and even, "then you are ignorant beyond belief."

Timothy rolled his eyes. "What is that supposed to mean."

"It means something like that"—Vivian jabbed a finger at the theater doors—"could *only* have been written by a white man."

"You're crazy," Timothy said, though the confidence had leached from his voice.

The crowd looked perplexed. Ingrid wondered if she'd heard Vivian correctly. Before anyone could ask for clarification, she stomped down the stairs. Zoe went after her.

"Wait!"

Zoe turned around.

"I think I should talk to Vivian. You know . . . Asian to Asian?" Ingrid tried desperately.

She didn't look convinced.

"Please. It will only take five minutes."

Zoe's eyes followed Vivian's shrinking figure as she retreated into the library. "Do what you got to do," she shrugged. "I'll be waiting outside."

Ingrid found Vivian in the basement, sitting on the floor outside the shuttered archive doors.

"Hey you," she said cautiously.

"What do you want," Vivian snapped. Her cheeks were damp.

"To see if you're okay." Which was true, Ingrid told herself. She had sort of come to care for Vivian after all this time, in the same way she had for the churlish classroom rabbit she'd taken home in third grade. But she also had to know—she couldn't sleep until she found out what she'd meant by—

"I'm fine. My ancestors were oppressed and I continue to be oppressed. It's part of the burden I have to bear," Vivian said nobly. "The cycle of neocapitalist violence goes on."

Ingrid nodded sympathetically and lowered herself onto the floor. She offered up a tissue from a pack in her purse, which Vivian turned her nose up at, then snatched a moment later.

"I'm sorry about what that student did. I mean, a conversation about censorship *would* be really interesting"—Vivian narrowed her eyes at her—"but of course, not by lying to you and stealing your megaphone." She brainstormed some terminology she'd memorized. "Not by *taking up space*."

"I'm just so tired," Vivian said. Her voice cracked on the last word.

Now Ingrid felt pity seeping into her. She realized she didn't know what Vivian lived through on a daily basis, what it was like to walk in her limited edition combat boots. Underneath, perhaps she was like everyone—unsure of herself. Frightened, even.

Good God, what had gotten into her? She had to stay focused—she was on a top-secret undercover mission!

"Hey, can I ask what you meant? When you said *Chinatown Blues* could have only been written by a white man?"

Vivian honked her nose into the tissue. "It's just a theory I have. It's stupid. Sorry, I shouldn't use that word."

"Nothing you think could be stupid. You're one of the most brilliant people I know." And it was true, she thought resentfully.

Vivian sniffed in agreement.

"So . . . what's your theory?" She held her breath.

"I think Xiao-Wen Chou"—Vivian sighed—"wasn't who he said he was."

"Metaphorically, you mean?" she whispered. Her heart was beating so hard, she feared it would exit her throat.

"Sure."

Her shoulders softened.

"Actually, no. If I could just find evidence, I could finally prove—" Vivian paused.

"Prove what?"

"That he was only pretending to be Chinese American."

Ingrid stopped breathing.

Vivian twisted the tissue in her hands. "It's this feeling I get when I read his writing. There's something about it that just doesn't seem . . . authentic."

"I see," she exhaled.

"But I wonder, since you've been researching him for so long, have you ever noticed anything 'off'?"

"Off?" Ingrid echoed faintly. She had somehow vacated her body and buoyed up to the ceiling, where she gazed down at herself and Vivian, crouched on the floor, talking in hushed tones.

"Yeah, like—"

"No," she said bluntly. "Never."

"Oh. I see." Vivian shredded the tissue into slivers.

"Have you told anyone else about this?"

"Not yet. I feel like I'm on the brink of this, this revelation—but I can't figure out the missing piece. If I could, everything would make sense; I know it would. I sound crazy, don't I? Sorry, I shouldn't use that word."

"You don't sound crazy," Ingrid said slowly and unconvincingly. "But you seem . . . overworked. Maybe you should take some time . . . for yourself. You can't, um—save the world in one day," she added distractedly. The gears of her brain whirled. How much of the truth had Vivian unraveled? And when did she plan to reveal it?

"Forget I said anything." Her voice had cooled from conspiring to icy.

"Sure, if you say so," Ingrid murmured, still distracted. Vivian's dissertation had intruded into her head: "Pleasing the White Master: Traditional Asian American Literature and the Good Little Immigrant Myth."

"Vivian?"

"Yeah?"

"I just realized I never asked: what's your dissertation about?"

"Oh." She crumpled up the tattered tissue and sat up straight, clearly pleased to be speaking from her usual position of authority. "Well, I argue Chou did a disservice to Asian American advancement by writing literature that upheld the model minority myth and other destructive stereotypes. That, rather than call into question his relationship to whiteness, he produced literature white people wanted him—no, *needed* him—to write." She tilted her head. "Why do you ask?"

Ingrid forced a smile. "No reason."

AT THE WAFFLE-DOG Factory, Ingrid dragged her feet behind Stephen, Azumi and Leila, who, judging by their oohing and aahing, were having the time of their lives. You would think they were at the Louvre, she thought sullenly. She couldn't fathom why Stephen looked so happy—he detested greasy food, preferring gently seasoned vegetables and skinless chicken breast. Ingrid either had to stash her junk food in odd places, or indulge at Eunice's, lest Stephen lecture her on the irreparable dangers of trans fat. But looking at him tucking into a second waffle-dog, you'd never know it.

Though she was consumed by more pressing matters, Ingrid wore the customary inflatable waffle-dog hat and inspected the whirring machines and assembly lines with feigned interest. She had only come because, well—something about Azumi just didn't sit right with her. Today she was corseted into a checkered pinafore accessorized with knee-high socks, a ten-inch hair bow and a teddy bear–shaped purse. What was this grown woman playing at?

A child screeched past Ingrid, splattering her with mustard, ketchup and spit. She would've been impressed by his gift for abstract expressionism if it hadn't revealed itself on her jeans. Today was Saturday, the worst day of the week to visit the factory, since families were among the most frequent visitors, as were, oddly, couples.

"Look what happened," Ingrid pouted, shouldering herself between the others. Azumi pulled a woeful face, which annoyingly served to enlarge her already large eyes, while Stephen remarked, "That'll come off in the wash." Ingrid's jaw dropped. That was it? No emergency stain remover pen? No fretting she'd contract a disease from the kid microbes on her person?

They slipped back into their translated conversation, Leila spinning like a third wheel between them. Ingrid lagged behind for a moment, then caught up, turning to Azumi and half shouting, "SO, A-ZU-MI. WHAT DO *YOU* THINK OF A-MER-I-CA?"

Leila translated her response: "'I think Americans speak too loudly.'"

Her single attempt at engaging Azumi trialed and failed, Ingrid turned to sulkily ponder a machine mixing batter when she heard a familiar voice. She curved her neck around, then back just as quickly.

It was Alex.

She drew her waffle-dog hat down and snuck another peek: his hand was sitting snugly in a woman's back pocket. But whose? She casually cantered backwards for an unbroken view of his date, knocking over a cardboard cutout of a life-size waffle-dog that smacked him on the shoulder.

He turned around. "Ingrid?"

"*Alex? Is that you?*" One would have thought she had just sighted an extraterrestrial. "What are you doing here!"

"I'm on a date. Oh, yeah, this is Tiffany."

Feigning shock was no longer required. Before her stood a statuesque whi—Caucasian woman with wheat blond hair grazing the middle of her back. Her skin was tanned to the color of toasted graham crackers and her eyes looked, incredibly, to be the exact size and shape of walnuts. She wore tight jeans and a crop top airing out her braless, evidently chilly breasts.

"N-nice to meet you," Ingrid finally choked out.

"Hi! Nice to meet you, too!" Tiffany squished her into a hug.

An uncomfortable silence ensued before Ingrid asked, "So, have you two been dating long?"

"About a week!"

"Where did you guys meet?"

"At the gym! I saw him doing squats and just had to get his number," Tiffany sighed.

Ingrid looked up at Alex, expecting to see a satisfied smirk. Who had accused who of being a "white boy chaser"? He was a textbook hypocrite. And yet . . . why was it so disarming to see him with a whi—Caucasian woman who'd slid out of the silken pages of a *Playboy* magazine? Ingrid did a double take: instead of a smirk was a look of consternation on Alex's face.

"Too many waffle-dogs?" she joked.

Alex turned to Tiffany. "Give us a sec."

She kissed him wetly, moaning a little, then flounced away to study a poster about cage-free eggs.

"She seems"—Ingrid struggled to find the word—"popular."

"What the fuck. You want to talk to me like everything's okay?"

She stared down at her clogs.

"I shouldn't even be talking to you. What you did to Yoon, that was a fucking dick move. I didn't know you hung out with that lame-ass PC crowd anyway."

"But it was all just a, a, plan—I can explain—"

"I don't want to hear it. You fucked up."

"I know I did. Just—can you ask Eunice to call me?"

"Why should I?"

Ingrid glanced around—though Stephen, Azumi and Leila were nowhere to be seen, she lowered her voice. "Please, Alex, I've tried everything. Texting, calling, emailing, postal mailing. I showed up to one of her classes. I even went to your guys' apartment."

"What the fuck—"

"But she won't talk to me."

"Can you blame her?"

"Well, if I could just explain—"

"Whatever, Ingrid. I thought you were cool. Turns out you're a fake-ass backstabber. Later."

She opened her mouth to protest when Alex brushed past her and returned to his date, who immediately reattached her mouth to his, emitting breathy moans every few seconds.

"For Christ's sake, there are children here," Ingrid grumbled to herself.

By the time she found the others, they were already in the coat check line. Stephen was feasting on his third waffle-dog of the day and looking the picture of health: eyes bright, cheeks flushed, a healthy sheen of sweat varnishing his nose. "Where did you go?" he asked cheerily.

"I got lost . . . near the intestine encasement area."

She waited for Stephen to express his concern, to sweetly remind her she should wander no more than six yards from him in public spaces. Instead, he reached down to pluck off her hat.

"Oh no, it deflated," he said.

The juicy and plump waffle-dog was now withered and limp.

How fitting, Ingrid thought.

THE OPENING NIGHT of *Chinatown Blues* was unseasonably warm. The pale February sun had peeked through the clouds earlier in the day, then scattered them completely by evening. The mild weather proved useful when forming a human chain. The protestors interlocked their arms as they stationed themselves on the concrete floor outside the theater doors.

"We will stay here all night!" Vivian cried.

The rest of the protestors, even Zoe, echoed her with halfhearted enthusiasm. The futility of tonight's protest was apparent to everyone besides her. Theatergoers gingerly stepped over the man-made barrier, making their way inside without any difficulty. Unfortunately, the theater also had more than one set of doors thanks to what Vivian called "oppressive" safety regulations.

Alas, the show was going to go on.

An elderly woman gripping a cane struggled to lift her skirt over the protestors while simultaneously protecting her modesty. When she dropped her ticket, Ingrid sheepishly handed it back—not without a sharp reprimand from Vivian.

She no longer knew how to act around her. Since she discovered Vivian was on the trail of knowing what *she* knew, that her secret was no longer a secret, she had been avoiding looking at her or speaking to her or, in general, appearing in her line of vision. Although she had resolved to maintain normalcy—covering her ears as the screams multiplied, keeping the cat firmly stuffed *in* the bag—the thought of Vivian stealing the fruits of her labor was . . . unthinkable. The long-bred streak of academic competitiveness had reared its ugly head. For so long, Vivian had outpaced and outwritten her. How would *she* like choking on the exhaust fumes of someone else's success? How would *she* like being overlooked and neglected? And besides, Vivian assuming credit for "unearthing" Chou's true identity when Ingrid had done it first was . . . unprincipled! If it were the inverse, Vivian wouldn't have waited before announcing the truth to the world. She wouldn't have hesitated to destroy a man's life in mere seconds, to piggyback off it for her own personal agenda—

"Hey, you okay?" Zoe nudged her.

Ingrid realized she was breathing heavily through her nose. "What? Oh. Yeah." She broke off from the human chain to dig around in her purse, then swallowed another Lucidax pill. Her fourth of the day. But she felt fine—she had eaten a balanced dinner of Samyang instant noodles, a microwaved chile verde burrito and a neon pink Sno Ball. Stephen hadn't been at home to stop her.

Almost eight o'clock—the show was about to start. The last group of theatergoers wove through the protestors, followed by a couple holding hands.

"God sees all your sins!" Vivian shouted after them.

The others exchanged concerned looks. This didn't sound like Vivian. Wasn't she a devout atheist? She looked unwell, too. Normally impeccably put together, with her short hair angled just so, her combat boots polished to a military shine, her dark lipstick imprinted perfectly on her lips—the Vivian before them sported purplish bags beneath her eyes and greasy, flat hair.

"I will now recite all of Assata Shakur's essay she wrote in prison," she announced in a teary, martyr-like voice.

They would be here for a while.

"Do you have any water?" Ingrid asked Zoe. She felt unbearably thirsty despite having drunk a thermos of water.

"Sorry, I finished it awhile ago."

Vivian's voice thumped inside her skull like a subwoofer. The sensation of other people's clammy arms was suffocating. The concrete beneath her felt frigid and damp. She felt an urgent need to lie down somewhere, preferably alone, preferably in a dry area.

"I have to go to the bathroom," she whispered.

"Go for it. I think we're pretty much finished," Zoe nodded.

Ingrid disentangled herself, studiously dodging eye contact with Vivian, whose glare she sensed, and stood up, coming face-to-face with a late arrival. He had long black hair plaited into a queue, yellow-tinged, cakey skin and eyes pulled back at the corners—

"Xiao-Wen Ch—Chou," Ingrid stuttered.

"What?" Zoe said.

"He—he's here."

"Who are you talking to?"

"No one's there—"

"Ingrid, *where* are you going?"

"Hey, is she okay?"

"Do not even *think* about going through those doors—"

"She doesn't look so good—"

"Does she understand the definition of boycotting?"

"If you go inside there, do *not* come back, Ingrid Yang—"

"Vivian, calm down—"

"I never trusted you anyway, fucking traitor!"

Ingrid trampled on several people's legs as she tottered after Chou. He wore the same changshan she had seen in the closet: black with royal blue and gold threading. A special changshan for a special evening.

"Wait!" she cried softly. She lurched through the theater doors after Chou's figure, anticipating a pair of security guards primed to tackle her.

But the lobby was deserted.

She crept into the theater, keeping low to the ground, and scanned the audience for Chou. There he was. Lightly skipping down the stairs, arms swinging merrily. What was he doing? She watched in disbelief as he hoisted himself onto the stage and vanished behind the velvet curtains. She waited for the audience to murmur and gasp, but they remained silent. As though hypnotized, Ingrid slid into an empty seat in the very last row, next to the fire exit.

The lights dimmed with a burst of music, a trilling, florid tune inter-spersed with gongs, chimes and clangs: *De de de de DA DA de de DAAA!* The curtains swished apart to reveal a backdrop of San Francisco's old Chinatown: buckled hills of cityscape framed by neon CHOP SUEY and MAS-SAGE signs vertically, zigzags of red lanterns horizontally.

Below the backdrop, a makeshift bedroom revealed Chou hunched over on a scanty bed and Mimi, played by Samantha, striking an insolent pose beside him. Her hair had been replaced by an ebony wig, her skin with clown-white face powder. She wore scarlet lipstick, excessive black eyeliner and a garish green qipao with a slit up the thigh. Was this also a hallucination?

Chou washed laundry in a bucket and croaked, "BOSS man tell me NO money TO-day!"

She rubbed her eyes. This was definitely a hallucination. And did Mimi just cry, "Me no LI-key!" and strike her folded fan against her ass?

For the rest of the play, Ingrid was trapped in a horror show à la *A Clockwork Orange*, her eyelids peeled and pinned back by shock and dis-gust. She couldn't look away, not even to surmise the audience's reactions. But she didn't have to—their feverish clapping and raucous laughter spoke volumes.

Before her eyes, scenes from the play were cut and collaged with mem-ories of all her years in the East Asian Studies department. She saw chop-sticks balancing over porcelain bowls paper lanterns silk pearls fortune cookies long braided pitch-black hair peonies fans koi fish bamboo gongs artificial zen garden fountains rice paddies the Great Wall of China chow mein conical hats golden dragons faceless masses mysterious clay teapots inscrutable egg rolls sneaky kung fu barbaric pear tree blossoms exotic tea cups seductive Baoding balls treacherous opium spies invisible jade brace-lets castrated sexless nunchucks broken English dirty unclean bound feet cheap alien goods pestilential plagues.

The scenes bled together in a surreal moving picture until she couldn't unscramble the play from her memories, fiction from fact. An inundation of images she had never wanted to see, images she had snipped from her conscious mind, looped through her one after the other, faster and faster.

"Make it stop," Ingrid moaned. She jerked wildly from side to side, but all her limbs were sewn tight to the seat.

As the play careened to its climax, she saw Xiao-Wen Chou's features slither from his face to the floor; saw John Smith preening before his vanity table, mangling his eyelids with tape; saw their two faces overlapped like sock and buskin, comedy and tragedy, grinning and laughing, crying and wailing, forming a colossal cave of a mouth deep enough to swallow her whole—

The curtains fell.

Ingrid was doused in cold sweat. Her tongue was numb. Her eyes were parched. Her ears rang.

"He's a fraud," she whispered hoarsely. "A fraud!" she tried, louder.

But no one could hear her amid the thundering applause.

AT 4:32 A.M., Ingrid sat up in the darkened bedroom with her laptop balanced on her knees. She stared into the screen, face awash in artificial blue, eyes webbed with pink veins, and hovered a tremulous index finger over the Publish button. She had set up a fake email account and bought an Internet domain, www.thetruthaboutchou.com. The anonymous homepage read:

XIAO-WEN CHOU IS NOT DEAD. HE IS A WHITE MAN
WHO IS STILL ALIVE. HIS NAME IS JOHN SMITH.

Below, she detailed the chronology of reveals and reversals. From the smiley face note to the obscure Chinese village, to the archive donation, to breaking and entering, to the makeup on the vanity table and the three photos in the mirror, to witnessing Smith scrub off his Chou face.

She knew what Vivian Vo would do. Now she knew what Ingrid Yang would do: take her hands off her ears and run headfirst into the screams.

She clicked Publish.

All that remained was patience as the hungry maw of the Internet digested her words and regurgitated them, over and over. She had done her part; the rest was up to fate. She snapped her laptop shut, snuggled under the covers and fluttered her eyes closed with a peaceful conscience, certain the universe would make things right in the end.

A SECOND LATER, Ingrid was pawing through a drawer of office supplies in a state of frenzy. She scribbled on a piece of paper and slipped it into an envelope, then stamped and addressed it. As she held the envelope up to the weak moonlight seeping through the window, she smiled what could only be described as a manic smile.

Ingrid Yang was nothing if not careful.

PART III

Spring Quarter

11

Chaos in the East Asian
Studies Department

REPORTER: I am standing outside Barnes University's East Asian Studies department, which has descended into chaos in the past week.

Footage of graffitied walls, overturned boxes of papers, a broken fluorescent light dangling from the ceiling.

REPORTER: The mayhem broke out on Monday, when the department's entrance was vandalized with offensive slurs. Surveillance video suggests the suspects of this Asian-on-Asian crime are two young men wearing dark clothing and nude stockings over their heads. The university has not yet apprehended them.

A blurred-out image of red spray-painted writing over glass doors.

REPORTER: Then, on Wednesday, the head archivist of the Xiao-Wen Chou archive, Margaret Hong, reportedly faced verbal harassment while performing her job. She has not returned since.

An image of a TEMPORARILY CLOSED *sign plastered over the archive doors.*

REPORTER: On Thursday, a department-wide walkout was staged by East Asian Studies faculty members. Now, today, on Friday, March third, police have been negotiating for five hours with a professor, Wenli Zhao, who has climbed to the roof of the Humanities Block and is threatening to jump.

Grainy footage of a woman in her sixties standing on the ledge of a twelve-story building, accompanied by sounds of crying in the background.

REPORTER: Professor Zhao has dedicated her life to the study of a Chinese American poet named Xiao-Wen Chou—who it turns out may not be Chinese at all.

A photo of Xiao-Wen Chou with a large question mark stamped over his face.

REPORTER: In February, an anonymous website claimed Chou is a white man who has been living as a Chinese American man by wearing "yellow-face" makeup—a tradition in Hollywood.

Photographs of Warner Oland as Charlie Chan, Mickey Rooney as Mr. Yunioshi and Christopher Lee as Fu Manchu.

REPORTER: Last week, the undergraduate student newspaper, *The Barnes Gazette*, published a story about the website in its "I Heard It Through the Grapevine" section. I am joined here by editor in chief Norman Duchamps. Norman, can you tell us more?

A nervous-looking student with round glasses and curly hair standing in front of police cars.

NORMAN: Uh, well, we got this letter in the mail with the website's address. And at first, we didn't do anything about it. We thought it was a joke.

REPORTER: Then what happened?

NORMAN: Then, uh, I decided to publish it in the "Grapevine" section. No one takes it that seriously, anyway. But after it came out, we started getting calls.

REPORTER: What kind of calls?

NORMAN: From former students and colleagues who said they were, uh, suspicious, too. About Chou.

REPORTER: Can you tell us more?

Norman adjusts his clip-on tie and removes a piece of paper from his pocket.

NORMAN: Actually, I can. My assistant editor transcribed all the calls:

"I took a poetry workshop with him one summer and he claimed my speaker wasn't Asian enough. In order for my poem to 'achieve authenticity,' he said I had to make my speaker 'identifiably Asian.'"

"I had been in Hong Kong for Tomb Sweeping Day and was showing Xiao-Wen some photos I'd taken of my grandparents' tomb. He admired the food on the altar and asked how it tasted. When I laughed, he became confused. Then when I said of course we didn't eat any of it, he criticized me for wasting food. I rationalized it at the time by assuming he was joking. But in retrospect, that was a moment I should have realized something was very wrong."

"I worked in administration for the E. A. department back in the nineties. And I noticed a pattern: Chou only recommended white students for the Xiao-Wen Chou postdoctoral fellowship. Even when we'd have exceptionally qualified candidates of East Asian descent, he ended up recommending a white candidate. Every single time."

"One summer, I saw Professor Chou at the YMCA pool, in the locker room, and I swear to God, his face was melting off. When I told the other students in his class, they said I should lay off the drugs, which—okay, fair point—but that day, I wasn't on anything."

"At every single department potluck, he brought this awful, tasteless potato salad. With *raisins* in it. I had expected, I don't know, mooncakes specially ordered from overseas! Or Christ, even Chinese takeout just once. Everyone else in the department went out of their way to cook East Asian delicacies; it had become a kind of competition. But without fail, Xiao-Wen would only bring that damn potato salad."

REPORTER: *Fascinating.*

NORMAN: But even after we got all these calls, we still didn't know what to believe. We thought this was like, uh, a really sophisticated prank.

REPORTER: What convinced you it wasn't?

NORMAN: One of our reporters reached out to that restaurant in San Francisco, the one formerly owned by Chou's "parents," and it turns out for a few years in the sixties, it *was* owned by a couple named Lingyu Gao and Shaoqi Chou. They had, uh, passed away, but our reporter tracked down their only living relative, a great-niece. And she said the couple *did* have a son but he died from tuberculosis when he was a baby.

REPORTER: That's some extraordinary investigative reporting for a student-run newspaper.

NORMAN, proudly: Thank you. Then we tried to contact Chou's biographer, Clark Thompson, but his name just led back to a bankrupt LLC,

"Year of the Ox & Co." And another one of our reporters found a photo of a John Smith in an old Fallowtown High School yearbook. If you put the pictures together, of him and that Chinese dude, the similarities are pretty obvious.

Side-by-side photographs of Xiao-Wen Chou and John Smith.

REPORTER: Incredible, Norman, just incredible.

NORMAN: Totally. So then, after some major discussion, we decided to publish a front-page feature. With the photos.

REPORTER, turning back to face the camera: That was the catalyst for the string of violent events that have taken place in the past week. Norman, do you have any regrets?

NORMAN, looking defensive: *The Barnes Gazette*'s motto is "Swear by the Pen, Die by the Truth." So, no, I don't have any regrets. The people deserve to know what really happened.

REPORTER: What's next for *The Barnes Gazette*?

NORMAN: Well, we're trying to track down where Smith is, find people who are close to him. Friends, family. But so far, no one's come forward.

If you have any information about John Smith, call 413-555-6215.

REPORTER: This is Tricia Perez of WQR7 Local News, reporting live from Barnes University. Tune in at seven p.m., when I'll be interviewing Walter Luke Gibson, a man who says he was personally bullied by John Smith.

Students holding hands and crying, standing behind yellow caution tape.

INGRID SAW THE fire from inside her office. Through the western-facing window, smoke bloomed into the cloud-studded sky. She hurried out, rode the elevator to the first floor with a jittery leg, then cut through the Social Sciences Block. By the time she arrived, a sizable group of students had already gathered. She stretched on her tiptoes to locate the source of everyone's gawking.

An immense fire roared in the middle of the quad. A figure leapt around it while tearing pages from a book and flinging them into the flames. Ingrid elbowed her way to the front of the crowd, coughing and fanning smoke from her face.

"M-Michael?" she gasped.

His untied and tousled hair hung limply down his shoulders. His white frog-button shirt, the same one he'd worn at her apartment, was soiled and burnt at the sleeves. Sizing up the pile of books, she estimated he'd murdered roughly half his library. The fire—or, rather, funeral pyre—was steadily engorging itself on Chouian sestinas and ballads.

"Thirty years!" Michael cried. "Thirty years of my life I gave to this hogwash." His eyes were bloodshot with delirium. "And for what? So he could make a fool out of *me*?" He cleaved apart the book in his hands—*Elegy of the Phoenix*—and chucked both halves into the fire, then fell prostrate on his knees and yanked at the ends of his hair. The man standing next to Ingrid, an E. A. administrator, imploded into tears. Michael turned his face towards the sky and howled noiselessly, his eyes crimped shut, his mouth a stretched-open square of pain.

Someone worried, "Should we call an ambulance?"

"No," someone else shouted, "call the fire department!"

As though possessed, Ingrid's feet drew her closer to the fire. Why was Michael destroying his life's work? His actions defied logic—

A headline from the morning news flitted across her mind: SMITH'S FRAUD UNDERMINES CHOU SCHOLARS. Oh. Of course. She understood perfectly now.

If Chou had been revealed to be as Chinese as Velveeta cheese, what did that say about Michael Bartholomew, PhD in Chinese American literature (and Chinese ancient history) and chair of the East Asian Studies department? Who was Michael, really, without Xiao-Wen Chou to prop him up?

Ingrid edged closer as he rolled around on the ground while hugging his sides, reciting verses from "The Love Song of J. Alfred Peng," one of Chou's earliest works.

"'I have measured out my life with porcelain spoons,'" he whimpered before wedging a stray page into his mouth.

The crowd murmured in concerned sympathy while exchanging knowing looks: the poor man had gone off his rocker.

Flames curled around the torn pages and lapped at the broken book spines. Michael's shirttail lay precariously close to a burning scrap of verse. Ingrid bent towards him, outstretching a tentative hand to move it aside, when he turned and looked straight at her. Her breath caught in her throat. Michael's eyes were blank, devoid of recognition. She recoiled and pushed back through the crowd.

ONCE HOME, Ingrid swaddled herself in a blanket. Despite the radiators clanking and hissing at full blast, she shivered uncontrollably. She threw herself facedown into a pillow and groaned. This wasn't supposed to happen! Telling the truth was good and lying was bad; even preschoolers knew that. And John Smith had lied to everyone for over thirty years. He had to be held accountable, right? A smidgen of accountability was all she'd wanted, was why she'd emailed Luke a link to *The Barnes Gazette* article with a casual, "Wow, have you heard about this?" in the hopes he'd corroborate the paper's claims. She hadn't taken into account East Asian Studies scholars and professors . . . people who'd dedicated their lives to Xiao-Wen Chou . . . whose livelihood hinged on the integrity of their research . . . Her mind flipped through the scenarios she'd instigated: Margaret tearfully stumbling home after being verbally accosted; Michael flailing around on the soot-covered ground; Wenli Zhao teetering on the ledge of the Humanities Block.

"No, no, no!" Ingrid cried aloud, cocooning deeper into the blanket.

She didn't worry Stephen would overhear her talking to herself. Last week, he and Azumi, along with Leila, had embarked on their US book tour. Their goodbye at the airport had been polite but emotionally strained, with Stephen handing her a list of important health and safety reminders, and Ingrid clinging to him for a full nine minutes like he was going off to war. Stephen didn't approve of crying in public (so disrespectful to everyone who had to look at you), but a few of her disobedient tears wet his pocket protector. This confused her. What was there to cry about? Stephen's translation was attracting recognition and praise. She, the supportive fiancée, was thrilled for him. Why should she care he and Azumi would be flying in the same planes, sleeping in the same hotels, showering naked under the same water source? That's right—she didn't care. She trusted Stephen. He was dependable, loyal, downright predictable. He wasn't capable of something as interesting as adultery. Still, she wouldn't mind hearing more frequently from him. She groped for her phone, wondering if she should call him. He was presently in Baltimore. Or was it Bloomington? No, pestering him was pointless. And how could she seek his advice when he was ignorant of the chaos she'd ignited?

She scrolled through her contact list and paused at Vivian Vo—she'd know what to do in this situation. Perhaps she'd penned a paper titled "Yellowface Damage Control: What to Do After Anonymously Outing a White Man's Racial Farce."

But she knew she wouldn't pick up.

When they last crossed paths on campus, Vivian had paused to talk to her instead of pretending she was a lamppost. Ingrid was overjoyed, given Vivian's recent declaration that she could not be forgiven for failing to boycott *Chinatown Blues*, that she was no longer welcome in the POC Caucus and finally, that she was a "treasonous sellout."

"Did you hear the news?" Vivian asked in an oddly sugarcoated voice.

This was just after *The Barnes Gazette* reported on www.thetruthabout chou.com.

"Oh, yes—did you?" Ingrid caught the illogic of her question a moment too late.

"Isn't it just *incredible*?" Vivian went on. She looked frenzied around the eyes, like she'd recently been electrocuted.

"Incredible?" Ingrid squeaked.

"That this story came out two days—just *two* days—after we had that talk in the library."

She gulped. "Yes, it is."

"I mean, what are the odds?"

"They must be very low?"

"So low!" Vivian eagerly echoed. "You wouldn't happen to know who sent in the tip about the website, would you?"

She struck a pose of intense concentration. "No . . . I can't say I do."

"Because all the time I've spent on Chou has been wasted. My plan to disprove his identity through his writing is garbage now."

"I wouldn't say that—"

"No, it is. I put it all in my kitchen garbage disposal."

"Can you put paper in there—"

"Since *allegedly*, this person found Smith's address and broke into his house like a *psychopath*!"

" 'Psychopath' is a strong word—"

"Oh, how rude of me, I almost forgot—I wanted to give you my condolences! I'm *so* sorry, Ingrid."

"Condolences?"

"I mean, you must be heartbroken." Vivian tugged her mouth into a dramatic pout.

"Heartbroken?"

"All your research—on the use of enjambment in Chou's poetry, wasn't it?—has zero value now. I mean, it's absolutely useless. You can put that in the garbage disposal, too!" she cackled.

"Oh—right. It's true I am very . . . distressed."

"Obviously you'll have to write a new dissertation now. Weren't you already in your eighth year? Such a shame. Oh, well, not everyone is made to withstand the rigors of academia."

"Actually—"

"Well, it was *so* nice running into you." Vivian pulled her in for a hug, the first time they'd ever touched. Her fingers alighted on her shoulders as if she were a slime-covered sea creature. "Let's keep in touch!" Her cheerfully frenzied demeanor wavered for a moment, replaced by a look in her eyes that made Ingrid pee herself, just a drop.

No, she could not ask Vivian Vo for help.

INGRID PACED CIRCLES by the elm tree in Wittlebury Park, bathed in milky moonlight. The night was clear and cool, and minus fireflies and magnolias sweetening the air, the scene was identical to episode sixteen of *My Once and Forever Springtime Love*, when Jung-Suk and Hae-Young dig a time capsule next to an elm tree, where they make a pact to reunite in ten years.

If Eunice had solved Ingrid's clues, left in her mailbox, graduate cubby and car windshield, she should be here now, at 10:00 p.m. It was already 10:12. Either her clues lacked precision (she had relied on an online English-to-Korean translator) or Eunice had decided not to come.

Ingrid sank dejectedly onto the damp grass, the blanket she'd brought long forgotten. From a picnic basket, she produced a bag of shrimp chips, meant to be shared postreconciliation, tore it open and shoveled handfuls into her mouth without tasting a thing. Stephen was gone and now Eunice wanted nothing to do with her. She was alone. Well, what else was new.

Next she reached for a box of chocolate koala cookies when she detected a distinctly artificial cotton candy scent. She knew that scent: Stripper Pole, a perfume banned in three countries. She leapt up and spun around.

"It's not fair," Eunice panted, clomping up the rest of the hill in wedge booties. "You know episode sixteen is my favorite."

"Yes." Ingrid tried to rein in the tears collecting in her eyes.

"I wrote a paper on it for Professor Baek's class. A really good paper."

"Yes." She gave up trying.

Eunice had reached the top of the hill. She delicately dabbed at her cheeks. "And you know when I see other people cry, I automatically cry, too. I didn't even wear waterproof mascara today."

"I'm sorry, Yoon."

Eunice sniffled. "I know you are."

"You're my closest friend," she began, "and you mean so much—"

"Oh, stop that," Eunice said briskly, though Ingrid could tell she was pleased. "Don't you remember Hae-Young only expressed her feelings through grand gestures? If you spell it all out, it ruins the moment."

Ingrid smiled through her tears.

"I do have some things I want to say, though."

She nodded fervently.

Eunice looked around, then said primly, "Well, are we supposed to stand here all night?"

Ingrid remembered the picnic blanket, flapped it open on the grass, then parked a cardboard tray with two cups of boba in the middle. Once they sat down, Eunice plucked the bag of shrimp chips from her timidly outstretched hands.

"So . . ." she prompted.

Eunice finished chewing and swallowed. "So. Why were you hanging out with Vivian?"

She faltered on where to begin. She couldn't explain everything without admitting she'd lied. "The night we broke into Smith's house, I saw him dressed as Chou. I saw him . . . take all his makeup off."

"No, *really*?" Eunice gasped and clapped a hand over her chest.

"Well, yeah—"

Eunice laughed. "Oh, come on, it was obvious you made the website—"

She paused, looking wounded. "But why didn't you say anything that night?"

Ingrid itched the eczema patch on her ankle. "I don't know . . . I guess I didn't want to believe it was true. I just wanted it to go away . . . Pretend it never happened . . ."

"You were probably experiencing PTSD," Eunice commented wisely.

"I should've told you the truth," she said. "I'm sorry, Yoon."

Eunice dabbed at her cheeks again. "So, what did that have to do with Vivian?"

"Oh. Right." She took a deep breath and walked her through the acrobatics her mind had conducted: her confusion about yellowface leading her to read Vivian's article resulting in her plan to figure out what to do about said yellowface by convincing Vivian to trust her through infiltrating the POC Caucus—all without Vivian catching on to Chou's real-life deception.

"So you see, at the protest, I was undercover. I was . . . playing a role."

"Oh." Eunice mulled this over. "But why didn't you call me afterwards to explain? I thought you were"—she glanced down at her boba—"avoiding me."

Ingrid stalled, her insides dunked into ice water. The truth was . . . the truth was, she'd been disappointed Eunice couldn't see why someone like Thad was . . . *problematic*. The truth was, she had started to change. The two of them had crouched at the same starting line and now Ingrid was on the verge of outrunning her. But how could she confess to such blasphemous thoughts? She didn't *want* to outrun Eunice.

"I felt too guilty," Ingrid made herself say. "I thought you hated me."

"I could never hate you. I just need you to be honest with me."

Ingrid sipped nervously from her boba—she'd lied to so many people now, she worried it had become a permanent fixture of her personality.

The two friends munched in silence and stared up at the moon. Though they had always comfortably passed the time together without needing to speak, now the silence assumed physical dimensions, squatting between them like an invisible boulder.

"So—what have you been up to?" Ingrid asked shyly.

"Oh, you know, the usual. Calling Thad when I want a booty call." Ingrid internally winced. "Being annoyed by Alex, teaching, writing. I'm on part three of the dissertation," she grinned.

"Eunice, that's wonderful! You just have one more part left, right?"

She started on the cookies. "Mmhmm."

"So what will you do—after?"

"I might move to South Korea for a while."

"What?" she cried.

"Well, I've been thinking about it, and I don't want to spend years chasing after a tenure-track position, you know? When I applied for the PhD, I mostly did it for my parents. I thought it was the only way I could, like, honor their memory, you know?"

Ingrid nodded, surprised. Eunice's parents had both been professors before they died in a car accident. But she rarely, if ever, alluded to the tragedy.

"There are other things I want to do," Eunice continued. "Don't you think I'd be a good K-drama makeup artist?"

Ingrid enthusiastically agreed, though she felt panicked at the prospect of Eunice leaving her behind in Wittlebury. One month without her and she'd fallen apart, hallucinations and all—what would happen if she stayed in South Korea for years?

Eunice took note of her downtrodden mien. "Anyway, it was just an idea," she said brightly. "Now tell me *everything* about Vivian and her 'social justice crusade.' Is she as horrible as she seems?"

"Huh? I mean yes—yes, she is!"

Not ten minutes after promising she wouldn't lie anymore, she was doing it again. But looking at Eunice, eyes still muddy with wet mascara, Ingrid launched into picking apart Vivian and her insufferable politically correct ways. She'd always performed the activity with relish, and it should've been easy to dip back into, but now the serrated words labored past her lips. As she spoke, she remembered how Vivian's voice had cracked with emotion on the library floor.

Just when she thought she had a handle on who someone was, on the exact shape and size of their character, on the precise quantity of their goodness and badness, they insisted on changing.

INGRID GINGERLY PICKED her way around the broken glass and coffee-stained flyers that patterned the floor of the E. A. department. She hadn't visited since news about Chou-Smith had (literally) destroyed the place. The corkboard lay fractured in two against the toppled water cooler. Framed photos of Chou and other illustrious East Asian writers had been vandalized and smashed. A single crushed egg tart lay facedown on the carpet. An involuntary shudder ran through her—she was responsible for this crime scene.

Ingrid gathered bits of trash, careful to skirt around the broken glass, and with her arms full, trooped towards the bathroom garbage can—then froze. Voices? She'd assumed the building was empty. The specter of Wenli Zhao poised on the ledge of the building still haunted the place.

She tossed the trash, then followed the voices into the lounge, relieved they weren't in her head. Six drawn faces looked up at her: two second-year masters students she didn't know well, an associate professor, a visiting lecturer and a friendly acquaintance, Gurti Lakra, an English fifth-year from London. For a moment, she frowned, wondering why the scene before her looked amiss, like a "What's Wrong Here?" picture game. Then she realized everyone present was Asian. In the E. A. Studies lounge, this was an exceptionally rare occurrence. They were huddled together in a circle like refugees after a civil war.

"Hi . . . I'm Ingrid," she announced hesitantly.

"Hi, Ingrid," everyone echoed in wan voices.

"Is it okay if I join?"

Gurti waved her over to an empty chair beside her. In the center of the circle was an overturned cardboard box supporting cold coffee, paper cups and stale donuts.

"What were you all talking about?" she asked, once she had selected a rock-hard donut and sat down.

"Just trying to figure everything out," a second-year said quietly.

The visiting lecturer nodded. "I think we're all feeling really conflicted."

"Conflicted how?"

"I mean, the whistleblower has a right to—"

"Whistleblower?" she interrupted.

"Yeah. The guy who made that website."

"Hold on, how do you know it's a guy?" Gurti asked.

The visiting lecturer shrugged. "I can just tell."

Gurti snorted.

"Anyway, he has a right to say what he said. But—" He paused.

"But?" Ingrid prompted.

"At what cost?"

"Yeah," a second-year agreed. "Look at what happened to Professor Zhao. Was this all worth it?"

Ingrid shrank back in her chair, clutching her donut like it was a shield.

"But the university is giving her tenure," the other second-year said.

"That's not the point . . . And they should have given it to her a long time ago."

"True. You know, when I heard that, I realized all the Asian teachers in the E. A. department are lecturers and adjuncts," Gurti reflected. "None of them are actual professors."

Ingrid furrowed her brows together. "And the chair of the department before Michael was Kenneth McDougal."

"The chair of the department has never been Asian."

The room stilled for a moment.

A second-year spoke up. "Those of us who've been researching Chou— what do we do now?"

"Stop, I guess."

"Why should we?" the visiting lecturer asked defensively.

"Yeah. A part of me, I don't know . . . I'm still skeptical."

"Same. I saw the photo on the news—but anyone can doctor a photo."

"Who's to say Norman what's-his-name didn't do it himself?"

"Right."

"But what would be his incentive?" Ingrid asked.

"This is the biggest news story of his life."

"Apparently *The Washington Post* offered him a job!"

"That's incentive to make up a story, if you ask me."

What was everyone talking about? Why were they acting like she—er, the whistleblower—hadn't told the truth? She fumbled around in her purse for her bottle of Lucidax. Empty.

"Wait a second," Gurti said. "The whistleblower is clearly a former Chou researcher. Why would they compromise themselves if they weren't telling the truth? They wouldn't ruin their academic career for the hell of it."

"That's *if* the whistleblower is who he claims to be."

"Stop saying 'he'!"

"Guys, come on. Anyone can go on the Internet and write a bunch of horseshit. People out there believe in UFOs but not 9/11. Should we just take this guy's word as a reason to destroy decades of honest work? I mean, serious consequences are happening based on hearsay," the visiting lecturer argued.

"Yeah, Margaret might quit for good."

"M-Margaret?" Ingrid stuttered. "The archivist?"

"Well, Vivian Vo and her army are demanding Barnes shut down the archive. She said it's 'a shrine to the practice of yellowface' and leaving it open is 'tacit support of yellowface.' Margaret told me she's afraid to come back. I don't blame her. So excuse me if I don't think so highly of this mysterious whistleblower."

Gurti crossed her arms. "Well, I think it was brave."

Ingrid blushed before aggressively smoothing her hair over her cheeks. The visiting lecturer cocked a wry eyebrow. "Brave?"

"They were committed to the truth! Even if it meant hurting other people." Ingrid flinched. "Even if it meant hurting themselves. But that's what a whistleblower does. They believe the people—we—deserve to know the truth. Isn't that, I don't know, what's the word—"

"Heroic?" Ingrid suggested, pouring herself a cup of cold coffee and trying to appear disinterested.

"That might be going a bit far," Gurti laughed. "I meant like, a sign of integrity. That's how we know they're telling the truth."

The associate professor finally spoke. "Actually, I want to personally thank them, whoever they are. I've wasted twelve years of my life on Chou. God forbid I waste any more."

Ingrid slurped happily from her cup.

"When you think about it," Gurti said, "isn't the truth that we're all a little embarrassed? That we didn't catch on sooner or figure it out ourselves? The fact is—the fact is"—she drew a weary breath—"we were conned. By a white man."

The room fell silent again.

"So why won't he—I mean they—reveal who they are?" the visiting lecturer challenged. "What are they afraid of?"

"Come on. Didn't you read the website? They broke into Smith's house. That's a felony."

The visiting lecturer tipped back in his chair, splaying his legs apart so his knee knocked sharply into Ingrid's. "I just think we should take things on the Internet with a grain of salt. Especially in this day and age."

"Hypothetically speaking," Ingrid said with a nonchalant air, "what would it take? For you to believe Smith is really Chou?"

The group glanced around at each other.

Gurti shrugged. "Who knows. At the end of the day, people will believe what they want to believe, won't they?"

INGRID FELT IMPOTENT and useless, but fortunately, a cure existed: magical little pale blue pills. At the drugstore, she chucked three bottles of

Lucidax into her basket, and as she waited in line, added six candy bars and a supersized bottle of electrolyte water to the party (even while drugged out, she'd never forget to hydrate). She looked forward to numbing herself into oblivion while zoning out before the TV. Goodbye problems, hello infinite void!

Then at the last minute, much to the cashier's frustration, Ingrid ditched her full basket and returned to her car empty-handed. Gurti had said she had integrity. Well, she hadn't addressed her directly—but still, she had used the word *integrity*. And here she was trying to take the easy, chemically enhanced way out. Gurti would be appalled.

Ingrid had set into motion events she couldn't control—a scientist whose invention surpasses what she'd thought possible. She couldn't twiddle her thumbs as it lumbered around, wreaking havoc. And she couldn't formulate a plan to stop it if she was half-sentient.

She passed her apartment, where too many temptations to mope lurked. She wound aimlessly through Wittlebury, cutting haphazard corners and U-turns, crisscrossing the small town's arteries until she found herself flowing into the freeway's bloodstream. As she flew past a picturesque cow pasture, she thought back to her old self, molting in the archive while tracking the clock's second hand rotation. To think, the only source of her panic then was over a document three people in the universe would read before it collected mold on a basement shelf. What did that matter now? How could it, in light of everything that had happened? She exited the freeway and knew: the days of footnotes and bibliographies were over.

Ingrid turned right at the light, zipped down an empty avenue, left, left again. When she hit the brakes, it was nearly six o'clock and she was outside her parents' house. The setting sun softened even the rough edges of Putterville. She stood outside the door for a while, acclimating to the peculiar sensation that always accompanied revisiting her childhood home: smothering nostalgia. She hadn't come alone in a long time, not since she'd hunted for her lucky rabbit's foot. And in tandem, it had been a long time since her parents had treated her normally, the way they did when

Stephen—no, when anyone who wasn't their immediate family—wasn't around.

Her mother opened the door and not twenty minutes later, Ingrid was ingesting a half dozen elaborate dishes her parents insisted had just been sitting in the fridge.

"How is your research?" Jean asked, heaping a pile of shrimp and walnuts into her bowl.

Ingrid frowned. From her last visit with Stephen, she had unconsciously prepared for another round of CSL lessons. Why are you speaking to me in English? she wanted to ask. When her parents spoke to each other, it was always in Mandarin or Hokkien. But that was a silly question. It was she, age twelve, who forbade her parents from speaking to her in their native languages.

"Fine."

"Just fine?"

She shrugged, tucking herself into a cross-legged position, and crammed more food into her mouth. In the company of her parents, regressing into the role of a brooding teenager came easily.

"How is everything at the university?" Jean asked, essaying a different angle.

"Fine."

Her mother patted her mouth with a napkin and settled it theatrically over her lap. Ingrid knew this precipitated some kind of speech.

"We saw the news," she said. Well, here it was.

"It is very concerning," Bo added. He had emailed her multiple articles from *The Barnes Gazette*.

"We called to ask if you were all right."

"But you did not return our calls," Bo said. Ingrid could tell his feelings were hurt.

"I was going to. But I was—I was—"

"Busy," both her parents said, glancing meaningfully at one another.

"Yes," she said stiffly.

"Well? What is going to happen now?" her mother asked.

"I don't know. I guess my dissertation is over." She laughed weakly.

Bo stopped eating. "Why?"

She looked at him, baffled, her towering forklift of rice paused in midair.

"Why?" Jean repeated. "You did nothing wrong."

"Mom, Dad," she groaned, "you said you saw the news, didn't you? That Xiao-Wen Chou is a white man who pretended to be Chinese?" She deposited the rice in her mouth and said in a distorted mumble, "It's all over."

Her parents were silent. Ingrid was about to ask if they wanted to watch *Jeopardy!*, when Bo abruptly announced, "This is America."

"What? What are you *talking* about?" she moaned.

"In America, you can be whoever you want."

Jean nodded vigorously. "So what, he put on some face paint and an ugly wig? He will never be Chinese. He is a—zenme shuo—clown. Why should we care about a clown?"

"Because, Mom, it's *offensive*. Yellowface is *offensive*," Ingrid whined, her teenage mannerisms in full effect. She blinked. Yellowface is offensive? She had never talked so openly about race-related topics with her parents. In fact, she hardly knew how they felt about race . . . or racism . . . or, come to think of it, white people. The handful of times race had come up at the dinner table, her parents had defaulted to her knowledge, if it could be called that, on the foreign subject. And when it came to politics, they concerned themselves with the elections in Taiwan over the ones in their adopted country. Instead of complaining about the left versus the right, they complained about blue versus green. She had never even asked if they voted in the US—the question had seemed intrusive, borderline rude. But maybe they didn't know how they fit into American politics precisely because they didn't know how they fit into American life.

Taken altogether, she had no meter to gauge how her parents would position themselves in a discussion about race.

Jean sighed and pitched her napkin onto the table. "American children like you are so easily offended. I think you like being offended. Because you have never been hungry or poor."

Ingrid choked on her rice.

"What? I'm serious. When people are starving and dying, Americans don't care. They go out to buy a big TV and a big car. When a man puts on a silly costume, everyone cares. Why?"

"So you're not mad? That a white man took—I mean, *stole* your culture?" she pressed. The severity of John Smith's crimes seemed to have eluded her parents.

"And we don't take from American culture?" Her mother pointed at the shrimp and walnut dish. "This has Miracle Whip."

"That's not the same thing as pretending to be Chinese—"

"Aiya, I know it's not. I'm not stupid!"

"Don't upset your mother, Ingrid," Bo chided her.

But Jean was already worked up. "Okay, you want another example?" She disappeared into the living room.

Ingrid guiltily nudged the food in her bowl. "Mom, just sit down and eat," she called.

A moment later, Jean returned with a paisley-clothed photo album. Ingrid's stomach kinked into knots as her mother skimmed through the plastic-covered pages before jabbing at a photo: seven-year-old Ingrid, wearing her best dress, her mother's high heels and jewelry, and atop her head, a misshapen, baby-duck-yellow mass of curls.

"What about that?" Jean said, both pleased and proud she'd found the evidence she sought. "You ripped it off your doll's head. The expensive one I—Santa got you for Christmas. I was very mad at you!"

"My Real Friend doll," Ingrid said quietly. She remembered how she'd peeled the wig from the plastic head with the end of a metal ruler.

"You liked to run around the house in it all the time. You looked very stupid—"

"Okay, okay," Bo interrupted, "I think she gets the point."

"—but it made me happy," Jean finished, "because it made you happy."

Ingrid half-wished Vivian had come to dinner. If she were here, she would say—something about colonization—the plundered Asian body—

"What your mother means," Bo said, looking at his wife, "is that you should not give up everything because of something you did not do."

Jean nodded ferociously again. "Why do they make the rules? And why can they change them whenever they want?"

She looked from her mother to her father. So they understood a "them" lived alongside an "us."

"Don't let them bully you," Jean added, her voice softening.

She felt oddly touched. "I—I won't. I promise." Her parents smiled, seemingly satisfied. Jean made to shelve the photo album, when Ingrid stopped her. "Actually, can I borrow this?"

That night, she flopped stomach-down onto her bed and leafed through the album. When she came to the photo of the little girl in the yellow wig, she dislodged it from its plastic sleeve to study her face. She is cheesing for the camera, all her teeth on display, save for a missing front tooth. Her smile screams happiness. But when Ingrid looked very hard, she could've sworn a pang of sadness ached behind her eyes.

Or was that only her imagination.

12

Good Old-Fashioned American Freedom

Ingrid was reluctant to meet with her dissertation advisor. Their last encounter—he writhing on the ground and eating snatches of verse—had deeply disturbed her. His behavior had been . . . unhinged. Michael had always been unerringly and reliably himself. Now she didn't know what to expect from him.

At first, Ingrid postponed responding to his urgent requests for a meeting, but, having already exploited five different illnesses in the past, could only improvise one legitimate illness (mumps) before she resigned herself to the inevitable. She also didn't want him to "swing by" her apartment again, especially with Stephen away (currently in Milwaukee).

Through the front window of the Old Midwife, Ingrid spotted Michael reclining in a leather armchair. She took several deep meditative breaths, hoping to steady herself, and instead caught a whiff of pollen, which set off a violent sneezing fit. For a moment, she considered this a timely development—she'd really *look* sick!—but then she sighed. Head held tremulously high, as though she were entering a competitive chess match, she marched inside and sat stiffly across from Michael. She looked him over: his cheeks were no longer drained of color and his eyes were no longer ominously blank. Perhaps he had recovered from his sooty episode.

"Ah, Ingrid, my prize PhD student! 'Neng shi tou bieren, suan you zhihui; neng shi tou ziji, cai you guangming,'" he chortled.

Evidently he was his old self again.

"Ha ha," she laughed, though she hadn't understood a word.

"How are you?" Michael asked. "I ordered you your usual." He nodded at a cup of hot chocolate. No whipped cream.

"Oh, thank you. I'm doing all right." Ingrid paused. "How are *you*?"

He fell back in his chair and massaged his eyes, groaning. "Oh, Ingrid, Ingrid, Ingrid. Where do I begin?" He sat up and shook his head. "At first, I went a little mad. The burning of my books and papers—that was a mistake. A great, great mistake."

"It's understandable—"

"But I was going through all the usual stages. Shock. Denial. Anger. Grief."

Ingrid's brow creased. Was she here to discuss his divorce?

"But now I have reached Enlightenment. And I say that with a capital E."

"Enlightenment?"

Michael dropped his chin and his voice. "I've done some digging and I have it on good authority we are being *sabotaged*"—he sucked in his breath, as if his next words caused him inordinate pain—"by the Postcolonial Studies department."

She blinked rapidly. "What?"

"I know. I know! I couldn't believe it myself. To think we once regarded them as intellectual equals. We've had our differences throughout the years, of course, and you know I've always considered their methodologies fallacious. But this—this is crossing a line. And that website"—here

Michael flung his head back and laughed, drawing concerned stares from the other café patrons—"that website's sole purpose was to defund the E. A. department."

"De-defund?"

"Oh, sure, they've always been a smaller department than us. Fewer endowments and fellowships and whatnot. No archive to speak of. They didn't even exist until some students kicked up a big fuss over it. But what does that have to do with us?" His eyes pleaded with her. "Clearly, they couldn't take the humiliation anymore. They knew the university was going through some, shall we say, financial redistribution. And what better way to pocket all the funding for themselves? To make our department appear"—he sighed grievously—"uncredible."

"I see . . ."

He frowned. "Are you not incensed, Ingrid?"

"Oh, I am! I am *very* incensed. It's just—Michael, are you suggesting the website's claims aren't true?" She registered his forbidding expression and hastily revised, "It's just that I saw the side-by-side photos and, well, the resemblance is uncanny."

He took a long and leisurely drink of tea, a bite from his orange scone, another long drink, then looked pointedly at her.

"Ingrid, let me ask you this. What is 'truth'?"

"Come again?"

"'Truth.' A loaded term, to be sure. But at bottom, one that is up for interpretation."

"I don't think I follow . . ."

Michael chuckled. "You see, during this whole . . . debacle, people have been focusing on the wrong thing. 'White man this, yellowface that.' But it doesn't matter if the poet who wrote 'The Cherry Blossom's Song' or 'Guardian Lions Asleep at the Gate,' or my personal favorite, 'The I Ching Sonnets,' was white or black! Green or pink!"

Ingrid worried she'd suddenly become hard of hearing.

"What matters is the *text itself*! You remember Roland Barthes's infamous essay 'La mort de l'auteur.'"

"Er, not really?"

"Well, Barthes believed when an author completes a text, he no longer has anything to do with it. When he relinquishes it into the world, he relinquishes all ties to it. The text is its own autonomous product. Who the author is—race, gender, class, age, etc.—is irrelevant. It's as if the author dies the moment he sets down his pen. All that matters is the *text itself*."

"But what does—what does that have to do with Chou?"

"Oh, Ingrid, it has to do with everything!" Michael's voice was so hypnotizing, with the narcotic flourish of a dictator, that a small audience had converged around them. "Chou's texts haven't changed, have they? If we judged his poetry as *worthy* yesterday but *unworthy* today, all because of a measly little name change, well—that would suggest we had poor judgment in the first place, wouldn't it?"

"Er—"

"And all this talk about suspending dissertations-in-progress on Chou. Shifting Chouian scholars to new areas of expertise. Permanently shutting down the archive. It's hysteria! Nothing needs to shut down. By God, have we forgotten what art is?"

Michael hoisted himself into a standing position and gesticulated wildly with his cup. Ingrid ducked to avoid a splash of scalding tea.

"Art should have no limitations! Art cannot *be* art with limitations! The very foundation of literature is the freedom to *imagine*. Or is this what we've become, a horde of narrow-minded thought police? Tearing away your books? Burning them when they challenge the thought police? Will we allow ourselves to be caught in the clutches of communist *censorship*? The last I heard, this was America. Do you know who else supported censorship? Do you?"

"Who?" the audience whispered.

"Hitler!"

The audience gasped. A few people covered their mouths. One woman made the sign of the cross.

"See, I believe in freedom. That's right. Freedom! The purest American virtue enshrined in the First Amendment. Freedom of imagination. Freedom to empathize. Freedom to become more than the material shackles we were born into!" He paused and raised his eyebrows, impressed by his own turn of phrase. "And I will be damned if America's freedom is compromised. I will fight for freedom until my dying day, so help me God!"

Applause erupted through the café. The man standing next to Ingrid, white-haired, strapped into suspenders and contoured like a kettle, had tears glistening in his eyes.

After Michael finished handing out his information, he sat back down, cleared his throat and faced Ingrid.

"Well, what do you say?"

"Er—to which part?" she stalled.

"To *joining* me."

"Joining you?"

"In this fight!"

She was speechless.

"Don't squander what you've worked so hard for! You're close to finishing your dissertation on enjambment, aren't you? And I've already made it clear something in the lines of a tenured professorship is very much in your future, should all go well. There's no need to 'upturn' your whole life! To 'dismantle the system'! It all comes down to how you frame things . . . As I said before, the 'truth' is up for interpretation. And, I know this appeals to your inherent sensibilities, Ingrid, our pursuit will be bound up in the ancient Chinese values of *honor* and *loyalty.* You and I, together, will defend Chou's poetry from the ravages of the less Enlightened." Michael sipped deeply from his cup, satisfied with the conclusion of his speech.

"Let me get this straight. You want me . . . to continue studying Chou . . . like nothing has changed . . . even though it appears he is a white man . . . who pretended to be Chinese American for thirty-five years?" Her hands strangled the arms of her chair.

"Well, that's a rather pedestrian way to put it, but yes."

"I—I don't know what to say."

"For those who haven't accessed the same plane of Enlightenment as I, the idea can take a little while to grasp." Michael patted her on the knee. "The fault isn't yours. We've all been conditioned to think of our physical manifestations in finite terms. But I—I have always been a profound believer in the transcendence of the self." He gazed thoughtfully through the front window.

Ingrid replied, "I'd rather stick needles into my eyeballs," which somehow came out as, "Could I get back to you in a few days? I just have to check—my schedule." She had already gathered her belongings and extricated herself from her chair, keeping as much distance as possible between her and Michael. On the coffee table, her lukewarm hot chocolate sat untouched.

"Naturally. But I know you'll come around."

THREE DAYS LATER, Michael was on TV, reconstructing the speech he'd given at the Old Midwife. The kettle-shaped man at the café was none other than Herbert Plimpton, seventy-seven years old and the beloved host of Wittlebury's longest-running local talk show: *Here's Herbert!* Michael's oration had thoroughly impressed him. His guests typically ranged from a spelling bee runner-up to the co-owner of a yarn store. He had never had anyone quite like Michael on the show.

"I've never had anyone quite like you on the show," Herbert rasped. "You possess a very strong charisma, young man!"

The two men were settled comfortably on opposite ends of a sofa, a synthetic backdrop of a bookshelf and fireplace behind them, an equally synthetic basset hound between them. Herbert flaunted, as he always did, colorful suspenders.

"You're such a flirt, Herbert," Michael chuckled.

"Oh, you should have seen me in my youth," he nodded. "I had myself a pretty bird or two. Show business attracts the womenfolk, you see—it's in their nature." Offstage, a PA waved a sign at Herbert: STAY ON TOPIC. "Oh, but here I am getting away with myself. Michael, your words the other day, they really, hm, spoke to my soul!"

"I'm not surprised, Herbert, I'm not surprised."

"Because I think we have it bad these days. Very bad. 'Don't do this,' 'don't say that,' 'don't touch the interns,' everyone says. 'Apologize for something that happened before the war.' And now they're shaming one of us for writing about, what was it, Chinese vases? I say, Michael, let the man write about Chinese vases if he wants!" Herbert's jowls quivered passionately.

"I absolutely agree."

"It wasn't always like this, you know!" Herbert warbled. "It's only in recent times people have started making up all these newfangled rules. An old friend of mine, Dougie Douglas, used to be a fine comedian. He sold out shows! Traveled all over the fifty states! Had a very popular character named Little Nappy Head. I tell you, looking at him onstage, you couldn't have guessed he wasn't born as dark as the bottom of my shoe—"

Michael coughed conspicuously and adjusted his tie. "Right—well, Herbert, what I'm concerned with is good old-fashioned American *freedom*. In America, you can be anything!" He gazed poignantly at the sound boom hovering above his head. "A doctor, an astronaut, the president of the United States. And yes, Herbert, the most well-known and widely studied Chinese American poet."

"I can't see the appeal, but to each his own," he wheezed.

"And I think it's important to emphasize the *dangerousness* of politics that divide people into such oversimplified categories. Nowadays, they say, 'You can only wear this and say that and do this if you have such and such percentage background.' This is cultural segregation! If we can't see beyond skin color, Herbert, and recognize that at bottom we are all *human beings* who share the same DNA, then we are doomed as a species. And if we continue down this slippery slope, it's only a matter of time before we become locked in a savage *race war*."

Herbert brightened at the thought. "I tell you, Michael, I didn't mind the days when we had our own water fountains. But I suppose all good things must come to an end—"

"But you were right, Herbert," Michael interjected loudly, "when you said we are presently under persecution. Do we not have the right to exist? To wonder? To dream? To become more than what we've been taught is possible?" He leaned forward breathlessly and clasped his hands together. "Imagine telling a young woman from *Me-hico* that she can never grow up to be a computer programmer because the majority of computer programmers are Caucasian men, and she was not born a Caucasian man. The double standards are very troubling."

"What's that about Mexicans?" Herbert squinted at him.

"Never mind that—I mean we should no longer feel *shame.* That's what you were talking about earlier, weren't you? Shame. People like you and I, every day of our lives, carry around shame. And for what? For being born in the bodies we were born in? For descending from a so-called "privileged" lineage? Oh, no, Herbert, no. This ends now. We will not be shamed for being who we are. And we will not be shamed for having dreams and doing our damnedest to reach those dreams. This is America— and it is our God-given right to pursue happiness at the expense of others!"

Once more, Michael had inadvertently risen from his chair.

"Sit down, boy, you're out of frame," Herbert scolded him, then turned to the cameras. "Now here's a word from our sponsor. *Tighty Whiteys: Even If You Leak, They Won't!*"

A CLIP OF Michael's episode went viral on the Internet, racking up over 50,000 views in three days.

In Defense of Freedom
@mbartho
Visitor Count: 20,549

March 12

Good morning, followers, new and old. To my new followers—
welcome! To my old followers—you may be wondering why I've
changed the name and design of my blog. That's an excellent
question. Where is the daily Laozi quotation in the sidebar? Or the
Chinese astrological predictions of the day?

As many of you know, I've been a Professor (and Chair) in the
East Asian Studies department at Barnes University for many years.
But I also want you to know: I'm more than that.

First and foremost, I'm a born and bred American. My parents?
Born and bred Americans. My grandparents? You got it—born and
bred Americans.

And I have many other interests besides Ancient China. Such as?
you ask.

First and foremost, freedom. The most sacred American right of
all time that we must safeguard at all costs. Second, Jesus Christ.
Third, barbecue. There's nothing I love more than a 32 oz flank steak
cooked medium well!

Check back for updates—I've got a special project in the works
I'm excited to share with you all.

March 18

The day has come! My manifesto is now available for sale:
In Defense of Freedom
$19.99 (not including shipping and handling)
Available here.

Anonymous unpaid reviewers have said: "It's a manifesto for the ages"
and "Michael Bartholomew is the savior we've been waiting for."

In the manifesto, I outline my philosophy on why anyone can be
anyone if they put their mind to it, plus *how* anyone can be anyone.

Included are examples of all the ways freedom of imagination has not only widened our worldview, but nurtured mankind throughout the ages.

Imagine, if you will, a world without Molly Bloom (written by a man) or Mr. Darcy (written by a woman). Imagine a world where every science fiction and fantasy novel vanished from the bookshelves (they were written by humans, not aliens and werewolves, after all). That's right—if it were up to the censorship police, countless works of art would cease to exist. If it were up to the censorship police, we'd be living in Jim Crow–era segregation: whites in their half of the bus, blacks in theirs, everyone else somewhere off to the side. Is this the world we want for our children? "Separate but equal" art?

My fellow Americans, the stakes are high. After all, if Harriet Beecher Stowe had never written *Uncle Tom's Cabin*, how would anyone have figured out slavery was bad?

Written in plain and simple language, *In Defense of Freedom* is for everyone, whether you have the reading level of a fifth grader or two PhDs like yours truly.

I'll be selling the manifesto at the Wittlebury Public Library tomorrow at noon. Stop by, snag an autograph and begin the journey to Enlightenment!

March 27

My, my, these past few days have been a whirlwind. Many of you may have read my front-page feature (with a full-length portrait) in *The Barnes Gazette*. Or you may have heard my speech when I was kindly invited to be the keynote speaker at Wittlebury High's graduation ceremony. Or you may have recognized my voice on the radio, having a lively conversation with DJ Mack on KZRY.

I am honored and humbled by your support. And if you haven't picked up your copy of *In Defense of Freedom*, click here (enter "DOFO" for a 10% discount).

But some of you may have also heard that as of late, I've been the victim of cyberbullying:

"Hypocrite."

"Fraternizing with the enemy."

"Commie sympathizer."

To these people I say: name-calling is wrong. And: I owe you an explanation.

Some followers are confused about my alleged "associations" with a "freedom-hating, Communist-loving" country. How can I be a supporter of true-blue American freedom when I've dedicated my life to researching the long-held enemy of America? you ask. To that I say: you're right.

Yesterday, I had a highly educational meeting with the author of the popular local newsletter *Yellow Peril 2.0.* You might think this meeting would have been argumentative. Far from it. This man opened my eyes to the dangers of the sitting Chinese government and the fast-multiplying Chinese population. You see, I had specialized in the Ming Dynasty (circa 1300 to 1600). Call me naive, but I had failed to understand China is a husk of its former self. The China of today is, as he informed me, "a direct threat to American democracy, freedom of speech and the open market." He warned we must all viciously guard ourselves against the inevitable "Asian Invasion."

I have seen the error of my ways. Forgive me. From this day forth, I, Michael Bartholomew, renounce all my associations with that treacherous country.

April 11

Good morning, followers! What a sight to behold, waking up and seeing you've *tripled* in size. As always, I am full of gratitude. I am touched so many of you have reached out with your personal stories of hardship.

To the man who wore a funny Halloween costume to work one year only to be slapped with a lawsuit: I sympathize with you.

To the woman who simply hoped to blend in with her exotic surroundings and was ejected from a destination wedding: I understand you.

To the young man who has an addiction to spray tanning and has been accused of committing a hate crime: I am with you in your plight.

So many of you have asked how you can help grow our movement (for this *is* a movement). The new DOFO headquarters will be based in Wittlebury, MA, although satellite headquarters are not out of the question in the future. I'm putting together a grassroots team, so please fill out this <u>form</u> if you're interested in volunteering. Schools, rallies, birthdays, christenings, you name it—Michael Bartholomew is open for bookings!

April 25

Due to popular demand, DOFO T-shirts are now <u>available</u> in sizes XS and XXL.

And don't forget to <u>subscribe</u> to the weekly DOFO newsletter! I upload a new video every Friday.

Today's "Food for Thought" question, posted by @derfuhrer69, is: "If people can be transgender, why can't they be transracial?"

I look forward to reading your comments below!

This blog post was sponsored by Halloween All Year Long™.

INGRID WITNESSED MICHAEL'S transformation from stuffy academic to "the voice of a forgotten generation," as one effusive commentator declared, with abject horror. With each appearance in public, each blog post and video (analyzed closely and agonizingly by Ingrid), Michael fine-tuned his speech, mannerisms and dress. He cottoned on fast to the four cornerstones of winning over the American public: 1. Accessibility—they responded well to short, snappy sentences and simple vocabulary; anything more was elitist. At the same time, they wanted 2. Respect—they hated being talked down to; they weren't *idiots* and 3. Efficiency—they had no time to waste on nuance or historical context; they preferred their causes and enemies summed up in one clean shot ("commie freedom haters," in this case). Finally, 4. Consistency—because they liked their public figures the way they liked their cartoon characters, Michael took to recycling the same outfit (a white button-down tucked into blue jeans, tucked into cowboy boots) and bookending each appearance with the catchphrase "Keep your hands off my freedom!"

Michael was learning, in short, how to be a politician.

The thought nearly provoked a relapse in Ingrid's Lucidax addiction. She had purchased another bottle at the drugstore (the last one she could ever purchase since, unsurprisingly, it had been discontinued following a class-action lawsuit). Though she hadn't yet succumbed to their allure, she frequently shook them out into her palm, mouth-watered over the pale blue pills, then released them one by one back into the bottle.

Nothing, not a thing, was turning out the way it should have.

Her website received fewer and fewer visitors each day. Someone had bought the domain, www.theREALtruthaboutchou.com, which was nothing but an animation on a repeating loop: a cruel caricature of Chou's laughing face (his eyes two slanted dashes, his skin neon yellow, his buckteeth outsized and menacing), whose mouth swallows his whole face before reemerging.

The parody website had replaced hers as the first search result.

On campus, the POC Caucus's protests to permanently close down the archive had petered out. Their attention was diverted when someone used permanent marker to cross out the eyes of professors—the only two black professors, that is—in the Africana Studies department's hall of photos. The POC Caucus was working together with the BSU to have the incident investigated as both a hate crime and a death threat, so far to no avail.

They protested daily outside the Office of the Dean until counterprotestors, Barnes students who moonlit as DOFO followers, showed up to "defend the First Amendment." The university responded by sending in campus police to deescalate the situation, which in practice, of course, escalated the situation.

Over in the E. A. department, classes had continued uninterrupted. Although a scant handful of professors and graduate students had permanently quit the department, most stayed. They drifted around campus with glazed expressions as they resumed their Chouian research, their Chouian lectures, their voices and gestures verging on ventriloquistic.

And the final punch in the gut: Vivian was nowhere to be found. A DOFO supporter had unearthed old photos and posts revealing her upbringing in an ultra-conservative, anti-gay family. Known as "Vinh Vo" back then, she'd even gained moderate popularity for her blog *Conserva-Teens*. The anonymous social media account was promptly shut down but not before Ingrid had scrolled through every upload. The news was shocking—yet it also furnished the missing context to Vivian's . . . unique brand of activism. The DOFO supporter, however, didn't share this perspective. The top post labeled her a "puppet paid for by liberal lobbyists." Word had it she'd taken a leave of absence following a mental breakdown.

The creation of the website was not supposed to lead to this down-is-up-left-is-right anarchy—and it *definitely* was not supposed to make way for Michael's twisted ideology.

When she'd hit the Publish button, Ingrid naturally hadn't planned for all the professors in the E. A. department to lose their credibility. But she also hadn't wanted everyone to prematurely pardon Smith, as if he'd been pronounced innocent without ever having to stand trial. The sheer madness of the past few weeks—from Wenli Zhao threatening to hurtle herself from the rooftop to Michael's budding romance with political propagandism to Vivian's precarious mental state—was John Smith's fault, not hers.

But where was he?

"Probably having the time of his life," Ingrid muttered as she paced her living room, "watching the news from inside his enormous house and laughing at this three-ring circus." She slumped onto the sofa and cradled her head in her hands. If only she could hand him over to the public like lobbing meat into a carnivore's cage. After all, the public was out for blood. They had such sharp teeth and such a developed appetite for righteous anger.

"THE STRAWBERRY BLOND is really flattering on you," Eunice complimented her.

Ingrid could hardly make eye contact with her reflection in the mirror. The photo of herself as a child, the ridiculous yellow mop balancing atop her head, skimmed across her mind.

"Actually, I think this one suits me best." She tugged off the strawberry blond wig for a dark brown wig, not dissimilar from her actual hair color.

"Ingrid, the point is for us to be *incognito*. Smith knows someone broke into his house so we have to be extra careful."

She reluctantly surveyed the other wigs laid out on Eunice's bed and shrugged, selecting a coppery chin-length one, and after some pleading, convinced Eunice to trade her violet wig for a wavy black one.

"We can't show up like we're going to a rave," Ingrid said reasonably. "Being *incognito* means *unnoticeable*, too. And besides, Jehovah's Witnesses probably aren't allowed to dye their hair."

"I guess so." Eunice examined herself in the mirror, turning from side to side. "Actually, I forgot I look really good in this color."

They changed into white blouses, black blazers, thick pantyhose and calf-length skirts, accessorized with a clipboard and copies of Eunice's old Bibles, and were about to head out when Ingrid asked, as casually as she could, "By the way, is Alex home?"

Eunice cocked her head. "No, I think he spent the night with some girl."

She felt a strange deflation in her chest. Probably the blonde from the Waffle-Dog Factory.

"Why?" Eunice peered curiously at her.

"Hm? No reason."

As they walked to Eunice's car, Ingrid tried not to remember how Alex had looked at her that day: such dripping disappointment it bordered on disgust. But she and his sister had made up; she had apologized; she had repented! When she saw him again, she'd show him she'd changed—

"Ingrid, are you listening?"

"Huh?"

"I asked if you remember your lines."

"Oh, right. 'Hello, sir. Are you interested in hearing about our lord and savior Jesus Christ?'"

"And if he says yes?"

"We'll ask him if we can come in."

"Then what?" Eunice steered the car out of her parking space.

"You'll start giving him the 101 on Jesus stuff and I'll ask to use the bathroom."

"Good."

"But I'll get confused about the directions and accidentally go upstairs. I was homeschooled, that's why. Then I'll take a picture of Smith's yellow-face vanity table." Ingrid whipped out her phone with a mischievous smile. "Later, we'll mail the photos to him with a note saying he has to publicly admit to his crimes or we'll tell everyone where he lives."

"And add that there's more where that came from."

"But . . . we don't have anything more."

"Saying that is just a mandatory part of blackmail."

"Oh, right."

"But if he says no, he *doesn't* want to hear about our lord and savior Jesus Christ?"

"We'll say—wait, I forgot." Ingrid chewed on a nail.

"We'll say we've been going door to door for six hours without any water."

"And could we please come in for some water."

"And then you'll ask to use the bathroom."

They grinned at each other.

The plan was flawless, sure to make Smith break his silence and condemn his past actions. Because no one cared if Vivian or the POC Caucus said yellowface was wrong; that was predictable, tired news. But if a *white man* said it was wrong, that you couldn't just wake up one day and slip on someone's race like a costume, and if he told *other* white men, surely they would listen. Surely Michael's theory of "Enlightenment" would self-destruct, exposing its shoddy scaffolding. Surely the good people of Wittlebury would side with common decency.

When Eunice pulled up to Smith's house, goosebumps tiptoed up Ingrid's spine. She hadn't been back in this neighborhood since December. The memory of that fateful night came reeling back. The metallic taste of horror coating her tongue. The nauseating, free-fall drop of her stomach. Part of her wanted to snatch the wheel from Eunice, grind down on the gas pedal and drive as far as she could away from John Smith. But a far greater part of her wanted him to look her in the eye.

They crossed the street, moving with brisk (but pious) steps, though Ingrid's thoughts were anything but. Playing on repeat in her head was the refrain "Come at me now, motherfucker." All her momentum was zapped, however, when they reached the sprawling green lawn. Smack in the middle stood a red and white FOR SALE sign.

"No," Ingrid mumbled, "this isn't possible."

She ran up the steps of the house, cupped her hands around her eyes and looked through the front window. Empty. Not a single piece of furniture in sight.

Eunice caught up to her and patted her back.

"I'm sorry, honey. I had a feeling this might happen, but—"

"You did?"

"You just seemed hopeful for the first time in a long time. And I was hopeful, too."

They gazed in silence at the dusty hardwood floors.

"Ingrid," Eunice said quietly, "I think you know what you have to do now."

"I do?" She scratched miserably at her wig.

"Listen, no one takes the website seriously anymore. They've forgotten all about it—isn't that what you said?"

"Yes . . ."

"Do you know why?"

"Er . . . why?"

"Because the person who made the website never appeared on the TV or radio or newspaper. They could never disprove all the bullshit *Michael* was saying on the TV, radio and newspaper. It's been a completely one-sided story."

"What are you saying?" She knew exactly what she was saying.

"You have to be the one who stands up to him." With her Bible pushed urgently against her breasts, Eunice faced Ingrid. "You have to come clean."

THE NEXT DAY, Ingrid dragged herself to *The Barnes Gazette* office as though the guillotine awaited her. Stephen would find out that instead of industriously plodding away at her dissertation all year, she'd been playing amateur detective. He hadn't brought up www.thetruthaboutchou.com, undoubtedly because he'd been too busy on his book tour to have heard about it, but once she professed to its creation, he would know she'd lied to him for months. Her parents, too, would find out their daughter was guilty of committing at least three separate misdemeanors.

When she'd spoken over the phone with Norman Duchamps, she'd offered him vague but tempting information: she had "exclusive dirt" on the website's author. After putting her on hold for an excruciating thirteen minutes, Norman said he doubted he could squeeze her into his tight schedule, but to come by anyway. She resented an undergrad treating her with such flagrant disrespect, but what could she do?

The walk from her apartment felt longer than usual. She couldn't count the number of times she'd taken this path through the cluster of semen-smelling trees, jumped over the Z-shaped crack on the sidewalk, cursed at the glitchy streetlight, passed beneath the university's gates where dozens of pigeons awaited their next target. She had given her adult life to this place. And for what?

Eunice stood just beyond the gates, smiling and waving. The sight of her soothed the quicksand sensation in her gut.

"Thanks for coming, Yoon."

She threaded her arm through hers. "Are you kidding? I couldn't let you do this alone."

As they crossed the main lawn, they heard an urgent voice, amplified through a loudspeaker, issuing from the direction of the library.

"—prevented me from coming forward [*something something*] damaged my mental health [*something something*] institutional oppression—"

They exchanged stunned looks, then hurried towards the library, rounding the Science Block to see a familiar figure holding court at the top of the steps.

"—Bartholomew's dangerous rhetoric is infecting the public. He's *intentionally* spreading bigotry and hate. Which is why I cannot keep silent. I *will* not be silent. We've had decades of being talked over because our oppressors were speaking for us. That stops today."

The onlooking crowd clapped and whooped. Ingrid elbowed her way to the front. Slow, queasy apprehension dripped through her.

Vivian closed her eyes and announced with somber gravity, "I am the one who created www.thetruthaboutchou.com. I am the one who discovered a white man has paraded in yellowface for over thirty years."

Ingrid stared up at Vivian in disbelief. She was dressed all in black, her lips immaculately painted, her voice brimming with confidence, clearly overjoyed to be speaking on the cruel injustices of the world again.

Vivian Vo was back.

INSIDE THEIR SHARED OFFICE, Eunice paced the room while shaking her head. "Ugh, I can't believe her. I mean, I *can*—this is the most Vivian thing ever, she really out-Vivianed herself this time—"

Ingrid leaned against the window.

"—take credit for something *you* did. Oh, that conniving little—"

From up here, she had a panoramic view of the quad. More people had swarmed around Vivian, high-fiving her, taking photos, demanding autographs. Was someone carrying a camcorder? And was that a *sound boom*?

"Actually . . ." Ingrid trailed off. The thought of being launched into the spotlight, of having microphones shoved under her nose, of regurgitating snippy sound bites while juggling what to say and what *not* to say—all of it was as appealing as being boiled alive. "Actually, maybe this is a good thing."

Eunice stopped her pacing. "What?"

"I'm not good at public speaking, you know that. I freeze up. I couldn't handle all the . . . attention." Vivian, on the other hand, thrived on it.

"She's a liar. We have to tell everyone she's lying!"

"Vivian's not perfect." She paused. "But she must have her reasons for doing this."

Eunice crossed her arms. "Why are you defending her?"

"Wha—what?" she laughed nervously. "I'm not defending her."

Eunice looked unconvinced.

"I just think things are um, better this way." The old desire to surpass Vivian had steadily ground down to a fine powder, hardly observable to the naked eye. She didn't care anymore if Vivian took credit for something she did. All that self-inflicted competition seemed so childish now. And, in a way, Vivian . . . *deserved* this moment. Racial justice and cultural reparations and whatnot—that was her dominion, no, her *identity*. She'd built it on years of organizing, protesting and educating herself. She'd put in the work to transform herself from the face of *Conserva-Teens* to "the darling of Postcolonial Studies." What right did Ingrid have to cut the line?

She braced herself and added, "And you know, Vivian's not as awful as I thought. I, um, I've actually started reading some of her articles. They're kind of interesting."

"You're being serious."

"Yeah. I am."

Eunice stared at her in disbelief. A prickly silence followed. Ingrid cleared her throat and transferred her gaze to Eunice's desk, which nearly sunk under the weight of a stack of papers: "Exploring Hegelian Ethics in Korean Dramas."

"Oh! Is this your dissertation?" she asked, absurdly grateful to have a reason to change the subject.

Eunice was scrolling through her phone. "Yeah, I finished the first draft," she said without disconnecting her eyes from the device.

"We should celebrate! Chimaek?"

"I can't tonight. I told Thad he could come over."

A drop of disappointment trickled through Ingrid. Was it because Eunice couldn't hang out or because she was still seeing that human-shaped crouton? Be a supportive friend, she commanded herself.

"How *are* things *going* with him?" she asked in an unnaturally effusive voice.

"Fine," Eunice shrugged. "How are things with Stephen?"

"Huh? Oh. You know, fine. He's still on his book tour."

She nodded sympathetically. "Long distance must be hard for you guys."

"Why?"

Eunice laughed. "You know, because you guys were always glued together. And because—" She pressed her lips shut.

"What?"

"Nothing—"

"Eunice, *what*."

"I was just wondering, is he still traveling with that Japanese author?"

The image of Azumi, accompanied with the bouncy tunes of a J-pop song, sprang into Ingrid's mind like the opening theme of an anime. "Yes. What about it?" she said more roughly than she'd intended.

"If my fiancé were gone that long with someone like her, I'd be worried." The words leaked from Eunice, as though she'd corked them inside herself for weeks. She slapped a hand over her mouth. "Sorry, I don't know why I said that."

Ingrid couldn't tell if she should be offended. Was Eunice doubting Stephen's commitment, a man who'd committed to the same brand of lotion for over *eleven* years? And who was she—Miss Lover of Alt-Right Tech Bros—to give relationship advice, anyway? I should brush it off, Ingrid thought, and come across as terribly sophisticated and above-all-such-worldly-nonsense.

Instead she grabbed Eunice's hands in both of hers. "Yoon, I think I need another makeover."

13

Exhibiting All the
Usual Signs

Ingrid launched the video chat software and sat patiently before her laptop, her smile fixed in place. Within the confines of her screen, her head looked plucked from her body and dropped on a cupcake. From the neck down, she was all frills and bows, strawberry pinks and vanilla creams. Her face, too, featured an ice-cream-inspired palette: peach eyeshadow, cherry lip gloss and a finish of milky face powder. A few days ago, when Eunice had first decorated her face in this style (gleaned from a fourteen-year-old's "Super Kawaii" online tutorial), she paid careful attention, even jotting down notes on her phone. Alone, she managed to achieve a passing approximation of the original effect, but while Eunice worked with a light hand, Ingrid layered it on under the assumption a makeover demanded total unrecognizability.

When the chirping ringtone stopped, a mess of pixels rearranged themselves into Stephen's face.

"Can you hear me?" he asked.

"Yes. Can you hear me?"

"Ingrid?"

"Stephen?"

"Can you hear me?"

"Yes! I *said*, can you hear me."

"I've been asking if *you* can hear *me*."

Ingrid sighed. "The connection is fine." Behind Stephen was a dismal-looking hotel room. "Where are you now?"

"Twin Cities."

"Oh. How's it going?"

Stephen studied her face. "You look different today. Did you change your hair?"

"Something like that." She waited. "Well, do you like it?"

"Oh, sure."

She smiled and batted her two-inch-long false eyelashes.

"What's the matter with your eyes? You haven't been forgetting to use your prescription eye drops, have you?"

"What? No. My eyes are—never mind. How's the tour going?" she tried again.

"About the same. Always asked the same questions. Eating the same hotel food. My back hurts from these spring mattresses." He glowered at the hotel bed.

Was Stephen being purposefully vague? Whenever she asked about the book tour, he always answered in the same platitudes.

"But a signing or reading or whatever probably only takes a few hours. What are you doing the rest of the day?"

"Sometimes I try a local sushi bar or do some light bird-watching. But most of the time, I'm working on the book—I don't think you realize how time-consuming it is. I'm not on vacation, you know."

"Right." She had momentarily forgotten about his new work in progress. The American publisher of *Pink Salon* had propositioned Stephen with a nonfiction book concept and he had gamely accepted the challenge. The working title was *Translating a Language I Can't Speak*.

Ingrid wondered how to backtrack and coax him into elaborating on these restaurant visits and bird-watching expeditions. Did he go alone? With Azumi and Leila? Or just Azumi?

Stephen's glasses had lit up with minuscule blue boxes. Was he browsing the Internet during their chat? Was she *boring* him?

"I caught a cold," she said loudly.

"Remember to drink lots of fluids."

She frowned. "Actually, I think it's the flu."

"Well, that explains why your cheeks are so flushed. You should see a doctor, dear."

Ingrid stared at him in shock.

Stephen didn't notice. "I'm actually not feeling well myself," he said in a petulant voice. "In fact, I've had a terrible morning."

"You have?" She'd assumed, just as he'd said, that a book tour equaled a vacation. "What happened?"

"I received my first"—he swigged dramatically from a water bottle —"my first bad review."

With all the success of *Pink Salon*, Ingrid hadn't thought it possible. "Oh, I'm sorry." She finally took in Stephen's disheveled appearance: he hadn't blow-dried his hair and his collar was ever so slightly lopsided.

"It's unbelievable the kind of drivel that gets published these days. I've never even heard of this woman—"

"What did she say?"

He flicked his hand dismissively. "Nothing—it could hardly even be called criticism—it was an unresearched, personal attack—"

"That sounds really serious, Stephen—"

"Well, I'm not going to waste any more time thinking about it and neither should you." Although he'd only just raised the issue, he was adamant on tabling it. "Oh, right—I wanted to ask you about this 'crisis' happening at Barnes."

She blinked. "Who—where—how did you—"

"Do you remember the professor I reached out to who specializes in Japanese translation?"

"I think so."

"Well, he teaches at the University of Minnesota. We met for matcha tea earlier and he asked what I thought of 'the Xiao-Wen Chou controversy.' I had no idea what he was talking about until he filled me in."

"Oh. I'm surprised anyone cares what happens here," Ingrid said, though, as she said it, she remembered academics universally adored one thing: academic scandals.

"What's surprising is you haven't mentioned it to me once. I mean, Xiao-Wen Chou is the man you've been researching for nearly five years now."

"I know . . ."

"Don't you think I'd want to be informed about a fire and a suicide attempt at your university?"

"Yes . . ."

"Don't you think I'd be concerned for your safety?"

"Yes . . ."

"So why didn't you tell me?"

"Well, it's embarrassing. I had been . . . fooled."

Stephen shook his head. "It's incredible this Smith fellow pulled it off for so long."

She frowned. Pulled it off? Like it was a feat?

"But people aren't even mad anymore!" she said in a rush. "I think they were mad for a week. Now everything's gone back to normal . . . except it hasn't. I feel like I'm trapped on *The Truman Show*."

He shrugged. "Humans are averse to change. They've thought of Xiao-Wen Chou as Chinese American for decades. They don't want to think of him any other way."

"I know. Believe me, I *know* it's hard to accept." Ingrid felt the sickening cold nausea crawl up her spine again. "But now people are *defending* him. Michael is defending him! He's become some kind of . . . yellowface advocate! People are saying Smith pretending to be Chinese has some-thing to do with, I don't know, American freedom! Can you believe it?"

Stephen pursed his lips. "You don't sound like yourself. You're being quite . . . political."

"I'm not being 'political.' I'm just summarizing facts. And I think Smith should face consequences for his actions. He isn't above the law! I mean, the law of public opinion."

"Well, Ingrid dear, it's complicated. I know it's tempting to paint Smith as a one-dimensional villain, but we have to remember he's a *person*. No one's heard his side of the story yet, right? Let's not stoop to making snap judgments—we're above that."

"Stephen—what are you saying?" Her neck was overheating from the enormous bow knotted around it.

"Look, I'm not saying the makeup and the wigs were acceptable. I can see why that offended many people with Asian heritage. But I think what we have here is a man who devoted his entire life to a foreign culture. Peo-ple only do that out of love, Ingrid. I'll admit his interpretation was extreme—but I think he deserves some sympathy."

Ingrid could not believe what she was hearing. "'Love'? Let's not give him such lofty ideals. What about 'boredom'? I think Smith just wanted to make himself more *interesting*. I suppose writing sonnets about, I don't know, Jell-O salad, wasn't *exotic* enough for him."

A sneer disfigured Stephen's face, so briefly she wasn't sure if she'd imagined it. "To play devil's advocate, isn't walking in each other's shoes how empathy is created? Everyone says they want to wipe out discrimina-tion. Eliminate the notion of 'the other.' Couldn't this be a means to that end? To advocate for inborn equality, but to punish those who outwardly manifest that very equality, seems like pure hypocrisy."

She tried to open her mouth but had momentarily lost her motor functions.

"I just think it's better when people are interested and invested in dif-ferent cultures than when we're not. When we're sharing rather than hoarding something for ourselves. I mean, what if someone said you could only listen to Chinese music? And wear Chinese clothes? And eat Chinese food? For the rest of your life—"

"I'm not Chinese!" she cried, on the verge of tears.

Stephen softly shook his head. "Ingrid, I won't speak to you when you're acting emotional like this. Please try to calm down or we'll have to talk another time."

"Don't call me 'emotional' right now, Stephen, I swear to God, or I will—I will—"

"Threatening someone you're in a relationship with is a form of emotional abuse," he said evenly.

Ingrid wanted to slam her laptop shut and pitch it across the room. But then Stephen would accuse her of "being emotional." Instead she smiled and twirled a pencil as she regulated her breathing. Finally she spoke. "You're right, Stephen. I *was* getting emotional. I apologize. If you want to talk without emotion, let's stick to the facts."

"Well, good. I'm glad you're seeing reason now." He crossed his arms behind his head.

Ingrid forced her smile to stay plastered on her face. "And the fact is you can't be objective when it comes to this discussion. You are biased." Stephen frowned. "I mean, you've made a living from becoming an 'expert' in a foreign language, haven't you? It's in your interest that remains acceptable in our society. Not just acceptable—*admired*."

"What does translation have to do with all this Chou controversy?"

"Well, Stephen dear, your job is like being the—the gateway for non-Japanese people to access Japanese culture. Have you ever considered you're taking away opportunities from Japanese American translators? Or Japanese translators? Who have an emotional connection to the text?" By the look on his face, her words had struck a sore spot. "Well, isn't that just a fact? Are you going to tell me you're Japanese now?"

"Please don't belittle me, Ingrid, I know I'm not Japanese. What point are you making?"

She kept her smile rigid. "So—so my point is you can't help but exoticize Japan even if you learn to speak Japanese or live in Japan. Or marry a Japanese woman. Or—or have half-Japanese kids! Because you're looking at it from the outside in. And you always will be. Even the presumption you can act as some kind of invisible, neutral filter into the Japanese language is—is laughable!" Where was all this coming from? Had her brief dalliance with the POC Caucus taught her to speak this way? But how— osmosis? She wasn't sure everything added up, but it was certainly provoking a reaction from Stephen. He was leaning forward now, his face gigantic on her screen.

"So, according to your argument, a non-Caucasian person could never translate French. Or Russian. Or German."

"That's completely different."

"How?"

"The fact that you have to ask—"

"So there is no difference." A proud little smile curved Stephen's thin lips.

Ingrid's face flushed. "Stephen, you're *white*."

He stared at her in horror. For several seconds, he did not say a word. She was about to ask if the connection had frozen when he said in a high-pitched, strained voice, "That is completely out of line. I've confided in you about how hard it was for me growing up wearing glasses. I've been discriminated against, too—"

"Oh, Stephen—are you getting emotional?" she snapped.

He looked like she'd punched him through the screen. "What has gotten into you? Do you need to talk to a professional? I know these accusations about Chou must have been hard on you, and I wish you'd confided in me for that very reason, but I couldn't have imagined . . . Ingrid, I think you're having some kind of psychotic break—"

A polite knock on the door interrupted them. She was trembling so hard, her vision had grown fuzzy. Blurry eyed, she watched him open his hotel door, revealing the silhouette of a woman: short, pale, dark haired.

"Who was that?" she asked when he sat back down. But she knew who it was: Azumi fucking Kasuya. All of this was *her* fault. Though Ingrid's thoughts were scrambled to bits, she was certain of this much: she and Stephen had never argued before he'd started spending all his time with the twenty-two-year-old ingénue.

"I have to go," he replied tersely. "The Biannual Japanese Literary Conference is starting in an hour."

"Right." She dug her nails into her thighs. "Have fun."

Stephen finally met her eyes. "I will."

His face disappeared from the screen, replaced by a travel booking website. In the search bar was a round-trip flight from Boston to Des Moines. Ingrid had hoped to surprise Stephen on the next leg of his book tour. Now she exited the window and searched "Pink Salon" plus "negative review." She clicked on the first result, "All Translations Have an Agenda— What's Stephen Greene's?" by Rin Saito, and read the first paragraph:

> *Stephen Greene's translation is tailored to titillate North Ameri-can audiences, and by extension, the North American market. His unfaithful adaptation of Kasuya's original text is not so much a failure of his language skills but a failure of his imagination to see Azumi's character as little more than a sentient sex toy. While full pages of "slice of life" scenes are cut, where Azumi cooks, cleans, sleeps, journals and dreams (in other words, scenes where Azumi is at last a desexualized body), sex scenes are consistently length-ened, sometimes to one and a half times their size. And if that isn't a clear enough indicator of Greene's personal agenda, "chest" is translated as "full breasts" seventeen times.*

INGRID HAD NEVER been one to rifle through her boyfriend's things in search of an unfamiliar perfume or lipstick stain. She believed respect and mutual trust were the bedrock of any healthy relationship. She looked down on women who thought their partners incapable of platonic friendships with other women, as if all men were so sex-starved that when a vagina was in the room, they could think of nothing else. That mentality was backwards, old-fashioned and (she'd have to double-check an article of Vivian's) *so* heteronormative.

She, on the other hand, prided herself on having evolved to a much higher plane of awareness.

All of that sailed out the window as Ingrid prepared to turn Stephen's PC inside out. She trusted him, of course—the trouble was that wretched anime-character-come-to-life. Popping up at his hotel door at all hours of the night. Fixing him with her moony eyes and tittering with her hand over her mouth and prancing about in her milkmaid clothes. How could anyone be so . . . *pleasant* all the time? Azumi probably never lost her temper the way Ingrid had during the video call, and if she did, her temper probably expressed itself through sparkles.

Naturally, Ingrid wouldn't resort to her supersleuth antics from last fall; like a former felon, she had put that dangerous way of life behind her. She just needed to know if Azumi was luring her hapless fiancé into a sticky web of seduction—in which case, she'd bat away any such illusions from her pretty head. Poor Stephen, completely clueless he'd been singled out as the victim of Azumi's lustful plotting!

Ingrid sat down at his desk and swung her neck in a circle, loosening out any cricks, then interlaced her fingers and stretched her arms forwards and backwards. She knew the password to his PC, just as he knew hers. Until this day, she'd never nonconsensually poked around in his electronic drawers and closets, but she'd been left with no other choice—her future marriage was at stake.

First, his email: nothing of interest. He had no direct correspondence with Azumi; everything was communicated through her agency or her interpreter. Second, his social media. Annoyingly, in this department, Stephen proved exceptionally difficult to spy on. His only account was for professional networking, which could hardly call itself social media, though the website did include a personal messaging system. She scoured his inbox to be safe—mostly old friends from boarding school named Brock and Hunter who asked what he was up to these days. Nothing from Azumi. Then she skidded to a stop on a message, sent a year ago, from a Sandra Lee. The name sounded familiar.

> Hi, Stephen! Oh my God, it's been so long. How are you? You look *great*. I see you're engaged now. Who would have thought! Well, congratulations. I hope you will be very happy. PS: Can I ask when you two met?

> Why, hello, Sandra, it's wonderful to hear from you. My, how time flies. I must say you are looking very well yourself. I don't mean to dredge up old wounds, but I want to apologize again for how things ended between us. As for your question, I don't entirely understand the reason behind it, but my fiancée and I met four years ago.

Of course—Sandra Lee was the name of Stephen's ex-girlfriend.

At the start of their courtship, he and Ingrid had responsibly briefed each other on their last relationship—which explained why "Sandra" rang familiar—and, this chore completed, neither of them had brought up the uncomfortable subject again.

She squinted painfully at Sandra's photo before remembering she could click on her name to access her profile. Her first reaction was confusion, then a lick of indignation, followed by another bout of confusion.

Because Sandra Lee was Asian. If Ingrid had to guess, maybe with Korean heritage . . .

But—but—she had always assumed—with a name like Sandra Lee—it had conjured up country music, poodle skirts and (she could not understand why) pie. All kinds of pie—pecan, lemon meringue, blueberry. Sandra Lee was supposed to be white. Why wasn't she white?

Although . . . her being Asian wasn't unusual, was it? The world had lots of Asians. Probability-wise, purely in terms of hard numbers, the odds of Stephen dating an Asian woman at some point in his life must be something like one out of five. And, well, wasn't life full of coincidences? Just the other day when she visited the bank, the teller's name had been Ingrid, too.

Perhaps the somersaults in her stomach had to do with Sandra's prettiness, not her Asianness. Ingrid zoomed in on her photo. She had prominent double eyelids (surgery?), a slim jawline and expensive-looking teeth. Ingrid checked her bio: a veterinarian living in Chicago. She glared at the screen; her parents had always hoped *she'd* grow up to be a veterinarian. What a little show-off.

She closed the browser to search for "Sandra Lee" in Stephen's computer files. Nothing. She tried "Sandra" and "Sandy" next, receiving no results.

To excavate anything on his ex-girlfriend called for the hard-won, meticulous research skills she'd earned as a PhD candidate. Ingrid glanced at the clock; she might have to stay up all night if she was going to complete the task in one sitting. She would even make color-coded spreadsheets if necessary.

With her sleeves pushed up, she scrolled through Documents: Bills . . . Jobs . . . Housing . . . Passport Photos . . . Taxes . . . Translation . . .

Wait a second.

Taxes. Taxes? *Taxes.*

Her thoughts flew to the hours she'd devoted to furiously narrating Marguerita's steamy tryst with Dante in the castle . . . She'd cached the erotica in a folder discreetly entitled Taxes.

What were the odds?

She opened the folder to find, as expected, taxes. Stephen's were perfectly organized by year. She clicked on the most recent file—a run-of-the-mill 1099 form—then breathed out a sigh. Perhaps she'd overreacted about Sandra's message . . . After all, neither of them had followed up on their platonic conversation. Perhaps she'd even been too hard on Azumi . . .

Was it her fault she was Japanese, attractive *and* spoke in a breathy falsetto? Come to think of it, she didn't even know if Azumi was interested in men.

She was about to exit the folder when she spotted a second embedded folder, also labeled Taxes. No doubt containing general information, such as how to file taxes in the first place. Doing it alone was a tricky business, she knew, which was why a career in accounting—

The folder was stocked with JPEG images.

She floated her mouse over the first image, her heart ramming against her rib cage.

An unfortunate fork in the road lay before her. She could choose to look and find confirmation of her darkest fears: Sandra propped against a bedpost in sheer lingerie. Sandra spread-eagled on a rotating heart-shaped bed. Sandra bent over in assless leather chaps, whip in hand. Stephen had never taken such obscene photos of Ingrid (clearly he respected her too much).

Or she could choose not to look and walk away with something in between: a tainted, less blissful flavor of ignorance. She had done it once before, when she uncovered John Smith's bamboozlement and had said nothing, had done nothing. That had worked out—well, it hadn't worked out at all.

"Oh, fuck it," she groaned. Scrunching her eyes shut, she clicked on an image, then cracked open an eye.

Looking back at her was a photo of a woman. A woman who was not Sandra. But, like Sandra, she was Asian. She possessed stringy hair and unflattering rectangular glasses. The scene looked dated; if Ingrid had to guess, it was captured during Stephen's college days. And sure enough, photos followed of the pair playing some card game at a party, sitting on a grubby dorm room bed, their limbs gawky and angular. Stephen's hair was spiked up with gel and his forehead was acne ridden.

This girl's photos—Annie, Ingrid decided to call her—were soon displaced by a second girl's, who she christened Jenny.

Among the pictures: Jenny in a bikini, lounging on a beach towel and slurping from a coconut. Jenny and Stephen smiling into the sun in match-ing wraparound sunglasses. Her face was round, with shallow dimples. Stephen's hair had been long then, past his ears—she'd never seen it like that.

Jenny's photos gave way, at last, to Sandra's, the most intimate of the lot: Sandra asleep on a sofa. Sandra kissing Stephen's cheek; Stephen kiss-ing hers. Holding hands at a formal dinner. Blowing out the candles on a cake. A ridiculous one of them rubbing noses.

By the time Ingrid got to the last of the photos, she had thrown up twice into the trash can. The floor had been pulled out from her. No—she had been wrung out like a wet rag. No, worse—bulldozed over. No, that wasn't exactly it, either—

No American English idiom could accurately convey the sensation of discovering her fiancé had not one, but three ex-girlfriends, who, all three of them, appeared, for all intents and purposes, to be, as far as the human eye could tell, of East Asian heritage, which was, incidentally, most coinci-dentally, what Ingrid Yang herself was.

FOR THREE HOURS, Ingrid lay in a comatose state on the office floor. She stared unblinkingly into the overhead light on the ceiling. A fly buzzed on her arm; she didn't bother to slap it away. Occasionally, she turned her at-tention to the carpet fibers and counted them. A few times, she shot up and laughed maniacally, clutching at her sides. Once or twice, she blew snot into her sleeve-turned-handkerchief.

She could call Stephen and demand clarification. Maybe the folder was a hilarious misunderstanding involving Photoshop or a long-lost identical twin. Or maybe he'd explain that where he'd grown up in Connecticut, and where he'd gone to college in New Hampshire, and where he'd worked afterwards in Massachusetts, the female population had been 99 percent Asian, so how could she argue with those numbers? And . . . well . . . was it really so bad if a white man exclusively dated Asian women?

Ingrid hauled herself up from the floor and back to the computer.

Head angled away from the screen as if it might blind her, she tentatively typed "asian women + white men" into the browser and skimmed the results.

MAIL ORDER BRIDES FROM CHINA—VISA INCLUDED! WATCH XXX INSATIABLE ASIAN SLUT GET ANNIHI-LATED BY WHITE DICK! LOVELY, CHARMING ORIEN-TAL LADIES WAITING TO CHAT WITH YOU! ASIAN FEMALE SEX DOLLS FOR SALE, NOW AVAILABLE WITH FULLY CUSTOMIZABLE PUSSY!

Ingrid gagged and leapt out of the chair, a second wave of vomit surfacing. Surely Stephen didn't have anything to do with all . . . *that*. Surely a logical explanation existed for everything she'd witnessed. She just needed someone to jolt sense into her.

ALEX ANSWERED the door. Ingrid waited for him to crack a sarcastic joke or make fun of her or even scold her, again, for how she'd mistreated his sister. But when she stepped into the foyer's light, his bemused smirk faltered.

"Is Eunice here?" she asked, failing to quell the tremor in her voice.

"Yeah, I'll go get her. Hey, are you okay?"

"No," she replied. Normally she would have pretended everything was fine in front of Alex. But now she slunk to the sofa, oozing moroseness, and flopped onto her side. She grabbed one of Eunice's throw pillows—screen-printed with her favorite Korean actress's face—suffocated it in her arms and closed her eyes. She opened them a moment later when she flopped onto her other side and felt something cold against her arm: a sports drink. She looked around for Alex. He was sitting at the kitchen counter with his laptop.

"Thanks," she whispered.

He nodded without looking up.

"Honey!" Eunice rushed out of her room, outfitted in pink hair rollers and a citrus-scented sheet mask. She perched on the sofa arm and stroked Ingrid's head. "Honey, what's wrong?"

She pointed a shaky finger at the manila folder on the coffee table. Inside was a collection of photos she'd printed out.

Eunice flicked through the photos quickly at first, then slowly. "Who are—" Her eyes bulged. "Is this *Stephen*?"

"Yes," she moaned.

"And these are . . . ?"

"What does it look like, Yoon?"

Eunice reached the last photo, of Stephen and Sandra rubbing noses, then set down the folder with a low whistle.

"Is three too many?" Ingrid whispered.

"Well . . . I read somewhere that the standard rule allows a white man to have one Asian ex-girlfriend."

"One?" she half shouted.

"Well, actually I think there's a clause that stipulates something like, if it's been seven years since his last Asian ex-girlfriend, he's allowed a second one, etc."

She hurled her face into the throw pillow.

Eunice shook her head. "I was never sure about Stephen."

"What do you mean?" she asked, her words muffled by the pillow.

"He didn't exhibit all the usual signs."

"Signs?" She bolted upright. "Eunice, what are you talking about?"

She peeled off her sheet mask and yawned. "Oh, you know, he didn't have a collection of samurai swords in his bedroom. And I've never heard him talk about anime or manga. I mean, he's really into classical music and bird-watching and old white man stuff like that, isn't he? But—"

"Yes?" Ingrid urged.

"He does love sushi . . ."

Alex snorted from across the room.

"And his job!" she cried. "Don't forget his job!"

"Oh, right." Eunice rubbed her arm. "I'm sorry you had to find out this way, honey."

"So—what do I do now?"

"What do you mean, what do you do now?" She gawked at her in disbelief. "Don't tell me you're thinking of—what—calling off the engagement? Are you insane?"

Ingrid returned to the throw pillow's embrace. "But he—he has—" She couldn't bring herself to say it. The F word.

"So he has a type!" Eunice laughed. "Who cares? Everyone has a type."

Alex snorted again.

Eunice shot him a look, then scooted down to sit beside Ingrid. "Tell me: What's my type?"

She made an effort to visualize the boy toys she occasionally saw swaggering out of her room.

"They work in tech?"

"Go on."

"They lift weights?"

"And they're white," Alex called out.

Eunice rolled her eyes. "I'm a woman who knows what she wants! It's called *empowerment*. I use these men and discard them after I'm done with them."

"But is that the same as this . . . pattern of Stephen's?"

She puckered her lips into a rosebud. "Oh. I'm not sure."

"And if these, um, white men only date Asian women—that wouldn't bother you?"

"We're two consenting adults. I get what I want. And he gets what he wants. It's modern dating!" She threw up her hands.

"You wouldn't feel . . ." Ingrid gulped. "Replaceable? Interchangeable? Objectified?" She scratched hard at her ankles—her eczema had flared up horribly within the past hour.

"Don't overthink it. We're animals. Creatures of lust! The body wants what it wants. Are you saying we should *force* ourselves to sleep with people we aren't attracted to? That's totally *not* feminist."

"I don't know . . ." Ingrid tapered off.

"Don't listen to my sister's bullshit," Alex announced. He had positioned himself in an armchair and flung his feet onto the coffee table. "She's a white-worshipping, self-hating *race traitor* only interested in white beta males who couldn't mate with white alpha females."

"Oh, shut *up!*" Eunice turned to Ingrid. "There he goes with his incel talk again. He gets it all from this creepy MRA forum—"

"Incel?" he scoffed. "I can get any girl I want. I've bagged more ten-out-of-ten chicks hotter than all the Chads you chase after."

"Wow, Alex. That's really healthy—to see dating as a competition and women as trophies to be won. I see you've matured since middle school."

"Gee, Eunice, where do you think Asian men learn that mentality? When Asian chicks tell us to fuck off as they go running into every Chad's pasty arms?"

"According to *you.*"

"Actually, according to *statistics.* Asian women rank white men the highest and Asian men the lowest. The dating world *is* a game. You said it yourself."

"No, I *said,* it's empowerment." Eunice's skin was now bright pink in addition to dewy and citrusy.

"Volunteering to be some dude's Oriental masturbation material is not 'empowerment,' it's retarded."

"You shouldn't say that word," Ingrid mumbled.

Alex looked at her. "Oriental?"

"The other one—both—"

"Whatever, PC police," he shrugged. "Listen, Ingrid, your white man is a standard beta male Asian fetishizer. Either dump him and get yourself some dignity and self-respect or be like my sister, a slave to mediocre Chads who can't get with white chicks and have self-esteem issues."

"So, you're saying no one actually finds Asian women attractive?"

Eunice snapped. "And white men only sleep with us as—as second options? Or consolation prizes? That's really fucked-up thinking." Alex rolled his eyes. "And honestly, you're one to talk. What about that weird white girl you dated last year?"

"Who?"

"The one who was always here playing video games in her cat-ear hoodie? Who was always calling you 'oppa' and trying to dye your hair blue like her favorite K-pop singer?" Eunice turned to Ingrid and added, "She claimed she had a 'Korean soul,' and I swear to God, she literally looked like a pancake." She turned back to her brother. "Sorry to break it to you, Alex, but *you* were fetishized."

He blinked disjointedly before emitting a strange, delayed laugh. "Yeah, whatever. I mean, I didn't actually like her. I was just using her, so—"

"Liar, you loved every minute of it! What was your nickname for her—'my European princess'?"

Alex laughed. "You're one to talk. Do you want me to tell Ingrid *your* nicknames for your exes?"

"Oh, just shut up."

"You shut up."

The brother and sister glared at each other for several moments.

Ingrid tentatively coughed to reinstate her presence in the room. "But what if Stephen still—I mean, he loves me—we love each other—maybe he was attracted to me at first because—but then, he fell in love—with my personality—so maybe—he doesn't even know I'm Asian anymore—maybe I'm just—a person to him—"

Alex leaned forward, his face very close to hers. He smelled of minty aftershave. "The sad thing is, Ingrid, you'll never know for sure."

She stared at him in silent terror.

"Good night, ladies," he singsonged as he drifted into his room.

"Eunice?" she whispered. Her head felt padded with insulation. "What just happened?"

Eunice cupped her cheeks in her hands. "Ingrid, snap out of it! Just ignore everything he said. I should have told him to fuck off the second he got started. I'm sorry about that—like I said, he gets it from this toxic forum full of angry virgins with mommy issues. You're going to listen to *them* for advice?"

"But Alex said—I mean—how *will* I know for sure?"

"You're in love! And happily engaged! Does it really matter why?"

"I love Stephen," she automatically repeated.

"Exactly! And he loves you. So what's the issue?" Eunice caught her eyes straying towards the manila folder. "Let's get rid of that thing. You don't need to think about those other sluts. He chose *you*."

Ingrid wordlessly followed Eunice into her backyard, where she dumped the photos into a metal trash can. The night air was warm and soft. Crickets hummed in the grass.

"You do the honors." She handed her a kitchen lighter.

Ingrid held the trigger down and lowered the flame to the edge of the photos. Annie, Jenny and Sandra smiled up at her. "I can't do it," she whispered.

A moment later, they were in Eunice's bedroom, feeding the photos through an automated shredder.

"Doesn't that feel good?" she encouraged.

Ingrid stared at the ribbons of paper and nodded, but truthfully, she did not feel a single thing.

14

The Ultimate Asian Woman

"Vivian Vo: Up Close and Personal"

The Barnes Gazette – Online Edition

By Avery Fairchild | May 14

At twenty-six, Vivian Vo should be enjoying the carefree life of a young twentysomething: blacking out at parties, disappointing her parents and making poor life decisions. But Vivian has no time for trivial matters. As the head of the Postcolonial Studies department's POC Caucus, all her time is devoted to her political and social causes. Her experience in community organizing is extensive and, among other projects, includes volunteering for a disenfranchised Hmong youth program, supporting tenant rights, donating to refugee camps, hosting workshops on building a police-free society and, a lifelong passion of hers, painting colorful street art murals of Black women and men who have been murdered by the police.

When I meet Vivian at her apartment, she looks tired but beautifully put together in a stunning plum áo dài by Vietnamese designer Ngoc Bich Pham. With her trademark dark lipstick and heavy eyeliner, Vivian might come off as intimidating at first glance. But sitting at her kitchen table, where she's laid out Vietnamese iced coffee for us, she appears vulnerable, anxiously twisting her onyx ring, a gift from her partner, Zoe Washington.

Avery Fairchild: Thank you for having me over, Vivian. I love how sparsely you've decorated your apartment.

Vivian Vo: I try to resist Eurocentric capitalist pressure as much as I can and support Indigenous artists.

A: You're truly an inspiration. I don't think I can ever give up my daily almond milk latte. (Laughs.)

V: I'm not trying to be an inspiration. Just living life to my ideals.

A: Of course. So let's talk about these ideals. You recently announced on the library steps you could no longer stay silent. You made the shocking revelation you discovered Xiao-Wen Chou was the invention of a white man named John Smith. Vivian—many people were surprised you didn't come forward sooner as the creator of www.thetruthaboutchou.com. What made you hesitate?

V: Well, victims of trauma undergo all kinds of psychological phenomena: denial, acute stress disorder, cognitive dissonance, memory loss. Finding out Smith had been openly living in yellowface for thirty-five years was, obviously, traumatizing. I had to first accept the reality of what I had witnessed before I could talk about it.

A: I'm so sorry you had to live through that harrowing experience, Vivian.

V: Thank you.

A: Can you walk us through that night? Only if you feel ready.

V: (Closes her eyes, breathes deeply, then nods.) First, I want to say that although private property is an imperialist invention, I don't condone breaking and entering without the homeowner's consent. But I was left with no choice at that point—and, when I made my decision, I reminded myself that I was acting in the name of a greater cause: truth and justice. I wasn't doing it for myself.

A: Of course.

V: And I hope that, should John Smith take me to court, the judge and jury will understand.

A: They'd be heartless not to.

V: Well, the American criminal justice system has been corrupt since its inception. I wrote a paper on it—"Incarcerate This: How Mass Incarceration Keeps Us Enslaved."

A: Excellent. And what was it like, entering Smith's house?

V: I could immediately sense the environment was toxic. Part of me wanted to turn around the moment I walked in. But then I reminded myself—of the greater cause—and kept going. Something made me head to the master bathroom. I'm not sure why; it could have been the guidance of a former ancestor. So I walked straight from the back door to the bathroom and found it—the vanity table.

A: But on the website, it says you looked around downstairs before going upstairs.

V: (Softly chuckles and points at her head.) Post-traumatic memory loss.

A: Right—my apologies. So what was your first reaction when you saw the vanity table?

V: Disbelief. Even though I had seen Smith leave the house earlier with my own eyes, I thought I had accidentally ended up at the house of an actor or circus mime. But then, when I had calmed down enough to examine the wigs, I recognized them. And when I saw the yellowface photos on the mirror, it finally clicked.

A: How did you feel when you saw Smith removing his "disguise"?

V: Like my body was cut in half. And those pieces were cut in half. And then those pieces were cut in half. And on and on.

A: That sounds incredibly violent.

V: (Nodding ferociously.) It was an act of violence. I'll have to suffer the consequences for the rest of my life. But I hope, with therapy, that I can work through it.

A: We're all rooting for you, Vivian. And if you had to make a guess, what motivated Smith's actions?

V: I don't have to make a guess. Smith was working under the assumption that there are "benefits" to being a POC, benefits denied white people. For example, the assumption that Chinese poets are "taking away" opportunities from white poets. This is false in every sense of the word and I don't have the energy, time or emotional bandwidth to explain why without compensation—FYI: I accept funds at @VisDecolonizing. Smith's supporters claim he suffers from "deep-rooted psychological shame" over his whiteness, which caused him to "disown" it. They think he's a victim who needs rehabilitation.

A: And what do you think?

V: I don't buy any of it. Assuming an oppressed race, which as a white man he's complicit in oppressing, has everything to do with power and domination. Period.

A: So can you tell us why you created an anonymous website, rather than go directly to the press?

V: Oh. Well . . . I was afraid Smith would come after me. Yes, that's right. I had to protect my identity.

A: And how did the website change things?

V: At first it was great, seeing all these people get their comeuppance. People who had worshipped at Xiao-Wen Chou's altar had to reckon with their former selves. Because *I* had always been suspicious about him, I want to make that very clear. I always knew his writing lacked legitimacy.

A: When you say "comeuppance," are you referring to the events in the East Asian Studies department?

V: Well, since the only person in my department researching Chou was me... yes, that's right.

A: So you're referring to Wenli Zhao's suicide attempt?

V: Oh, well, no, I wasn't.

A: So—

V: I mean, even though Professor Zhao insisted on producing *Chinatown Blues*, and after the reveal of Chou's identity, she was probably so horrified she'd propped up this white man's Orientalist trash—no one should be driven to such despair that they'd want to self-harm. I honestly wish her the best.

A: I see. Did you consider revealing your identity at that point?

V: No. I thought the E. A. department would sort itself out.

A: So what was the tipping point that made you come forward?

V: Well, as you know, Michael Bartholomew has become Smith's spokesperson, defending him as he continues to hide out who-knows-where. When I heard about his "Enlightenment" theory, I figured it would die out. But after Michael went on that xenophobic talk show, he just—blew up. I shouldn't have been surprised, given our country's past, but I never expected it to go this far.

A: On the library steps, you said Michael's rhetoric is "dangerous." How so?

V: He's hijacking and profiting from this traumatic moment—that the Asian diaspora is still healing from—and rebranding it into a white nationalist movement.

A: Can you elaborate?

V: The language he's appropriating—about the American right to freedom—is couched in white nationalist rhetoric. Look at the people coming out to his rallies—all white men and women who happen to subscribe to the same reactionary politics. A coincidence? I think not. Michael's finally saying everything they wished they could say without fear of being called "racist." Now they'll just be called "patriotic" and—

A: I would just like to state, as a white woman, that I totally do not condone their behavior.

V: ...

A: Sorry, please continue.

V: As I was saying, his supporters don't actually care about John Smith's right to a Chinese American identity. They just want to hide behind a slogan that claims to be ultra-American and anti-Communist but is really an excuse for them to openly celebrate white supremacy.

A: Speaking of which—

V: I mean, for decades, POC have been hurt by images of ourselves we couldn't control; images whiteness propagated. We couldn't play ourselves; we couldn't speak for ourselves. These images became popular discourse. But now that there are more of us, collectively condemning this racist behavior, they're panicking. True white supremacy is predicated on white people doing whatever they want, whenever they want, without consequence. Being prevented from assuming a different race is a direct threat to centuries of white supremacy. That's what this boils down to: fear of the death of white supremacy.

A: I didn't know "white supremacy" could be used so many times in just a few sentences! It's very... inspiring.

V: Thank you.

A: Before we wrap things up, Vivian, I want to ask about your future plans. What happens now?

V: My plans are simple: stop Bartholomew at all costs.

When Vivian walks me to the door, the tiredness I had seen in her at the start of the day seems replaced with renewed determination. Although she is a controversial figure on campus, with supporters and detractors, it's undeniable Vivian Vo will leave her mark on Barnes.

WALKING INTO PLATINUM Investigative Associates—with the same gum-smacking receptionist, the same Garfield calendar, the same jelly bean jar with the same amount of jelly beans—Ingrid was waylaid by an attack of déjà vu.

Darlene, decked in a camel power suit with gaudy ivory buttons, hadn't changed, either. Around her throat, a beaded necklace encircled a small wooden mask. She caught Ingrid staring at it. "Got it on safari in Tanzania," she winked. "Please, sit."

Ingrid gingerly lowered herself down, trying to circumnavigate the patchouli-infused currents of air.

"Well, I'm surprised to see you again, I thought we found your man. Or are you looking for someone else now?"

"No, you—we didn't find my man. But I was able to myself through some digging—" Darlene raised her eyebrows. "I mean, through pure co-incidence, I finally found him." She handed her a piece of paper with Smith's name and address. "He was living here, but he recently moved. I don't know where."

"Did you try talking to his real estate company?"

"Er—no."

"Interviewing any of his neighbors?"

"No?"

"Contacting local moving companies?"

"No . . ."

"Leave it to the professionals, then," Darlene laughed. She rubbed, rather sensually, the African mask on her necklace. "Any other information you have on him?"

"You mean—you haven't heard?"

"Heard what?"

"I thought it was all over the local news."

Darlene frowned.

"John Smith pretended to be a Chinese American man named Xiao-Wen Chou."

"Write down the name for me."

Ingrid complied, though it was the second time she'd spelled it out for her. Darlene didn't seem the least bit shocked about Smith's con. Perhaps she came across all sorts of unspeakable deeds in her line of work.

"That's why he was so hard to find," she continued. "I think he tried to bury his old identity when he became Xiao-Wen Chou."

"I can put two and two together, sweetie."

She eked out a smile. "If you find him, could you please give him this?" She slid an envelope across the desk.

"Not if, *when*." Darlene got up and throttled her hand. "I'll be in touch soon."

Ingrid left the office in a daze, unsure of what had driven her back to Darlene after her past incompetence. Perhaps she'd become disenchanted with sleuthing. Or perhaps she simply had more pressing thoughts nagging at her.

She got in her car and drove haltingly in the direction of Barnes. The E. A. department administrator had sent her a series of sternly worded emails about her dissertation paperwork. Was she defending in June? Would she need to appeal to extend her PhD into an exceptional ninth year? Was she staying in the program at all?

She didn't know. Her parents told her while they wouldn't mind bragging rights about their daughter becoming *Dr.* Ingrid Yang, she should do what was right for her. Eunice told her to "trust her inner voice." Stephen told her—well, she could hardly sustain a conversation with him.

Ingrid sat in her car and gazed at the university's redbrick buildings and green lawns. She had been, perhaps unconsciously, putting off speaking to someone, someone who'd been affected by the events she'd instigated more than anyone else. She walked to the Humanities Block, rode the elevator up to the fourth floor and stood outside office number 400.

"Professor Zhao?"

Wenli's brilliant white hair was styled in a smooth chin-length bob. She had soft features and bright, inquisitive eyes. Today she wore scarlet lipstick and jade drop earrings. As an undergrad, Ingrid had taken one class taught by her—a class on Romanticism in Chou.

"Come in. Oh—hello, Ingrid. It's been a long time."

"Yes, it has. How are you?"

Wenli gave her a wan smile. "I've been better."

"I'm so sorry about—about everything that's happened."

"It's not your fault." This somehow seemed both true and false.

"I just can't believe Smith conned me . . . you . . . everyone."

Wenli's voice turned bitter. "Everyone keeps saying they've been 'conned.' What I feel is betrayed."

"Betrayed?"

She gestured for Ingrid to sit, then turned her full gaze on her. "The person known as Xiao-Wen Chou was my mentor. He took me under his wing. And because he was one of the only Chinese people in the department, I trusted him. I confided in him. I looked up to him. When he passed, I mourned for months. I visited the archive on the anniversary of his death every year. And left flowers!" She shook her head. "Everyone talks about having lost a teacher or a colleague or 'the father of Chinese American poetry.' But I lost a friend—twice."

Ingrid's eyes stung with the force of tears. She had never—not once—conceived of Smith's actions in this light. "Thank you for sharing that with me, Professor Zhao," she said quietly, her voice cracking on her name.

Wenli smiled sadly.

They sat in silence for a moment before Ingrid noticed the paper mountain obstructing half the desk. "Are you . . . still teaching?"

"Oh, yes."

"How have you . . . managed to go on?"

"How have I managed to go on," Wenli repeated faintly. "I don't know if I had much of a choice."

"Oh?"

"I'm sixty-one, Ingrid. I couldn't exactly quit and pursue a new career. It's nearly impossible to switch paths after a certain age. So I get on with it. I bear it."

Her heart wrenched at the somberness weighing down Wenli's voice.

"And I remind myself there are worse things in the world." She stared into space, then refocused her gaze. "Was there something in particular you wanted to discuss?"

"Oh, right," Ingrid said, gathering herself. "I was hoping to ask you for some advice. You see, I've been struggling with my dissertation . . . on Chou. I've written about a hundred seventy-five pages. I just—I just don't know if it's worth finishing. Will a degree in Chouian studies have any value—"

"Finish it."

"What?"

"The dissertation."

"Oh." Ingrid felt a drizzle of disappointment. Perhaps what she'd really wanted wasn't advice but permission to quit.

Wenli removed a small, handsome pipe from her desk drawer, lit the bulb at the end and drew a long breath. "Would you like a hit?"

She accepted, then nearly choked upon realizing it was exceptionally potent marijuana. "Thank you," she coughed hoarsely, tear ducts leaking, and passed the pipe back. "So—you think I should defend?"

"The university will take and take from you. *You* have to take from it. That's the only way to survive."

"Survive?"

Wenli took another hit and exhaled. "Barnes is backed by wealth, prestige and power. Take what you can and leverage it for yourself. You're right the degree might carry less . . . significance in the world now. But you'll be a doctor. No matter how facetious it is, the world runs on titles and awards. People only want to invest in what's already been invested in. That's been my experience, anyway," she shrugged. "So use those three little letters behind your name to your advantage. Think of what Barnes can do for *you*."

"I see . . . I've never thought of it that way. You've given me a lot to think about, Professor Zhao. Thank you." She considered asking Wenli about *Chinatown Blues*, about what her intentions had been approving Samantha's casting . . . Was it supposed to have been ironic? A form of social commentary? Or had her belief in Chou's identity resulted in complete trust of his art—just as it had for Ingrid?

Wenli stared out the window with a stricken look. No, Ingrid decided, now wasn't the time. She got up from her chair. "Well, goodbye. And . . . take care."

Wenli nodded, then called her back as she was about to close the door. "If you defend, and I hope you do, Ingrid—I'd like to be there."

"Of course. I'd be honored," she said, though her head was already tumbling with competing thoughts. Wenli had a point, certainly, one she hadn't considered before—but could she coerce the remaining seventy-five pages from herself?

Truthfully, she was tired of taking the hard way out. Why was "sucking it up" and "pushing through to the end" perched on such a high pedestal, anyway? These were the same so-called values that sent PhD students running headfirst into the open arms of antidepressants. For once in her life, she wanted to be selfishly and deliciously *lazy*. To embody the most abhorred word of her generation: *unproductive*. She, yes she, wanted to be the person who walks away as a car combusts into flames in the background. This was her chance.

Downstairs, Ingrid flung open the main doors, striding so purposefully, she slammed into Vivian Vo.

"Vi-Vivian," she stammered. "Sorry, I wasn't watching where I was going."

"Oh, hello, Ingrid. Do you have a minute to talk?" she asked, her voice dreamy.

"Uh—sure?" The last time they'd interacted, Vivian had given off the energy of a paint sniffer. Now her energy was oddly . . . zen. She glided to a nearby cluster of cement benches.

Ingrid followed behind her with a curious mix of gratitude for being rescued from the spotlight and disbelief at the presumptuousness of her interview in *The Barnes Gazette.*

Vivian sat down on a bench and patted the spot next to her. "How are you, Ingrid?"

"I'm dropping out of the PhD!" she beamed.

The zen look in Vivian's eyes withdrew for a moment. "Oh," was all she said. Then she blinked and slipped back into the same dreamy voice. "Well, I'm so glad I ran into you."

"You are?"

"I've done a lot of thinking and growing lately," she said, nodding gently off into the horizon. Ingrid looked her over—when had she started dressing like a hippie witch? And, was it her imagination, or did she smell like a palo santo diffuser?

"Oh? Well, that's great."

"And I want to forgive you and forgive myself for the way I treated you."

"Forgive me?"

"I'm at a point in my life where I am no longer repressing my truth. Honesty, Ingrid, is the only path forward."

"Of course—"

"And the truth is I've always looked down on you. Not because I felt threatened or anything," Vivian hastily added, "but because I thought my beliefs, my politics, were superior to yours."

"I could tell—"

"I rejected East Asians who so readily worshipped at the false Xiao-Wen Chou altar—"

"I had no idea he was white—"

"And as you know, I've long held the belief that light-skinned East Asians are the white people of POC—"

"Er, I didn't know that—"

"But now I see I've taken the wrong approach." Vivian faced Ingrid and clasped her hands in hers. "It is not your *fault* white supremacy has conditioned you to be who you are. It is not your *fault* you play into the destructive myth of the model minority. It is not your *fault* you have shucked and jived for the white man. I forgive you. I forgive myself."

"Thank you?"

Vivian yawned and stretched luxuriously. "Oh, I feel so much better now. Are there any honest revelations you would like to share?"

She laughed nervously. Across from them, a pair of undergrads were greedily making out.

"This is a safe space. You can tell me anything."

"Anything?" Maybe Vivian would find the truth nothing short of hilarious, and together they would revel in the hilarity of it all. "You're going to laugh so hard when I tell you this," Ingrid chuckled. "I mean, it's so—I don't even know where to start—"

"Speak with intention."

"You don't have to pretend with me." She paused and waggled her eyebrows. "I know your secret."

"Excuse me?"

"That you didn't create www.thetruthaboutchou.com. That you didn't break into John Smith's house," she whispered.

"Ingrid, what on earth are you talking about?"

"I know you didn't do any of that—because *I* did!" She fell over herself, even tacking on a couple knee slaps and snorts, and awaited Vivian's surprised laughter.

"What did you just say," she replied stonily.

"Er—that you don't have to pretend with me anymore—because I did those things—not that I want you to *tell* people—this way, *you* can take down Michael instead of me—and honestly, I'm grateful to you—I mean,

I *hate* public speaking—it gives me indigestion—plus I'm not really photogenic—but you, you always look fantastic—"

"I have no idea what you're talking about," Vivian said in clipped tones. She stood up, then turned around to hiss, "And if you say otherwise, no one will believe a pathetic PhD dropout."

"But what about speaking one's truth?" Ingrid called after her. "What about forgiveness?"

For a response, she got Vivian's middle finger.

Ingrid's jaw dropped. She leapt up from the bench. Stomped around on the grass. Crossed her arms and uncrossed them. Kicked a couple of medium-sized rocks. Started a few, "Why, that little—" only to leave her thoughts unfinished. The undergrads divided in two to gape at her before fusing back into a single organism.

Ingrid sat back down on the bench and composed an email on her phone: "Michael, I'd like to schedule my defense for next month. Please let me know the date and time." She closed her eyes and waited. A few minutes later, she received a response: "Ingrid, my foremost Chouian scholar in the making! I took it upon myself to book a room some time ago, knowing you'd come around. June twentieth, eleven a.m., conference room 105 in the Humanities Block."

Her defense was confirmed.

If Vivian thought she could just cast her aside, if she thought she could scrub her from Barnes and hoard all the degrees and publications and acclaim for herself, well, she didn't know who she was dealing with.

The hit from Professor Zhao's pipe had finally kicked in. She lay back on the bench. At first, a giggle or two escaped her. She caught the undergrad organism eyeballing her again. Act normal, she commanded herself. She giggled a third time. This set her off, each giggle somehow funnier than the last, until she was laughing so hard tears rolled down her face and bloomed on the cement bench.

Then Ingrid sat up and blotted away her tears and snot. She was going to write the fuck out of those seventy-five pages on Chou's use of enjambment.

STEPHEN WAS CALLING again—the seventh time in two days and the seventh time she hadn't answered. She wasn't *avoiding* him—she'd just been awfully busy, talking to Eunice and Alex, meeting with Darlene, going to campus, not to mention needing to eat, shower and sleep on occasion . . . And now she had a hankering for a leisurely walk.

She let the call go to voicemail.

The day was balmy and cloudless. Waiting at a stoplight, Ingrid was needled by the realization she *was* avoiding Stephen. She had never, in all five years, ignored his calls. But what was she supposed to say to him? "Hello, dear, how's the weather over there and do you even love me for who I am?"

Naturally, he knew she was upset, but he attributed it to their combative video chat. He had texted he was sorry. She had drafted a dozen replies before deleting them all.

On the one hand, her self-induced panic attack over his three ex-girlfriends was ludicrous. Was it fair to bring charges against him for his past relationships? And was his offense, if it could even be called that, serious enough to warrant a breakup? After all, she loved Stephen. She counted on him tremendously. His actions and words had an overwhelming effect on her. Their lives and possessions and habits were inextricably enmeshed. And she felt an intense attachment to him, like she was a non-cancerous growth on his thigh. That was love, wasn't it?

Ingrid was physically incapable of picturing the future without also picturing the future of Mr. and Mrs. Greene. They would marry, get preapproved for a mortgage, retire, grow old, die in their sleep, ideally at the same stroke of midnight. Like Judith Newman and her husband, they would constitute the quintessential academic couple: a literary translator and a professor, their personalities (bookish, nitpicky, socially awkward) one and the same, quiet nights at home spent completing a 3-D clown puzzle or enjoying a documentary on the behavior of feral cats. Theirs was a foolproof blueprint for happiness. Ingrid had coveted this future for the two of them, had waited impatiently for it. And now, because of some old photos, she was willing to toss it all out the window? Eunice's words rang in her head: "Are you insane?"

She stepped onto Ainslie Street, pausing to stare blankly at the butter sculptures in a window display.

And yet, she couldn't expel Alex's declaration from her head, either: "The sad thing is, Ingrid, you'll never know for sure." How *could* she know for sure? Like Eunice had explained, something as superficial as taste in food and pop culture was meaningless. This sort of man was becoming craftier. He knew better than to showcase his collection of samurai swords on his bedroom wall or advertise his encyclopedic knowledge of 1990s anime on the first date. Like all mammalian predators, he had adapted to his environment.

This sort of man could be *anywhere*. Ingrid glared suspiciously at the white men passing by on the sidewalk.

Should she put Stephen through a series of tests? Attach him to a polygraph machine while thumbing through photos of women from every conceivable ethnicity, taking note of who made his heart rate quicken? Make him sign a binding legal document prohibiting him from dating another Asian woman should they ever break up in order to save her the humiliation of being relegated to number four on the list? Persuade him to relocate to a country with so few Asians, the odds of him straying from her would be next to none? Poland? North Dakota?

Because ever since the Three Asian Ex-Girlfriends Incident, Ingrid had begun eyeing her fellow Asian women in an unsettling new way. Here was another one, traipsing down the street while listening to music on earbuds. Ingrid glowered at her, even bared her teeth a little. A month ago, she would have been an unremarkable pedestrian; today, she was a direct threat to her impending marriage.

All her life, Ingrid had dutifully held up white women as the embodiment of beauty and, it follows, had compared herself to them and, it follows, had come up short. But white women's elevated position in her hierarchy of beauty had now been unseated. After all, if Stephen had a—F word—for Asian women, then every single one alive on the planet, between the ages of eighteen and, say, sixty-two, must be irresistible to him since race was the defining pull of attraction. She didn't think individual attractiveness played a major role, since Annie was dowdy and Jenny was plain and Sandra, Ingrid hated to admit, was more conventionally attractive than herself. But then, what was the deciding factor between more than one Asian woman? Was the only way to avoid replacement by another Asian woman to somehow become . . . the ultimate Asian woman?

Ingrid froze in the middle of the street.

So why *had* Stephen chosen her? Because she happened to be in the right place at the right time? If he'd met another Asian woman five years ago with roughly her same age, education and prospects, would he have ended up with her? Would he be just as happy?

Her thoughts were interrupted by her buzzing phone. Eunice had texted her: "*A New You*'s season finale just started—want to come over?" Oh no. *Eunice was an Asian woman, too!* Though this was an obvious fact, the knowledge drizzled over her as if for the first time.

She frantically flipped through a mental catalogue of all the times Stephen and Eunice had occupied the same room. Did he ever hug her for a second too long? Did his eyes lustily glaze over at the sight of her cherubically round face? An unsettling impulse overcame her, like she wanted to shove Eunice off a swing set. Was she *jealous* of her? She had never compared herself to her closest friend in that capacity, as if they were two (straight) female primates tussling over the last (straight) male primate. She had always protected their friendship from such base instincts. What was wrong with her?

"For fuck's sake!" Ingrid cried aloud. She charged into an ice cream shop and reemerged with two cones, groaning unhappily as she licked away at both, then stormed up the street towards Wittlebury Park. Passersby dodged out the way, aware this woman was not to be crossed. She plopped on a bench, hardly tasting her sea salt caramel and hazelnut swirl.

But Eunice had debunked her brother's theory. According to her, the reason why a couple *started* dating didn't matter; what mattered was why they *stayed* together. In which case, Stephen had to love her for who she was. He wouldn't date someone for five years and propose to her simply because of her ethnicity, would he? And yet . . . all those times he'd commented on how "cute and small" Ingrid was, on how she was his ideal partner, on how he loved her hair, eyes and skin . . . What had he been saying—really saying? That if she *didn't* have her hair, eyes and skin, he wouldn't love her? And the fact that he'd cycled through three Asian women in a row—was he trying to "upgrade" on the standard model each time?

The sad thing is, Ingrid, you'll never know for sure.

It was hopeless. If she chose to stay with him, she'd go insane testing him 24/7, trying to figure out definitively and without a doubt that he loved her not because of what she looked like or what she represented but because of the part of herself that was incorporeal.

If she chose to stay with him *and* hold on to her sanity, she'd have to . . . accept her own objectification. She shivered, not from brain freeze, but from knowing she'd be split apart, never certain if the submissive and docile figure in the mirror was a reflection of her true self, or the ghostly affect of someone telling her her entire life: this is who you are, this is all you can ever be.

The memories came tumbling back: the white colleague who said, "Ni hao piaoliang" the first, second and third time they met. The white-haired veteran who leered, "You remind me of the sweetheart I had back in Vietnam." The white male cop who pulled over when she'd been waiting for a cab one night, demanding, "What are you doing on this corner?" as he eyed her bare legs. The drunken group of men who sidled up to her at a bar, asking, "How much?" Thinking they meant the drink in her hand, she responded, "Um . . . Twelve dollars, plus tax and tip?" ignorant of her mix-up until one of them smirked, "Do you give group discounts?"

How was it possible to be so desired and so hated, the two intertwined like heads of the same beast?

Ex-boyfriends, male teachers, men on the street, former bosses, older businessmen in airplanes—the way they'd treated her, talked to (or rather, over) her, insulted her as they pretended to compliment her, the presumptive and invasive questions they'd asked her, the attention and coddling and patience they'd demanded from her, the limitations and one-dimensional roles they'd placed on her—all of it had groomed her into accepting *their* conceptions of herself.

Ingrid had been zoning out for so long, her ice cream had melted over her hands. Embarrassed, she straightened up and hoped the mess looked purposefully artful.

Say she *wasn't* with Stephen and ventured back into the wilderness of modern dating, wouldn't she find herself mired in the same predicament? Even if she handed out "How Many Asian Women Have You Slept With?" quizzes on first dates, a man could always surprise her later down the line. She could come upon his porn-viewing history and find unsavory titles like "Barely Legal Asian Teen Bangs Hairy Old White Expat." Say a man had never dated an Asian woman before and Ingrid is the first so she thinks she's in the clear, but they could break up, and he could date another one after her and another one after that . . .

She could be someone's Asian starter kit.

And therein lay the hidden clause in the contract: as long as she was in a relationship with a white man, she would never know beyond the shadow of a doubt if he *had been* infected, *was* infected or *would become* infected. She'd simply have to live with the uncertainty.

Ingrid threw her head back, ramming both ice cream cone ends into her mouth with wild abandonment. A child stopped on the sidewalk to gawk at her in admiration. His mother shielded his eyes and yanked him away, whispering something about saying no to drugs.

She looked warily around the park. Oh God, Asian women were everywhere. Since when had they all descended on Wittlebury?

So far, she'd seen one couple composed of an Asian woman and a white man.

A second one.

A third.

A fourth.

After two hours, Ingrid had counted twelve such couples, three Asian and Asian couples and one inverse couple, of an Asian man and a white woman. What did it mean? She wasn't gifted at math, but surely those numbers were telling, even damning. A sudden intense interest in dating statistics hooked her—maybe she *was* cut out to be an accountant.

But why, she fretted, was her instinct each time she saw a couple like her and Stephen to pity the woman and loathe the man? To tell her, "Run and save yourself before it's too late!" and to tell him, "Do us all a favor and buy yourself a sex doll. At least it won't have to endure years of therapy." She realized, with a swell of sadness, she could no longer give these men the benefit of the doubt. She could not even give it to her own fiancé.

Ingrid wiped the ice cream stains on her jeans and wondered if everyone sweated through such strenuous mental gymnastics when it came to matters of the heart. What was it like to date while white?

A WEEK LATER, she received a voicemail.

"Darlene Woods here. Good news: I made contact with your man. Call me back."

15

Serial Killers Want
to Be Caught

The motel was to the northwest of Wittlebury, across state lines. Ingrid flew past fields, dense constellations of trees, gas stations guarded by wooden bears. She stopped once for a cup of sour coffee and a cloying whoopie pie. After three hours, she turned off an exit towards a state park. Buried down a forested road stood the motel, a sullen rectangle with low eaves and chipped blue paint. By the entrance, a sun-broiled woman reclined in a plastic lawn chair, staring openly as Ingrid searched for room 11.

When she knocked on the door, her hand was trembling uncontrollably. Her tongue felt inflated to twice its volume; her head, shrunk to a fourth of its size. What could she say to the man who had consumed so many of her waking hours, a man who had, for better or worse, changed the course of her life?

"Come in."

Smith sat on the edge of the bed, a single armchair facing him. He wore jeans, a faded T-shirt and the same white baseball cap from the last time they'd been in such intimate proximity, when she observed him from inside his closet.

The room was close with the smell of salt and grease; she guessed Smith had recently ordered takeout. The walls and carpet were tan, the bedspread and towels a striped burgundy pattern. Dust motes swirled in the square of sunlight on his lap.

"Please, sit." He gestured at the armchair.

Ingrid stole a glance at him. His eyes were the same severe brown, his mouth drawn heavily downwards, sun spots and raw patches crowded on his cheeks and neck.

"Ingrid, is that right?"

"Yes." Listening to John Smith speak was eerily jarring. His voice—a voice she knew by heart—had, until recently, belonged to a different man.

"I appreciate you coming all the way out here. I assume you're wondering why I asked to meet in person. I could've very easily answered you by email." He paused. "Well, I admit I was curious. I wanted to meet you—the one who figured it all out."

In spite of herself, Ingrid felt disturbingly . . . flattered.

Smith smiled and looked her over carefully. "You're smart, that's clear. Determined. A little reckless, too—not many people would go to the trouble of breaking in. That's a felony." He paused, then laughed a surprisingly warm and capacious laugh. "Oh, don't look like that—I'm not here to turn you in. I found it admirable, the lengths you were willing to go."

"You're not . . . mad?" she asked suspiciously.

Smith shook his head. "I'm curious—how did you get in? Old credit card trick?"

"No, a lockpick."

"Ah." He leaned back and nodded. "Very good."

Confusion spread over her. What was his angle?

"Well, I figure you have some questions. Whatever you want to know, ask. It's the least I can do. Thirsty?" He went to the bathroom and returned with two plastic cups of tap water. "This is all I have at the moment."

Ingrid accepted the cup and took a lukewarm sip. "Why?" She cleared her throat. "I mean, why did you do it?"

Smith chuckled and rubbed his chin. "It's a long story."

"I have time."

I GREW UP in a military family. My dad was in the Air Force, my mom was stay-at-home. I was an only child. We lived all over the place—North Carolina, Hawaii, Texas, DC. I got used to it—never had an issue leaving a new school or my friends. And I loved it, living in all those different places. Every time I moved, I could be someone else. I even changed my name a few times—my favorite was Beau. Don't ask why.

When I was nine or so, my dad left us. Mom moved us back to her parents' house not far from here, in Fallowtown. Started dating a stream of assholes, drinking a lot, probably doing drugs, I wouldn't have put it past her—the usual. My grandparents raised me. I won't bore you with the details.

The kids at my new school didn't believe my dad was in the Air Force. They had all seen my mom reeking of alcohol after school. They also didn't believe I had lived in all those places. I guess that's when I started lying more, probably around sixth grade or so.

Psychologists say compulsive lying is a way to get attention, right? I don't know if that's why I did it. I realized it was easy fooling people—especially lying about small stuff. And every time I wasn't caught, I'd get this high—a sweet, short-lived high. I thought, everyone around me is a goddamn idiot.

I was good at school, you know. Favorite subject was English. I liked reading, liked it a lot. Not that my mom cared if I got good grades. I doubt the teachers even cared. No one amounted to anything in that town. The other kids said I thought I was too good for them, started making life hard for me. I couldn't wait to leave them and that sorry little town. So when I graduated from high school, that's what I did. Took the money I'd saved from shitty jobs—gas station clerk, dishwasher—and bought a ticket to Beijing.

Why China? I don't really know. I've been trying to trace it back. Was it a book I read or a movie I saw? Bruce Lee. Something we learned in history class. The Great Wall of China. No idea. Maybe it was just the farthest place I could think of. Completely different from boring, middle-of-nowhere America. And people in this country have always talked about China that way, right? If you dig a hole through the ground, you wind up in China. If you throw pots and pans down the stairs, it sounds like you're in China. The inverse of America. Maybe that was it. I don't know.

I stayed there for three months. I liked it, I did. I was both stared at and ignored. I lived in my head most of the time. Did a lot of thinking. Didn't have to interact with anyone besides handing over money. Well, eventually, money ran out. Plus, my tourist visa was going to expire. So I found myself on a plane back to Fallowtown. Couldn't believe it had come to that. I don't know what I had been thinking—that I could just start a new life in China? I didn't know how to speak any Chinese so I couldn't get a job, even if it was under the table. This was a long time ago, you understand. Now most people in the major cities know some English.

So I was still stuck in my sorry little town. I stayed with my grandparents, had nowhere else to go. My mom was gone. My grandma said she'd left with one of the men she had on rotation. Said she would call me sometime and visit. She never did.

I got a job at the supermarket, bagging groceries and mopping, that kind of stuff. I wrote at night. In the beginning, I just catalogued what I remembered about China so I wouldn't forget the time I'd spent there. Faces, smells, sounds, everything. The trip had already started to feel like a dream. Then I fooled around with writing poems. I had already written some when I was still in school, for English class. My teacher,

Mr. Thompson, chose just one to display on the wall and it was mine. I was cocky, I'll admit it. I thought they were good. Real good. Looking back now, I'm not so sure. But I was serious about poetry. I borrowed books from the library and learned all the terms. You know, I was insecure I hadn't gone to college. I had something to prove.

The librarian had gotten used to me checking out anything poetry related. She was always setting aside books she thought I'd like. A nice woman—Patty, I think her name was. One day, she showed me a new section next to the newspapers. "Literary magazines," she called them. They weren't for checking out, but I sat in the library reading them from cover to cover, every month.

After a couple years, I sent out my poems. The possibility of rejection didn't figure into my thinking, I'm embarrassed to admit. Publication felt . . . inevitable. I was twenty-one. What can I say. So when the rejections came, I was indignant. I'd write it off as the editor's poor taste or some intern's mistake. But even when I rewrote and rewrote a poem, and was so sure it was goddamn perfect, I'd get another rejection.

I think it was . . . around thirteen rejections—I know now that's not a lot—when I got another one. The editor mentioned some horseshit about "the authenticity of the speaker's voice." I thought, well, I'll just change my name. I figured, writers use pseudonyms all the time. This wasn't any different.

So I went to the library, found a book on Chinese philosophers and came out with the most Chinese-sounding name I could piece together: Xiao-Wen Chou. My third time submitting with that name, I got accepted. And again and again.

Sure, I still got rejections—but fewer than before. Was it because of "Xiao-Wen Chou" or because I'd already been published? To this day, I'm not sure.

I was pretty pleased. I didn't even think I needed anything more than the magazine acceptances. I liked looking at the poems printed on nice paper and thinking, I did that. I'm a real poet.

And then I won a contest for "Cedar Trees at Dusk," you remember that poem? A prize was included, three hundred dollars—a lot of money back then—and this publisher is asking me to write a book. So I thought, why the hell not? My own book. I doubted it would actually be published. So I did it—wrote more poems, the best I'd ever written, worked on them with an editor. We did everything through correspondence and telephone. Didn't even meet in person. And I proved myself wrong—the book was published.

I thought it would be like the journals: my poems would be printed on nice paper and that would be that. Hardly anyone would notice.

Maybe there weren't a lot of Chinese American poets around at that time, but I proved myself wrong again. People ate it up. I was asked to do interviews, readings, talks. I turned them all down. I told myself I wasn't interested in that aspect of it—the public aspect.

But then the awards came. And the publishers asked for a second book, *Elegy of the Phoenix*—that one changed everything. After it came out, the Chinese Cultural Heritage Association nominated me for an award, to be presented at a ceremony in Philadelphia.

So what could I do? Three years had gone by since I published that first poem under Xiao-Wen Chou. If I revealed myself now, I would end up losing everything. I didn't want to work at the supermarket until I died in a drunk-driving accident or drank myself to death on the couch, like everyone else in Fallowtown. I wanted a different life. A better life.

And I realized . . . maybe I'd lied to myself about the public aspect of it all. Maybe I did want fame.

So I mailed in my RSVP. I had about two months before the ceremony to start researching. Not a lot of information was available—the Internet didn't exist back then, you understand, so I had to request books at the library. That's how I found out about William Ellsworth Robinson. You know him? He was an American magician from the turn of the twentieth century. Had an act where he was an old Chinese man named Chung Ling Soo, stole it from an actual Chinese magician named Ching Ling Foo.

Guess which Chinese man people liked more? That's right. So Robinson started living like a Chinese man. Never spoke English in public and always used a fake translator. Claimed he was the orphan of a Cantonese woman and a Scottish missionary. Claimed his assistant was his Chinese wife, Suee Seen. In reality, she was just a white person in disguise, like him. No one even figured out Robinson's identity until he got shot onstage during an act and shouted in English. Faulty bullet catch trick.

So I thought—if he can do it—if he *did* do it, so can I.

I couldn't find any information on how he'd pulled it off, so I turned to Hollywood. I came across a microfilm of a little booklet called *Denison's Make-Up Guide*—that had some good tips, though nobody was using greasepaint anymore—and a magazine with pictures of all the different actors who played Charlie Chan. And whenever "useful" movies played at the theater, I bought a ticket. I think I managed to see *The Mysterious Mr. Wong*, *The Good Earth* and *The Teahouse of the August Moon*. But the Fu Manchu movies were the most useful—they were new releases at the time. What I was doing, you have to understand, was considered acceptable.

So I practiced and practiced. The wig wasn't too difficult, just hot and a little itchy to wear. The face makeup was pretty simple once I landed on the right color combination. But the eyes were the hardest. That's why I started wearing thick glasses. Never needed them. But they helped obscure any tape if it came a little undone.

I experimented by going outside, to the supermarket, then the post office and the bank, and seeing if people reacted. No one did.

And so when the ceremony came around, I put on my makeup, my "Chou face," and got on a bus to Philadelphia. I remember I wasn't even nervous. Like I said, I had always been a little cocky. And, if I may say so myself, I was convincing. In another life, I would've made a damn good actor.

But I was still amazed—that I had gone undetected. Just like Robinson. People were shaking my hand and saying how nice it was to finally meet me and asking to take pictures with me. I thought again, everyone is a goddamn idiot. Fooling people had been too easy, maybe because they made it easy. I felt some disdain for them, honestly.

And yes, I won the award.

Soon after that, I got an offer to teach at Barnes. I thought someone was pulling something on *me*. The offer came packaged with a tenure-track position, healthcare, retirement. I was still living in my grandma's spare room (my grandpa had passed away). And I thought: my grandma's had a long, shitty life. If I can make some real money and take care of her, treat her to a nice vacation, I should.

And I didn't want the sad, sorry me, anyway. "John Smith." I was glad to see him go.

I made things easier for myself by dying my hair black—that got rid of the wigs, at least until I was supposed to go gray, then white. I could just put on the makeup and the tape. Women around the world do stuff like that every day. If they could do it without complaint, so could I.

I started teaching the next year. I was only twenty-six at the time, but my students didn't seem to mind, maybe because they assumed Chinese people aged slower, and that I was older than I looked.

I know, I know, it is hard to believe. But you have to understand, we had very few Asian students back then. And I don't mean to stereotype when I say this, but the few who attended Barnes weren't in the English department. The East Asian Studies department had just been formed. So I wasn't really around Asian people. The people I *was* around—the people publishing, teaching and writing about me—they were all white. I don't know if I could have succeeded if they hadn't been.

But then, as the years went on, students like you came. And you can bet I was starting to get nervous. I probably didn't have to be—you had all seen my face in your textbooks. You had grown up believing I was like you. One of you. Why would you question it?

But I was still on edge during office hours. Lectures were all right, since I stood far enough away from the students. But I couldn't get out of office hours. I had a very large desk and I would sit with my chair against the wall, to maintain the maximum amount of distance between us. I also kept these meetings short: ten, fifteen minutes at the most. The university let me get away with what I wanted. I was their prize Chinese American poet, after all. I even acquired a reputation for being unusually private.

I felt a little easier about it when I got older. I had an excuse to wear thicker and thicker glasses.

Oh, sure, I regretted it at times. I had no one I could confide in. My grandma passed away when I was thirty-one. I tried to have relationships when I wasn't Chou, but they never worked out. Women called me secretive, always assumed I was unfaithful. I had a "no staying the night" rule in case they found my makeup and wigs. They knew I was hiding something.

The best way I can describe it is like getting lowered into a well. The further and further down I went, the more impossible it became to pull myself back up.

All I could do was wait to retire—but I was getting impatient. I knew when that time came, I'd be "Professor Emeritus." I'd have to dole out awards, judge contests and make speeches every year. Better to kill myself off. For me. For everyone.

Nope, never actually had pancreatic cancer. I'm healthy as ever, though my doctor says I have to watch my cholesterol.

Oh, sure, people's gullibility would sicken me. Ironic, I know. I counted on them to make my living, and yet I wanted—subconsciously, if I can get a little Freudian—to test people's stupidity. Maybe it was self-sabotage. I was going through one of those phases when I wrote *Chinatown Blues*. I must have thought, no way people won't see through this. But they didn't. And I was still stuck way down in the well. I had the impression I could do anything and get away with it.

Killing myself off was the best thing that ever happened to me. Surprisingly easy, too. I just issued a statement that the body was flown back to China.

Any other questions?

Oh, you've met Luke. Well, I admit I used his name to spite him at first. Then it just became a habit—I couldn't go around using John Smith anymore. If you talk to him again, give him my apologies.

Ah, yes. I thought you'd ask about that night. The gym? No, that can't be right. I must have been headed to the Imperial Seafood Garden. It's the only place I can go as Chou—no one recognizes him there; I'm just one Chinese face among many. Early December, wasn't it? I remember arriving one night and finding out they were closed. I think I even called the next day to complain. I was angry I had gone through the trouble of putting everything on and driving all the way out there. Ah, well, the answer's simple. I get better service as Chou. They give me choice cuts of meat, the freshest seafood, too. The one time I went as myself, they stuck me by the bathrooms and served me reheated General Tso's chicken. Never made the same mistake again. Remember, I lived in China—I know how it's supposed to taste.

Well, I just want to say, Ingrid, that I'm grateful to you. Honestly. I was getting a little desperate. I would visit the archive from time to time, without any of the makeup, naturally, and mess around with the boxes: mixing up documents, stealing documents . . . I kept hoping someone would get suspicious, dig a little deeper. But they never did. I thought my clues weren't obvious enough. Too obvious would have killed the fun, of course.

So when I saw your notes stuck in one of the boxes, I thought I'd leave you a little note of my own.

Why? Oh. I suppose the guilt got to me. Or maybe it was that same old desire to prove I was a little less stupid than everyone else. But if I'm being honest . . . and look, I'm really trying here . . . I wanted credit. In the same way serial killers want to be caught, eventually. I wanted people to know *I* had pulled off a magic trick for thirty-five years.

The only good thing, I think, that came out of this whole mess is that— I understand now. During those years, not everyone was respectful and polite to me just because I was a poet or even a professor. I knew what it was like to be the butt of a joke. What it was like to be mistrusted and dismissed. To be invisible. The way I got treated when I was Xiao-Wen and when I was John—it was like night and day. I didn't have to *pretend* to be discriminated against. I guess what I'm trying to say is: Ingrid, I know what it's like to be you.

Oh, that's right. I haven't even answered your question in the letter. I've thought about it and my answer is yes. To hell with it.

Now the real reason why I wanted to meet you in person is to . . . apologize. On my hands and knees, Ingrid, I'm sorry. I was a cocky twenty-one-year-old when I signed "Xiao-Wen Chou" under a poem. But you have to believe me when I say I never meant it to go this far. I never meant to hurt anyone. And I tried my best, honest to God, to get the facts right. To portray Chinese people in a positive light. I even thought, in a strange way, that I was helping—helping America fall in love with China.

No, you're right. I know there's no excuse. And I understand there's nothing I can do now that will fix the past, but I'm prepared to pay the price for it. Whatever you believe is a measure of justice, I'll see it through.

I know I don't deserve forgiveness, I shouldn't even ask for it—Ingrid, please, wait—but do you think you can find it in your heart to forgive this foolish old man?

PART IV

Summer

16

All Hail Emperor
Bartholomew

Standing beside the podium, Michael broadcast his hundred-watt smile to the audience. He glowed with newly purchased, youthful vitality: his skin was tighter and tanner, his teeth, brighter and whiter. He had chopped off his signature salt-and-pepper ponytail in exchange for a wholesome sidelong swoop à la John F. Kennedy.

Ingrid rubbed her eyes. Had he ever shuffled around the E. A. department in a silk overcoat, puffed smoke rings from a Japanese pipe, juggled Baoding balls in one hand while quoting Laozi in Mandarin? The man onstage wouldn't be caught dead gnawing on steamed chicken feet, much less lecturing people on the proper way to gnaw them.

Dean Clemmons finished reeling off Michael's long list of accomplishments and clamped a hand on his shoulder. "—which is why I'm so pleased to announce Michael Bartholomew is Barnes University's new dean of students!"

The audience of students and faculty on the main lawn broke into applause. Ingrid kept her arms crossed and shrank farther into her metal fold-up chair.

"Thank you, Dean Clemmons. Or should I say, Mr. Clemmons, ha ha. And thank you to everyone for your *overwhelming* support." Michael rested his hand over his heart as the June sunlight bathed his upturned face. "Barnes University has been my home for many, many years. And it is with great honor that I accept the position of dean of students—a responsibility I do not take lightly. As your dean, I promise not a *single* student on campus will feel excluded. I promise *everyone* can safely express their opinions, no matter what they are. And I promise *no one* will be shamed or silenced for their background. Because I believe higher education has a duty to cultivate an atmosphere of open, unfettered discussion. A university must be protected from the ravages of current politics and transitory trends; it must fully commit to upholding freedom of expression; it must remain an *intellectual* sanctuary. Censorship, in any shape or form, will not be tolerated."

Two aisles ahead of Ingrid, the men's rowing team was vigorously nodding. "Fuck yeah! Bartho rules!" they woofed while pumping their fists into the air.

No other explanation existed: Ingrid was hostage in a surreal, collective nightmare that would not end no matter how many times she pinched herself.

As Michael's popularity steadily rose, the rumors circulating him had as well: he was to replace Herbert Plimpton on his talk show; travel around the country as a one-man motivational speaker; run for city council; dabble in politics . . . national politics. But any imagined scenario would have been preferable to reality.

With Michael as dean of students, Barnes would become his little kingdom, and he, the little emperor on the throne. Unchecked, he could exponentialize what meager power he'd accrued as chair and professor of the E. A. department. He could abuse, on a far greater scale, his fondest pastime: grooming the young minds of tomorrow.

Ingrid would know; he had done it to her.

"—true equality means no one group is given special preference over another. The future at Barnes is not dividing ourselves into smaller and smaller categories, so that we feel further and further apart. So that we feel like different *species* instead of members of the same race—the *human* race. Under my watch, students will celebrate what binds us together, not what tears us apart. Universalism, not division, is our new guiding principle—"

She scoffed. Already Michael was refashioning the university in his image: the DOFO image.

"—and together, we will shepherd the next generation into the future! Thank you and God bless!"

Before the clapping had abated, Ingrid stormed to the refreshments table to sublimate her rage into hunger. She scarfed down a few canapés, then produced a one-liter Tupperware container from her purse and stocked it full.

"Ingrid!" Michael called.

She froze en route to the pigs-in-blankets. How had he picked her out in this crowd? Had he rigged a homing device to her?

"Congratulations!" she said, stretching her smile as far as it would go. Keep your friends close, etc.

He glanced down at her Tupperware and chuckled. "You are nothing if not resourceful."

"I'm a poor graduate student."

Michael ignored this. "I'm having a little gathering at my house tomorrow night." He drew closer. "Invitation only. I'm asking all my advisees, naturally."

At the mention of him as her advisor, she waited for him to prod her on her dissertation's progress. He hadn't brought it up in months. Now that

Michael had bigger ideological fish to fry, his advisor duties had sunk to the bottom of his prioritiess.

"Are plus-ones allowed?"

"For you, I'll make an exception."

She repressed an eye roll. "By the way, I realized I never gave you an answer." He wrinkled his brow. "To your question—to join you on your journey to Enlightenment?"

"Ah, yes, to join the DOFO movement," Michael beamed.

"Right." She grit her teeth behind her smile. "My answer is yes—I'm in."

She couldn't be sure, but for a half second, his expression dimmed before he clapped her jovially on the back.

"Excellent, Ingrid, excellent. I knew I could always count on you." He strolled off, turning around to call, "Seven p.m.!"

When he turned back around, Michael was immediately accosted with high-fives from YAACC, the Young Asian American Capitalists Club. As Ingrid watched the social cavorting unfold, she narrowed her eyes in disbelief: all the members sported DOFO pins on their collars. Why did the world refuse to make sense anymore?

TWO WEEKS AGO, in a live interview with Tricia Perez of local channel WQR7, John Smith had publicly denounced himself under Ingrid's tutelage. At first, her forgiveness was purely transactional. Taking Wenli's advice, she sized John up like the famous old institution he was and asked what *he* could do for *her*. She also figured working with John, rather than against him, was surely the best way to halt Michael's rise to power. Now that John had come out of hiding, it was only a matter of time before he tried to convert him into a soldier for the DOFO cause.

Before John got cold feet about his symbolic self-immolation, Ingrid had to capitalize on his guilt. She started calling him on the phone every few days to hash out her "Operation DOFO Must Die" strategy. But even as he listened politely and agreeably to her instructions, disgust simmered in the pit of her stomach.

She knew what Vivian would call her if she got wind of her collaboration with the yellowface devil himself: "traitor."

And yet . . . whenever Ingrid's thoughts meandered back to that afternoon in his motel room, she remembered John's pleading, tear-lined eyes. His vulnerability and repentance. His heartfelt, sincere confession.

In this manner, pity eventually overrode disgust. And as the days wore on, John grew less villainous, less mythical, in her eyes, until he dwindled down to a lonely, elderly man who had made a foolish mistake when he was young.

Still, her forgiveness was conditional; one false move and she'd revoke it. She decided what outlets John could and couldn't speak to, in addition to what he could and couldn't say. Anything she hadn't explicitly approved, he had to run by her. And when it came time for his interview, the words he spoke were hers.

After a lengthy apology, where he listed every grievance he had ever committed from "malicious deception" to "cultural exploitation," Tricia asked if he had any last comments. John looked squarely into the camera and said, "While I understand many of my longtime supporters feel the need to defend my actions, I ask that they stop immediately." This was, of course, a not-so-veiled reference to Michael. "Defending me only continues to harm a community that's suffered enough."

And then John went off script.

From her living room sofa, Ingrid looked on in shock as he hoisted himself out of his chair and, just like he had in the motel room, got down on his hands and knees. He hangdogged his head (the camera frantically zoomed out to spotlight the pathetic figure he cut), then clasped his hands together and whispered, "Asian Americans—I'm sorry."

Soon after followed a slew of online essays with catchy titles like "No Pain, No Name: Why My Chinese Name (and Identity) Is Not Up for Grabs," "They Want to Claim Oppression Without Experiencing It,"

"John Smith's Racial Cosplay Is an Insult to My Ancestors," "White People's Insatiable Greed for Everything, Including Our Lives" and Eunice's favorite, "They Either Want to Fuck Us, Kill Us or Be Us."

As Ingrid predicted, John was stripped of his many accolades, titles and honorary degrees. Once one organization started, the others followed suit or else risked tacitly condoning his past transgressions.

John appeared unfazed. Of his own volition, he returned his midcareer one-hundred-thousand-dollar grant back to its foundation with a note stating that the funds should be awarded, this time, to a real Chinese American poet. Since he'd caught the philanthropic bug, Ingrid suggested he establish a new scholarship at Barnes and just like that, he did. Every year, one incoming Asian American student would receive a full ride (with room and board *and* a meal plan).

Against all her assumptions, John had gracefully accepted his public ruination. Forgiveness, Ingrid realized, could lead to transcendence after all.

What neither she nor John predicted was Michael's televised response on the same channel a few days later. Sporting his new signature cowboy hat, he announced, "The DOFO movement does not endorse or acknowledge John Smith's recent statement. We are not associated with him, nor do we plan to be in the future."

"Does that mean you're disavowing Xiao-Wen Chou?" Tricia prompted.

"The movement started by my manifesto, *In Defense of Freedom*, was inspired by the Xiao-Wen Chou allegations. He remains a central example of our core tenet: anyone can be anyone. And as I explain in my latest video, which you can view on my blog, Chou is in fact a superior Chinese American poet compared to a poet with Chinese ancestry."

"How so?"

"Simple—his profound understanding of Chinese culture, despite *not* having Chinese ancestry, makes him far more remarkable. It just goes to show—in America, if you work hard enough, you can accomplish *anything*."

"Why—"

"But I also want to clarify that DOFO is more than Xiao-Wen Chou, much, much more. It's an ideological belief system that's surpassed the figure who inspired it. I encourage anyone who's interested in freedom of speech to stop by one of our events—I guarantee we have something for everyone."

"And would you care to respond to claims you're a quote unquote 'unapologetic racist?'"

"*Racist?*" he hooted. "My wife is Chinese!"

The light left Tricia's eyes. "I see. Well, that wraps up our—"

"I just have a quick announcement," Michael interrupted. His voice shed all professionalism and turned jangly and energetic, like a street hawker's. "Make sure to check out the new DOFO merchandise on our website. We've got bumper stickers, key chains, mugs and beer bottle openers!" He winked and flashed his bleached smile. "I'm Michael Bartholomew and until next time, 'Keep your hands off my freedom!'"

A few hours later, having stayed silent for months after chaos overtook the E. A. department, Barnes issued its first press release:

> *The allegation that Xiao-Wen Chou is a man named John Smith has shaken all of Barnes University. We pride ourselves on our commitment to the progressive ideals of diversity, equity and inclusion. The Chancellor's Advisory Board is conducting a special investigation into the matter. In the meantime, the Xiao-Wen Chou archive will remain open. Summer classes with Chou on the syllabus will continue until further notice. Student failure to comply with readings, assignments and exams on Chou will result in disciplinary action. We appreciate your cooperation as we assess this urgent matter.*

The press release proved Dean Bartholomew still had use for "Xiao-Wen Chou" as long as he could milk him for tuition and funding. But he no longer had any use for John Smith. The very person—well, the person behind a name—who he had researched, taught and lauded for so many years had been ditched on the side of the road the moment he no longer served his needs. Michael's only allegiance was to himself.

Then a new batch of online essays arrived, with titles like "The Witch Hunt Against John Smith Must End," "When Did the Outraged Left Become Judge, Jury and Executioner?" "Identity Politics Will Be the Death of America," "Will No One Think of the White Man? Compassion, Mental Illness and Healthcare Access" and "John Smith Is All of Us."

Her plan to stop DOFO had skittered to a miserable stop. Ingrid blamed her naiveté—of course *she* wasn't the person who could take Michael down. Only one person could.

Vivian had upped protesting to a level never before seen on campus. An online fundraiser was set up. Walkouts and die-ins staged in the middle of exams. Barricading and overnight squatting of the Registrar's Office (Vivian's rallying cry was "No justice, no transcripts!"). Local celebrity support was brought in. Slam poetry was slammed. Once, a trapeze was utilized to astonishing effect.

But Vivian's campaign to label and expel DOFO as a hate group had been met with lukewarm support at best, chilly apathy at worst. No one was listening anymore. No one *wanted* to listen anymore. Those personally unaffected were eager to return to eating their cereal without also chewing over racial injustice at eight a.m. People only cared until—well, they stopped caring.

Even members of the POC Caucus—citing finals, senior theses and summer internships, not to mention emotional burnout—showed up less and less. By all accounts—truly, the world had been flipped on its head—Vivian had lost and Michael had won.

Ingrid's fragile state of optimism was punctured, a poor deflating balloon. What else could she do? She had (unwittingly) ferreted out the truth. Created a tell-all website and sent its address to *The Barnes Gazette*. Supported Vivian's decision to pose as the website's author. She had hunted down the man at the center of it all and convinced him to slap a colossal I'M A BAD PERSON sticker on his forehead—metaphorically, anyway.

Instead she had birthed a monster: DOFO, helmed by Emperor Bartholomew. All her attempts at decapitating the six-headed thing only strengthened it. Now the monster had eclipsed Xiao-Wen Chou, John Smith, Barnes University, even Wittlebury. Its tentacles were reproducing and spreading . . .

"The fight's not over yet," John reassured her on the phone.

Ingrid tried to let his words bolster her, but in her lowest moments, she suspected the rise of DOFO was her fault and hers alone. If only she'd seen the smiley face in the archive and thought nothing more of it, how different things would be now. Michael would be safely ensconced within the four walls of the E. A. department, his visions for power extending only to his literary egg tart salons. Ingrid would be receiving her doctorate and applying for the Xiao-Wen Chou postdoc fellowship. She and Stephen would be in the blissful throes of wedding planning.

This was her punishment for questioning the world as it was, instead of swallowing it blind like an obedient child taking her medicine.

THE LIVING ROOM SOFA was littered with unfolded laundry, pillows, half-empty bags of chips and torn-open boxes of cookies. At two in the afternoon, the apartment was quiet. No sign of life disturbed the sofa's landfill surface. When Ingrid's ringing phone lurched her awake, the scene called to mind the start of a zombie movie: a single arm thrusting into the air, groping around wildly. She answered the video call with a groggy, "What?" She hadn't washed her hair in five nights and it clung to her scalp in oily, slick strips, along with a few errant cheese puffs. Long gone were the days when she showered, curled her hair and consecrated forty-five minutes to her makeup before a scheduled chat with Stephen. The outfit from several weeks ago—the frilly, high-collared, bow-necked atrocity—was now living at the bottom of her recycling bin. Today she wore an oversized Snoopy T-shirt with a tear in one side and a taco sauce stain on the other.

"Hello, dear," Stephen said. "Did you sleep on the sofa?"

"Huh?" she looked around, yawning. "Oh, I guess I did."

He peered closer at his screen. "Have you been eating cheese puffs? You know they make you gain weight."

Out of habit, Ingrid started to say, "thank you," to his usual well-intentioned reminder about her health. Instead, she ate an enormous handful, locking eyes with him as she chomped away, pieces tumbling out of the corners of her mouth.

Concern rippled across his placid face. "Is everything okay?"

Ever since the Three Asian Ex-Girlfriends Incident, he'd been attempting this question with mounting worry in his voice. Even after Ingrid could no longer avoid him, their conversations were cut short; she always had somewhere to be, something to do. He had to know everything was very much *not* okay, despite her insistence to the contrary.

"Yes," she sighed. "I'm just stressed about the dissertation."

"Right. It's always the dissertation when I ask what's going on with you. Your mysterious dissertation. The never-ending dissertation." He didn't bother to hide his annoyance.

"Actually, I'm getting close to finishing it." Stephen raised his eyebrows. "Anyway, you'll see soon enough at my defense."

He nodded. "I'm looking forward to seeing what you've been so busy doing this year."

Ingrid arranged her lips into a smile. She wanted to demand, "Are there more than three? Will my images be slotted into the Taxes folder one day?" Instead she said with faux cheer, "I'm looking forward to it, too."

"Well, besides the dissertation, is anything else new?"

She chugged from a room-temperature can of root beer and let loose a baritone burp. "John Smith went on TV and denounced his actions. But, get this, Michael denounced *him*. His white nationalist propaganda tour is more popular than ever. They have . . . beer bottle openers for sale! And now that he's dean, he can spread his gospel at Barnes. It'll become the new DOFO headquarters." She sank dejectedly into the pile of snacks.

"White nationalist propaganda?" he repeated skeptically.

"What?"

"Nothing."

"Stephen, *what.*"

"You say that so easily."

"So?"

"So I just thought that little . . . political outburst of yours the other week was . . . a temporary phase you were going through. But now, am I to understand, your longtime trusted advisor is a supposed 'white nationalist'?"

"Yes."

"Could you define the term for me?"

"Well—um, not off the top of—"

"Or tell me how a white nationalist is different from a neo-Nazi or a skinhead or a KKK member—"

Ingrid said nothing. She felt like she'd been caught unaware on the day of a pop quiz.

"—think you should be very careful making such a serious accusation. After all, our country's legal system is predicated on assumed innocence until guilt is proven—"

She stopped listening. So maybe she didn't know the differences between all those variations on the same hate group—but she could learn! Was it fair of Stephen to trip her up, just so he could make a point? She had no energy to launch into another argument with him; they were always "theoretical" for him, "emotional" for her. The time she'd attended his family reunion in Connecticut, a contentious debate over immigration broke out at the dinner table yet everyone spoke in upbeat voices as though they were chatting about the weather. She had sat through it, trying to look unbothered, trying to be likable, even as the spaghetti casserole in her stomach churned. He hadn't considered the toll the debate had taken on her then, either.

"How's Azumi?" she asked when he stopped for breath. "Tell her I said hi."

"She's fine."

"What has she been up to?"

"I don't know, you'd have to ask her yourself." He paused. "Ingrid, why do you always ask about Azumi?"

She shrugged and examined her artificial-cheese-dust-encrusted nails.

"Are you . . . jealous?" A tender, teasing look came over him. "I'm flattered."

"I'm not *jealous*. She dresses like a ten-year-old. Why would I be jealous of a child? That's gross."

Stephen chuckled. "Rest assured, dear, I have no interest in Azumi. I regard her as a worthy writer, certainly, and we have a strong professional working relationship, but she's simply not my type."

Not his type? Ingrid burst into a belly-deep laugh, then converted it into a hacking cough. When she recovered, she asked, "Does *she* understand that? She's always hanging around your hotel room, isn't she?"

Azumi, Azumi, Azumi. Lately she'd encroached into Ingrid's nightmares: she'd turn a corner and there she was, tittering and squeaking in an orgy of lace and bows. Even in her waking hours, she unwillingly pictured her and Stephen entwined in bed: Azumi mewling and writhing beneath him as he performed his steady up-down-up-down percussion on top of her.

"Please, Ingrid, we go to the hotel conference room together so we can work on our Q and A preparations. She's also proving extremely invaluable to the new book project."

"I'm sure she is."

"I don't think you realize what we're doing is *work* and it's tiring and—"

"That's funny, because I saw on her social media page you visited the giant yarn ball in Kansas together."

"You know Azumi is intensely interested in getting the full American experience."

"How could I forget," she said flatly. "So will I be seeing her next week?"

"No. She's flying back to Tokyo."

"What a shame." She hesitated. "By the way, you still haven't sent me your flight info."

"You're coming to the airport?"

"Why wouldn't I?" They had always picked each other up whenever one traveled without the other.

"Because you haven't been yourself. I don't know what to expect from you anymore. To be perfectly honest, dear, it's quite worrying. I was recently reading an article about mental breakdowns—"

For a brief moment, the sight of Stephen's pale face and wire-rimmed eyeglasses filled her with disdain. She had the urge to slap him.

"—I'll forward them to you—"

She blinked; the urge had disintegrated into shame. The experience was so disorienting, she lied about a medical emergency—explosive diarrhea, when he demanded clarification—and quickly ended the call.

She walked into their bedroom. Stephen's clothes were arranged on the left side of the closet. His shoes were lined up on the left side of the door. His specially lubricated tissues for sensitive skin were stationed on the left nightstand. Then she allowed herself to visualize all his belongings disappearing one by one, sucked into an invisible vortex. With the same temerity as a nun entertaining blasphemous thoughts for the first time, she wondered what shape her life would take without Stephen filling it. What kind of person would she be if he, too, vanished?

Her mind glitched, unable to process the concept. Ingrid and Stephen; Stephen and Ingrid. Like a mathematical proof, one could not exist without the other.

To imagine living without him would mean unsealing the trapdoor to a bottomless basement where she'd tossed the Film Studies Major, Engineering Grad Student, Investment Banker and Medical Resident. Where those pesky feelings of being unwanted, alone and abandoned had been tucked very, very far down.

She glanced at Stephen's socks, still neatly folded from a wild night of color-coordinating their undergarments. Above them hung a striped shirt and navy pants—Stephen's half of a matching couples outfit. Hers consisted of the same shirt in a smaller size, paired with a calf-length navy skirt. Holding it up, her eye snagged on a note pinned to the skirt's tag: "Hand-wash with half detergent, half fabric softener. And remember to take your vitamin D."

Ingrid shut the closet door, laughing a little. What had she been thinking? Of course she couldn't live without Stephen.

MICHAEL'S NEW HOUSE WAS so extravagant as to be deliberately rude to all the neighboring houses. The facade was constructed of stones in muted grays, purples and blues, with roses and vines choking the sides. On the corner was a three-story turret and on the curving front lawn, a Roman-style fountain featuring a drowned, but upon closer inspection, still-drowning, mermaid.

"I didn't know professors *or* deans made enough money to live in this kind of house," Eunice remarked in awe.

"I have a feeling Michael is the only one at Barnes who can," Ingrid said. His DOFO sponsorships and sales must have been skyrocketing.

They stopped in front of the imposing door, embellished with a brass knocker in the shape of a harpoon, which seemed insensitive given the mermaid situation a few yards away.

"Well, let's just hope we make it out alive," Ingrid said. She pulled the knocker three times and braced herself. But instead of Michael, his ex-wife greeted them.

"Cixi?" they gasped.

Gone was her Cultural Revolution cotton-padded jacket. The Cixi before them had stepped out of a 1950s suburban housewives catalogue, complete with a floral cupcake dress, sheer stockings and kitten heels. Her lips were frosted pink; her eyelids, baby blue. Her black bun had mutated into a tightly curled, platinum blond helmet.

"Hello, girls!" she said with a beatific smile.

What had Michael done to her? The Cixi they knew did not smile, much less inflect her voice. She waved them into the foyer, where she offered to take their purses.

"It's—it's fine, Cixi," Ingrid sputtered.

"I go by Cindy now. But please, call me Mrs. Bartholomew. This way!" she trilled, sashaying farther into the house, heels click-clacking against the polished wood.

They fell back from her.

"I thought you said they were getting a divorce," Eunice whispered.

"Hypnosis?" Ingrid suggested.

"Lobotomy?" Eunice countered.

Cixi led them to the massive living room, where guests were spread throughout, standing up and nibbling on hors d'oeuvres, sitting down and sipping from cocktails. Inoffensive jazz looped in the background.

Cixi asked what they'd like to drink.

"Whiskey, straight," Ingrid said. She suspected punishingly strong alcohol was needed tonight.

Eunice raised her eyebrows. "Same."

Cixi sashayed away again, reappearing a moment later with their drinks. "Enjoy the party, girls. I'm *so* glad you could come," she cooed, then sailed off to attend to new arrivals.

Ingrid was about to restart the hypnosis versus lobotomy debate when Eunice announced, "Oh, there's my old undergrad advisor—hi, Professor Baek!" After she scampered away, Ingrid installed herself in a discreet nook beside a grandfather clock. She had always imagined Michael's house as a grander version of his office, with silk screens and bonsai trees accenting every room. She wouldn't have been surprised, in fact, if he had uprooted an authentic plot of Chinese land from across the Pacific into his house.

But, with its paintings of romping wild horses and eight-foot-tall stuffed grizzly bear, the house looked awfully . . . white.

The other John Smith, purveyor of *Yellow Peril 2.0*, had taught Michael well. His former beloved area of expertise was now associated with card-carrying, red-wearing, capital-C Communists, staunch upholders of censorship, the natural enemy of American freedom. How easily the Chinese vacillated between ally and enemy every hundred years depending on who America was mad at or what America wanted. When needed, they could stand in as white, or at least, white enough to slaughter other Asian men and women in America's wars, but with the snap of a finger, they were yellow again—the color of a disease, the color of a warning. Indistinguishable from the yellow men and women they'd slaughtered. Any temporary acceptance into whiteness revoked as quickly as it'd been granted.

Because that was the thing: they were never white to begin with.

Looking around, it was clear Michael had capitulated to his DOFO supporters' tastes—they preferred golf over Go, hot dogs over lap cheong, cowboy boots over silk slippers. No wonder he'd performed an aesthetic makeover to parallel his ideological makeover, Cixi included among his possessions. But how long before accusations of "fraternizing with the enemy" returned to plague Michael's choice of spouse? Was he trying to reverse-Xiao-Wen-Chou his wife? Did he believe if she put her mind to it and spritzed on enough peroxide, she would turn as white as him?

"Ah, Ingrid, there you are."

She jerked forward, sloshing whiskey on her dress. Michael was forever creeping up on her when she least expected it. He was like a malignant mist.

"Thanks for . . . the invitation," she said slowly. "Your house is very . . . spacious."

"Oh, this old thing?" he laughed.

She took a burning gulp of whiskey. The man was insufferable. "You know, Michael, I mean, *Dean Bartholomew*, I couldn't help but notice you seem . . . different. And Cixi, she seems different, too. I remember you saying she had left you for a Chinese man—"

"*Cindy* finally came to her senses," he said, in a voice that drew a hard line around the topic.

"Is that s-so?" she slurred. The alcohol had shot an arrow straight to her head.

"That little stain of a man will not be bothering my wife and I any longer. He's gone back to China," he sighed happily.

"Isn't that convenient." She scrutinized him. "You always seem to get what you want, don't you—*Dean Bartholomew.*"

"You'd do well to remember that, Ingrid." Michael's threatening words jarred with his dulcet tones. "I actually came over because I want to introduce you to someone." Hand against her lower back, he steered her towards a congregation of students. Leaning against the fireplace was a tall, bow-tie-clad student.

"Ingrid Yang, this is Timothy Liu. He's the president of YAACC and the new DOFO assistant director. Timothy, Ingrid is a newly joined DOFO member. I'm sure you two will have plenty to talk about!" With that, Michael excused himself.

She stared blankly at Timothy before she remembered where they'd crossed paths before: he had commandeered Vivian's loudspeaker during the *Chinatown Blues* protests!

"Please, join us, Ingrid," he said.

She perched unsteadily on the end of a sofa.

"Go on with what you were saying," a redheaded girl urged. Ingrid realized that besides her and Timothy, the other students were all white. They were dressed in a homogenous assortment of pastels, cardigans and bow ties. Her eyes hunted around for Eunice—why had she left her alone with these people? They looked like they'd escaped a haunted amusement park.

"Right, well, as I was saying," Timothy continued, "my father came to this country for his PhD in physics. He could barely speak English and had twenty dollars to his name. So how did he do it, you ask? Because he got a perfect score on the GRE's math section. Because he received a full scholarship. *That* is how my parents succeeded—by pulling themselves up by the bootstraps. America didn't care they were Asian. They cared about their grades and test scores. Because America is a *meritocracy*!" As people nodded and mm-hmmed in appreciation, Timothy paused for dramatic effect. "Now this is difficult to talk about, but my younger sister was denied entry to Barnes this year." Several students shook their heads, aghast. "My sister had a 4.2 GPA. She took eight AP courses. She received an SAT score of 1600. But that's not all. She volunteered with the community service club for four years. She played ice hockey for three and the saxophone for six. She speaks fluent English, Mandarin and Dutch. She distributed measles vaccines in Bombo, Uganda. So tell me why she wasn't accepted into Barnes?"

"Discrimination!" someone spat.

"Tell me why *some* newly admitted students at Barnes only have a 4.0 GPA, with a low SAT score of 1590?"

"Affirmative action!" someone else snarled.

Timothy nodded triumphantly. "So you see, if African Americans and Latinos want to succeed, they just have to look down at their boots, find the straps and *pull them up*. My parents did it, so why can't they?" The others crowed in approval. "And if they want to get into Barnes, they have to do it like the rest of us: with their grades and test scores. *Not* with their race."

The other students finished applauding as Ingrid's jaw unhinged.

"For sure, dude," a square-shaped man spoke up; even his hands were meaty squares. "I've always known what you're saying, right? But, like, I couldn't say it out loud—I mean, not without someone calling me 'racist.'" He wiggled his fingers in the air to signify quotation marks. "But, like, now I can say my Chinese friend—I can call you my friend, right?—"

Timothy winked at him. Ingrid frowned. Wasn't his family from Taiwan?

"—that my Chinese friend thinks what *I* think. It's fucking awesome!"

"Well, that's the wonderful thing about America. You see, I don't have to *agree* with a vandalizer inaccurately calling me 'gook' in the dust on my car windshield, but I can still respect the vandalizer's *right* to free speech."

"That's what *I've* been saying for years!"

"You're the man, Tim! You're the fucking man!"

He soaked in the applause, then carefully adjusted his bow tie. "This is what DOFO's all about: the freedom to openly debate our ideas without being shamed for them." He pulled out his phone. "Which reminds me of DOFO's newest initiative: the Sanctuary—"

The bow-tie-necked students all crowded around him, oohing and aahing.

"I have to go to the bathroom," Ingrid mumbled, though no one was listening. She was disgusted, incensed, outraged—and yet, she hadn't said a word. For all they knew, because she'd stayed silent, she agreed with them. Granted, she had to keep up DOFO member appearances, but surely she'd crossed an invisible moral line. What was wrong with her? Did this mean she hadn't changed at all? A year ago, would she have been enthusiastically nodding along with Timothy? Oh God—would she have been Michael's right hand? The thought made her positively ill. And yet . . . what was she talking about? She *had* acted as white people's right hand on so many occasions—laughing at their jokes, making the kinds of jokes they laughed at, staying silent when they cut racist remarks about other minorities in her presence, letting herself be patted on the head for being the *right* kind of minority, then *becoming* the minority they expected of her. She had been complacent. She had been complicit. Perhaps she still was. Perhaps, and this was harder to admit, no matter how much she changed, she always would be in some ways—simply by virtue of what she lived through and what would forever remain a secondhand story to her.

Ingrid looked back at Timothy, surrounded by what weren't adoring fans but supervisors making sure he stayed in line, and scoffed. No safety could be found in hedging their bets with white people, in believing they could be protected by them, as if their approval emitted some kind of special failure-retardant coating. Because while the light-skinned and affluent among her lot weren't turned down for loans and followed in stores and unable to walk through a white neighborhood without having the cops called on them, they didn't have power. Of course they didn't. They were mocked, trivialized, dehumanized. So self-effacing, they were simply effaced. They were given the illusion of power for being "allowed" to work in the same companies and live in the same gated communities. But if they were to rally together with fellow minorities instead of letting themselves be pitted against each other, distracted from a common enemy—oh no. If they were to surpass white people—oh, no no no no. *That* was Yellow Peril 2.0—or any peril of any color. The fear that, if given the chance, they would wrest power away from white people for themselves, relegating them to an inferior rank for the first time in history.

"Excuse me," said a snippy voice.

Ingrid realized she was standing stock-still in the middle of a hallway. She turned the corner and squeezed past gaggles of drunk students, hunting for the bathroom before discovering it was in use. The idea of forcing small talk with the people waiting in line—still more DOFO members—was unbearable. She extricated herself and headed upstairs, passing a lurid row of mounted skulls and antlers.

"There you are!" Eunice cried.

"*I've* been looking for *you*."

"Come on, I have to show you something." She walked purposefully down the hallway.

"Yoon, it's even worse than I thought," Ingrid moaned. "Michael's recruited Timothy Liu as his new henchman. He's Taiwanese, I mean Chinese—well, anyway, he's saying all this problematic stuff and everyone is thrilled because now they can say it, too—"

"Oh, he's a racism shield. Just like Cixi."

She stopped in midwalk. "A what?"

Eunice's eyes focused on the distance, as if she were about to recite a poem for show-and-tell. "It's when white people prop up a person of color who says racist things to deflect claims they themselves are racist when they say the exact same thing. Or in Cixi's case, when white men claim they can't be racist because they've had sex with, dated or married a woman of color."

"Where'd you learn that?" she asked incredulously.

Eunice smoothed her hair behind her ears. "Well, I didn't forget what you said about Vivian. I read some of her articles."

"Really?"

"Okay, I lied. I read all of them."

"Oh! What did—what did you think?"

She scrunched up her nose. "I was confused most of the time. But . . . I guess it made me see Vivian in a different way. She seems to really care about all that . . . political stuff," she shrugged.

At that, Ingrid remembered Timothy's speech.

"We have to stop Michael. We have to stop DOFO! He's roping in Asian students to back him up—even though DOFO's turning into this anti-Chinese, white nationalist haven—I don't even know anymore—"

Eunice stopped in front of a door and planted both her hands on Ingrid's shoulders. "Deep breaths. In . . . and . . . out. In . . . and . . . out. Good. Listen, I know how to take Michael down." She slipped through the door.

"How did you get in?" Ingrid asked.

Eunice brandished a bobby pin and winked.

The room was dusky, lit only by the moonlight shining through the windows.

"Is there a light switch?"

"Don't be silly, no one can find out we're in here."

They were inside a cavernous room, one side stacked with filing cabinets and cardboard boxes, the other side with furniture: Ming-style vases, tea tables, bamboo chairs.

"So this is where Michael stored all his 'chinoiserie,'" Ingrid whispered. "I knew it had to be around here somewhere." She poked at a porcelain figurine of a Chinese girl twirling a parasol, her eyes vacant, and shuddered.

"Come over here." Eunice was stationed by the filing cabinets. "Look at all this! There has to be *something* we can use against Michael."

Ingrid surveyed the long row. "I guess so."

Eunice nodded excitedly. "White men like him have all tried to get around the rules at least once, right? We just have to figure out Michael's secret." She jerked open a drawer and riffled through it, then glanced impatiently at her, "What are you waiting for? We have at least a couple hours before the party ends."

"Right now?" Ingrid hedged. She had snooped around in someone's house before and look what good it had done. "I don't know if I'm up for this kind of thing again . . ."

"You just said we have to stop Michael!"

"But what am I supposed to look for?"

"I don't know, tax evasion, offshore bank accounts, illegitimate children—"

The overhead light flicked on, rendering the room unbearably bright. Ingrid and Eunice stiffened like figurines, as if hoping to pass for Michael's collection.

"Can I help you girls?"

"We were . . . looking for the bathroom?" Ingrid tried.

Cixi flashed a pleasant smile. "Oh, I see. Well, please let me direct you to it. And when you're finished, do come down for dessert. I made lime-flavored cottage cheese with maraschino cherries and Vienna sausages!"

Eunice rushed up to her. "What did he do to you? Why are you acting like a blow-up doll that's come to life? Hello, Cixi, are you in there? Blink twice if you can hear me!"

For several moments, Cixi's smile remained stitched in place. Then it fell, replaced by her usual blasé expression. "Don't be so melodramatic, Eunice, it's not attractive on you."

Their mouths sagged open.

Cixi shut the door, flicked off the light and sat down on a flat jade jar.

"Are you okay? Did Michael kidnap you?" Ingrid asked. "We can— we can save you!"

She turned to her. "It's not attractive on you, either."

"Just tell us what we can do," Eunice urged, trying to sound less frantic.

Cixi kicked off her kitten heels and rotated her neck a few times.

"What you can do? Bring me a jar of chili oil. Oh, and some hoisin sauce, too. I'm sick of flavorless chicken breast and steamed vegetables."

"Got it," Ingrid said quickly. "Anything else?"

"Forged documents stating I was born in the US."

"Jesus, Mary and Joseph!" Eunice gasped, all attempts at taking it down a notch gone.

Cixi looked sharply at her, then continued, "Michael had Hsing-Kuo deported."

"Your—your Chinese lover?" Ingrid asked.

She nodded. "He can have me deported, too."

"But aren't you married?"

"Yes. But I came to the US on a K-1 visa." She noted the girls' perplexed faces and clarified, "A fiancée visa. We had known each other only for a few months. Michael can tell immigration our marriage is not a real one. That it was a—what do people call it—a green card marriage."

"So he *is* taking you hostage!"

Cixi tapped her nails against the sides of the jade jar. "I am choosing not to go back to China."

"Why?" Eunice asked.

"Yeah, what about your lover?" Ingrid pressed. "You could be together—"

Cixi's nostrils flared. "I do not have to justify anything to you two spoiled Asian *American* girls. It's not so simple. You don't know what—" She paused to dab at her eyes. "I have things I need to do here. If I go back, it will be my choice."

They exchanged remorseful glances.

"I'm sorry. You're right," Eunice said. "If there's anything else we can do—"

"Don't hesitate to ask," Ingrid finished. "Especially if Michael tries to make you do anything you don't want to." If he was forcing himself on Cixi—she couldn't bear to follow where the thought led.

Cixi smiled ruefully. "My husband is a man who does not like being wronged. He wanted me to come back not because he loves me but because I disobeyed him." She stood up. "If I need your help, I'll ask for it. But . . . *you* can ask me for help, too."

Ingrid and Eunice exchanged puzzled looks.

Cixi gestured at the filing cabinets. "I have keys to all the rooms in this house."

17

Total Immersion

BE CAREFUL
DON'T DO ANYTHING YOU MIGHT REGRET
I'M WATCHING YOU

The individual letters mimicked the classic layout of a ransom note: eclectically multicolored, snipped from the pages of magazines and pasted onto a blank sheet of white paper. Like the ones before it, the note was enclosed in a manila envelope missing both a return address and a postage stamp. Someone had slipped it directly into her mailbox. Through her kitchen blinds, Ingrid peered uneasily around the apartment complex. She felt plunged into a frozen lake, her entire spine numbed to ice.

When the first note arrived, she'd written it off as a harmless prank. A roaming pack of youths in her neighborhood were notorious for ding-dong ditching, stealing pacifiers from babies, drop-kicking jack-o'-lanterns and the like. When the second note arrived, she made a point of calling out, "Ha ha, *very* funny!" though she sounded unconvinced, not nearly as contemptuous as she'd hoped.

But the third note confirmed its author was not playing around.

"I'm watching you."

Who was "I"?

The number of potential culprits made it tricky to narrow down a single perpetrator: Timothy—who, beneath his gummy smile, seemed skeptical of her commitment to DOFO. Vivian—who, most recently, had flipped her off. Even John Smith—who, despite assurances he'd *wanted* to publicly grovel on his hands and knees, could resent her for it. After all, people kept turning out to be who they weren't.

Stephen walked into the kitchen, yawning and scratching his side. "You're already up?"

"I couldn't sleep. Jet lag?" she asked.

He nodded.

"Would you like some coffee?" She spoke stiffly and formally without being able to stop.

"Thank you, dear."

Stephen moved to hug Ingrid from behind when she stood up, pushing her chair into him.

"Sorry," she mumbled.

He came around to kiss her on the cheek and she swiveled in the opposite direction.

"Is everything all right—"

"Sugar? Cream?"

"No."

"Are you hungry? I got bagels—"

"Ingrid, what's going on?"

She set down the cup of coffee and pointed at the table. "I've been getting these—these notes. This one came today."

Stephen stared at it for an unnecessarily long time.

"I don't understand," he finally said. "Ingrid, I know you need attention after I've been away these past few months. Buying all that new makeup and clothing. Pretending to have the cold and then the flu. But this kind of manipulative behavior is very troubling."

A flicker of anger kindled in her before it died out. "No, Stephen, I am not doing this for 'attention.' Someone's been sending me these in unmarked envelopes."

He raised an eyebrow. "All right, suppose this is true—why would someone send *you* these notes? It's not like you've done anything wrong." The idea was comical to him; he thought her capable of so little.

"Perhaps this will come as a shock to you, Stephen *dear*, but women are threatened *all the time*. For things like not smiling when we're told to smile. How wonderful you don't know what that's like."

His dubious expression soured. He was unused to sarcasm from Ingrid, having once remarked it was a side effect of toxic masculinity and therefore didn't suit the gentler sex. "Well, what are you waiting for? If someone is threatening you, we have to go to the authorities."

She pressed down on her lips to keep from laughing. "You want us to go to the police precinct, wait for hours and fill out a report so they can tell us there's nothing they can do? Or maybe you'd like an officer to tell me I was 'asking for it.'"

"How could you possibly know that? Have you already gone to the police?" Stephen frowned. "I want to believe you, Ingrid, I do, but something about this feels off—"

"Forget it," she said coolly. "I'll take care of it myself. I've had to do that for months while you've been admiring giant balls of yarn with *Azumi*." She marched into the bedroom and slammed the door.

She needed space, not only from Stephen but in order to process the notes. They'd shaken her more than she would've liked to admit. And yet . . . she was almost grateful the notes had arrived just before his return. What else would they have talked about?

When she picked him up from the airport the night before, a tepid hug had been the extent of her affection. She was grateful, too, for his late flight—they'd quickly gone to bed, sex the furthest thing from anyone's mind. The idea of him touching her made Ingrid want to unzip her own skin. She'd lain in bed with the awful sensation that the person sleeping beside her was not Stephen, but a foreign and inanimate object passing itself off as her fiancé. Like a crash test dummy or a CPR manikin.

THE NEXT DAY, Stephen proposed an excursion to the Dampwood county fair, an hour outside Wittlebury.

"I understand it hasn't been easy, knowing that Azumi and—that I've been sightseeing around the country without you. This will be nice, just the two of us. What do you think, dear?"

Ingrid suspected he felt guilty for having accused her of inventing an elaborate conspiracy (in cahoots with USPS no less) for "attention." All yesterday, he'd treaded carefully in her wake, leaving little snacks and cups of water by the bedroom, where she remained stubbornly sequestered. He had slept on the sofa.

She thought of saying no, first and foremost because she doubted he'd atoned enough, and secondly, because she had plans to meet Eunice later. Even with Cixi on lookout, they'd only managed to upturn a single filing cabinet, and the only illicit activity they'd unearthed was an underground mahjong ring Michael had operated in the nineties—something, but not enough of a something to take him down.

"I don't know . . . I have a lot to do for the dissertation defense," Ingrid waffled.

Stephen's face crumpled. When sad, his thin lips disappeared into a trembling line and his eyes bulged behind his glasses. He looked quite pitiful, like a wet cat. She felt a twinge of remorse. Perhaps her investigation could wait. What had Eunice said? "He loves you and you love him. That's all that matters."

She trotted out her warmest smile. "Actually, I think I have time."

Relief washed over his features.

This cagey behavior around her own fiancé had to stop. She couldn't very well marry someone she felt repelled by, could she? And what had Hae-Young and Jung-Suk in *My Once and Forever Springtime Love* taught her? What had *Eunice* taught her? People deserved second chances.

She was about to head out in what she had on (gym shorts and her Snoopy T-shirt) but made an effort with her appearance at the last minute. She brushed her hair and patted on some makeup (nothing based on an online tutorial), then tried on several sundresses before settling on a checkered black-and-white one. She looked in the mirror and resolutely set her jaw: today was the day she'd snap out of her anti-Stephen funk. Like a self-cleaning oven, she would restore their relationship to factory settings. To normalcy.

On the drive over, he asked if she remembered the time they'd passed a strawberry farm, pulled over and abandoned their plans in favor of picking strawberries instead. The sweet memory resurfaced in vivid patches: the skimpy dirt road, the ache in her back as she squatted low to the ground, how Stephen's lips had tasted like pesticide-flavored strawberries.

She tentatively twined her hand in his. The solution to her conjugal troubles was simple: page through more of these snapshots in the album of their relationship until they erased all impressions of the Taxes folder.

With the morning sun streaming in from the east, Stephen's muddy hair glinted gold at the edges and, having tanned from his travels, he appeared less anemic than usual. Ingrid's heart swelled cartoon-wolf style. This was the man she was going to marry.

"Thank you."

"For what?" he asked congenially.

For choosing me. "Nothing," she smiled.

THE AIR WAS thick with barbecue smoke, artificial sweeteners and the trademark odor of petting zoos. Ingrid leisurely browsed the concession stands, mulling over what to indulge in first: bacon-wrapped turkey legs or deep-fried s'mores or funnel cake bathed in Coke. Her junk food proclivities were given free rein at county fairs, nothing nutritionally balanced within miles.

Besides enough food to end a famine, the fair featured an amusement park erected with all the usual rides: Ferris wheel, carousel, bumper cars. Another section was reserved for fair games: ring toss, water coin drop, balloon darts. At the far end of the grounds stood a stage where local musicians performed as couples square-danced or swayed to the Electric Slide.

Ingrid and Stephen watched a pig race, thrilled their pig, Porky Pine, stole first place from Sir Ham-A-Lot. They ingested three times the recommended amount of daily calories. They screamed alongside teenagers in the Tilt-A-Whirl. Stephen took a crack at a water gun race as she cheered him on. Ingrid petted rabbits, pygmy goats and llamas as he monitored her. Behind a life-size wooden cutout, they transformed: he into a giant ear of corn, she into a giant stick of butter. In the ten-dollar memorabilia photo, their smiles are goofy with bliss.

"Let's go on the Ferris wheel," Ingrid announced. She was having "fun"—a foreign sensation. For the past year, she'd been wilting inside a sunless basement, haunting the stale halls of Barnes, lying on her office carpet locked in a staring contest with the ceiling light, all while trying to resist the allure of psychedelic allergy pills. She still kept an emergency one in her purse. No, she and "fun" had become strangers.

Stephen nestled his arm around her. As the Ferris wheel rose into the sky, her head sheltered against his bony shoulder, Ingrid's heart quaked with joy. This was happiness. Yes, of course—how had she forgotten? Once she passed her defense, she could unshackle herself from Chou, John and Michael for good. She could cultivate a life outside the university's orbit—the novelty of the concept downright tickled her. She had never pursued hobbies during the PhD (she'd always wanted to try wood chainsaw carving) and she hadn't visited her parents nearly as much as she should have. And maybe she *had* been neglecting her relationship. Stephen was always accommodating *her* schedule, dropping by for *her* lunch breaks, worrying about *her* chronic lower back pain. She had never considered the trials of being engaged to someone already married to her research . . .

When the Ferris wheel lurched to a stop, the sky a brilliant blue above them, she knew: now was the moment. They kissed.

"I love you, dear," Stephen said.

"I love you, too."

How easily it tripped off the tongue! To think she had entertained thoughts of leaving him. Stephen was right—she must have been experiencing psychosis. Everyone said they were a perfect match—the dating website's foolproof algorithm included! How could she have doubted it? Their future unfurled cleanly before her eyes: Mr. and Mrs. Ingrid and Stephen Greene to be, standing at the altar, tearfully reading their handwritten vows beneath a canopy of twinkle lights—no, moss—no, twinkle lights *in* moss! The second they got home, she'd begin the cutthroat (but fun!) task of securing a wedding venue. She and Eunice would pore over bridal catalogues until their vocabulary consisted exclusively of exotic words like taffeta, organza, tulle. She'd schedule a cake tasting of her and Stephen's favorite flavors (subtle matcha and yuzu, of course); she'd even ask her parents to come along. The thought of devoting herself to a purpose besides the *dissertation* made her laugh aloud from sheer relief. Stephen grinned, looking as ecstatic as she felt. The Ferris wheel began its slow, jerky descent.

"When we get home, let's . . ." Ingrid paused. What was that homogenous mass down below? She squinted and leaned forward, sipping generously from her fresh-squeezed lemonade.

"When we get home?" Stephen prompted.

Her heart knocked loudly against her rib cage as sweat pearled on the nape of her neck. The mass of figures was arranging itself into identifiable parts: White sweater-vests. Plaid skirts. Knee-high stockings. Mary Jane shoes. Headbands. Pale skin. Pink lips. Black hair.

They were Japanese high school girls.

Ingrid spit out the lemonade, spraying it across her and Stephen's legs.

"Are you okay, dear?"

What the fuck were they doing here? she seethed. Am I hallucinating again? The second the Ferris wheel ground to a halt, she unbuckled herself and stormed down the platform to the gate. She overheard the girls' chatter—Japanese as suspected.

Her throat was dry, her underarms damp.

"Huh," Stephen remarked, looking amiably in the girls' direction. "They must be on a school trip. A lot of ESL programs teach 'total immersion' now, an interesting approach, though not without its difficulties. I should ask what school they're with—"

Ingrid sank her nails into his arm. "No!"

He looked curiously at her. "Why not?"

"Speaking to them in Japanese will—will ruin their total immersion!"

"I was planning to ask in English. You know I can't speak Japanese, dear—"

"I'm hungry!" she nearly shouted in his ear. She towed him away from the horde of Japanese girls, back to the concession stands.

"Really? We just ate"—he checked his watch—"half an hour ago. You know you get gas when you eat multiple times within the hour."

"But I really want to try"—her eyes fell on the nearest ten-foot sign—"deep-fried ice cream!"

He smiled. "Well, I suppose we could indulge just this once."

They stood before the massive board of flavors, Stephen gaily debating between chocolate and vanilla, Ingrid straining to reply in coherent, human sentences. Her heart hadn't stopped hyperventilating, her entire body had broken out in a cold sweat—

"Oh God," she moaned.

"We don't have to get butterscotch," he chuckled.

"Get whatever you want," she hissed. Two Japanese schoolgirls had popped up a few feet from them. This was a nightmare. She glanced across the pathway: another two.

"Although, the mint chocolate chip does sound refreshing—"

Ingrid glared at the nearest girl. She looked like Azumi—or was she conflating all Japanese girls together? Attributing all the same features and characteristics to them? Surely that was racist. Surely they were all individuals with distinct histories, personalities, fears, dreams—she snuck another glance—but look at her stupid stockings and her stupid sweater-vest and her stupid matching headband and oh, what would I give to wring her stupid pretty little neck—

"Ingrid, is vanilla all right?"

"No—I want—I want to watch the pig races again!"

But there were more. More Azumi look-alikes. More short skirts, more gigantic bows, more tittering. This was hell. Yes, she had descended into Asian Women Hell.

As if trapped in a parody of her Wittlebury Park episode, every single Asian woman appeared to Ingrid as a threat. She passed one with cropped hair and a nose piercing, armored in studded pumps and fishnet stockings. She immediately studied Stephen for his reaction—did he have a type within a type if his type was so broad? There, again, waiting in line at the fishbowl game: an older Asian woman, with her grandchildren, but still—she was trim about the waist and her hair was dyed a youthful chestnut shade—even if he didn't want to *date* her, he wouldn't necessarily be opposed to masturbating to her. She had a right to know if he was mentally committing adultery! But how *would* she know? She eyed him suspiciously as he cheered for their pig.

If only she could pry open his brain and poke around. Extinguish every thought about an Asian woman who wasn't herself. Better yet, install a device in his occipital lobe inhibiting him from visualizing other Asian women altogether. When he looked their way, he'd see only formless, staticky blobs. Yes! She'd seen it before on a dystopian TV show. Now they just had to hurry up and invent the technology—

"Dear, are you feeling all right? Porky Pine won and you didn't even clap."

"What? Oh. I think I have gas," she made herself say.

Stephen sighed. "I told you this would happen."

But even after splashing water on her face in the bathroom, Ingrid knew—the day had been ruined.

Everywhere she went, an Asian woman was bursting out from behind a concession stand or a garbage can or a tree. The entire fair had been transformed into one enormous fun house, complete with a shifting hall of mirrors. She was dizzy from her eyes darting from them to Stephen, then back again: Was he just looking at that woman? Or was he avoiding eye contact precisely because he *wanted* to look at her? Did he think she was pretty? On a scale of one to ten, how high? Prettier than me? Will he think of her when we're in bed? How can I surpass her? How can I be—the ludicrous question ballooned above her head—the ultimate Asian woman?

She abruptly froze in the middle of a busy pathway. The Azumi in the pages of *Pink Salon*—busting through the seams of a schoolgirl uniform, always on her knees, incapable of saying no, existing only to please—oh God, was *that* a white man's ultimate Asian woman?

"Ingrid, dear? What's wrong?" Stephen entreated.

She covered her mouth and made it just in time to a porta potty. When she came out, he presented her with a stuffed anteater he'd won.

"Thanks," she growled. "I want to leave now."

In the car, Ingrid ransacked her purse for the emergency Lucidax pill and dry-swallowed it. She had to calm down—no Japanese schoolgirls were locked inside the car with them, no gracefully aged Asian grandmothers, no bestselling kawaii Japanese authors.

But when she closed her eyes, an onslaught of images hurtled through her: Stephen giddily masturbating to Asian porn on his computer; Stephen obtaining a TESL certificate and moving to Japan to teach a classroom of chirping schoolgirls; Stephen falling from the sky onto a pile of breasty maid café hostesses; Stephen, wearing only a bib, an obasan spooning homemade torijiru into his mouth; Stephen embracing Eunice for just a second too long—fuck. She had gone insane.

"We're home. Ingrid? Hello?"

She slowly cranked her head to look at him.

His bemused tolerance had morphed into clear-cut annoyance. "Well? Are you coming or not? I've been trying to get you out of the car for five minutes."

Ingrid inched from the car to the front door, her limbs iron-heavy, then collapsed on the bed, Stephen's voice faintly blipping in and out of her consciousness. "I'm just—going—sleep—" she mumbled.

INGRID WOKE FACEDOWN. Through bleary eyes, she looked to her left and saw Stephen lying beside her.

"You're up," he said softly.

"Ergh . . ." she groaned. She felt incapable of rousing her muscles or producing saliva.

He nuzzled her rigid neck with his nose.

She tried to flex a toe—it was paralyzed.

"Would you like a massage?" he asked gently.

"Help," she rasped. Her throat was so parched, the entreaty came out a rattling wheeze.

Stephen interpreted this as a yes.

He swung his leg across her butt and kneaded her lower back, then traveled upwards by increments. Her shoulders and neck were incredibly tense. After a few minutes, as her connective tissues unknotted, Ingrid realized she'd been in dire need of a massage.

"Feels—nice," she said into her pillow.

"Good," Stephen murmured.

She was about to sit up when he whispered, "I missed you," and kissed her down her neck. He slid both his hands under her dress. She twisted away but his weight pinned her to the mattress. "I missed your eyes, your skin, your hair . . ."

His words snapped a taut cord inside her. She bolted upright, toppling him to the floor.

"What's wrong?" Stephen asked after re-coordinating his glasses. "You've been acting erratically all day. I've done my best to put up with your mood swings, but I'm getting a little tired of it. On the Ferris wheel, I figured you had motion sickness. But now I'm beginning to think you don't even want me to touch you—"

"Are you attracted to Azumi?" The words spilled from her.

He stared at her in disbelief. "What are you talking about?"

"Just tell me the truth."

"Why is this relevant—"

"I asked you a question."

He blinked several times before carefully selecting his words. "Azumi is a beautiful woman. Anyone can see that. It's not so much a question of attraction, but—appreciating a painting's beauty."

Ingrid's heart stopped. Azumi was a beautiful painting?

"And like I said, she isn't my type," he continued. "She isn't who I thought she was."

"What?"

"Do you really want to get into this right now? I was hoping to explain everything later—"

She folded her arms. "Talk, Stephen."

He stood up and combed a hand through his hair. "Fine. But you have to promise not to repeat this to anyone."

Ingrid nodded impatiently.

"The night we stayed in Salt Lake City, I couldn't sleep and went outside for some fresh air—you know I find uncirculated air intolerable. And that's when I saw Azumi talking on the phone—*and smoking a cigarette*. She was cursing—*in English*. Even her voice in Japanese was deeper instead of . . . breathless. She'd become unrecognizable." He stared off into space for a moment, as if reliving his shock. "Then when I confronted her, I found out it's all fake."

"What?"

"The sweet, modest persona. The 'autofiction' novel—it's just fiction.

She's from an ultrawealthy family, not an orphanage. And she grew up between Tokyo and New York, not the Japanese countryside. She never worked at a pink salon when she was eighteen, either." His voice slid from perplexed to pedantic. "When I said her dishonesty was indefensible, she had the audacity to tell me she was 'capitalizing on fictions of the popular imagination' and 'reclaiming the spoils she was rightfully owed'—"

"What?" Ingrid knew she kept replaying the word, but her head was spinning like a top. Why did everyone insist on changing who they were?

"I know, it's hard to swallow. That's why you have to keep this a secret, my reputation as a translator could be damaged if this gets out—"

"Stop—stop talking about that. You're changing the subject. You—you said Azumi is beautiful . . . Is it because she's Asian?"

"Where is this coming from, Ingrid?"

She shut her eyes, steeling herself. "Why do you have a folder with photos of your three Asian ex-girlfriends?" She couldn't believe she'd uttered the words aloud. She folded her knees to her chest and covered herself with the sheet, waiting for remorse to assail Stephen's neutral expression.

"You looked through my computer," he said flatly.

"That's not the point—"

"You violated my privacy." He paced the bedroom in agitation. "I thought we trusted each other. This destroys all of that. You've destroyed any foundation of trust we have."

"Me looking through your computer destroyed our 'trust'? What about the fact that you never told me?"

"Told you what?"

"That you only date Asian women!" she practically screamed.

"You're being hysterical."

"Why?" she choked out, swiping at her cheeks. She hadn't realized they were wet.

He looked a little frightened of her. "Why," he repeated.

"Why only Asian women?"

Stephen stopped mid-pace. "Ingrid, that is an absurd question. Are you going to ask why some people prefer redheads? Or people with tattoos? Or why some people want to fuck stuffed animals? What about people who were born attracted to the opposite sex?" He waited, as if challenging her to dispute this false equivalence, but when she remained stone-faced, he pivoted to a softer tone. "Having preferences is completely normal. And no one knows 'why' we have them. Even in the animal world, mates will seek out mates with brighter feathers or—"

"Don't do that," Ingrid interrupted. "Don't make me feel like I'm crazy. I'm allowed to be upset and—and paranoid after finding out all *three* of your ex-girlfriends before me are also Asian! Don't you understand how that would make me feel—I don't know—replaceable? I have no idea if you even love me for who I am—" Fresh tears fell down her face.

After a moment, Stephen spoke in a quiet voice. "It's true I like Asian women. But it's a *compliment* to be liked. And I will not be made to feel like a monster when I have done nothing wrong. I never hurt anyone. I didn't force those women to date me. Ingrid, they *wanted* to date me."

"But you must have targeted them because they're Asian! You have a fe-fetish," she sobbed. There, she had said the dreaded word aloud. He had to see things from her point of view now. He had to understand why—

What was that sound? Was he *laughing*?

She watched in horror as his chuckle steadily intensified into a full-body laugh. He was laughing so hard, he crashed backwards into the dresser, knocking a glass frame to the floor. The photo inside was taken on the night of their engagement at the Imperial Seafood Garden, the night he told her, "I've been looking for someone like you my whole life."

"Oh, that is rich, Ingrid."

"Excuse me?" she said, in between blowing her nose.

"That is rich coming from *you*."

"What are you talking about?" she snapped. She hoped to come off authoritative but sounded like she had a sinus infection.

"Let me ask you this—what race are your ex-boyfriends?"

For a moment, the room spun as though she were back on the Tilt-A-

Whirl before she scrambled for a quick recovery. "Don't change the subject. We're talking about you and your sick, twisted 'preference'—"

"Answer the question. What race are your ex-boyfriends?"

She remained silent.

"White. They're white," he said. "Aren't they?"

She opened her mouth to argue it wasn't the same, it wasn't the same at all—but the words evaded her.

"That's what I thought." An awful little smirk marred his face. "I think before you go around pointing fingers at people for having a 'fetish,' you need to take a good long look at yourself."

Stephen went into the closet and returned with a duffel bag. He started calmly folding underwear, shirts and shorts inside. "I'm going to stay with Hunter for a few days. I think we need some time apart to cool down."

When he left, he didn't slam the door.

18

Fever Dream

INT. THE COURTRQOM OF INGRID YANG'S MIND - NIGHT

A dark and wood-paneled courtroom, lit only by flickering
candlelight. Long shadows dance against the walls. All
those present wear a white wig, a black robe and red
rouge on their cheeks.

                    JUDGE MARGARET
          Plaintiff, please state your case.

                    STEPHEN
          Ingrid is a hypocrite. She accuses me of
          having an "Asian fetish" when she is the one
          with a white fetish!

                    JUDGE MARGARET
Define "fetish."

                       STEPHEN
Gladly, your honor. It's when a person of
color exclusively dates or sleeps with white
people.

                    JUDGE MARGARET
Prosecution, you may begin your
cross-examination.

                        ALEX
Thank you, your honor. We are gathered here
today to crucify Ingrid Yang.
                      (laughs)
Kidding, kidding. Ingrid, is it true that in
your thirty years, you have only dated white
men?

                       INGRID
Yes.

                        ALEX
Slept with white men?

                       INGRID
Yes.

                        ALEX
How many?

                    JUDGE MARGARET
Irrelevant.

                    ALEX
Would you say you
                    (pauses dramatically)
hate your own people?

                    INGRID
What? I don't hate my own people!

                    VIVIAN
Leading.

                    JUDGE MARGARET
Sustained.

                    ALEX
Explain then why you have never dated an
Asian man.

                    INGRID
I . . .

                    ALEX
                    (glances down at file)
I have it on record you have said the phrase
"I'm just not attracted to Asian men" a total
of three times in your life.

                    INGRID
        . . .

ALEX

I have it on record you have said the phrase
"He reminds me of my cousin" a total of two
times when friends tried to set you up with
an Asian man.

Ingrid wears a hunted expression on her face.

ALEX

Ingrid, is it not offensive to suggest all
Asian men look alike? Are your words not the
textbook definition of Asian emasculation? Are
you not directly responsible for mental
health issues relating to self-esteem and
self-worth existing within the Asian American
male population?

VIVIAN

Leading!

JUDGE MARGARET

Sustained.

INGRID

But I did date an Asian guy!

The courtroom gasps.

JUDGE MARGARET

Order, order!

INGRID

I mean, kind of . . . in sixth grade.

The courtroom groans.

JUDGE MARGARET

Please continue.

INGRID

So I was the only Asian in my class, right?
Then this boy--Jacky Ma--transferred to my
school. And everyone made fun of him. He
didn't know a lot of English and he had an
accent. So I was like, "Ha ha, yeah, what a
FOB!" My friends loved it when I said stuff
like that. One day when Jacky tried to talk to
me in Mandarin, I pretended I couldn't see
him. And so everything was going great until
Austin Krantz started saying me and Jacky were
related. And I was confused because Austin
also said we were boyfriend and girlfriend.
Did he mean I was dating my own brother? When
I would walk past Jacky, the other boys would
whistle and make kissing noises. But Jacky and
I still had never talked. And on top of that,
I didn't want anyone to think I liked Jacky. I
was in love with Austin. I don't really know
why. He was always punching desks and walls
and he kicked our third grade teacher in both
shins. But all my friends--no, all the girls in
our grade--were in love with him! So I had to
prove me and Jacky weren't actually boyfriend
and girlfriend. I had to prove I wasn't like

that FOB loser! I was the same as Britney,
Amber and Megan. If we all laughed at Jacky
and made fun of him, how could I be like
Jacky? But obviously they weren't getting it,
which is why I cornered Jacky after school one
day and made him cry.

                    ALEX
How?

                    INGRID
    . . .

                JUDGE MARGARET
Answer the question.

                    INGRID
I called him a chink. And I spit on him.

Condemning stares and headshakes from the courtroom.

                    INGRID
But I checked on social media and he's a
billionaire now! He-he's married to a
Brazilian supermodel!

                JUDGE MARGARET
Irrelevant.

                    ALEX
                (triumphantly)
So it seems the root of this is self-hatred.
Do you plead guilty?

                    INGRID
I don't really know what you mean--

                    ALEX
How do you plead?

                    INGRID
I-I know it was wrong, those things I said
about Asian men. But in my defense, I was
just trying to survive!

                    ALEX
Survive what?

                    INGRID
I don't know--

                    VIVIAN
White supremacy!

                JUDGE MARGARET
Order, order! Ms. Vo, please wait your turn.

                    ALEX
Ingrid, do you admit your proclaimed lack of
attraction to Asian men does not have
anything to do with Asian men but your own
insecurities?

                    INGRID
                 (mumbles)
Maybe . . .

                    ALEX
Do you believe yourself capable of attraction
to Asian men?

                    INGRID
                  (blushes)
I think so.

                    ALEX
                  (smirks)
No further questions, Your Honor.

                JUDGE MARGARET
Defense, you may begin your
cross-examination.

                    VIVIAN
Thank you, Your Honor. To begin with, I'd
like to address the Prosecution's statements.
I will give him that disavowing physical
attraction to an entire population based
on race alone is racist. But I also want
to emphasize that no one is owed sex
simply <u>because</u> they share the same race.
Asian women's sexual agency has been
policed enough as it is by white men;
we don't need our fellow Asian men
joining in.

                JUDGE MARGARET
Relevancy.

VIVIAN

Right. Ingrid, I'd like to paint a scene for
the courtroom. Please describe your first
relationship with a white man.

INGRID

Oh . . . I guess it happened my freshman year
of college. Before that, all the boys--I
mean, all the white boys--ignored me.
Actually, when I think back on it, a lot of
them were mean to me. After Austin, I was in
love with this guy, Ethan. I don't think he
even knew my name. Then at the start of
ninth grade, we were at Amber's birthday
party playing seven minutes in heaven. I
spun the bottle and got matched with Ethan--
I couldn't believe my luck! When we were
alone in the bathroom with the lights off,
I closed my eyes and waited for him to
kiss me. I thought, maybe after we kiss,
Ethan will like me back and I'll have my
first real boyfriend! But Ethan just asked,
"Is it true?" And I was like, "Is what true?"
And he said, "My brother told me Asian
girls have slanted pussies. So is it true?" I
told him I didn't understand. Then Ethan
tried to lift up my skirt so I ran out of the
bathroom and called my parents to take me
home.
                (frozen expression)
Oh. I think I repressed this memory.

                    ALEX
              (in a posh English accent)
Can everything be traced back to repressed
memories and childhood trauma? Isn't that a
bit . . . reductive?

                  JUDGE MARGARET
                    (shrugs)
Don't ask me. This courtroom is all over the
place.

                    VIVIAN
                  (impatient)
Ingrid, your first relationship. How would you
describe it?

                    INGRID
Oh, right. Well, freshman year, this guy who
was a film studies major asked me out on a
date. I was so shocked because, I'm being
objective here, he was really attractive.

Alex rolls his eyes.

                    INGRID
Even my white girl friends said so! I was
used to guys like him ignoring me and going
for them. But this guy was into me! So I was
surprised but also really . . . grateful.

VIVIAN
(turns to audience)
Do you see how white supremacy taught her to
love her oppressor?

ALEX
This isn't Postcolonial Studies 101.

VIVIAN
(ignores Alex)
Would he comment on your ethnicity?

INGRID
Well, he would say things like, "I'm normally
not attracted to Asians" and "I've never been
with an Asian before."

VIVIAN
And how did that make you feel?

INGRID
Special. I thought, wow, I can't believe he
chose me to be his first Asian girl. What a
privilege!
(stilted smile)
And my white girl friends—they were just as
surprised. When I told them he'd asked me to
be his girlfriend, they looked at me like I
was explaining a complicated equation and
kept asking, "But why?"

                    VIVIAN
White women.
                (long sigh)
So more generally, why did you only date white
men?

                    INGRID
It made me feel special?

                    VIVIAN
You already said that.

                    INGRID
Western beauty standards?

                    VIVIAN
That's true for everyone--I'm asking about you.

                    INGRID
My neighborhood had a lot more white guys
than Asian guys?

                    VIVIAN
Please--think, Ingrid.

                    INGRID
            (slowly, after several moments)
I guess in some way . . . it made me feel
less Asian to be with a white man. If I was
with an Asian man, then my Asianness doubled.
But if I was with a white man--the hero who

everyone in the universe looks up to--then I couldn't also be the villain. You know, the greenish-yellow Chinaman on those old pulp book covers with long fingernails, who are always trying to kidnap a white girl and take her to his den of sin? I couldn't be who Americans mocked and banned and interned and deported and lynched. Not if a white man chose me--because white men were the ones who did all those things. His whiteness could . . . protect me. Make me an exception. Bring me onto his side, the good side. Maybe I didn't really want the love of a white man. Maybe what I always wanted was the love of a good man. That is, "the good guy" in the story--and he'd always been white. I don't know. It's just . . . a theory.

The courtroom falls into a reflective silence.

                    EUNICE
              (calling out from audience)
But what if you mutually objectify each other!

                    VIVIAN
The balance of power is unequal. One is always the colonized, the other, the colonizer.

                    ALEX
Here she goes, Ms. Thinks-She-Knows-Everything.

                    VIVIAN
          (rolls eyes and turns to Stephen)
Which brings me to the plaintiff's original
claim: that Ingrid is a hypocrite for
accusing him of having an Asian fetish when
she has only dated white men. While her
former disavowal of Asian men remains
inexcusable--Your Honor, perhaps we can work
out a plea bargain--the plaintiff's original
claim is unfounded. Mr. Greene, do you see
how it is virtually impossible, given the
historical trajectory of the last four
hundred years? Any fetishization of white men
or women could only happen if they had not
colonized, enslaved, raped, bombed and
incarcerated the majority of the world. A
"white fetish" could only exist if we had
done that to you.

                    ALEX
Don't directly address my client!
                  (frowns)
Wait a second, why the fuck am I arguing on
behalf of this lame-ass weeaboo? I quit.

Alex throws his folder to the ground. The courtroom
cheers.

                    VIVIAN
Stephen, when did you first develop a racial
fetish for Asian women?

STEPHEN

(looks around in horror)

What the hell? How did I get up here?

Stephen now sits inside the testimony box.

VIVIAN

Answer the question.

Stephen folds his arms.

VIVIAN

Was it movies that portray Asian women as
exotic flower fuck dolls or seductive dragon
ladies or heart-of-gold sex workers or just
hypersexual fiends?

STEPHEN

I don't know.

VIVIAN

The Toll of the Sea (1922)? The Thief of Bagdad
(1924)? A Girl in Every Port (1928)? Shanghai
Express (1932)? China Girl (1942)? Japanese War
Bride (1952)? House of Bamboo (1955)? Love Is a
Many-Splendored Thing (1955)? Teahouse of the
August Moon (1956)? Sayonara (1957)? The Barbarian
and the Geisha (1958)? China Doll (1958)? South
Pacific (1958)? The World of Suzie Wong (1960)? A
Girl Named Tamiko (1962)? Tamahine (1963)? You
Only Live Twice (1967)? Madama Butterfly (1975)?
Shōgun (1980)? An Officer and a Gentleman (1982)?

Year of the Dragon (1985)? Tai-Pan (1986)? Full
Metal Jacket (1987)? Come See the Paradise
(1990)? Indochine (1992)? Madame Butterfly (1995)?
Chinese Box (1997)? Charlie's Angels (2000)? Rush
Hour 2 (2001)? The Quiet American (2002)? Austin
Powers in Goldmember (2002)? Kill Bill: Vol. 1
(2003)? The Last Samurai (2003)? Lost in
Translation (2003)? The Sleeping Dictionary
(2003)? Harold & Kumar Go to White Castle (2004)?
Mean Girls (2004)? Memoirs of a Geisha (2005)?
Silk (2007)? Gran Torino (2008)? Machete (2010)?
The Social Network (2010)? Scott Pilgrim vs.
the World (2010)? The Wolverine (2013)? Ex
Machina (2014)? Miss Saigon: 25th Anniversary
(2016)?

STEPHEN
(sighs)
I haven't seen most of those movies.

VIVIAN
Japanese anime, then, where Japanese women
who do not look Japanese are hypersexualized
and hyperinfantilized?

Stephen looks bored.

VIVIAN
What about porn, where one of the most highly
searched terms is "Asian"? Hidden Pussy,
Flying Penis? Or perhaps hentai? Revenge of
the Tentacle Monster?

                    JUDGE MARGARET
I think we get the picture.

                       VIVIAN
Or perhaps you're into the search term
"torture," which brings up videos of Asian
women on porn sites?

The courtroom falls into a stunned silence.

                       VIVIAN
No? Was it the Page Act of 1875 that banned
Asian women from immigrating to the US under
the presumption they were all disease-ridden
whores? Was it the history of US military
occupation in Asian countries, when white men
first conflated Asian women with sex through
"comfort women"? When they associated "wife
back home" with white women, and "overseas
mistress" with Asian women? Was it through
the "mail-order bride" trade that began as a
direct result of the rise of western
feminism, convincing white men that Asian
women could still be subjugated and enjoy it,
indeed, prefer it? Was it through the sex
trafficking trade that is heavily composed of
Asian female victims?

                       EUNICE
What if the exotification of Asian women has
been so deeply rooted in our culture for
centuries, the source of a fetish can't be

pinpointed? What if the source is our
culture?

Vivian hands out papers to the judge and jury.

VIVIAN

These are statistics showing the elevated
rates of domestic abuse and rape of Asian
women by white men. I think we can all agree
it's much easier to hurt someone if they are
a something.

Judge Margaret places her hand over her mouth.

VIVIAN

Mr. Greene, will you admit a racial
fetish is, by definition, racist? Will you
acknowledge it has violent and dehumanizing
consequences--both physically and mentally?
Mr. Greene?

Stephen tries to talk. Nothing comes out. He points at his
throat, panicked.

VIVIAN

That's all, Your Honor.

THE NEXT MORNING, Ingrid woke from a dream so intense, she'd pitched
all her blankets to the floor and managed an impressive 180-degree spin,
with her feet facing due headboard. Though she couldn't recollect a thing,

from the moment she sat up, she was struck by an inexplicable desire to talk to four people.

A LEX OPENED THE DOOR looking distracted, but signaled with a lift of his chin for Ingrid to come in.

"I'm in a live game," he explained over his shoulder as he dashed back to his bedroom. "Eunice isn't here."

"I know. I want to talk to you."

She plopped awkwardly next to him on a beanbag, marveling at his index finger's implausibly rapid-fire pace and at the figures on his screen: elves, warlocks and the US military. She felt shy, as if she were twelve again and entering a boy's bedroom was a thrilling dare, an extension of the boy himself. Alex's was a testament to cool (a towering sound system, posters of rappers) and cute (an oversized panda plushie, a jar of paper lucky stars). His unmade bed, his imprint still legible on the sheets, was overwhelming in its intimacy—she flushed and looked away.

"What's up?" he asked without ungluing his eyes from the screen.

"I had a fight with Stephen. About his Asian ex-girlfriends." She carefully monitored his reaction. What did she expect from him? Congratulations? Validation?

"Okay," was the extent of it. Alex shouted into his microphone, "Behind you! Two-twenty!"

"He's staying at a friend's place right now."

"So you broke up?"

Had he asked the question with a hopeful lilt? Or had she simply hoped he had?

"I don't know. Maybe." Ingrid cleared her throat and picked at a questionable spot on her jeans. "Anyway, I came to ask you something. According to that online forum, how does an Asian woman stop being a 'self-hating, white-worshipping whore'?"

His expression shifted uncomfortably. "I don't really go on there anymore."

"Why?" He didn't say anything. "Alex, what happened?" she tried again.

"Fuck, I died." Onscreen, blood splattered behind the words PLAYER DEAD: THREE KILLS.

He rolled backwards in his ErgoChair and finally looked at her. "A while ago, someone posted about an English guy who murdered a Thai woman. He chopped her up and put the pieces in a suitcase with a dead dog. And then he threw it in a river."

"Oh my God."

"Yeah. And everyone was saying she deserved it and how it wouldn't have happened if she didn't chase after white dick." He coughed. "I guess it was kind of immature of me to get sucked into all that." Alex glanced back at his screen. "Anyway, maybe you could, I dunno, try going on dates with guys who aren't white and just see how it feels."

She fiddled with her car keys. "I'd love to hear what your experience with dating has been like . . . as an Asian guy and all that."

Her palms were sweating so much, she dropped her keys and suddenly forgot how hands worked, why were hands so *weird* and why had she said "experience" like she was a customer service survey—ugh, she really had reverted to adolescence—

Alex was looking at her funny. "Do you need some water or something?"

"Huh? No, I'm okay, I just, well, would you—like to get Mexican food? At that restaurant you wanted to check out?"

"On a date?"

Her cheeks singed. Before she had a chance to answer, Alex continued, "We can definitely talk, it's just—I'm actually seeing someone."

Her shoulders slumped. "Oh. Tiffany—the *Playboy* model."

He laughed. "Are you kidding? She's not someone I want to get serious with."

"Really? I thought—well, why were you seeing her, then?"

A pinging sound came from Alex's computer and he turned away to type in an instant messaging program. She worried her question had upset him, when he said, "Honestly? That conversation we had after you found Stephen's photos, it got me thinking. And I guess dating a white girl like her, it made me feel . . . I dunno, like I was taking something nobody believed I could take. Like I was proving everyone wrong. I know it's kind of fucked up."

She sighed. "A lot of things are."

They were both quiet for a moment.

"So . . . who's this new girl?" she asked.

"Her name's Ji-Eun—"

"She's Asian?" Ingrid interrupted.

He laughed again. "Yeah, she's Korean. We met at church—"

As Alex talked, a dreamy, dopey look misted over him. She thought back to the night after the open forum when *he'd* asked *her* out. If she'd been single then, if she'd said yes—would she inspire the same dreamy, dopey look now?

"Oh. Well, I'm really happy for you, Alex," she said. And she was (mostly).

"Maybe we can all hang out sometime. With Yoon, too."

"Okay," she smiled. "I'd like that."

VIVIAN WAS AT a meditation retreat for trans, femme and nonbinary POC, but said Ingrid could drop by.

When they met outside the recreation center, Vivian looked well, though a shade fatigued around the eyes. Ingrid followed her to a lavender-colored mat, bordered by various crystals and a sage smudge stick.

"Are we allowed to talk in here?" she whispered. All around them, people sat cross-legged or lay on mats with their eyes closed.

"It's fine—this space is very antirestriction."

She lowered herself onto the other end of the mat. "So, Vivian, how are you?"

"Tired. End of the school year—you know how it is."

"I'm really sorry your Chou protests haven't . . . panned out."

She shrugged. "It's never-ending."

"Maybe you should take it easy for a while. You know . . . take care of yourself?"

Vivian cocked an eyebrow. "That's what my therapist says. She also says my 'self-worth isn't bound up in others perceiving me as virtuous,'" she sighed. "But that's the thing: I can't live with myself if I stand back and do nothing. People always say, 'If I were alive when the Nazis were around, I would have done something.' But that's not true—most people aren't willing to sacrifice themselves. They just want to repost an article on social media and call it a day. I'm actually writing a new paper about it: 'Still Thirsty: Why Boba Liberalism Will Not Save Us.'" She left an expectant pause in the air.

"Oh, I can't wait to read it," Ingrid duly rejoined.

"Anyway, I have to do *something*, even if it doesn't change *anything* . . ." She trailed off, then looked her fiercely in the eyes. "The Black and Brown students at Barnes are counting on me." Her voice cracked. "Aren't they?"

Oh, Vivian. Ingrid was glad, thankful even, that they'd gone from coldly brushing past each other like potted plants to being in each other's lives. She doubted they'd ever be close friends and she'd always feel *a little* inadequate around her (she still had so many terms to look up), but—she would miss seeing her around campus.

"Um, can I ask you something?" she whispered.

But she had now closed her eyes and appeared to be meditating.

As Ingrid studied this Vivian—smaller and frailer without her loudspeaker—she was temporarily overcome with astonishment at her existence. In a way, if the world had had its way, Vivian—fearlessly proud of who she was and where she'd come from and what she believed—was not supposed to exist. She was resiliency embodied.

Ew, what was this feeling? Was she . . . *proud* of Vivian? The cheesiness of the thought was *disgusting*. She cast a glare around the retreat—all the positive energy in the room was to blame.

"Um, Vivian, can I ask you something?" Ingrid tried more loudly.

She nodded and swung a smoking bushel of sage above Ingrid's head. "I forgot to cleanse you of the outside world."

"Cleanse away."

When this act was completed, Ingrid asked, "Is it okay to single out nonwhite men to date?"

Vivian opened her eyes and frowned. "Is this some kind of weird social experiment?"

"No. No! I mean, I don't mean it to be?"

"Oh. Well, I used to date white women." She stroked her hair back, laughing. "I know, can you imagine?"

"So, was it really different—dating an Asian woman?"

Vivian looked ill at ease. "Well, I've only dated Zoe since I stopped dating white women."

"Oh, right. So . . . is it okay?"

"Hm. I don't know. If race is the biggest qualifier in looking for dates, does it mean you're using these men to make yourself feel better? As if dating someone of a certain race gives you credibility? Then you're just using the person for their race, which one could argue is a form of fetishization."

"Oh. I hadn't thought of that . . . Have you ever felt that way before?"

"Why?"

"I mean, with you and Zoe—"

"We're talking about *you*, not me," Vivian said a bit brusquely. "Anyway, what was I saying? Oh right. But since you're both Asian, you're coming together because of your shared culture and, most likely, shared trauma of dating white people. There's nothing wrong with that. And I'm all for dating within a white-free space—no unpaid labor teaching what you already know. Plus, no white supremacist relatives and *way* better food during the holidays." She paused. "But just because someone's a POC doesn't mean they don't hold white supremacist values."

"Timothy Liu," they blurted out at the same time, then broke into laughter.

"You've given me a lot to think about," Ingrid said. "Thanks, Vivian. Really." She prepared to get up when she felt a tug on her sleeve.

"Hey, before you go . . . um, I owe you an apology," Vivian mumbled. "My therapist says I need to stop thinking of apologies—real apologies—as a sign of weakness. So, I'm sorry. That I pretended you hadn't created the website. And I know it's not an excuse, but I had switched to a new antidepressant and—"

"You don't need to explain—"

"—I just felt so powerless. None of the protests were changing anything and I thought I could finally make a difference—"

"You did," Ingrid insisted.

"It's been a rough year," Vivian said. As though instinctively, she petted one of her crystals.

"I can't wait for it to be over."

"Hey—are you still dropping out?"

"I'm not sure yet."

"Well, let me know if you decide to defend. If you do, I want to be there. For support."

INGRID CONVENIENTLY ARRIVED at her parents' house when they were about to eat dinner—it was turning into a habit. Tonight her parents had prepared congee with pork floss, fried gluten and pickled celtuce, plus a side of smashed cucumbers.

"Ingrid, this is a nice surprise," her mother said.

Her father asked after her fiber intake and the last time she changed her car's oil, then proceeded to hand her two articles on the subjects.

At the dining table, she pushed aside a stack of floppy disks and a plastic bucket of Happy Meal toys, then ate a second helping of everything. For dessert, she helped slice up yellow watermelon.

After the dishes were washed, she cleared her throat. "Mom, Dad. I want to ask you something—"

Her parents looked up at her in alarm, already concerned.

This gesture alone made Ingrid tear up. "When I was a kid, do you think I—hated myself?"

"What do you mean?" Jean asked.

"I mean—did you ever get the feeling I hated being Asian?" Saying the words aloud was awful, as if that alone gave credit to the notion. She thought of her last visit home, her mother brandishing the photo of her in the yellow wig, evidence of wishful thinking enacted through make-believe.

Her parents traded glances.

Bo finally spoke. "You never wanted to eat Taiwanese or Chinese food." He nodded towards the kitchen. "Not like you do now. You wanted to eat—what was it, that microwave food in the blue box . . . Kid Cuisine."

Jean smiled, lost in her memories. "Oh! When we used to speak Mandarin in public, you would just walk away and pretend you didn't know us. Remember?"

"I got lost at the mall one time because of that," Ingrid said, sheepish. "And I had to go to the information booth to call you on the PA system. It was so embarrassing."

Bo leaned back in his chair and rubbed his head, chuckling. "Remember my colleague's daughter, Yifan? She came over one day to play. You must have been . . . ten, eleven? When you saw her, you ran to your room and shut the door. Yifan watched cartoons with us until her parents picked her up."

"You were a . . . zenme shuo . . . brat!" Jean cried.

"My colleague told me the next day, 'Yifan wants to have a playdate with you and your wife again. But not your daughter!'"

Jean was laughing so hard, she was crying. Bo's face was bright red. He dabbed his eyes and forehead with a handkerchief. Even Ingrid laughed until she had a stitch in her side.

When everyone had settled back down, Jean said softly, "Remember when we asked if you wanted to go to Saturday Chinese school? You said—"

"I said I would rather die," Ingrid finished. "I'm sorry I was such a—a brat."

"But you did not mean it. You were a teenager!"

"We knew it wasn't easy for you, growing up here," Bo added in Mandarin.

"You did? But you never talked to me about it."

Jean sighed. "You're right."

"We never talked to you about a lot of things," Bo said.

"Like what?"

"Like, it wasn't easy for us, either," her father continued in Mandarin. "The things we had to endure at our jobs—it was humiliating. Always passed over for promotions. Not having friends—"

"Our coworkers never invited us to their barbecues or baby showers," Jean said, miffed.

"—people talking down to us like we couldn't understand them. Shopkeepers treating us rudely," Bo continued. "Strangers shouting and spitting at us from cars." Ingrid's heart clenched—it was the first she'd heard of this. "But we could not complain to you. You were born here. We wanted you to be born here. We just hoped it wouldn't happen to you." He looked at his wife. "Maybe we should have told you how we felt."

Ingrid dried her eyes with the back of her wrists. Her father had never spoken so much in one sitting.

"Thanks, Mom. Thanks, Dad."

"Do you . . . want to speak Mandarin with us again?" Jean asked tentatively.

"I—give me some time."

She patted her daughter's hand. Bo nudged the plate of yellow watermelon towards her.

WHEN INGRID ARRIVED home, the only available parking was in the overflow lot. She yawned as she crossed the leaf-strewn street, savoring the pleasant rustling of her steps, and fell into a steady one-two-two rhythm before coming to an abrupt stop. A small gray rabbit sat in the grass, a single glowing eye fixed on her. Ingrid stood still, not wanting to scare it away.

A sharp rustle came from behind her. She whipped her head around in the darkness as her stomach plummeted twenty stories. Was someone following her? She sprinted towards the mailbox, dreading another ransom-style note. Whoever left it must have just been here—oh, why hadn't she installed a security camera? She wrenched open the rusted metal door, breath held.

No note.

Her shoulders softened. Maybe whoever was leaving her the notes had finally quit. She went inside the apartment and flicked on the hallway light.

"Ste—" she started to call before shame pinched at her. Right. Stephen was gone.

She bolted the door, tried the handle, tried it two more times, then verified all the windows were locked. You are an independent modern woman of the twenty-first century, Ingrid chided herself. Get it together. Even so, she squished three pillows together on Stephen's side of the bed, forming a lumpy approximation of a human body, and curled around it.

Despite being an independent modern woman of the twenty-first century, old habits were hard to kick.

19

A Priori, A Posteriori

C ome on, this will be fun," Eunice urged. "Like old times."

Ingrid reluctantly shoved a black beret over her ears, looking less chic detective and more frumpy toadstool.

"Here, put these on, too." Eunice passed her a pair of black cat-eye sunglasses.

Ingrid doubted they had to be incognito when everyone in the E. A. department still ambled around like dazed zombies. The broken ceiling light hadn't been repaired yet; no one seemed to notice, much less care.

Eunice looked over her shoulder to check the hallway was empty, then jammed a key into the door.

"We're in!" she cried happily, as though they'd burglarized Michael's office.

The artificial bonsai zen garden fountain was gone, as was his collection of clay teapots. The empty walls were checkered with faded squares and rectangles, vestiges of his Chinese scrolls and paintings, to make room for his new decorations: a glass rifle display and a five-foot sea bass mounted on a wooden plank, if Ingrid had to guess. Cixi had informed them he was staying overnight in Boston for a speaking engagement. "Kick him where it hurts," she'd said when she handed over the key.

Eunice plopped down in Michael's desk chair, spun around a couple times, then turned on his computer.

"Password ideas?"

"DOFO," Ingrid suggested. She opened a cardboard box stacked with papers and halfheartedly skimmed the first page.

"No. I only have two more tries now," Eunice pouted.

"I don't know, Yoon."

She tilted her head, thinking. "I could ask Thad if he has access to hacking software. You know how in spy movies, they just plug in a USB key and download everything in ten seconds?"

At the mention of Thad, repulsion bled into her. Eunice hadn't sloughed him off yet? Even after reading Vivian's article on white men utilizing Asian women as racism shields?

She made her voice light. "Okay. But do you really think Michael would keep top-secret documents in his computer? When it's so easy to hack someone long-distance nowadays?"

Eunice wrinkled her nose at the Windows 95 logo on the screen. "You might have a point." She rolled up her sleeves. "Old-school style, it is."

But two and a half hours later, their sole discovery was a common interest shared by Michael and Ingrid's parents. For a paper published nine years ago, he'd written over twenty drafts and saved every one—an anomaly they assumed—but Michael kept to the same exhaustive practice for all his papers. Each draft recorded his meticulous edits and corrections, always in the same bright red ink. When it came to his academic books, instead of manila folders, his revisions filled entire boxes. He never junked a single scrap of paper, no matter how insignificant. No wonder he couldn't bear to part with his "chinoiserie" collection—he was an incurable hoarder.

"Are you hungry?" Ingrid asked. "Let's get lunch." She needed a reason to leave—standing inside four walls of pure Michael Bartholomew was pressing on her claustrophobia.

"But we just got here," Eunice said, lifting the lid off another box. "Plus I brought Cup Noodles."

"I don't know how much longer I can keep doing this, Yoon." She pulled off her beret and tossed it onto Michael's desk, but the flaccid statement piece hit the edge and slid into the trash can.

Eunice looked horrified. "Ingrid, what's going on?"

"Nothing—"

"So why are you acting like this—"

"Acting like what?"

"Like you're not even here—"

"I am literally here—"

"Oh come on, you know what I mean—"

"Just forget it—"

"What's really going on? I can tell you're hiding something from me." Eunice hesitated and spoke in a gentler voice. "Did something happen with Stephen? I know he's back from his book tour. But every time I ask you how things are, you change the subject."

Hearing his name in her mouth made Ingrid stiffen. Her obsession with Stephen's hypothetical attraction to her was absurd, and yet, why was she still looking at Eunice askance, as though she were constantly measuring her friend's desirability against her own? She wasn't ready to have this conversation with Eunice, not when she'd packed away a dozen worries in her own cardboard box to agonize over later. Not when she was in denial over Stephen's absence.

Just lie, she thought. Pretend everything is fine.

Instead, with the reckless shot of adrenaline that accompanies starting a fight with a stranger on the subway, she found herself saying, "Actually, I confronted him. About his fetish."

Eunice's eyes widened. "Oh. What did he say?"

"He said exactly what you said. That everyone has 'preferences.'"

Tension expanded into the room.

"Well . . . isn't that true?" Eunice said after a moment.

"No. There's a difference between liking guys with tattoos and fetishizing an entire race."

"But what if you can't help who you're attracted to? There's nothing you can do about that," she shrugged.

Her indifference sent a rip of anger through Ingrid. "You should at least, I don't know, examine it and confront it—instead of just acting like it's perfectly okay to date an alt-right tech bro," she snapped.

Now the tension pushed against the walls until the pressure could pop.

Eunice's voice hardened. "Excuse me?"

"I can't believe you're still seeing Thad after he made that incredibly offensive app!"

"First of all, me and Thad aren't sleeping together anymore. You would know that if you paid attention when I talk instead of only thinking of yourself." Her words stung like an open wound. "Second of all, I wasn't interested in *dating* Thad. I was *using* him."

"What does that even mean?" Ingrid countered. "Your attraction to him still means he had power over you. Have you ever considered *he* was using *you*?"

She narrowed her eyes. "Do not try to turn this around on me. You're the one who feels guilty you've only been with white men. *I've* slept with a half-Filipino guy! And a black guy from Ghana!"

This information came as an unexpected slap. "You have?"

"Yes." Eunice looked smug. "I was in the International Students Club when I was an undergrad. They encouraged a very sexually liberated space."

Ingrid blinked. "But—but just because you've slept with them doesn't mean you don't still have . . . problematic feelings about white men. And it doesn't mean you're not being fetishized!"

"Stop talking about me when you're really talking about yourself.

You're mad because you, Ingrid Yang, are not so different from me. But I've come to terms with who I am and what I want."

Her whole body bristled. "Well . . . I don't know if you have."

"I guess we'll have to agree to disagree."

"Great."

"Great."

The tension in the room had ruptured, but Ingrid didn't feel any release. An ambulance's blaring siren passed by.

"Well," she said awkwardly, "I'm going to get something to eat." She fidgeted with her sunglasses. "Do you want anything?" She'd reverted to a tactic her mother had perfected: patching up an argument by pretending it never happened.

Eunice flipped open a manila folder and stuck her face in it. "No. I'm going to stay here and keep working. *Someone* has to stop Michael."

"Okay. Thanks for helping me, Yoon," Ingrid said, hoping her sincerity shone through.

"Don't thank me. I'm not doing this for you—I'm like, trying to be a good person or whatever."

As Ingrid left the room, syrupy guilt had already begun to replace stodgy anger. She was in an irritable mood and she had lashed out at Eunice. Rather than apologize, which would have simply confirmed she was a bad friend, yet more proof she spoiled everything she touched, she had chickened out. She loitered outside the door, contemplating going back in to say, "I'm sorry." She was always apologizing—to the mailman for having so much mail, to her doctor for making her do her job, to a stranger on the street for being in his way. So why was apologizing to Eunice so hard?

She moped towards the elevator. As the metal doors cinched shut, her words rang in her head: "You're mad because you, Ingrid Yang, are not so different from me." What had she meant? Eunice was her closest friend— why *wouldn't* she want to be like her?

When the elevator doors parted, a memory seized her: the first time she'd laid eyes on Eunice.

Five years ago in the E. A. Studies lounge, Ingrid had been braving another forgettable meet-and-greet for new students when Eunice walked in. She automatically zeroed in on her like a target floated above her head. Because she was another Asian woman. And there were so few of them in the department.

The pasty and bespectacled men in the room flocked around Eunice, obscuring her from view. But Ingrid had already dissected her—colored contacts, dyed hair, skin-tight clothes—under a harsh surgical light. How could someone like *her* have gotten into the program? she stewed to herself in a corner.

When Eunice was assigned to her office, she was livid. Of course the department had slapped the two of them together. Of course they were mixed up for one another, though they looked nothing alike. Ingrid was civil but cold to Eunice as they worked in silence, only occasionally asking if the other wouldn't mind opening or closing the window.

Then, at the start of Eunice's second year, Ingrid walked in to see her head flat on her desk, crowned by damp tissues. She had just given a presentation followed by a Q & A session. An "Asian chick from Postcolonial Studies" tore down her argument with the same ease as tearing down papier-mâché. Eunice abruptly fled the conference room to keep from crying in public.

In the aftermath, they divulged their mutual hatred of Vivian, the spark that gave rise to their inseparable friendship—and yet it had been constructed on the hatred of another Asian woman. A woman who, Ingrid knew now, had always weathered issues of her own.

Standing outside the elevator, she deliberated pressing the up button and confessing everything to Eunice: When I met you, I judged you and disliked you. Forgive me.

But what good would that do?

In spite of how Eunice could drive her up the wall; in spite of how she knew she treated Eunice worse than she had ever treated Stephen because maybe she *did* see too much of herself in her; in spite of how Eunice was always trying to improve and upgrade her—Ingrid had never been more grateful that five years ago, they'd been assigned the same office by chance, or maybe not by chance.

She drove across town for Eunice's favorite boba and shrimp chips and left them in a bag outside Michael's office. On the front, she wrote, "I'm sorry."

THE END OF final exams heralded a festive mood on campus. Though the forecast was in the low seventies, students were playing shirtless Frisbee, sunbathing on the main lawn and shotgunning Natty Ice. The carefree strains of a guitar coasted on a light breeze towards Ingrid. As she crossed the quad, the acoustic chords were replaced by an irksome, repetitive whine. She identified the source when she came in sight of the Student Union: drilling and hammering. Scaffolding had been erected around the building, but streams of students still swam in and out of the revolving doors. She covered her ears and hurried inside.

WELCOME TO THE SANCTUARY! shouted a sign above the computer lab. The room looked unchanged save for a folding table loaded with coffee, tea and pastries. Timothy's grand unveiling was . . . refreshments?

Then her eyes landed on a poster:

THE SANCTUARY: COMMUNITY RULES

1. **All viewpoints are welcome!**

2. **Don't judge an idea until you've tried it out.**

3. **Censorship will not be tolerated.**

4. **Opinion-shaming will not be tolerated.**

5. **There's no such thing as a stupid question. For example: What is "Islamophobia"? Is it real? Is it a propaganda campaign created by ISIS? Who knows! Let's debate!**

6. **Listen to each other. Really *listen* to each other.**

7. **Interrupting and speaking without raising your hand is allowed as long as it's done respectfully.**

8. **No name-calling! (E.g., "that's racist," "that's sexist," or alternatively, "you're racist," "you're sexist," etc.)**

9. **What happens in the Sanctuary stays in the Sanctuary.**

10. **Keep this space a safe space—for everyone.**

So *this* was the Sanctuary. Not an upgraded computer lab but a school-sanctioned, free-for-all, no-accountability gathering place for bigots. She snapped a picture—she needed proof she hadn't nightmared it into existence.

"Good to see you, Ingrid!" a chipper voice called from behind.

Fuck.

She turned around to see Timothy striding towards her. He pumped her hand up and down. "Sorry about the noise. Construction should be over in a month." He gestured at a group of students arrayed on foam cushions. "This is our makeshift meeting room until the Sanctuary is completed."

"Er—I just stopped by to check it out, I actually have to go—"

"Nonsense, have one of these!"

He beckoned her to the refreshments table. Egg tarts? Michael had apparently shut down the literary salons in the E. A. department in exchange for funding the Sanctuary. Timothy lifted one onto a napkin and wafted it under her nose. She was assaulted by the fresh butter in the flaky crust, by the slight undulating jiggle of the silky custard. Goddamnit, Timothy had identified her soft spot.

Ingrid accepted the egg tart, cursing her gluttonously weak will, and observed the group. Except for a couple YAACC members, the color scheme skewed beige. A vague pressure told her to listen in, collect useful information for her and Eunice's covert operation. But a far more ir-

resistible pressure told her to inhale her egg tart, go home and lie facedown on her bed.

"Everyone, you remember Ingrid."

She tried to smile normally.

"Are you okay?" Timothy asked with concern. "You know, I've also suffered from facial muscle spasms. I can recommend an excellent specialist."

"Oh—no, it's fine."

He patted an empty cushion for her, then indicated a perky student in
pigtails. "Taylor was just saying Barnes is missing a Caucasian Studies
department."

Ingrid wedged the entire egg tart into her mouth.

"I mean, the blacks have their own department. The Asians have one,
too. I don't know why we're being left out," Taylor complained.

"It's discrimination," someone chimed in.

"Caucasians have made a lot of contributions to the world," she went
on. "Literature, math, world history. Everything!"

Ingrid swallowed without chewing, half hoping the egg tart would suffocate her.

"We should create a Caucasian History Month!"

"Let's start a petition."

"Yeah!"

"Dean Bartholomew would approve it, for sure."

"Bartho rules!"

Everyone clapped and hooted. One guy pounded his chest.

Without a word, Ingrid got up and piled all the remaining egg tarts
onto a paper plate. The least she could do was steal from these fascists. She
waited for the group to object, but her departure didn't make a dent in their
discussion.

As she made her way to the exit, she caught the overture to Timothy's
next sentence: "—which reminds me, I'd like to bring back the anti–
affirmative action petition I started last year—"

What in God's name was wrong with him? He had the dimensionality of a cartoon. Did he feel no shame colluding with white supremacists? she huffed, feeling especially lofty on her moral high horse. She shook her head in despair. Ending affirmative action would *not* help Asian students, if that's what Timothy was after. In fact, some Asian communities made up the lowest income bracket in America and denying this only served to deny the vast variety within—

Wait. Why did that sound familiar, like hearing a song with jumbled-up lyrics? Ingrid froze, her brain doing skips and hops. Hadn't *she* once put her name to a "Equal and Fair Admission to Barnes University" petition?

Oh God. *She had signed Timothy's petition.*

Though she was alone, her face inflamed from mortification. She'd have to scour and bleach her Internet footprints, somehow expunge her name from the list of signatures. She couldn't have anyone finding out the kind of person she'd been—

Ingrid stopped and turned around. Through the building's glass exterior, the Sanctuary was still visible. Something about Timothy's smile (tightly sewn in place) and the way he gestured with his hands (overeager) reminded her of . . . herself. Doing "Ying Ying" whenever her white girl friends commanded her. Trying desperately to befriend her freshman roommate, a legacy student named Bathsheba who owned two horses. Ingratiating herself with her doughy E. A. department colleagues.

Who did she think she was? How dare she pretend she and Timothy were cut from a different cloth?

She continued walking across the quad, struck by an unexpected swell of sadness for young Ingrid, for Timothy, too, even as his actions repulsed her. Should she try to rescue and convert him? Would that be presumptuous? But didn't she have a responsibility to try? Or would she only push him further away? Did Timothy just have to . . . work things out on his own? But what if he never did, what if he amassed power in Michael's shadow, emerging as a figurehead himself one day . . .

She wanted to take a nap.

How did Vivian do it? Shoulder all the injustices at once? Just trying to rectify the injustices *she'd* committed was exhausting enough as it was. The moment Ingrid felt overwhelmed, her instinct was to crawl into bed and smother a pillow over her ears. A part of her, though she knew it was wrong, still craved the soothing balm of apathy.

"INGRID!" JOHN SAID at the door. "Come in, come in."

When she looked at him, she was no longer tipped over by vertigo, as though Chou's face lurked beneath his. Now she saw the same nondescript man she'd met in the pan-Asian supermarket.

John's house was as sparsely filled as the first time she'd encountered it. Cardboard boxes and pyramids of bubble wrap leaned against the living room wall.

"Moving again?" she joked.

"No, I'm moving back in," John said, perplexed. He glanced down at the paper plate in her hands. "Oh, are those for me?"

She watched regretfully as he ferried the egg tarts away. She hadn't meant to give John all of them, she just refused to leave egg tarts inside a hot car as a matter of principle.

"Well, have a seat." He nodded at the sofa as he disappeared into the kitchen. "I just bought a juicer. What'll you have? Orange? Tomato? Spinach?"

She shrugged. "Whatever."

John returned with a tray bearing all three. He sat down, drained his glass of tomato juice and sighed contentedly. "So what's on your mind?"

Ingrid chose the glass of orange juice and finished it in three gulps. She stared glumly at the fireplace across the sofa. "Michael can't be stopped. It's over."

"Now, now, don't say that. We just have to keep trying."

She considered sharing her and Eunice's (loosely termed) plan to incriminate Michael, then changed her mind; it would only make them look unequipped to take down DOFO.

"How? What else can we do?"

"Well—I'll have to keep thinking about that one. The best ideas take time," he winked.

They sat in silence for a minute before Ingrid asked, "Are you mad at him?"

"Who? Michael?" He bit into an egg tart. "I suppose I feel sorry for him. In a way, what I did ruined his career."

"Oh."

"I don't . . . appreciate what he started in my name. I wish he'd stop, you know that." He brushed a few crumbs from his lap. "But I can't help but pity the man. He's trying to salvage something from the remains of destruction, so to speak."

That was certainly one way to put it. Ingrid thought back to Michael's largest photograph in his old office: him and John as Xiao-Wen Chou, standing side by side, draped in traditional changshans.

"When did you first meet him?"

"Oh, my, that was years and years ago." He abruptly went to the kitchen, returning with another tray of glasses. "Refill?"

She shook her head and got up to stroll the perimeter of the room. On the fireplace mantel was a set of Baoding balls in an engraved wooden box.

"A gift from Michael," John said when he saw her examining them.

"Were you friends?"

"Friends? No, I wouldn't say friends. More like equal admirers. He admired my poetry. And I admired the academic work he was doing. For a time, anyway." He cleared his throat. "And now he wants nothing to do with me—the real me, that is. Why do you ask?"

She raised an eyebrow. "It almost sounds like you miss him."

He laughed. "Please, Ingrid, give me a little credit."

The compulsion to drive to John's house remained unclear even to herself. She had simply gotten in her car and it had brought her here. Her thoughts felt muddled, like the contents had been stirred with a spoon. She sensed some part of herself struggling to single out the missing piece to a puzzle, but she had no idea what the completed puzzle was meant to resemble. Whenever she tried to get a closer look, the image fractured.

"Sorry for barging in like this. I don't know where my head is lately."

"I imagine you're feeling lost."

She nodded.

"Confused and scared."

She nodded again.

"Well, Ingrid, I don't have the answers. But what I can say is this—you can count on me. We'll get through this together, I promise."

"Thanks, John," she said, and meant it. She returned to the sofa and closed her eyes. "I guess our DOFO plans will have to wait for now, anyway. I have to finish my dissertation."

"What's it about? I don't think I ever asked."

She recited her usual three-sentence summary.

"Well, I have to say, from having read a lot of dissertations in my time, that's a top-shelf idea."

Ingrid smiled, then sat up very straight, gripped by a sudden thought. "Actually . . . would you like to come to my defense?"

Somehow—somehow John Smith sitting in the audience during the bizarre performance art piece that entailed her hypothesizing about the man he'd purported to be for thirty-five years was not only a strangely symbolic act but a fittingly cruel and unusual punishment. His presence would also make a mockery of the university's policy to continue teaching Xiao-Wen Chou as if John Smith weren't real, as if Chou were an incorporeal poet who existed on a separate plane of time and space where being dead or alive, white or yellow, made no difference.

"I assume Michael will be there," he said.

"Yes. Will that be weird?"

He hesitated, only for a moment. "We're both adults. I'm sure it'll be fine." John raised his glass. "Ingrid, I would love to come."

THAT NIGHT, Ingrid saw two missed calls from Stephen. Her hand hovered over her phone as she contemplated calling him back. Then she powered it off and turned on her laptop. On the desktop was a job application from the Waffle-Dog Factory. She'd downloaded it during a "total and utter hopelessness" phase, when she felt convinced endeavoring to obtain her degree was a hamster wheel's exercise in futility. She scrolled through the form and got as far as filling in her first and last name. Then—catching sight of herself in the mirror above her desk—sighed and opened up "Dissertation: Draft Three" instead. Twenty-seven more pages to go.

"COME OVER TO Michael's house—now," Eunice whispered urgently into the phone. They hadn't spoken since their quarrel in his office three days ago.

Ingrid wicked the sweat from her forehead. She'd been furiously editing her Works Cited list for the past hour.

"I can't, I'm working on my—"

"Listen, there's some kind of DOFO meeting happening downstairs. I'm trapped in the 'chinoiserie' room—Michael came home early. I'll keep looking around up here, but you need to sneak into that meeting."

Ingrid had tried to tell Eunice last time—all that supersleuth business seemed childish now, and worse, pointless. She began to protest, "But I'm in the middle of—"

"Please, Ingrid, I need you."

Hearing these words from Eunice destabilized her. For once, she was asking *her* for help. Ingrid winced, remembering how she'd lashed out at her in Michael's office.

"I'm leaving now."

"And come undercover."

"What? Hello?"

Eunice had hung up but she had an inkling "undercover" didn't mean all black with a black beret. On the way over, she cut a detour to the campus bookstore.

Fifteen minutes later, Ingrid arrived at Michael's back door replete in a DOFO T-shirt, fanny pack and trucker hat. She convincingly passed as an advertisement for the American flag.

Her original plan was to ring the doorbell, whereupon she'd be graciously led into the meeting, then admonished herself for even thinking of it. Top-level DOFO secrets would never be leaked to a low-level member like her and though she'd technically joined their ranks, she hadn't been outright enthusiastic about it.

She shot off a quick text message and a moment later, Cixi—still startling to witness in all her 1950s suburban housewife glory—cracked open the back door. She took in Ingrid's DOFO-inspired wardrobe, price tags still attached, and arched a perfectly waxed eyebrow. She signalled for Ingrid to follow her to the end of the hallway, then quickly pulled her into a room and shut the door behind them.

They stood inside a wood-paneled office of a long-ago secretary: clunky typewriter, Rolodex, rusty wire fan. Ingrid looked around in confusion before Cixi dropped to her knees and motioned for her to do the same. On the wall, just an inch above the floor, was a baroque metal grate opening up to a formal dining room on the other side of the wall, where some half dozen people sat around a table—all white men and women. No Timothy Liu in sight, or anyone below the age of forty-five.

If she pressed her ear against the grate, she gained the ability to listen but lost her ability to look.

"I'll keep watch outside," Cixi mouthed, then slipped from the room.

Ingrid peered through the grate again, angling her head this way and that for a better view.

The faces were familiar—wait, she knew them. They were Barnes professors: Kenneth McDougal, who she'd taken for Japanese Imperialism. Patricia Lombardi, who taught introductory Cantonese. Noah Steiner, who specialized in colonial Korea. And three others she couldn't name, though she'd seen their faces in the department's hallway of framed portraits.

She gave up looking for listening.

"—more and more people are saying it should be."

"—totally unacceptable."

"We know that, Kenneth, but the university is facing public pressure."

"From?"

"Journalists—"

"Anyone can self-publish on the Internet; it doesn't make them a 'journalist'—"

"—claim it's like 'living in an emotional war zone.'"

"Nonsense—"

"—radical leftist propaganda—"

"The point is, we need to come up with a new PR strategy."

"Isn't that the purpose of the chancellor's 'special investigation?'" At this, Ingrid's spine tingled. She wiggled her phone from her pocket to turn on the Voice Recording function.

"But that was weeks ago—now people are following up."

"If we ignore it, it will die down—"

"Can we at least discuss the other option? Closing down the archive. What would that look like?"

"And lose everything? Absolutely not—"

"I don't know how much longer it can go on, Patricia—I'm trying to be realistic."

"And I'm trying to keep Bancroft's legacy intact."

"He'd be rolling over in his grave if he knew we were even considering—"

"He'd be rolling over in his grave if he knew what *John's* done—"

"If you ask me, Bancroft was naïve to trust John could get away with it for so many years—"

"You think he would've been more grateful for that costly little archive Bancroft gifted him—"

Ingrid's head throbbed. The dean of Barnes all those years ago *knew* about John's racial charade? And *supported* it?

"Well, he believed John when he swore he could keep it up." The hair on her arms stood up at the sound of Michael's voice. "Never thought he'd kill himself off and start mucking around in the archive. The definition of self-sabotage if I ever saw it."

"Well, I always had a funny feeling about Xiao-Wen—I mean John."

"Likewise. He had a . . . carpetbagger quality to him—"

"Ladies and gentlemen, let's stay on topic. We can be frank here. What we all want is to maintain control. This is, after all, *our* university," Michael said.

A round of agreement traveled through the room.

So that explained his play at becoming dean: keeping the bastion of power at Barnes white . . . ivory white.

"—what I meant when I said the department cannot handle any more of them. We take an enormous risk each time—"

"But we face just as much criticism when we *don't* enroll any of them—"

"This is exactly why we have students like Ms. Yang—"

Ingrid forgot to breathe.

"Michael, how can you be sure?"

"I told you, I have everything under control."

"But how do we know we won't have a situation like Wenli's again—"

When Ingrid finally remembered to breathe, her oxygen-starved lungs bucked, provoking the inhalation of an enormous dust bunny. The maddening tingle of a sneeze keened in her sinuses. Don't you dare, she ordered herself, pinching her nose and eyes shut—hold it, hold it, hold it. A tremendous, wall-shaking sneeze burst forth from her. She clapped her hands over her mouth.

"What was that?"

She scrambled to the door and threw it open, coming face-to-face with Michael. Cixi hung behind him, one polished hand tugging anxiously at his shirttail.

"Ingrid." Michael stared at her in her DOFO T-shirt, fanny pack and trucker hat, now fashionably turned askew.

"Michael! How *are* you? T-Timothy told me about a DOFO meeting this afternoon!" Cocking her head, she pretended to study a message on her phone. "Oh—I got the wrong meeting place. Whoopsie!" She hesitantly lifted her gaze to his with what she prayed was an innocent mien.

Michael still stared at her, unamused.

"Well, I should get going now," she chuckled.

Ingrid flattened herself against the wall, edged past him and ran full-speed towards her car.

EUNICE WAS WAITING by her front door. Ingrid was so overcome with what she'd just witnessed, she instinctively hugged her. A look of relief flitted across Eunice's face. They pulled apart and smiled at one another before Ingrid snapped back to the issue at hand.

"Yoon, you will not *believe* what I heard," she babbled, "they called John a carpetbagger and they even started talking about me but I didn't get to—" she paused to gawk at the ornate wooden box by Eunice's feet. "Did you steal that?"

"I had to."

"But if Michael finds out it went missing on the day I was there—oh, shit, oh, shit—"

"That will be the least of his worries."

Ingrid didn't pick up on the foreboding nature of her words. The moment they were alone in the apartment, she took out her phone. "I even taped part of the meeting—listen!"

When the recording ended, Eunice shook her head but didn't say anything.

"Bancroft knew *all along*! Can you believe it? You don't seem surprised. What's going on?" she asked curiously.

Eunice was having trouble meeting her eyes. "I think you should sit down for this." Ingrid impatiently complied. "Well, you know we've been finding really useless stuff, right? Yesterday, Cixi told me she caught Michael poking around in his 'chinoiserie.' So I searched everywhere on that side of the room and found this box hidden inside an armoire, the kind with a false bottom. I mean, it *looked* like the bottom, but it was too high off the ground. That's when I saw an opening just big enough for a finger to pull up the plank of wood."

"And?"

"The box had receipts for eyelid tape. Foundation. Wigs."

"Could you repeat that?" Ingrid frowned. "I don't think I heard you right." Why would John have sent receipts to Michael?

Eunice paused for a beat, then went on. "There's more. I found all these Xiao-Wen Chou poems edited in red pen."

"Oh. Well, lots of professors annotate poems."

"They weren't annotations. They were suggestions."

Why was Eunice acting like Michael's years of Chouian research were some sort of revelation?

"They sent each other letters—for years."

"I know, John told me they admired each other's work."

"Ingrid."

"I don't understand what you're trying to say," she said, her voice barely audible. She felt herself dissolving into a slow spiral. Eunice was sliding up the wall and onto the ceiling. Was her vision tilting or was she deflating to the floor? If she was on the floor, how was she also standing upside down on her head?

"Ingrid, you know what I'm saying. You just don't want to hear it."

20

Be a Good Girl

I saw this in the mailbox," Stephen said, a little apologetically.

She considered chucking it directly in the trash, but instead asked him to read the note aloud. He ripped open the envelope and frowned.

"Well?" she said.

"'If you stop now, nobody will get hurt.' I don't understand, Ingrid. What's going on?"

She snatched the piece of paper from him—still the same ransom-style cutout letters—then jammed it in her pocket. She understood with crystalline clarity who had been sending her the notes all this time: a certain dissertation advisor turned dean turned aspiring cult leader.

"It doesn't concern you," she said, pretending to examine the floor. "What are you doing here anyway?"

"I need my car back."

"Oh."

"And I forgot my electric toothbrush charger."

She watched him walk to the bedroom, swerving her head as he rounded the corner. She had expected a slovenly and unshaven Stephen, stinking of alcohol and takeout fumes, his outsides mirroring his tormented insides. But he looked . . . great. As he strolled back down the hallway, she observed his crisp new haircut and spiffy new pocket protector. Even his chin acne had cleared up.

Ingrid marched to the kitchen; she needed a snack. Several snacks.

With his electric toothbrush charger in hand, Stephen cornered her as she rummaged in the fridge. "This is ridiculous, Ingrid. We need to talk about what happened."

"I don't know what there is to talk about," she said into the freezer.

"We both said some things we regret. That's all."

"Actually, I don't regret anything I said." She gave up snack hunting and maneuvered around him towards the front door. He followed on her heels.

"I can forgive you. No—I *have* forgiven you."

"*You* forgive *me*?"

"Well, it took me some time, but"—he paused and searched her gaze—"Ingrid, I love you." His bottom lip trembled. "Do you still . . . love me?"

When she looked in his eyes, she saw fear tangled with hope. This was the most vulnerable Stephen had ever made himself before her. She knew he loved her, even if she didn't know why. And while this was once enough, *more* than enough, it no longer was. For the first time in years, she felt extraordinarily calm, as though afloat in the halcyon eye of a natural disaster.

"I want to break up" she said evenly.

For a second, something akin to a spasm of pain opened in Stephen's face and she felt compelled to say, "I'm sorry"—because she *was* sorry to have to hurt him—but then his face warped with confusion. "What?"

"I want to break up," she repeated.

"No." The word hit like a clenched fist. All traces of vulnerability she'd beheld a moment ago had dissolved. "Listen, you have to believe me when I say I don't have 'yellow fever.'"

Yellow fever.

Why did people call it that? As if an attraction to a nonwhite person was a sickness, an abnormality that necessitated a cure. As if, once the fever took hold of you, you were powerless to it and therefore, guiltless.

Because she wasn't screaming or crying, he seemed encouraged.

"This suspicion I have a 'fetish' is all in your head," Stephen happily explained, as though this was supposed to be a great comfort to her. He clasped her hands in his. "Ingrid dear, I don't think you have a lot of confidence. I've been reading this self-help book and it's true, you need to love yourself before you believe you're deserving of love. If you're open to it, seeing a psychiatrist is absolutely nothing to be ashamed of. It's completely up to you if you want to go, of course, but I already set up an initial consultation for you next week. Ingrid, I'm your *ally*."

She opened her mouth to laugh but could not rally the energy for this simple task. She looked at Stephen as if for the first time: a medium-brown-haired man of medium height and medium intelligence with a below-average-sized heart.

"You think I'm breaking up with you because of your Asian fetish?" she said disbelievingly. "You think that's the only reason I can't stand to be with you any longer?" He assumed he had a monopoly over self-help literature—well, she had read an article or six herself. She had taken an online quiz called "Is your partner emotionally abusive?" and received a clear-as-day answer. She had learned the vocabulary and used it to translate their relationship. And wasn't translation the truest form of empathy? Oh, she had empathy—not for him but for the Ingrid who had formerly loved the Film Studies Major, Engineering Grad Student, Investment Banker, Medical Resident and now Japanese-to-English Translator—men who had thrown her bones and convinced her she should be grateful to lick them.

She yanked her hands free and stepped closer to Stephen, who shrank against the door. "Stephen Greene, you are the most gaslighting, micromanaging, patronizing, manipulative person I have ever met, whose need to dominate someone else is so pathetically obvious, it's textbook pathological." Ingrid tottered a little in shock—that had unfolded more smoothly than she could have ever hoped. "And now," she coughed, "I would like you to take all your things and leave."

Stephen's mouth dipped open and closed like a goldfish. After a moment, he wordlessly skulked into the office. He gathered his remaining things into a cardboard box she'd left on the floor, his movements stiff and halting (perhaps he *was* getting carpal tunnel). Then he migrated to the bedroom and transferred his clothes into a suitcase.

Ingrid followed after him and plucked a familiar article of clothing from the closet. "Oh, but not this. I'm keeping this." She waved the schoolgirl outfit he'd bought her in the air. Stephen jerked back as if it had been poisoned. He nodded rapidly, his lips pale and dry.

"And you can have this back," she said, before plunking her engagement ring in his palm. She felt instantly lighter, like she'd just unloaded a week's worth of constipation. The very notion of marriage, once a comforting security blanket, had morphed into a blanket that could asphyxiate her in her sleep.

From the living room, she heard the front door close and a minute later, the Oldsmobile sputtering to life. She sat very still for a moment, clamped her eyes shut and waited—now that Stephen had left, for good, would she implode?

A few seconds passed. Then some more seconds. A whole minute ticked by.

She felt fine. Tired, but fine.

The truth was, she had said goodbye to Stephen months ago.

She stood up and studied the schoolgirl outfit in her outstretched arms. The woman who'd enjoyed wearing it, who'd had zero misgivings over wearing it—she had said goodbye to her, too.

Ingrid tried to run it through the paper shredder, but the fabric was too thick. Then she packed it into the kitchen garbage disposal, but this manufactured a terrifying clicking instead of the usual ear-splitting roar. Next she considered donating it—but circulating tainted clothing seemed unethical, potentially cursing its subsequent owner.

Finally, she went out to the balcony, removed the round lid of the charcoal grill and tossed the outfit on top. She touched a lit match to a corner of the shirt, but it refused to catch—the polyester material must've been coated in layers of fire retardant. She went back inside, dug under the kitchen sink for a bottle of lighter fluid and doused every inch of the outfit. Then she set it on fire.

Entranced, Ingrid stared into the flames, admiring their merciless attack on the fabric, which oozed and bubbled before melting into a black carcass. The fire rippled the air around it, blazing against the bright summer sky. She had never seen a more beautiful movie.

Five minutes later, she leaned back in a lawn chair and crossed her feet against the balcony railing. She took a swig from a can of Calpico, bit into a jumbo microwaved corn dog, then chased it with a square of fudge. She unbuttoned her jeans with a satisfied sigh. No one was there to remind her about calorie intake, sugar-induced mood swings or intestinal tract movements. If this was the single life, well, what had she been so afraid of?

She dispatched the news to Eunice and her parents by text: "I broke up with Stephen."

Within seconds of each other, they replied. Eunice sent back a volley of emojis: strong arm, heart eyes, sparkles, 100%. In the group chat with her parents, her mother likewise answered in emoji language: shocked face, questioning face, shocked face. Her father wrote back, "Good. I never liked him."

THE MORNING OF June twentieth was clear and hot, without a single smudge of cloud in the sky. Ingrid Yang was dressed in a loose black dress and white sneakers. Her hair was freshly shampooed and secured in a low ponytail. She was thirty years old and on her way to defend her dissertation. She walked with painstaking steps towards Barnes University—partly because she dreaded her arrival on campus and partly because her backpack weighed a staggering amount. Inside was a two-hundred-fifty-page dissertation and a garbage bag bulging with incriminating papers—papers she planned on handing over to *The Barnes Gazette.*

The previous night, she had received an email informing her the Humanities Block was closed for emergency fumigation (black mold). While this was all well and good for people's respiratory systems, her defense had been moved from conference room 105 to the adjacent auditorium, a far more expansive and intimidating venue. She was nervous enough as it was, not least because both Michael and John awaited her. But friendly faces would also welcome her: her parents, Eunice and Alex, Vivian and Zoe, Margaret and Daryl, Professor Zhao and Gurti. A few members of the POC Caucus had said they'd come, too.

She passed beneath the university gates, making her way across campus for the last time: the library, the archive, the quad, the theater where she'd first protested. She had spent nearly half her life at Barnes. This town, this university, had been her home for a long time. But it had been an inhospitable home; a home not meant for someone like her. Michael wasn't a malignant mist—Wittlebury was. The whole country was.

Outside the auditorium, a spray-tanned figure was schmoozing into a cell phone. Her heart took a nosedive. Michael ended his call. "Ah," he smiled, "my prize PhD student."

She glared at him.

"I wanted to catch you before the defense. Say a few encouraging words," he chuckled. "You're a very intelligent woman, Ingrid. I've always known you to have excellent judgment. I'm sure you get it from your parents—I just had a little chat with them. They live in Putterville, don't they? On Quail Street? The lovely little house with a eucalyptus tree, if I'm not mistaken." Her chest contracted. "Now, I know it's an ancient custom for Chinese parents to worry about their child's future, but I assured them that they have nothing to worry about when it comes to you. I told them, 'I'm watching her very carefully.'" He forcibly embraced her, gripping her tight around her waist and panting into her ear, "Be a good girl."

Ingrid wrenched herself away, heart palpitating, and stomped towards the auditorium's second-level entrance. How dare Michael—how dare he speak to her parents! She couldn't fathom how he'd recognized them; she'd never introduced him to Jean and Bo. The knowledge that he'd wormed his way to their address curdled her breakfast. All the determination she'd felt that morning fizzled out.

Forget going to *The Barnes Gazette*. To the dumpster, it was. She slammed her palms against the auditorium door's push bar and stumbled at the threshold. A handful of people had transformed into a half-full auditorium. Some hundred faces turned around to look up at her. She slowly descended the stairs, everyone's gazes sticking to her.

In the front row, Eunice hopped up from her seat. Ingrid hugged her, breathing in her cotton-candy-scented hair.

"Who are all these people?" she asked in a daze.

"I invited everyone. The E. A. department, Postcolonial, Africana, Gender and Queer Studies. Even English and Comp Lit. Undergrads, grad students, faculty. Admin, too."

"Why?"

"Because. This is your day," Eunice beamed.

"Thank you, Yoon. For everything." She hugged her again, hard.

Behind Eunice, John was slipping into a seat in the third row. He waved effusively at her. What a sorry excuse for a person he was. She faked a smile back.

"Go," Eunice whispered, giving her an encouraging pat on the butt.

Ingrid climbed the short flight of stairs to the stage, wracked with nervous nausea, her breath uneven and her head faint—her constant state of being for the past year. When was she ever not feeling this way? As though she were a giant walking, talking marshmallow that absorbed whatever pricks and punches were thrown its way. A marshmallow that bent and twisted into the shape of whatever mold it inhabited. Too sensitive, too weak-willed, too . . . passive.

To the far left of the front row presided the dissertation committee, composed of Patricia Lombardi, Kenneth McDougal and, of course, Michael. He sat with his legs crossed while leisurely scrolling through his phone, as though he hadn't been outside threatening her and her family minutes ago.

"Ingrid Yang, you are here today to defend your dissertation in the East Asian Studies graduate department," Kenneth intoned in a listless voice. "You have a thirty-minute presentation, after which you will be subjected to two hours of questioning. I mark the time as June twentieth at 11:01 a.m. You may begin."

"Thank you." She spoke too closely into the microphone, emitting a high-pitched squeal. "Sorry."

Ingrid busied herself arranging notecards on the podium, then hunched over to fish for a pen in her backpack, all the while calming her breathing. What had she been thinking, that someone like her could take down someone like Michael? She lived in *this* world, a world where injustice prevailed.

She straightened back up, trying to exude composure. From the audience, her parents caught her eye and flashed her two exaggerated thumbs-up each, their faces shiny with pride. Reassuring warmth swelled up in her. She could do this. Just two and a half more hours and finally—finally—this chapter of her life would come to a close.

"Calligraphic Gestures: The Influence of Chinese Grammar on Xiao-Wen Chou's Use of Enjambment," Ingrid announced, then cleared her throat. "In my dissertation, I explore the ways in which Chou's formal stylings are inseparable from his linguistic heritage as a Chinese American first-generation son of immigrants—"

For the next fifteen minutes, she dutifully trudged through her presentation. The committee nodded approvingly, her parents smiled pleasantly.

So this was the path she had chosen: covering her ears as the screams multiplied.

"—exemplified in 'The Ancestral Hearth,' which references Chou's mother's side of the family . . ." Her sentence petered out.

"Chou's mother's side of the family?" The words tasted gluey and false on her tongue. Her eyes drifted towards John. He was smiling strangely at her—a familiar lopsided half smirk, like a long-ago smiley face drawn beside "No, stupid."

She looked down at her notecards and frowned. Why *was* she treating Xiao-Wen Chou as though he were real? As though he were a Chinese American man born from Chinese parents when he was a collection of pigment and tape and one man's hubris? What was this grotesque charade, this—this nationwide farce? She clocked Michael staring at her, a grin halving his face. He was enjoying her performance of the part he'd written for her, a scurrying mouse trapped in a cardboard box of his own construction. He was gloating.

She uncreased his note from her pocket: *If you stop now, nobody will get hurt.*

Michael must have known she'd nicked the box. Must have figured out awhile ago she was snooping on him. But how? She knew Cixi would never tattle on her. Perhaps he had video cameras installed in every square foot of his house. Perhaps, the whole time she thought she'd been tailing him, he'd been tailing her . . . The night she had seen the rabbit by her apartment . . . A shudder sliced through her.

Michael's message to her was plain: he held the power in this situation and she held none. After all, he had the entirety of Barnes backing him. Authority. Institutional weight. Money. Lawyers. Like cronies who show up swinging baseball bats and crowbars. Just like Professor Zhao had warned her.

Michael had the power to crush her into nothing with a mere flick of his pen. She'd be expelled from academia forever. And what did she have? A box of evidence he'd accuse her of forging.

On the other hand, she had the secret recording on her phone (even if it wasn't legally obtained evidence). And she had seen the meeting through the grate; wouldn't that make her an eyewitness? Perhaps she'd emerge victorious, after all . . .

And yet, every time she read the news, she came across more and more stories of men getting away with murder—literally. Men with a nickel badge and a high school diploma could kill with impunity. Heinous crimes like pedophilia, sex trafficking and gang rape were forgotten, buried under more identical news stories. In exchange for their exorbitant bails, these men were rewarded with ankle bracelets and the luxury of lounging around their million-dollar estates. They got paid time off, retired or moved to a country with lax extradition laws. They got to hit "Start Game Over." Just like the Barnes professor who'd sexually assaulted a freshman five years ago and continued to teach in the Economies department.

Absolutely no prior evidence suggested Michael, or Barnes, would be punished for what they'd done—even if Ingrid amassed all the evidence in the world.

But at the same time, in all those news stories, didn't someone have the courage to speak up, to put themselves at risk? Wasn't there someone who said, "He hurt me. And I have to tell the truth because I don't want him to hurt others."

She crumpled up the note.

"Ms. Yang? Ms. Yang?" Kenneth called irritably. "Anyone home? *Hello?*"

"Oh, um, yes, sorry."

"Please continue, Ms. Yang, preferably without taking any more naps." The other members of the committee chuckled.

"Of . . . course," she said uncertainly. She glanced at her parents, her heart nearly rending from the worry etched in their faces. "Sorry, I forgot to state my presentation requires a projector."

Kenneth sighed heavily. "Ms. Yang, you were supposed to request materials a week in advance. Someone set up the projector—now."

Daryl scampered on stage, wheeling out a projector from behind the curtains. He flicked a switch and a screen descended from the ceiling, flush against the high wall.

"Thanks, Daryl."

"Good luck," he nodded from beneath his mop of blue-black hair.

"I'd like to say," Ingrid murmured into the microphone, "my dissertation is actually about—" She swallowed and, against her will, locked eyes with Michael. His low brow was even lower than usual, shading his eyes into a menacing ridge.

"My dissertation is about"—Kenneth and this time Patricia sighed again—"the crimes Michael Bartholomew and Barnes University have committed."

Whispers stirred through the audience.

"Excuse me, Ms. Yang?" Kenneth frowned.

"Michael Bartholomew found out John Smith was, um, pretending to be Xiao-Wen Chou approximately thirty years ago." She could hear herself speaking clumsily and quietly when she should've been speaking with gusto and fervor. "They met at a Chinese Cultural Heritage Association award ceremony in Philadelphia. Instead of revealing John's harmful secret, he, um, colluded with him." She tugged the hefty stack of evidence from her backpack, plopped it on the podium and rummaged through the pages. Under the overhead projector, she placed John's poem "Playground Porridge," marked up in red pen. "Michael had recently graduated from Barnes with a—a history PhD but was struggling to find a job, given his obscure specialization in Ancient China. To establish his career as a professor of East Asian Studies, Michael worked with John to make Chou the greatest, the—the most canonical Chinese American poet who would overshadow all other, um, real Chinese American poets."

Gasps skipped from one row to the next.

"Go, Ingrid!" Eunice yelled.

She smiled gratefully at her, then placed a copy of a letter onto the projector and read: "'It's better than the first draft, but you need to insist on the trauma of growing up as a minority, John. Academia is positively devouring that sort of thing right now. I've already started outlining the paper I'm going to write on the finished poem: "East-West Identity Crisis as Aesthetic Form in Xiao-Wen Chou's Poetry.'"

Ingrid paused before moving on. "John consulted Michael on everything, including his makeup and wig choices." She presented another piece of correspondence: "'I don't know, John, from a distance it's all right, but from up close, the eyes are still a little off. Did you receive that new eyelid tape I ordered from Japan?'"

Ingrid allowed herself to look in the offenders' direction: Michael's spray tan had completely evaporated and his eyes kept beelining towards the exit. When she got to John's seat, she did a double-take: empty. She knew he wasn't scared of her—so who was he running from? Michael? But why would he—oh. New knowledge sank to the bottom of her stomach. If *she* was afraid of Michael, John must be even more afraid of him. After all, what did he have on John that ensured his mouth was stitched shut? In fact, just how much of the Xiao-Wen Chou personage was *Michael's* invention? But rather than own up to conspiring with him, John had made a run for it. A spineless coward until the end, she seethed. Like some bootleg nihilist, he acted like he had no skin in the game—in any game. She couldn't tell what was sincere or insincere with him, ironic or unironic. Had he meant his yellowface or had he meant his apology? Both?

John, she realized, was a real-life Internet troll.

How could she have ever forgiven him? Believed he wanted to redeem himself? He was a compulsive liar, the only truthful statement he had ever uttered in her presence. She had no idea if his dad had been in the Air Force, if his mom had abandoned him, if he had even set foot in China. When she visited him at his house, he had lied through his teeth about his relationship with Michael. Why? For trollish shits and giggles? Or so he could boast he had pulled off a "magic trick" for thirty-five years all by himself? Had he lied for the sake of his *ego*?

And he had lied to her another time, in the motel room, when he said, "I know what it's like to be you."

Give me a fucking break. Paint washes off. But her face wasn't painted on. She was born with it and she would die with it.

Already she suffered from existing in a world where she was infantilized even at age thirty. Where every representation of her was one she had had no say in. She had to put up with the five-dolla-sucky-suckys and the me-love-you-long-times not through any choice of her own. She had to live with the consequences of a dead white man's whims when he ended the story with Cio-Cio San choosing the love of a white man over her child's life, over her own life. That burden, the consequences of these popular narratives, was hers to carry. Never to those who created them. After churning out a day's worth of harm, they got to go home and live untouched by it. They got to be free.

And then, as if that weren't enough, they still wanted to *be* her. To slither inside her skin, to annex not just the exterior self but the inner self, like hands orchestrating puppets. That was total domination, wasn't it? Ensuring the other was rendered powerless, forced into docility, kept under careful and strict control. Was that what Vivian meant when she argued yellowface was an act of colonization . . .

The sound of the auditorium, people talking excitedly, plunged her back to the present.

"And it gets worse," she said, confidence finally seeping into her. "Barnes University knew about John's lie."

Epithets flew from the audience.

Ingrid made her voice louder still. "Michael persuaded Dean Bancroft to hire John and form an East Asian Studies department, which he would head. Bancroft had no interest investing in—in Asian writers. But Michael knew he was worried the university protests on the West Coast, the creation of the Third World Liberation Front, would infect East Coast schools. Michael claimed this was a way to—to maintain control of the growing number of Asian students, to keep them interested in 'good and honest traditional immigrant literature,' rather than anything that questioned the status quo or Barnes's history of oppression, as Vivian Vo argues in her dissertation, 'Pleasing the White Master.'" She glanced up to see Vivian clapping her hands above her head. "Bancroft agreed. He had no—no qualms taking tuition money from the Asian students he was scamming."

Kenneth and Patricia turned to stare at Michael in mock horror.

Ingrid pulled out her phone and slid the volume up to max before hitting play. "This was taken during a meeting at Michael's house." In the acoustically gifted auditorium, the professors' voices resounded clearly. Kenneth and Patricia now blanched a different shade of horrified.

Zoe rose from her seat. "Fuck you!" she shouted at the committee.

Wenli sprang up beside her and hollered so deafeningly, the walls trembled, "YEAH, FUCK YOU, MOTHERFUCKER!"

At this, Michael lurched out of his seat and clambered onto the stage. He seized Ingrid's phone from the podium and launched it at the ground, smashing it over and over with his heel until the black screen was splintered white. The recording had played only for some thirty seconds.

The auditorium was stunned into silence.

Ingrid could hardly look at Michael. The whites of his eyes bordered on feral; his slicked-back hair hung across his face; his mouth seemed ready to foam at the corners.

"You're going to listen to her?" he defied the audience.

"Yes," Vivian cried. "Fuck off already!"

When the POC Caucus started booing, the others joined in, their shouts echoing through the auditorium.

Michael scanned the audience, looking knocked off-balance. He wasn't used to heckling instead of cheering, Ingrid thought, to people tossing insults at him instead of bouquets. Then he whirled around to face her. "You think you can hurt me?" he spat, her microphone amplifying his words. He ripped it off its stand and hurled it to the floor, setting off a nail-scratching screech.

"Tell me, how are you going to do that? How is little ol' Ingrid going to do that? Ingrid Yang, everybody—who can't make up her own mind!" He looked wildly around at the audience, then turned back to face her. "Whose favorite hobby is being walked on by other people! Tell her to jump, oh, she'll jump! Yes, she really is that pathetic, folks. A true specimen of the Oriental race. *Meek*," he sneered. "You know, Ingrid, you should be thanking me for giving you direction in life. For trying to save you from a miserable little existence. I was setting you up nicely to inherit the department, too. You could have had a comfortable situation if you had just done what you were told—" He flexed his hands and took another step towards her.

Tears fell down her cheeks. All the oxygen in her lungs was escaping through an invisible puncture—

"Don't touch her!"

"Call the police!"

"Don't be stupid!"

Michael threw his head back and laughed with theatrical flair. Ingrid couldn't bear how close he was to her, but she couldn't dislodge her feet; they'd been cemented onto the floor.

"Oh, the police chief is a very good friend of mine. Call him. I'd *like* you to call him."

Of course the Wittlebury police were personal friends of DOFO's leader; how could they not be? When the town's entire history was founded on maintaining the power of—

Michael abruptly lunged at Ingrid, pretending to pounce on her, instead smacking everything off the podium. Papers shot up into the air. She screamed and ducked her head as they floated and swirled down to the floor. He staggered back, laughing and pointing at her.

"That's enough!"

At the sound of her father's voice, Ingrid's feet regained agency. She hastened across the stage and down the steps, where her mother wrapped her tightly in her arms.

"Mama," she sobbed.

"Arrest that man!"

Ingrid looked up. She had never seen her father so angry, so powerful. He stormed up to the security guard and pointed at Michael. "He tried to assault my daughter. Arrest that man—now!"

The security guard was one of two patrolling both exits. Ingrid had only cursorily registered their presence, too distraught by the unfolding events to look closer. Now she observed them: both massive and over six feet tall, white, with shaved heads. Their polo shirts were patterned in red, white and blue. Were they . . . DOFO members?

Michael cackled. "'Arrest that man!'" He mocked Bo in an obnoxious faux accent, one that didn't sound like Ingrid's father at all but a gag from a bad Hollywood movie, where white men could only pretend to be Chinese—but would never be fortunate enough to be something that wasn't vacant and hollow. For how else could they make room in themselves for such heinousness.

Ingrid's father crossed his arms before the stoic security guard, who wasn't coming towards the stage to arrest Michael, but moving closer to Bo.

"We are leaving now!" her father shouted.

The security guard blocked the door.

"No one will be leaving until I say so," Michael said. He suddenly appeared much calmer. He dusted off his pants, smoothed back his hair and stood up straight.

"What the fuck is happening?"

"Let us leave!"

"There's a hundred of us and three of them—what are we waiting for—"

"Don't you watch the news? These skinheads are trigger-happy domestic terrorists—"

"If they call for backup, someone *will* die—"

"Well, I do *not* plan on dying today—"

If people were hurt, it would be on account of her bringing them here. She had no other option—she had to get them out. Her eyes darted between the two exits. If she could distract the guard blocking the first-level exit, he would have to leave it unattended, creating an opening for everyone to flee through the exit at the top of the stairs. But how could she distract him? If only she could formulate a foolproof plan—she didn't have time to think—

"Everyone run!" she bellowed.

Ingrid rushed the stage, charging full-speed at Michael. His smirk turned to terror in seconds. She head-butted him so forcefully, he toppled to the ground like a toothpick. She wrapped her hands around his throat, squeezing with all her strength. His own hands copied hers, flailing at her neck, but she bit hard on the skin between his thumb and index finger, and his scream externalized as a muzzled whimper. She had only wanted to create a temporary distraction, but strangling Michael Bartholomew beneath her, adrenaline kicking through her veins as his eyes twitched with disbelief, she underwent a brief ecstatic experience—it was near religious. She felt possessed, hardly in control of her own movements, unsure if the two hands still latched around his flabby throat belonged to her. They tightened their vise, pushing hard towards the floor, and after what felt like a fast-forwarded eternity, his arms went limp and his eyes stared past Ingrid, as though emptied out—

Then the second security guard was hauling her away by the armpits and digging his fingernails into her flesh, his hands rough and calloused.

Sirens sounded in the distance. She spun her head around: a blur of bodies poured through the top exit. Eunice and Alex, Vivian and Zoe— she couldn't see them. Good, that meant they were safe. As she was dragged through the exit, she caught sight of her father wrestling the other security guard, who was also taking a fierce thrashing from her mother's purse.

"Let go of me!" Ingrid cried. She kicked backwards at the guard's groin just as two cold metal handcuffs slammed down on her wrists. He punted open the door on the ground floor, sunlight cutting into her eyes, and tossed her onto her stomach. She landed halfway on the grass, but the impact still hurt terribly, her restrained arms unable to break the fall, her bare knees scraping her to a stop, her face smacking hard into the ground. What was that flooding her mouth?

She recognized Cixi's face for a blurry moment, whispering, "Thank you," in her ear before dashing away.

"Ingrid!" Eunice gasped. "Are you okay?" She bent over Ingrid and petted her hair, her face contorted with distress.

"I'm—fine," she gurgled. "Go—help—parents."

She spit out a mouthful of blood and saw a pale object bounce away on the grass, then struggled to raise her head. Campus police in riot gear had swarmed the auditorium. People were trying to jostle their way towards her, but the police clogged the path with their clear shields, shouting through their megaphones to stay put—they had tear gas and rubber bullets and they wouldn't hesitate to use them.

Ingrid closed her eyes. Where was Michael? Was he planning to skip town? A horrible image gripped her: Michael racing to the airport and hopping on the next flight to Panama, peacefully living out the rest of his days in a hammocked grove of palm trees. Or was he still lying motionless and pale on the stage floor—

A sudden explosion of cheers reopened her eyes: Was that—*Ma-Margaret?* Launching a succession of perfectly executed roundhouse kicks into the heads of one, no, two, no, *three* cops? Oh, Margaret—you beautiful, complex creature.

Once this gap formed, people surged through the police barricade, breaking it entirely.

"Get out of my way!"

"That is my daughter!"

"Mom, Dad," she cried a moment later, seeing the outlines of their anxious, proud faces peering down on her. Her relief was so immense, tears spilled down her face again. "Did he hurt you?"

"We're fine," her mother said shakily, "you know your father wrestled in college—Ingrid, your tooth!"

"Are you okay?" her father asked urgently, laying the back of his hand against her forehead. "Ingrid, ni hai hao ma?"

She had broken off her engagement; she had failed her dissertation and no longer had a source of income; she had choked a white man and accused a powerful institution of fraud; she was newly missing a front tooth, which she would no longer have healthcare to fix; she had, she realized from the warmth soaking her legs, pissed herself in public—but Ingrid Yang could not remember ever feeling so happy.

She twisted to lie on her back, lifting her blood-smeared face towards the sun, and laughed.

Epilogue

A New You

"W elcome to the Waffle-Dog Factory! How can I help you today?"

A frazzled-looking woman armed with a fanny pack, Velcro visor and cell phone lanyard ransacked her shoulder bag for her wallet. "Hi," she grunted. Two children ran circles around her while clasping their throats and pretending to suffocate. After extracting every conceivable object from her bag, including what appeared to be a spatula, she slapped her wallet on the counter and hissed, *"Behave."* She jerked her head in their direction. "Made the mistake of giving them juice in the car. Three tickets. You got discounts for kids?"

"We sure do! Children under the age of twelve are half price."

"Great." She held out her credit card between two fingers.

"Are you part of our membership program?"

"Nope."

"Would you like to join?"

"Nope."

"And would you like to add a guided tour for only $15.99?"

The woman looked down at her kids, now twitching and spasming on the floor. They'd segued to fake seizures. "Nope."

"All right, that will be a total of $32.17. Credit or debit?"

"Credit," she said, tapping her card impatiently against the counter.

Ingrid swiped it through the machine. "Could you sign here, please?" She returned the customer copy of the receipt as the tickets printed.

"Bathrooms?" the woman asked, stifling a yawn.

"Restrooms and coat check are to your right, and the restaurant and gift shop are to your left." She enclosed the warm tickets in a paper sleeve and handed it over along with a map of the factory.

"Thanks," the woman nodded, then snapped her fingers. "Brandon! Dylan! That's enough now." She fed the tickets into her fanny pack's mouth and veered to the right, children in tow.

"Have a delicious day!" Ingrid called after them. She turned to the next customer in line and readjusted her inflatable hat. "Welcome to the Waffle-Dog Factory! How can I help you today?"

AT 3:00 P.M., Ingrid switched from front desk duties to gift shop restocking. Her shoulders sagged upon entering the stockroom: the sickly green metal trolley sat empty. Whoever completed the last restock was meant to fill it up again, but it contained only a foam waffle-dog squeeze toy and a copy of *The Official Waffle-Dog Factory Cookbook*. Hanging from the side of the trolley were an inventory clipboard and a ballpoint pen.

She scanned the list and reached for the ladder, then scaled the top shelf to retrieve seven boxes of waffle-dog–shaped chocolates. They weren't intended to be comical, or erotic, but the hot dog ends of the chocolates were extraordinarily phallic and, if she dared say so, anatomically correct. She had to exert inhuman self-control to maintain a neutral face when ringing them up at the register.

Ingrid was on a full-time schedule, working eight-and-a-half-hour shifts, with a half hour unpaid break in the middle, five days a week. For ten dollars an hour, she greeted customers, operated the cash register, oversaw the coat check, gave tours, restocked the gift shop and cleaned the taste-testing area. She had two opening shifts, two closing shifts and one midday shift. The job didn't come with benefits or any paid sick/holiday leave, but she was allowed one free waffle-dog or any side dish (cheese fries, macaroni salad, corn balls) per day. Plus, every sixty days of work, she accumulated two free admission tickets.

Today was June twentieth, exactly eleven months since she'd started working at the Waffle-Dog Factory. Between the end of her dissertation defense and the start of her new job, she authorized a monthlong vacation for herself: binge-watching as many reality TV shows as she could stomach; taking advantage of all the free trial classes in town (hip-hop dancing, fencing, chainsaw wood carving); sunbathing at Wittlebury Park while reading novels composed almost entirely of sex scenes; going on a seaside daytrip with Eunice to indulge in overpriced lobster.

At the end of the month, she received an eviction notice: since she was no longer a graduate student, she no longer qualified for graduate student housing. She'd either have to live with three to five roommates in order to pay her rent, bills, student loans and save up for a car, or she could move back home with her parents.

She moved back home with her parents.

Her first decree was a family viewing of a (sensitively directed and award-winning) documentary on hoarding. Her parents conceded that true, perhaps they could do with a bit of organizing and decluttering. But when they procrastinated, promising they'd get around to it another day, then *another* day, she decided to tackle the project herself. She finished entire audiobooks while sorting mountains of objects into "keep" and "donate" hills, until her parents, frustrated with her arbitrary decisions, swapped in for her. They even confronted, of their own volition, the behemoth that was the garage. Once cleared out, it housed all the storage boxes in Ingrid's bedroom, reverting the latter to its former high-school-era state.

She untacked her old posters, photos and certificates, then painted the faded pink walls a bright white. The last step was a yard sale for her old furniture, and to her surprise, her parents pitched in several boxes of their own.

Ingrid liked living at home again. Everyone bemoaned moving back in with one's parents as a palpable sign of having failed adulthood. But to her, the supposed downgrade was analogous to winning a chance at a do-over. Having never engaged in prolonged conversation, they now had ample time for it, even if their attempts were peppered with periods of clumsy silence. She learned that her mother concealed a sly and wicked sense of humor. That her father, when given a few beers, could belt out Teresa Teng songs with such tenderness, it moved her to tears. And she was beginning to let them see her, too, beginning to tell them, little by little, the parts of her life she'd withheld.

On her days off, Ingrid helped her parents cook, clean and mow the lawn. On days she worked, her parents insisted on packing her a lunch (then lightly bickered over who got to pack it). When their schedules aligned, they planned group activities like board game nights, feeding the mean-spirited geese at Wittlebury Park or bowling at the local alley during seniors night (her parents pocketed an excellent discount). Of course, she still lapsed into the role of the moping teenager when she was nagged just a little too often about how she stacked the dishes or how she forgot to empty the dryer lint box again or how she once again finished all the Twinkies, but on the whole, they fell into a familiarly unfamiliar coexistence.

And she was thankful her parents didn't begrudge her choice to not only leave Barnes but academia altogether. She had no desire to transfer to a different university like Vivian, who now lived with Zoe in a Brooklyn apartment along with thirty houseplants and an ex-bodega cat named L Train. They supported her decision to work a minimum-wage job. They didn't badger her every few weeks with the dreaded reprimand disguised as a question, "When are you going to get a *real* job?" They knew she liked working at the factory. Even if her manager always assigned her and none of her coworkers to Asian tour groups, even if the occasional customer complimented her on her "impressive" English, she liked her job. She did.

Ingrid just needed time to drift, time to feel lost, time to waste. Having never considered another career besides academia, she wanted to avoid blindly rushing into a new one, propelled by panic and guilt. Above all, she needed time to savor her freedom from Barnes. From Michael.

The news of his acquittal eight months ago had been seared into her brain.

DEAN CLEARED OF ALL CHARGES

The Barnes Gazette

By Norman Duchamps | October 17

This morning, the Chancellor's Advisory Board acquitted Michael Bartholomew of all charges. The dean of students faced allegations of having intentionally deceived students and faculty on the true identity of John Smith (formerly known as "Xiao-Wen Chou").

At a press conference, the chancellor issued the following statement: "After months of thorough investigation, we have determined no evidence of wrongdoing on Michael Bartholomew's part. He will depart on a yearlong sabbatical to heal from his injuries and will resume his position as dean of students next fall."

Barnes was rocked by events that took place on June 20 during the dissertation defense of former PhD candidate Ingrid Yang (East Asian Studies). After Bartholomew accused her of slander, premeditated assault and emotional distress, she faced a hearing of her own and the possibility of expulsion. Yang quit the PhD program and forfeited her doctoral degree rather than face trial.

Given Barnes's history, she shouldn't have been surprised at the outcome of Michael's so-called investigation (for months, he'd paraded around campus with a neck *and* back brace, both of which she surmised were purely for show). But she was still disappointed. The only positive news concerning him had come by way of Cixi, who'd divorced him and taken all his DOFO assets with her.

As for John, no one ever heard from him again. Well, Ingrid did receive a Johannesburg-stamped postcard with only "Thinking of you" written on the back. Was the sender John or some other estranged figure from her past? Ingrid never knew for certain.

Ingrid navigated the trolley in the direction of the gift shop. A squad of teenagers strutted towards her with their phones suspended before their faces, live-streaming their commentary of the factory.

"Kill me if I ever end up working here," one of them quipped as he passed her. The others laughed.

"Have a *dee-li-cious* day!" she called, loud enough for her supervisor to hear, then stuck her tongue out at the teenagers a second later.

HER BREAK WAS at 5:30 p.m. She set a timer on her phone, made a quick stop at her locker, then nearly ran to the back of the factory. Squatting against the side of the building, next to the loading dock, were scratched-up picnic tables with striped umbrellas in mint green, yellow and red.

She opened her insulated lunch bag to find a turkey wrap, a hard-boiled egg, sliced apples and a thermos of cold green tea—definitive proof her mother had packed it. Whenever Bo was on lunch duty, he snuck her egg roll cookies or sweet rice crackers or some other sugary treat. Still, she tucked in eagerly, eating with her right hand while scrolling through her phone with her left. At the top of her social media page, a "Nine of your mutual friends 'liked' this post!" notification blinked above a photo of a white man and an Asian woman holding hands at a protest. With their two other free hands, they hoisted a cardboard sign into the air: SAVE LITTLE TOKYO! STOP ALL EVICTIONS TODAY!

Ingrid selected "Do not show me similar notifications."

She heard Stephen had met Marie Fukushima, a prominent activist, while volunteering at this year's Day of Remembrance for Japanese internment. Stephen was smart, she had to give him that—he had learned to level up his camouflage. Ever since moving to San Francisco, his social media posts were no longer factoids about Japanese cuisine but scathing tirades against anti-Asian racism. He'd also started wearing knitted beanies, traded in his round wire-framed glasses for square plastic frames and—oh, how she cringed to witness it—was nursing a paltry little beard.

As for Azumi, she had released a manga adaptation of her novel, still under the ruse of her false identity, to an even greater bout of international success. Ingrid had to hand it to her—her dedication to the character of Azumi Kasuya for the purposes of cultural revenge was awe-inspiring. She also appeared to have cut ties with Stephen—at least, Ingrid had deduced as much from the sudden discontinuation of their online interactions.

Although she had left academia firmly in the rearview mirror, its former habits still clung to her: obsessiveness, overanalyzing meaningless incidents and a deep pleasure derived from sleuthing, or as it was usually known, "researching." Up until a few months ago, she had kept abreast of Stephen's whereabouts and subsequent transformation—not because she missed him or wanted him back but to satiate her naturally inquisitive personality.

Not above pettiness, she also wanted to say, "Told you so!" to anyone who might care.

She was impressed Stephen had dove so fearlessly back into the infested waters of dating. A while back, she logged into her old account on the website where they'd matched, but in less than twenty-four hours, deleted the account with welcome relief. She had received three dick pics and two messages referencing "soy sauce" (not in a good way)—one of which was sent by none other than Austin Krantz from elementary school, now sporting a comb-over and working for a pyramid scheme.

She screenshotted the photo of Stephen and Marie and sent it to Eunice before remembering the time in South Korea: 6:40 a.m.

Ingrid had managed to ward off crying until after Eunice passed through airport security, waving ecstatically to her, Alex and Ji-Eun. She was not about to spoil Eunice's voyage with her "don't leave me" woes.

And after that one time, Ingrid didn't cry again. She was happy for Eunice, proud of her for knowing what she wanted and going after it, two skills she could only dream of replicating in her lifetime. Eunice was a freelance makeup artist (and could add PhD to the back of her name to boot) but hoped to eventually join a company that catered to celebrity clientele. Ingrid could tell she loved living in Seoul. During their weekly video calls, she described the wonders of belonging to the majority, of being utterly and sublimely unremarkable, of the safety it afforded. But of course, "returning to the motherland" wasn't the magical cure-all she'd imagined, either. Every so often, she came down with a bout of "third culture diasporic blues" (Eunice's words). She also lamented the ubiquity of "icky white male expats."

Ingrid wondered if she tried to downplay the sheen of her glossy new life in Seoul in order to ease the sting of her very unglamorous, very uncosmopolitan life. "You're never coming back, are you?" she sometimes teased her. Eunice assured her she wasn't planning on staying forever. But Ingrid knew things could change. People—they were always subject to change.

Her phone buzzed. She checked it in a panic, worried her text had woken Eunice up, but the notification was from a language learning app stating it had been thirty days since her last Beginning Mandarin lesson. Did she want to continue lesson 3.8 now? She swallowed a bite of apple and hit "Ask me again later." She intended to finish the class, she did—but after the first few weeks, without deadlines or teachers reprimanding her, she'd caved under another teenage habit: slacking off on homework. Still, she was proud of herself—Ingrid Yang, learning how to read and write Mandarin. Her parents half joked that after she completed the course, she could start Hokkien next.

Her phone buzzed again; her break was over.

THE MOST COVETED duty was coat check. Since two people managed the booth (one taking coats, the other returning them), employees could freely

chat with one another. Coat check was also the only place she could discreetly text without fear of a supervisor materializing behind her back—
which somehow always coincided with the *one* time she peeked at her
phone or forgot to sponge up a condiment overflow or snuck a waffle-dog
sample.

Joan was already in the booth. She asked if Ingrid had plans after work.

"Not tonight," she smiled. "What about you?"

Her coworkers were mostly younger than her, in their late teens and
early twenties, but a few were around her age or older. Sometimes after
closing, everyone gathered at a bar two streets down, where they traded
gossip about annoying customers or micromanaging bosses or salacious
in-factory hooking up.

Ingrid wouldn't say she was especially close with her coworkers, but she
delighted in hanging out with people from the "real world," a.k.a. people
who didn't live inside the stuffy bubble of Barnes. She didn't have to listen
to them bandy around the word "discursive" in casual conversation, much
less name-drop obscure eastern European theorists. Not that she couldn't
engage in esoteric discussions with her coworkers—but any pressure, or
desire, to perform her intellect had fizzled out.

Outside of work, her social life consisted of third-wheeling with Alex
and Ji-Eun, still a nauseatingly cute couple, and sharing the occasional cin-
namon bun over coffee with Gurti at the Old Midwife. Every once in a
while, she stopped by Margaret's boutique specializing in high-end brocade
fashion (and was invariably greeted with an enthusiastic "may I help you").
When the POC Caucus hosted a defund-the-police info session or a Black
and Asian Solidarities workshop, she made an effort to attend. She always
sat quietly in the back, petrified of accidentally saying or doing anything
vaguely offensive, and received cautious "hi's" from the other participants,
but was not invited to the after-parties. She didn't mind. At least now she
could maintain eye contact with the posters on the wall.

"Do I need a drink," Joan whistled, rotating her neck a few times. "Are
you going to come out tonight?"

"I think so," Ingrid said. Her phone buzzed in her pocket. Eunice had replied: "Could Stephen be more of a hypocrite?" She laughed under her breath and started formulating a response, when Eunice sent her an article: "Top Twenty-Five Things to Do in Taiwan's Capital."

Ever since Eunice moved away, she had hinted at a hypothetical two-legged visit: Ingrid flying to Seoul for a week before they spent another week in Taipei together. At first Ingrid assumed these discussions were a collaborative fantasy, co-imagined purely for the joy of it—after all, planning how they'd eat this and try that minimized the distance between them.

But living with her parents, Ingrid was able to set aside a decent portion of each paycheck, even after her monthly student loan payment. If she kept it up, she could afford the trip in just a few weeks.

Her avoidance of international travel, not even for a quick dip into Canada, was a puzzling fact to those around her and even to herself. The extent of her world had been limited to Wittlebury, its surroundings and a handful of nearby states. What lay beyond her known world had always frightened her. But now that she'd experienced breaking and entering *and* aggravated assault, well, flying eight thousand miles across the ocean wasn't so frightening anymore.

Three months ago, she had applied for her first passport. Before she fell asleep, she liked running her thumb over the embossed cover and paging through the thick, blank pages. With the passport in hand, her trip to Taiwan had gone from hypothetical to real. She would meet never-before-seen aunts, uncles and cousins, and reunite with her grandparents for the first time since they visited when she was a teenager.

"Let's do all of them," she texted Eunice and, a second later, added a smiley face.

SHE WAS ASSIGNED the last guided tour of the day, a boisterous group of assorted ages, ethnicities and nationalities. Her feet ached and her stomach already longed for the half-eaten lunch in her locker, but she slipped on her brightest smile and cheeriest voice.

"Hello, everyone!" she said into her headset microphone. "My name's Ingrid and I'll be your tour guide today. If you have any food allergies, please let me know. Now if you'll just follow me up these stairs, or if you'd like to take the elevator right over there, we'll start the tour on the second floor."

She had memorized the official guided tour script, but sprinkled in her own little asides and anecdotes. When the group would chuckle or shake their heads at the precise moment they were meant to, her insides would hum with satisfaction. Even more than coat check duty, she loved giving tours.

She led the group through the second-floor history of the factory, then the different processes of waffle, hot dog and cheese production on the third floor, before arriving at everyone's favorite part of the tour on the fourth floor: the taste-testing room. Besides the original waffle-dog flavor were seven others: chili, ranch, dill pickle, cheddar, jalapeño, garlic and, for the adventurous, dark chocolate.

"Please discard your toothpicks in any of the trash cans you see around you," Ingrid said pleasantly, eyeing the squad of teenagers, who hoarded seconds and thirds of the samples.

At the end of every tour, she stationed herself at the exit with a basket of complimentary pins cradled in her arms. The pins were printed on a mint green background, with a plump waffle-dog in the center, and came in various shapes.

She smiled at each person who plucked a pin from the basket, sending them off with a mandatory "Thank you for visiting!" or "Come back again soon!" or "Have a delicious day!"

One kid asked for two pins, the teenagers sauntered by without a backwards glance and an older man with a cane held up the line, taking his time selecting a pin. He bent over the basket and scratched his chin. Ingrid smiled; he looked like someone's doting grandfather who stored peppermint candies in his pocket. He wore corduroy pants and, despite the ninety-degree heat outside, a long-sleeved dress shirt beneath an argyle sweater-vest. He had light brown skin and a short, graying Afro.

"I had a wonderful time. Thank you," he said, looking up at her and holding her gaze.

"You're welco—" she began to say, then froze. She stared at the man, flattened by a sudden wave of disorienting dizziness. For a moment, she swore she'd swallowed too many of her old Lucidax pills as reality turned slippery at the edges and crossed into the threshold of fiction. The man had three faces, one layered over the other like tracing paper.

The first was the face of America's former greatest Chinese American poet. The second was the face of a con artist responsible for a thirty-five-year-long hoax. And the third was the face of a newly fabricated person— so new, he wasn't even real.

But seen altogether, he was just another white man taking what wasn't his to take.

"J—John," she stammered.

"Good seeing you," he winked, and before she could say another word, he faded into the crowd.

Notes

Chapter Eight: Chinatown Blues

137 **"Let's stay on topic: the casting of Samantha Prochazka as Mimi Lee":**
From "The Yellowface of 'The Mikado' in Your Face" by Sharon Pian
Chan (*The Seattle Times*, July 13, 2014): " 'The Mikado,' a comic opera, is
playing at the Bagley Wright Theatre from July 11 to July 26, produced by
the Seattle Gilbert & Sullivan Society. Set in the fictional Japanese town
of Titipu—get it?—the opera features characters named Nanki Poo,
Yum-Yum and Pish-Tush. . . . All 40 Japanese characters are being played
by white actors."

Chapter Twelve: Good Old-Fashioned American Freedom

219 **Their attention was diverted when someone used permanent marker:**
From "Black Tape Over Black Faculty Portraits at Harvard Law School"
by David A. Graham (*The Atlantic*, November 19, 2015): "When students
and faculty arrived at Harvard Law School's Wasserstein Hall Thursday

morning, they found a disturbing sight. On a wall of portraits of the law school's tenured faculty, black tape had been placed over each of the African American faculty members."

Chapter Fifteen: Serial Killers Want to Be Caught

273 **That's how I found out about William Ellsworth Robinson:** Excerpt from *The Glorious Deception: The Double Life of William Robinson, aka Chung Ling Soo, the "Marvelous Chinese Conjurer"* by Jim Steinmeyer (New York: Hachette, 2006): "If Soo had really been Chinese, if his act had been authentic and not exaggerated, his tricks and costumes would not have pleased his overeager public. As an impersonator, he was better than Chinese—he was free to match the public's fantasies of an old China" (p. 214).

274 **I came across a microfilm of a little booklet:** Excerpt from *Denison's Make-Up Guide: For Amateur and Professional* by Ward MacDonald and Eben H. Norris (Chicago: T. S. Denison, 1926): "The Chinaman—The 'ground tone' of the yellow man is Chinese grease paint. This is freely applied to face, neck and hands. The actor should, of course, use a wig with queue, such as that on page 68, and the connection between wig and forehead should be hidden by grease paint the color of the face. Wrinkles should be lined in to help the disguise. The eyebrows can be raised, blotted out or modified as necessary with the 'ground color,' and their outer corners should be turned up in oriental effect. This should be done skillfully, as on it depends the success of the make-up. Use the artists' stamp for all finer touches. The eyes should also receive an upward slant by careful shading at the outer edges. In this connection a study of the Chinaman, from an actual make-up, on page 53, will be instructive. The ears should be prominent and the cheek bones high, which is a matter of careful shading with the brown lining pencil and use of nose putty. The Chinese face is often deeply wrinkled, and if as in some plays he wears a mustache, the upper center of the lip is bald" (p. 21).

Chapter Sixteen: All Hail Emperor Bartholomew

296 **How easily the Chinese vacillated between ally and enemy:** "How to Tell Japs from the Chinese" (*Life*, December 22, 1941) and "How to Spot a Jap" by US Army (*A Pocket Guide to China*, 1942).

Chapter Eighteen: Fever Dream

335 **What about porn, where one of the most highly searched terms is "Asian"?:** From Pornhub's "Most Searched for Terms of 2018," released on December 11, 2018:

Most-searched-for terms (all genders): "Searches for 'Japanese' gained 3 positions to become the 5th most popular search, with 'Asian' gaining 6, 'Korean' up an impressive 16 and 'Chinese' up 14 positions."

Most-searched-for terms (men): First place: "Japanese." Third place: "hentai." Fourth place: "Korean." Tenth place: "Asian."

From *Orientalism* by Edward W. Said (New York: Vintage Books, 1987), p. 281: "[The local] women are usually the creatures of a male power-fantasy. They express unlimited sensuality, they are more or less stupid, and above all they are willing [. . .] When women's sexuality is surrendered, the nation is more or less conquered."

From "White Sexual Imperialism: A Theory of Asian Feminist Jurisprudence" by Sunny Woan (*Washington and Lee Journal of Civil Rights and Social Justice* 14, no. 2 [2008]):

"In a 2002 study conducted by Jennifer Lynn Gossett and Sarah Byrne, out of thirty-one pornographic websites that depicted rape or torture of women, more than half showed Asian women as the rape victim and one-third showed White men as the perpetrator. The study further uncovered a strong correlation between race and pedophilia, advertising with titles such as 'Japanese Schoolgirls' or 'Asian Teens.' Furthermore, images of Asian women in pornographic forms consistently came up through a keyword search for 'torture'" (p. 292).

"To colonize the Asian nations, countries such as the United States flooded Asia with military forces. As an inevitable result of military presence, prostitution centers consisting of local civilian women sprung up to cater to the White servicemen. With these sexual experiences as their main, if not only, encounters with Asian women, White servicemen returned home with the generalization that Asian women are hypersexualized and always willing to comply with White man's prurient demands. This germinated even more interest in Asian women as sexual objects. To sustain this increased interest, the Asian sex tour industry developed" (p. 293).

"Thus, while Blacks most often fall victim to Black offenders and Whites most often fall victim to White offenders, Asians most often fall victim to White offenders, not Asian" (p. 297).

From "Domestic Violence High for Mail Order Brides" by Jackie Northam (*All Things Considered*, NPR, July 2, 2003): "Federal officials report that many of the immigrant women suffer abuse at the hands of their new husbands, and those particularly at risk are women who meet their husbands with the help of mail order bride agencies."

From "Project AWARE: Asian Women Advocating Respect and Empowerment" by the Asian/Pacific Islander Domestic Violence Resource Project (DVRP) (2013): "Approximately 41–61% of Asian women reported experiencing physical and/or sexual violence by an intimate partner during her lifetime."

From Global Slavery Index 2018: Asia and the Pacific, Region Highlights: "The Asia and the Pacific region had the highest number of victims across all forms of modern slavery, accounting for 73 percent of victims of forced sexual exploitation, 68 percent of those forced to work by state authorities, 64 percent of those in forced labour exploitation, and 42 percent of all those in forced marriages."

339 **A while ago, someone posted:** From "Briton Wanted over Murder of Thai Dancing Girl" (*Times* [UK], February 2, 2015): "A British former nightclub owner is at the centre of an international manhunt after the body of a dancer was found chopped up in a suitcase in Bangkok. Shane Looker, 45, is believed to be the last person to have been in contact with Lazami 'Pook' Manochat in the red-light district of the Thai capital. The remains of Miss Manochat, 31, were discovered stuffed in the suitcase together with a dead dog in the Mae Klong River in Kanchanaburi, 70 miles south of the capital Bangkok."

Chapter Twenty: Be a Good Girl

368 **Why did people call it that?:** Excerpt from *Madame Butterfly* by Giacomo Puccini (1904), libretto translated by Dmitry Murashev:

> *"To think that this little toy*
> *is my wife! My wife!*
> *But she displays such grace*
> *that I am consumed*
> *by a fever*
> *of sudden desire!"*

378 **But Michael knew he was worried:** From the University of California, Berkeley's Center for Race and Gender's "Third World Liberation Front" web page:

"In 1968, a coalition known as the Third World Liberation Front (TWLF) is formed between the Black Student Union and other student groups at San Francisco State University to lead a five month strike on campus to demand a radical shift in admissions practices that mostly excluded nonwhite students and in the curriculum regarded as irrelevant to the lives of students of color.

"In 1969, a multiracial coalition of UC Berkeley students comes together and forms the third world Liberation Front (twLF) to demand that the University acknowledge the histories of communities of color as vital scholarship through the creation of a Third World College dedicated to the underemphasized histories of African Americans, Asian Americans, Chicanos/Chicanas, and Native Americans. The three month long protests that followed resulted not in a Third World College but in the Department of Ethnic Studies."